A Conclave of Crimson

BEVERLEY LEE
&
NICOLE EIGENER

This is a work of fiction. Any reference to historical events, real people, or real places is used fictitiously. Other names, characters, businesses, places, events, locales, and events are either the products of the author's imagination or used in a fictitious manner, and any resemblance to actual persons, living or dead, places, or actual events is purely coincidental.

©2024 by Beverley Lee & Nicole Eigener

All rights reserved, including the right to reproduce this book or portions thereof in any form whatsoever.

Rights or media inquiries: nicoverley@thevampire.org

First Edition: March 2024
Also available in ebook and hardcover

Excerpt from "Les Chercheuses de Poux"
by Arthur Rimbaud, in the public domain

Book and jacket design by Nicole Eigener
Cover photograph by Box of Kittens
Design and photography ©2023-2024
by Beverley Lee & Nicole Eigener

This book was written and published simultaneously in Oxfordshire, UK and Palm Springs, California, USA

Library of Congress Control Number: 2023917302

ISBN: 979-8-9873802-7-7

For wine, blood, ink, and soul-sharing
... for our vampires, forever

✝✝✝

Pour le vin, le sang, l'encre et le partage de l'âme
... pour nos vampires, pour toujours

READER'S NOTE

✝✝✝

This book is not YA — it contains graphic content and is intended for mature audiences.

This book is a sequel to two existing series: the Gabriel Davenport Series by Beverley Lee and the Beguiled by Night series by Nicole Eigener. A guide to the characters from the previous books is available on page 382.

CONTENT WARNINGS

✝✝✝

Blood (both descriptive and consumptive), bones and catacombs/crypts, allusions to vampire suicide and self-harm, arson, explicit sexual scenes between male vampires, brief mention of non consensual touching (past), violence and gore, and vampire abuse (past).

SOUNDTRACK

✝✝✝

Music lovers: turn to page 385 to enjoy the official Spotify soundtrack for *A Conclave of Crimson*.

REVIEWS FROM THE PREVIOUS BOOKS

THE GABRIEL DAVENPORT SERIES

I just want to say that if you've been looking for a horror series to jump into and become totally enraptured - this is the one for you. It's compelling, heart racing, sexy, terrifying, brutal and entertaining. Pick up all three.

— SADIE HARTMANN
@mother.horror / author of
101 Horror Books to Read Before You're Murdered

CRIMSON IS THE NIGHT: A VAMPIRE NOVELETTE

I love the works of both of these authors, so this little crossover where Vauquelin meets Clove and the Bloody Little Prophets was perfect.

— JEN YOUNG
Bookstagrammer

THE BEGUILED BY NIGHT SERIES

The series is lush, lavish, resplendent. The prose is rich, sensuous, and violent. The main character remains as torn by his inner turmoil as ever. Themes of finding yourself and accepting yourself take the spotlight. Eigener's voice demands that every step of the way is validated by the realisation of self and self-worth and finally acceptance.

— AUSTRIAN SPENCER
author of *The Sadeiest*

EPIGRAPH

OUBAITORI
*(n.) The idea that people, like flowers,
bloom in their own time and
in their own individual ways*

*We've always been about burning stars.
All about us is unearthly and radiant.*

— ANNA AHKMATOVA

*We talk so much of light,
please let me speak on behalf
of the good dark.*

—MAGGIE SMITH

1 / NIGHT 1:

THIS IS PARIS, THE CITY OF LOVE

The sleek, obsidian car sweeps along the rain-slicked roads, the driver effortlessly navigating the early evening streets. Busy, of course, because this is Paris, the city of love, where all things are possible if you only dare to dream.

The windows of this vehicle are blacked-out, a precaution in case the occupants are delayed on their journey. They could, in fact, spend the daylight hours inside, should the need arise.

Flynn Frenière, who has acquired the vehicle, and who sits behind the wheel, will not take any chances with his passengers, given their importance. When the message had arrived from Clove, asking for his assistance, Flynn had immediately set the wheels in motion.

Although his penchant for acquiring fine art and other valuables for the world's elite has waned a little over the years, he still has his finger on the pulse of where to go if someone needs an item, however bizarre. It had taken him three hours to locate the car, and another hour to arrange the necessary amendments to make his passengers comfortable, and, more importantly, safe.

By the end of that first night tickets on the Eurotunnel were booked, fake passports were in process, and the boot of the prestigious car was stacked with luggage.

Now new clothes grace the master vampire beside him and the three boys on the back seat. He glances across at Clove, his gaze taking in the tailored black trousers and forest green silk shirt, open at the neck, a jacket slung across his lap. Tonight Clove's long, dark hair is tied back neatly in a high ponytail, his nails cut short. But despite this elegant glamour the power resonates from him in waves.

'How much longer?' Clove asks, without turning to Flynn: because, of course, he has felt the gaze upon him.

Flynn glances at the sat nav map as they pull up to a set of traffic lights. 'Twenty minutes tops.' He pauses and checks the door locks are in place as they come to a halt. 'Does he know that we're close?'

'I suspect Vauquelin knows of our impending arrival.' Clove doesn't add that Vauquelin had probably known the instant their car drove out of the Eurotunnel onto French soil.

Clove has not undertaken this journey lightly. For five years he has kept his boys at Gehenna, their only respite when they went out to hunt. Five years in which they had learned, under the tutelage of Elijah, how to fight with dagger and rapier, how to dissect a human body and the many ways to dispose of it efficiently, how to steal and drive a car, how to bend a human mind to their will, a demanding skill only Gabriel had fully mastered.

Clove turns his head slightly towards the rear of the car, feels his first-born's mind-touch reach out to him.

I'm ready.

Not that Clove has any qualms about that particular point. He had taken Gabriel aside earlier and impressed upon him the need to be vigilant.

'We will be in a strange place and although I have taken all necessary precautions you must be aware that unless Vauquelin or myself are with you, there might still be danger present. It is up to you to keep your brothers safe, and out of trouble.'

The last part of that had been a direct reference to Moth, and Gabe's lips had quirked as he nodded his understanding.

The snarky, rebellious member of the Bloody Little Prophets is barely keeping his agitation under restraint. Although the prospect of an adventure with his brothers is something he has seized with both hands, the fact that they are visiting Vauquelin at his home has Moth in a flurry of turbulent nerves.

The last time they'd met, at Gehenna, Moth had called Vauquelin out on his need to return to the past: and afterwards the master vampire had found a chink in Moth's armour, exposing his vulnerability, a fact that dances along the edges of his memory. Vauquelin had been gracious but Moth isn't sure if that was because he had been a guest at Gehenna. Now the tables are turned — and a vampire never forgets.

A warm hand settles over his, warm because they had all fed before they left the stone walls of their fortress.

'It's okay, we'll be there soon.'

Gabe knows he hates being cooped up, that he's nervous about this meeting: because this time, it's not just Vauquelin.

There's a new vampire in town, one who carries the master's blood in his veins. Had Vauquelin told Éric about Moth? He balls his hands into fists and stuffs them into his lap, angry at himself for getting so worked up, angry that he has to wear clothes that make him feel less like himself, although he had flatly refused to wear dress trousers: opting instead for eye-wateringly expensive jeans and a plain black shirt.

Gabe sits beside him, dressed in those fucking tailored trousers that cling to his legs in all the right places and a designer polo in the same forest green as Clove's shirt.

So. Fucking. Beautiful.

Even if he does look like an ad for a prep school social.

The car moves off from the traffic lights and turns onto a side street, travelling from smooth tarmac to ancient cobblestones.

Gabe exhales a small breath of relief. He hadn't liked cruising along the main roads where people could see them, where they were on display, where other vampires might turn their heads from darkened alleyways and watch them pass. And wonder.

Because Clove is the necromancer, no matter how much he tries to keep this part of himself stowed away, and that power moves with him, vibrating in the very air. It had taken Gabe a while to fully comprehend that the same blood runs in his own veins: but it's part of his heritage.

He's very much looking forward to meeting Vauquelin again — or V as the master had said to call him — and is curious about the vampire who had won his heart. Gabe hopes that Moth will accept Éric and not be too *Moth* about it all: otherwise Gabe will spend this visit keeping the peace. He wants time with both of their hosts, to talk and to learn... without worrying that Moth is somewhere destroying a priceless antique or having a meltdown in a dark corner.

He casts his gaze to Moth's profile, sees the hard line of his jaw and the way his mouse-brown hair falls over his brow, and his heart flips over.

Fuck, we've been through so much together. He rests his cheek against Moth's shoulder and feels his lover relax into him.

Teal sits at the other side of Moth, his head against the window, golden hair silvered in the lights of the city as they flash by: although now those lights are mainly to be found in the apartments and garrets lining the side street. He wishes he was out in the open air so he could thrill to the sights and the sounds of a new city, that he could wander past windows and absorb the pulse of this new life, that he could visit art galleries and museums.

Do they have evening hours? He wants to go so much that it makes his fingers tremble. He pushes his hands under the satin bolero jacket laid across his lap, and a smile touches his lips.

Of all the clothes Flynn had brought for them to choose, this one had caught his eye: the fabric gleaming in the moonlight as Flynn carried it across. The edges are piped in a colour that almost matches his eyes, and when he had slipped it on it fitted him like a second skin.

He'd teamed it with high-waisted black trousers and a slim fit T-shirt and both Moth and Gabe had whistled their appreciation.

Teal doesn't really like being in the limelight, but he basks in his brothers' love.

He plays with the embossed logo on the side of a pair of designer sunglasses — not just for effect, a necessary addition for his eyes, eyes that still swim with the two fireflies that had elected to stay with him — and presses his open palm against the window.

The car turns left, and then immediately right. After two hundred yards Flynn brings it to a halt outside two imposing, heavy gates, and turns off the engine.

The atmosphere inside begins to thrum with three coiled energies.

Teal looks across to Moth, and Moth graces him with a lop-sided grin.

'We wait for Vauquelin,' Flynn says.

He hopes the master comes quickly — this car in its resplendent shininess doesn't exactly blend into the background.

Its very presence screams Look At Me.

Moth's mind settles on the luggage they'll have to unload.

It's messing with his reality.

Why the fuck do we need luggage? We're vampire. Moth glances to the rearview mirror and catches Flynn's unwavering gaze.

Flynn's mind-whispered reply slams into Moth's brain like a fist. *Your first lesson, Moth, is to understand that things are not what they were.*

Moth's lips tighten as he sinks further into the leather seat.

Flynn knows that luggage is a very human thing, but they will need clothes for their time here and the ones they have donned for their trip are meant to exude luxury, that if they were stopped they could say they were on their way to the opera, that any gendarme would surely wave them on given the obvious wealth on display and a touch of vampire persuasion. He understands that this new situation is difficult for Moth, but, as always, the young vampire will have to think on his feet.

Gabe opens his door and breathes Parisian air for the first time.

Two towering, embellished black and gold gates stand before him.

And behind them the grandiose house that had belonged to Vauquelin for centuries.

Moth appears at his shoulder, his gaze tracking Gabe's.

'Fuck.'

It's a single word that speaks volumes.

What the fuck is going to happen now?

2 / NIGHT 1:

MON PAPILLON DE NUIT
{ MOTH }

A whirr breaks the tension as the gates unfold and Vauquelin comes into view, striding across the pathway through the front gardens, wielding a remote control.

But Vauquelin is alone.

He reaches the gates, nodding and smiling at the boys, and immediately grasps Clove by the elbows, a hint of a smile playing over his face.

'You all have arrived safely. My greatest hope,' Vauquelin sighs.

He inclines his head to Flynn, a sign of respect, the modern equivalent of a bow: Flynn is the architect, so to speak, of all Vauquelin's current happiness. Had he not encountered Flynn in 1929, and again last year, Éric would not be inside the house, waiting.

A long time coming, indeed.

And now Vauquelin swivels his head to the boys.

There is an unspoken etiquette amongst vampires.

Elders first.

Assistants second.

Youth last.

But it would be impossible to overestimate the strength and influence these boys, teenagers in body but not in mind, had on Vauquelin at their first meeting.

In no uncertain terms, Gabriel, Teal, and, surprisingly — *especially* —

Moth, effectively altered Vauquelin's perception.

He owes them all an inestimable debt.

And that is why they are here: so that he might repay them even a soupçon of his gratitude.

Vauquelin turns once more to Flynn. He despises the thought of treating this magnificent vampire as a mere assistant, for he has accepted a great honour: that of transporting Clove and the boys outside the shelter of Gehenna, assuring the safe arrival of precious cargo.

Irreplaceable cargo.

If something had happened to them in transit, Vauquelin would never have forgiven himself. So Flynn is included in his great debt.

Trust.

Such a rare commodity. Among humans, yes: but even more so in the revenant world. So many opportunities for betrayal, for gain at another's expense. Trust is hard-earned for a vampire.

Clove had brought Vauquelin into his circle of confidence.

The fact that he *allowed* Vauquelin to meet them in the first place, that handful of years ago in Gehenna, was the ultimate privilege.

And Vauquelin had no comprehension at the time how much that meeting would change his life.

He wants each one of them to know how important they are to him.

'How very fetching you all look.' He surveys the lot of them but looks away from Clove when he finishes that statement.

The boys are one thing. Clove is another.

Vampires never lose significant memories, and Vauquelin has not forgotten the effect Clove had on him.

Hélas,[†] it is hidden away as one would save a beautiful photograph of a wonderful evening, an evening one knew could amount to nothing: he knew it then as he knows it now. A bittersweet memory, a cinder that

---
† ALAS

will not quite extinguish itself, although the flame for Éric dims its light.

The spark between Clove and Vauquelin has been sufficiently acknowledged. It passed between their eyes and no others.

If only...

Some words need no utterance.

And so Vauquelin moves on.

As he is wont to do.

He begins with Teal.

'My young friend, I cannot wait to see your face when you encounter the delights within these walls. Please know that you have free licence to wander and discover. This is a home for you. Perhaps not as fortified as Gehenna, but you always have our protection. I give you my word.'

Next: Gabriel.

Vauquelin only strokes Gabriel's jaw with his thumb — he relishes, as he observes from the corners of his eyes, the sight of Moth bristling.

As the reacquaintances proceed, Vauquelin visualises Éric pitching a fit inside the heavy stone walls of the house — even at the *thought* of witnessing such an intimate gesture with someone who is not him: yet Vauquelin is glad Éric did not come outside.

They both need this time for themselves.

Vauquelin and Gabriel... their words will remain unspoken for now, and understood.

At last he turns to Moth.

They both fold their arms.

'Well, *mon papillon de nuit*, has the cat got your tongue?'

'What the fuck does *that* mean?' Moth whispers through gritted teeth.

A memory washes over him, Vauquelin dragging him to the floor in Gehenna.

A moment of reluctant kinship.

He buries it with a scowl.

He isn't going down again so easily.

A sharp elbow in the ribs from Gabe.

Vauquelin is stone-faced. 'Moth. *En français.*'[†]

Gabriel laughs, and Moth shoots him a Look.

« *Étonnant* , »[‡] Vauquelin says with a clap of his hands, 'Let us go inside. Éric is anxious to meet all of you.' He clears his throat. 'Flynn, may I ask you to bring the car to the front of the house? We can unload the luggage there.'

Inside, Éric paces to and fro across the marble tiles, biting on the string of pearls around his neck — at the last minute he decides to unclasp it and shoves it in his pocket. They know nothing about him... but *pearls*? Never mind that he loves the contrast with his white tank top and half-buttoned black shirt, his cargo pants and heavy boots.

What would *they* think of him?

He's been dreading this moment as much as he's been anticipating it.

So fucking confusing.

Like everything else in his revenant life so far.

Ever since Vauquelin told him about this visit, he's been a nervous wreck. He's met so few vampires, and the ones he has have proven to be untrustworthy. Deceptive, even.

He thinks of Olivier, V's dead vampire brother, and thrusts out his chin. So different from V.

Why should he trust *these*?

But ultimately he respects V's judgement. V has never once let him down... he's always been true to his word.

Even so, Éric is madly jealous of Vauquelin's other connections, of other vampires that mean something to him.

It's stupid, he knows... but still!

[†]- IN FRENCH
[‡]- MARVELLOUS

So while the guests are milling around in the courtyard, Éric is stomping on the floor, digging his fingers into his hair. He can't even take a peek: there are no windows in the foyer. His heart thrums in his chest — the sound of voices increases in volume behind the front doors.

The doors fling open, and suddenly they're all inside.

3 / NIGHT 1:

JUST BE YOURSELF

Éric's eyes widen: they're drawn to Clove at once, and then he turns his head to each of the boys.

Oh my god, he thinks. *They're so young.*

His jaw slackens… he isn't sure what to make of them.

'Hi. I'm Éric.'

He stops there, but quickly adds 'Castañeda de Vauquelin,' biting his lip. His frenetic energy is muzzled, tamed by the unfamiliarity of these new vampires standing in their foyer. He moves behind V and encircles his arms around his maker's waist, resting his chin on V's shoulder.

He can't take his eyes off the boys, but he sends a message to V, dropping a kiss on his neck with a silent whisper.

I don't know why I was so worried. They're just kids.

A fraction of Éric's tension erodes. So why does he still want to jump out of his skin?

Vauquelin nuzzles Éric's cheek and replies: *You have much to learn about our guests, my love.*

Teal draws down his sunglasses and drinks in the room, his bright, blue-green gaze drifting across the ancient, gilded walls. It lands on a huge porcelain urn filled with fresh blooms, resting on top of a circular marble table. The heady scent of lily and rose reaches him and he smiles.

He's only slightly aware of Gabe and Moth exchanging incredulous glances because he's awestruck at the beauty of the house, and they're only in the entrance hall.

'Vauquelin.' The hint of a smile as Clove steps forward, opening his arms as he takes in the opulence of the foyer.

'Thank you for inviting us into your beautiful home.'

He glances down at his feet, resting on a black marble tile, the chequerboard effect stretching along the long hallway, lets his gaze travel to the others present — only Teal and Éric stand upon white.

He turns his scrutiny upon Éric. For all of his apparent easy grace, there is a turmoil of emotions within Vauquelin's new lover: a certain tension in the cords of his neck, a definite rise in Éric's heartbeat as his attention settles on Gabriel, Moth and Teal.

He sends a mind-touch to Vauquelin.

Does he know of their history?

Vauquelin replies at once.

He knows very little. I thought it best that he hear their struggles from their own lips.

They have many nights in which to get to know each other better, but Clove will be alert for any confrontations that could be awkward. From the corner of his eye, Clove observes Moth undertaking his own appraisal of Éric.

The word *confrontation* is supremely Moth-shaped.

Teal moves closer to Gabe, resting his shoulder against his brother's. He's always happy to be the one who stands in the shadows, letting Gabe and Moth take centre stage. From here he sometimes sees things that might have passed by anyone closer to their nucleus; his brothers have a way of burning when they are together, a molten heat that frequently incinerates those who get too close.

Teal hadn't missed Gabe's sharp intake of breath as he took in the grandness of the foyer. It looks like The Manor, if that particular place had been dialled up to maximum and showered with gilt, and it's a gut punch to the boy who left all that behind.

He focusses his thoughts and sends a whisper of a mind-touch to Gabe.

I understand.

Gabe's eyes widen as Teal brushes against his senses.

A rush of love floods through him. He slings his arm around Teal's shoulders, damping down the unexpected anguish that had caught him out of nowhere.

This isn't The Manor.

This is Vauquelin's home.

But still the tremor in his chest flutters like a caged bird.

He's well aware of Éric's scrutiny but Gabe's shields are down and locked tight. Not that he isn't curious about this new vampire.

Vauquelin's need to surround himself with magnificent things doesn't stop with his possessions. Éric is incredibly beautiful, like a marble statue that Vauquelin had coaxed to life, dark Michelangelo curls falling over his face, and those riveting copper eyes. But there must be more to him than beauty.

Gabe realises that he's staring.

He straightens his shoulders and moves forward, a small bow of his head towards Vauquelin before he faces Éric.

'Gabriel. It's an honour to meet you, Éric.' He lets the smile on his lips travel to his eyes, as behind him Moth mumbles something that begins with an F.

'Hi, Gabriel,' Éric replies, stepping away from Vauquelin for the first time. Gabriel seems cool. Maybe this won't be so bad, after all. He reaches out and they awkwardly shake hands. Éric shoves his clenched fingers back into his pockets.

Moth wants to run.

Not into the hallways of this insanely extravagant house but out into the night air. Despite the high ceilings he feels them closing in, wanting to trap him inside this fucking clumsy social bubble forever.

It doesn't help that his mind can't stop replaying the clash that had happened at Gehenna between him and Vauquelin, and seeing him again only makes everything seem so much more now and not in the past.

The name Vauquelin had called him grates along the raw edges of his nerves, too. Gabe had understood, had laughed, and, for a moment, Moth had felt ostracised from the boy he loves more than life itself.

And now Gabe is introducing himself to Éric like they could be fast fucking friends. Moth catches the panic in his gut and his eyes darken as they look Éric up and down.

Sure, he's a pretty boy... but how often are they empty?

And Éric has something they don't. He has a few more mortal years that give him height and muscle tone. A few more years that Moth and Gabe and Teal will never have. Moth hates him with a passion that wants to claw its way from his throat and scream its fury.

Teal watches the explosion as it works its way through Moth's veins. He moves close and grabs Moth's hand, letting his gaze rest on the painting hung on the wall by the left-hand staircase, one of two that grace this incredible space. It's an oil painting of a grand house — not this one, but one surrounded by trees — and the light from the chandelier plays against its surface, making it seem almost ethereal.

The firefly glow in his eyes shimmers as the beauty of each stroke plays upon his senses. Beside him Moth has reached critical *Moth* stage, one that there will be no coming back from if he explodes now.

Teal has to diffuse the situation. He gives his fireflies unbridled permission to shine as he turns his gaze towards Vauquelin, well aware that Éric can't miss the way they flicker and dance.

'What year was this commissioned? It's stunning.'

Vauquelin takes Éric by the hand and walks to the painting, extending an arm to invite Teal to join them.

'This was painted before my human birth, in the year 1615. It is my father's ancestral home, the Château de Renonçeau. It was taken from me in 1685 because I refused to heel to the King. And along with it, I lost my title. I was a Duc, then. Now I am only Vauquelin.'

He smiles down at Teal, and beside him, he notices Éric is lost in Teal's eyes, leaning toward him slightly as if he could slip inside them and never return.

In fact, Éric almost wishes he could.

But Moth... *oof.*

He's afraid Moth wants to rip his throat out.

At least, that's what his expression indicates.

No fear, my love, Vauquelin mind-whispers to Éric.

His lover's dread is escalating and he draws it into himself, attempts to overwrite it. He caresses Éric's shoulder, ending in a comforting grip.

Just be yourself.

And with that, Vauquelin throws him right in the deep end.

'Éric, take the boys on a tour of the house. I have matters to discuss with Clove and Flynn.'

4 / NIGHT 1:

A RED VEIL SWALLOWS HIM WHOLE

Éric's jaw falls open and he crosses his ankles, hanging his thumbs from his pockets.

Are you fucking kidding me right now?

He isn't ready to be alone with them!

He thought they'd all hang out and get to know each other a little more, with Clove and V. But he knows better than to argue.

Besides: Clove, Flynn, and Vauquelin have already disappeared into the salon, leaving him standing there like an idiot, facing down these three strange teenagers.

He folds his arms, lifts a hand to fidget with one of the silver hoops adorning his earlobes. He drills his gaze into Moth's bizarre eyes: one is brown, one a light grey.

Hmm, he thinks. *Fucking weird*.

'So what are you guys, like fifteen or something?'

Moth is up in Éric's face in an instant, mismatched eyes blazing.

He's only just got a hold of his fuse after Teal gave him a moment to decompress, but now it's lit again and a red veil swallows him whole.

'You have no fucking idea what we've gone through together. And don't let our looks deceive, we've spat out better vampires than you in our fucking sleep.'

'Whoa, whoa, whoa, little man!' Éric shoves Moth backward. 'Who do you think you are? It was just a question!'

They lunge toward each other, mouths tightened, chests puffed out.

Éric's bravado is on thin ice.

He wasn't expecting this, and he's never been a fighter.

But he can't yield now.

He chokes back what he really wants to say.

His breath intensifies.

But what did he expect?

That they'd all just be instant vampire pals, and everything would be a fucking blast?

Well, yes. Yes, that's exactly what he was expecting — not this.

So he bumps Moth's chest with his.

He's not letting him win.

Not here.

This is *his* house. And they just fucking got here!

Gabe is a millisecond too late to stop the contact between Éric and Moth. He grabs a fistful of Moth's shirt and hauls him backwards so quickly that Moth almost loses his balance.

And then Moth is up in *his* face, fire in his eyes, spittle on his lips.

'Fuck it, Gabe. I'm not letting him talk down to us just because we look wet behind the ears!' Moth tries to free himself but there's no way Gabe is letting him loose right now.

'May I remind you that we're guests here?' Gabe hisses. 'And it was only a question.' His eyes flick towards Éric. 'Even if it was badly worded.'

Tension hangs in the air of the grand foyer, thick and threatening, thrumming with negative energy.

'Moth.' Teal's quiet voice finds its way through the charged atmosphere, and everyone turns to face him. 'Can you come with me? I want to find the library.'

Everyone — or at least the Bloody Little Prophets — knows it's a ploy. Moth, especially, knows it's a ploy... but he never refuses Teal anything.

He shrugs himself free. The look he fires towards Gabe quite plainly says they will talk later: and don't expect it all to be hearts and flowers.

Teal moves to Moth's side, inclining his head towards Éric.

'The library?'

Éric thinks for a moment, squeezing his lips with his fingers.

They have to start over.

Things can't be like this!

'Actually... I have something *much* cooler to show you guys. Come on.'

He takes off down the long hallway between the staircases.

5 / NIGHT 1:

WHAT'S IN THE COFFIN?

They wander down ancient passages, taking twists and turns, and the house grows gradually darker until they stop in front of a menacing door.

Éric squats and lifts a panel from the stone floor, extracting a key and wielding it like a knife.

'Get ready.'

He opens the door with a flourish, and beyond is pitch black.

'Hang on...'

He steps inside a moment and re-emerges with a lit torch.

'Follow me... but watch the steps. They're really old and concave in the centre.'

When they hit the landing, they find themselves in a wine cellar.

'Big fucking deal,' Moth says. 'A bunch of bottles.'

'Nope,' Éric says. 'Check it out.'

He walks further, holding the torch up high so they can see the formidable archive of bones. Éric lights more torches and gives one to each of the boys. He stands proudly in the middle of the room, perched on top of the hatch to the acid pit.

That explanation will come a little later.

Now, he awaits their reactions with his lop-sided grin.

Gabe lets his gaze settle on the shelves of bones.

A shiver runs through him.

This is what V and Éric do with their victims, but how do they strip them down to pure bone?

He's grateful to Éric for doing his own damage control in bringing them here. It gave Moth time to cool down a little, although his lover is silent and in prime brooding mood. That's definitely better than the pure aggression he had shown, though.

Gabe isn't sure what had prompted it.

He'll try to get it out of Moth later when they're alone.

Teal drifts to Moth's side, his jaw slightly open as his bright eyes take in the macabre contents of the cellar.

That's all Moth needs right now: Teal's presence.

'This is pretty impressive.' Gabe turns his gaze towards Éric. 'There's a myriad of tunnels under Gehenna and some have old bones in them, but we've never put them on show.'

He glances towards Moth.

The flickering light from the torch he holds reflects in Moth's eyes and Gabe's breath hitches in his throat.

I love you.

A hint of a smile quirks on Moth's sullen lips.

However challenging Moth can be, Gabe loves him with a fierceness that makes his heart ache.

'It's not exactly on show,' Éric says. 'No one knows about this except me and Vauquelin. And now you guys.'

He hopes they'll appreciate this gift, that including them in a secret of this magnitude will help heal the rift between them.

Éric doesn't get why Moth is being so aggressive. And he really wishes he hadn't asked that question right off the bat... it didn't come out the way he'd meant.

He's never gotten to show off the house.

He doesn't have any friends.

He doesn't want to blow this chance to maybe have *real* friends for the first time in his life, friends that understand him... especially the way he is now.

Whatever.

There's more to explore in the catacombs.

'Back up just a bit, guys. And you might want to cover your nose and mouth.' He steps off the hatch and heaves it up by its thick, iron loop.

The repulsive, bitter stench of acid fills the air, and Gabe turns his head away.

'So this is how you strip them.' He nods his approval to Éric, knowing that their host is trying his level best in what has to be extremely difficult circumstances, given Moth's antagonism.

He needs Moth to cut Éric some slack.

Éric glances around the room.

Shit, I wish I had something to drop in here.

He hadn't exactly planned to show them the catacombs so soon.

Without a body it's not as impressive as he'd hoped.

'Anyway... you'll definitely get to see this in action later, but yeah... we drop them in here and the acid does the hard part. And then we stack them on the shelves. It's fucking sick, you guys are gonna love it!'

Teal's eyes flick towards the coffin in the back of the chamber, and Éric follows his glance.

'What's in the coffin?'

'Uh...' Éric dashes his tongue across his lips. 'Don't go near it. So, Teal. You mentioned the library. Let's go.'

The fireflies in Teal's eyes brighten at Éric's words.

Of the few things Vauquelin had told him about the boys, one standout was that Teal loves books: Éric can't wait for him to see them.

Maybe — just maybe — he'll show them *his* books, the volumes of pages he had written while V was away.

Vauquelin had them bound in leather.

But not tonight.

Éric eases the hatch down on the pit. He knows to treat the pit with the utmost respect. A bit of sizzled flesh will do that for a person.

At the top of the stairs is a receptacle to douse the torches. Éric dips his in first and returns it to its hook on the wall, waiting for the boys to follow. He slams the heavy door behind them and locks it.

'Come on.'

They retrace their steps through the same dark passageways, leading them to the foyer and the foot of the bisected staircase.

Éric sprints halfway up the left side before he stops and looks down over his shoulder: the boys are still on the ground floor.

'Well... what are you waiting for?'

Moth lags behind, his expression unreadable. He doesn't want to follow Éric *anywhere* but Teal is already on the bottom stair.

Moth's face says everything he isn't voicing.

'It's okay,' Gabe says, urging him forward, and this time Moth decides to roll with it — because really what kind of bad things can happen in a house owned by a vampire? Something inside him tells him that he knows exactly what kind of bad things could happen...

Double floor-to-ceiling doors await them at the top of the landing.

Éric rests his hands on the knobs and smiles at Teal.

'Are you ready?' He opens them with a flourish and steps inside, extending an arm to welcome them all to enter.

Shelves of books reach as high as the ceiling.

A rolling ladder.

A harpsichord sits at an angle in one corner, its closed fallboard keeping it silent, awaiting fingers to free its notes.

Large, gilt-framed paintings are scattered between the shelves, and a fire is already roaring in the fireplace.

V knew this room would be important to Teal.

Teal steps inside and the welcoming scents of leather and parchment overwhelm him. This is the place he would willingly spend every minute of his night, and the light in his eyes glows far brighter than it did downstairs. He's almost afraid to walk over to the shelves and touch them, in case they disappear and he's left holding nothing but wishes.

Éric watches Teal in awe.

It reminds him of his first night in this house, when he had arrived fresh in Paris, having never been in a place like this.

The library was the first place he wandered off to that night.

It's still one of Éric's favourite rooms.

But at this particular moment, he's edgy from all the conflicts.

He's anxious for something to settle, so that they might actually talk to each other… but that seems far away right now.

'Do you guys want to see your rooms?' he asks.

Gabe hasn't missed the tension that surrounds Éric's genial manner, and he knows that much of it is because of Moth's earlier aggression. And now he's about to say something that Moth will most definitely not like.

He takes a quick breath.

'Moth, I'd like you to stay here with Teal for a little bit. I don't want him to be by himself.' His words are quiet, but after they settle a silence drapes over the vast room.

He knows full well that Moth can't say no to this, although he's opening up a whole can of worms for when they're alone.

Moth's eyes darken and his lips set into that thin line that Gabe knows so well. It's the silent affirmative that is an explosion in his mind as he turns to Éric.

'Okay, Éric, lead the way.'

Éric quirks his eyebrows.

He's not sure what's going on between Moth and Gabriel, but it's pretty obvious where the authority lies.

And Moth's eyes burning into his back as they walk out of the room is an unmistakable sign.

6 / NIGHT 1:

WE'LL TAKE THIS ONE

Éric quietly draws the doors closed and laces his hands behind his back. It's a flash of V: sometimes he's astonished by how much he's adopted his mannerisms.

Is Éric copying him? Or is it in the blood?

He may never know.

'So... Gabriel. Or do you like to be called Gabe?'

'Gabriel will do for now.'

He wants to explain why, that Gabe has to be earned... but Éric is trying his hardest so he follows it with a warm smile.

Éric relaxes for the first time all night and replies with his own crooked grin, hanging a thumb on his pocket as he flings open the first door they come to.

The room is stultifyingly lavish.

Gabriel gawps.

'This is Clove's room. It's the largest room on the wing. It's only fair for him to have this one, don't you think?'

Gabe's gaze flicks around the grandeur of the room, and he nods in approval. 'I think he'll be more than okay here.'

'Okay, cool.' Éric begins walking down the hallway, opening doors left and right. 'You can pick the next best one for yourself.'

Gabe looks into each open doorway, trying not to let his jaw drop at the staggering opulence. One room in particular appeals to him, one where the wallpaper depicts an ancient hunting scene; he knows Moth will appreciate that.

'We'll take this one.'

'Wait... what? There are like ten rooms in this hallway. You guys don't have to share! Who's *we?*'

Gabe sees the confusion in Éric's eyes and it suddenly dawns on him that Éric doesn't have a clue about his relationship with Moth.

'Yeah, we... me and Moth.'

'Oh. My. God. You and *Moth?*'

Éric is absolutely flabbergasted.

Okay, deep breath.

His mind has been fractured all evening, but now it's fucking *blown*. He had hoped at the outset, before they arrived, that maybe he'd end up with some friends who knew what it was like to be him, but DAMN.

Now they're even closer than he had imagined.

Éric has no poker face.

He knows that Gabriel can see his shock.

'Moth isn't all sharp edges.' Gabe can't take his eyes off Éric. A grin breaks on his lips at his expression of pure horror. 'I know that's pretty hard to imagine given how he reacted tonight.'

He pauses and wonders how much to tell Éric at this time. It's probably not the moment to launch into the whole "well, I was hunted by a demon from when I was a baby" spiel, and explain just how he and Moth met, and also the absolute antagonism between them at the start.

'How long have you two been together?' Éric asks.

He's drawn into Gabriel's navy-blue gaze, his dark, floppy hair... in some ways he's like a miniature V, only V's eyes are almost an exact opposite blue, so pale, like arctic ice rimmed with midnight — except when he's angry, and they almost rival the night sky. His mind is swirling with Gabriel's revelation: Éric was never out. And now he's even more *in*, as a vampire. Doubly in. But he wouldn't change it for the world.

Now he has a place to belong… with V.

And he can feel Gabriel's belonging, too.

They have a place.

They can be themselves here.

His heart swells.

'About five or six years, I think?' Gabe's brow creases as he calculates. 'But where we live we don't have clocks or phones, so I'm just going on moon phases.'

Éric brings his hand to his lips, gnawing the tip of his thumb.

Seriously? Just exactly how old are they?

Teal's firefly eyes and now moon phases… their English accents…

The slacker from L.A. is suddenly extra self-conscious.

'You guys aren't really teenagers anymore, are you?'

'I was almost sixteen when Clove saved me.' Gabe says quietly.

Because if Clove hadn't shared his blood, Gabe would have died on that night from his injuries.

For the first time since his turning, Éric ponders his own age, and V's first loaded question: *could you imagine being twenty-four forever?*

At the time, it was a no-brainer. Twenty-four is a perfect age. He isn't that much older than them. Still, he's in a golden swagger era: no longer a disrespected teenager, yet still not having the worries of adulthood. It's a threshold. Toeing the line. Now, looking at Gabriel, the reality of a forever age sinks in for Éric — he winces as he recalls the first words out of his mouth to them.

They're not just kids.

Gabriel's words echo in his ears and he applies them to himself.

And I'd be almost twenty-fucking-NINE.

Does V ever think about this stuff? When will it stop?

Gabriel, Moth, and Teal will be teenagers *forever*.

Jesus.

But then his mind goes right back to Gabriel and Moth being a couple. He can't quite wrap his head around that! Now he realises what a gift Vauquelin has given him by arranging this visit. Not only for Éric to meet other vampires, but vampires that understand his particular kind of *love*.

'You know Vauquelin isn't just my maker, then.'

'Yeah... that was fairly obvious when I saw you with him in the foyer,' Gabriel says with a wry smile.

'Well... this is beyond awesome,' Éric says, his crooked grin in full force. But it quickly morphs into a frown as he casts his gaze to the floor. 'Even though it's pretty clear Moth hates me.'

He wonders if they know about V's time-slips, especially the last one that left them apart longer than they've been together. How could anyone believe that? But he hopes he has a chance to tell them... or Gabriel, at least — somehow he just *knows* he'd understand.

Éric is burning to confide in him already, but shyness drapes over him like an iron blanket and he shuts down.

He leads Gabriel further into the room and opens a jib door, set into the wall. It's covered in sea-green wallpaper, the edges blending almost seamlessly into the tree-strewn pattern.

Gabe lets Éric's words bounce around his head.

Even though it's pretty clear Moth hates me.

'Don't take it too personally about Moth. Trust isn't something he gives easily.' He wants to add that his own beginning with Moth had been like walking over a minefield, but it seems too personal when he and Éric have only just met.

Éric exhales, puffing his hair out of his eyes.

'I asked for it, though. I have a really bad habit of shooting my mouth off before I think. Vauquelin repeatedly warns me that it's gonna get me in trouble one of these nights. I guess this is the night.'

He side-eyes Gabriel and rolls across the wall toward the door, stepping inside to turn on a small lamp.

'This is an anteroom,' Éric says. 'There's another bed. Do you think Teal might like to stay in this one? That way he can still be close to you guys. But not *too* close.'

'I think he'd like that very much.' Gabe peers around the door.

The room is draped in darkness but he can already feel the safety within it, and having Teal close in a strange place is of utmost importance to both him and Moth.

'There's one more thing I want to show you,' Éric says. 'Come on.'

They walk back out into the hallway, and at the end, Éric opens yet another door.

'This is another bathroom for this wing. And the door locks… just saying.' Another crooked grin as he flips on the light switch.

A long bathtub is the centrepiece, with a fireplace at the end. It's unlit now, but Gabriel can easily imagine how this room would look with a roaring fire.

'Check this out.' Éric walks to a wheeled pulley on the side of the wall and lowers the chandelier. 'You just turn this wheel down to light the candles, and again to lift it back up. I've gotten to love candlelight more than electric lights. It's just so pretty. And you don't have to worry about burning them. We have about a gazillion candlesticks. There's more right here.'

He nudges a wooden trunk with the toe of his boot.

The absolute luxury of V's house suddenly overwhelms Gabe. He's got so used to how they live at Gehenna with its cruel austerity … being in a place that is exactly the opposite is messing with his head. He lowers his gaze for a moment to regroup his thoughts.

Éric reaches out to touch Gabriel's shoulder. He conjures the best he can to try and reassure Gabriel, whatever it is that's going through his mind. It's just to buy some time as he tries — and fails — to interpret the expression on Gabriel's face. He finally pieces some words together, and hopes he doesn't come off as a total fucking idiot.

'There's a smaller bathroom off the room you chose, but it doesn't have a fireplace ... or a big-ass chandelier like this.' He swallows hard, and wonders if he's making it better or worse.

'Don't worry if this is all bizarre for you. Trust me, it was wild for me, too. It still is, and I've lived here for almost five years. I'd never known anything like this. I was sleeping on a friend's couch at the time I met Vauquelin. Sometimes it's like living in a fucking museum, to be honest.'

Gabe reaches to hook his thumbs into the belt loops on his usual jeans, then realises he's wearing dress trousers. He's itching to change, to don his usual skin, but their luggage must still be downstairs.

'I know all about living in a museum,' he says.

His eyes flick to Éric's, and, for an instant, he sees the honest openness within them before Éric glances away.

'I was brought up in a house like this. Well, not quite as "Vauquelin" as this, more comfortable antique English eccentricity.'

Maybe one day he'll tell Éric about Noah and Carver and Olivia — and of Beth; *your mother, Gabe, she was your mother.*

'It truly doesn't get much more Vauquelin than this place,' Éric says, raising a brow.

He flops down in a chair, fidgeting his fingers.

It's obvious that Gabriel has swallowed some words — so has he.

God, there's so much I want to talk to you about, Éric thinks. He has no idea how long they're staying... V had never mentioned an end date.

Please let there be enough time...

Gabriel starts for the door, and Éric leaps up, grabbing his elbow.

'Gabriel, wait a minute. I know things got off on the wrong foot.' He hoists up a palm. 'I don't know what you've been through, but I do know how much Vauquelin loves you all. I'm so lucky to have this chance to get to know you, because you're all really important to him. I hope I didn't fuck everything up.'

He drops his gaze. He isn't used to being so open with others, but something about Gabriel gives him a sense of total safety.

'Anyway... we should probably get back. Moth's probably blowing a gasket by now, am I right?'

Gabe's eyes widen and a grin touches his lips.

'Rule number one you've just learned about Moth. His default is blowing a gasket.'

At last Éric laughs, showing his teeth.

It dawns on him that, since becoming vampire, he's never laughed this way with anyone besides Vauquelin.

At least no one that had *lived*.

It feels so good!

For a moment Gabe wonders if this might be a betrayal on his part, laying Moth's emotional make-up on the line, but it's better Éric knows up front: because they all have to live under this roof, for however long Clove and V decide.

But one thing he knows for certain is that Éric's unfortunate question earlier had fanned Moth's hostility to a point where even Gabe will have trouble talking him down.

It hasn't escaped his notice that Éric has two sets of razor sharp canines.

'Your fangs,' he says, as he runs his tongue over his own. 'Double sets?'

Éric pokes them with a fingertip, wrinkling his nose.

'What do you mean? Is that unusual?'

His fangs are exactly like V's... they're like Olivier's.

'Don't all vampires have the same kind?'

Gabe bares his own. He doesn't need to say anything.

'Wow,' Éric whispers, leaning in for a closer look.

His knowledge of vampires is limited to what he's seen with V — until now, he's never had any reason to question it.

Gabe could probably expand upon this topic but he wants to get back to Moth and Teal, before Moth does something that will get them all grounded.

'Shall we go back to the library?'

As they approach the doors, a completely irrational idea for a prank enters Éric's mind.

What would happen if I just walk in there with my arm around Gabriel's shoulders?

He rolls his eyes.

Yeah, no. That would be a death sentence.

He laughs again.

'What's so funny?' Gabriel asks.

'Trust me,' Éric says, 'you don't wanna know.'

He flings the doors open wide and they step inside.

Teal looks like he's in heaven and Moth is sitting on the floor by the fireplace, punishing a fallen log with a poker.

7 / NIGHT 1:

WHO ARE YOU TO BE WITHIN THESE HALLS?

Moth had heard Gabe and Éric approach. He could pick out Gabe's footfall amidst a crowd of thousands, and to hear it flanking Éric's fills him with a nauseous fury he isn't sure how to handle.

For the past few years at Gehenna he has lived alongside his brothers, with Clove and Elijah, and the lost vampires that came to the fortress walls in search of safety. They never stayed for long; Clove found new places for them and they always left with their hearts full of gratitude.

Moth's favourite nights were the ones he and his brothers disappeared into the tunnels running under Gehenna or went out hunting together: he didn't want to make new 'friends', didn't want their eyes upon him — one of the infamous Bloody Little Prophets.

It's obvious to him why Gabe and Teal are special, but he never feels special: just fucking lucky that somehow he has found his way into Gabe and Teal's orbit.

But in the gloom of Gehenna or out on the midnight moor he can be who he wants to be and he never has to hide or pretend to be something he isn't. Sitting here, clutching the poker so tightly that his wrist aches, he feels the old palatial walls and their memories judging him.

Who are you to be within these halls?

Moth doesn't turn his head as Gabe and Éric enter the room, but he feels Gabe's gaze settle upon him. He knows, without looking, that Gabe has already scanned the room looking for any perceived threat, because he's Gabriel Davenport, Clove's first-born, and pure-bred blood runs in his veins.

Gabe half-expects Moth to welcome them with some kind of snarky comment. But the silent silhouette of his hunched form by the fire is much worse, and it takes all the breath from Gabe's lungs. A dozen different emotions seize him: he closes his eyes for a second.

Éric is lost in the backlash of Gabriel's reaction.

Right away, he senses something is off: and potentially really, really bad. Standing there, in this now very-familiar library, his home seems like it isn't his. Instead, it's like he's an intruder: because he's walked into something so private, something he's absolutely locked out of, and he's surrounded by three others who are still complete strangers.

The intimacy of his exchange with Gabriel across the hallway recedes... the brief budding of their friendship closes like a failed bloom, and he folds back into himself. He sits in the farthest chair from all of them, tilting his head up to the ceiling, wishing he could just leave and go to V... but he's behind closed doors with the other elders.

This is how it always ends up for Éric... he can be flanked by people and still be the loneliest kid in the room.

Right now Gabe wants nothing more than to grab Moth's hand and take him out onto the night streets of Paris: so they can hunt with the air of another land caressing their skin... yet he's very aware of the importance of this visit, of V's invitation, because Clove had told him V *never* invites other vampires into his home. There's an expectation on his shoulders and he desperately wants to make Clove proud of him.

Gabe's focus shifts as Teal's glance flicks towards him, butterfly-kiss soft, as his brother raises his head from the book open on his lap, acknowledging their entry.

Happiness radiates from him, the joy of being amongst all of these ancient words, his immortal presence blending with the voices of the dead.

He crosses to Teal, presses his hand against his brother's shoulder and Teal leans into him.

The movement plucks Éric out of his lonesome reverie, promptly plunging him deeper into his darkness as he tunes into their closeness, their brotherhood. V is the closest he'll ever come to that. It's more than enough... he just hadn't known that there was *even more than that*: a totally different kind of connection.

He has to look away from them: it's too painful, and his emotions propel him up — he hugs himself, his long legs compulsively pacing.

He has to get his body moving or he'll explode.

'Moth,' Gabe says softly. 'You're not going to believe what's waiting for us down the hall.'

He can feel Éric's anxiety as he tries to unpack what the hell is going on here, knows that, to an outsider, Moth's behaviour is churlish and unsociable: but Éric doesn't understand what Moth has been through, doesn't understand that this shield he throws down is only Moth panicking behind it as he tries to stop himself from drowning.

'Gabriel,' Éric says. 'Why don't you show Moth the rooms? I can keep Teal company.'

A wave of relief passes over Gabe at the suggestion.

It's obvious that Éric has picked up on the elephant in the room and Gabe is mortified that he has to deal with this disturbance in his own home.

'Moth.'

But still Moth refuses to look at him. Whatever is bothering him is soul deep. Gabe will take a snarky, cornered, angry Moth, over the one sitting miserably by the fire. He walks across, dips his gaze to Moth's profile.

His lover's jaw is set tight, mussed hair hanging over his face.

The poker in his hand trembles.

I need you.

Gabe sends a mind-touch. He could have demanded that Moth look at him, could have appealed to the love they hold for each other. But these three words seem right, because Gabe could never not need Moth.

An instant where Moth closes his eyes tight and hangs his head. He rises to his feet, dropping the poker onto the marble hearth. The sharp noise ricochets around the library like a wayward bullet and both Teal and Éric spin to face them.

'My apologies.' Gabe finds a smile and turns it towards Éric as he grabs Moth's hand and drags him out into the hallway.

8 / NIGHT 1:

DON'T STOP

No words pass between Gabe and Moth as they stride towards their room, the only eyes upon them from the paintings hanging on the wall.

I'm handling it. Gabe sends another touch, this time to Clove, who can't have failed to pick up on his emotional yoyoing.

He closes the bedroom door, finds Moth standing by the huge bed, his fingers trailing over a silken tassel hanging from the bed curtains.

'Out with it.'

It's useless to beat around the bush when Moth is in this mood.

'What? Right here?' Moth's hand drops to the zip in his jeans.

But there's none of the usual teasing written on his face, none of the usual sensuality that always passes between them when they're alone. He's trying to bury what's wrong, and this one fact alone sends Gabe's alarm bells into overdrive.

A lump forms in Gabe's throat. He crosses the few feet of floor space between them, reaches out his hand and lifts Moth's chin with one finger, just as Clove does to him when he needs Gabe to be truthful.

'Tell me,' he says softly. 'Tell me what's eating you up inside.'

A flicker of panic dances behind Moth's eyes, his whole stance as inflexible as marble.

Gabe lets his finger drift along Moth's jawline, lets it drop to caress the column of his neck, lets it rest in the hollow of his throat, where Moth's pulse beats softly. He presses against the pale skin, and the pulse beat quickens under his fingertips.

His eyes never leave his lover's face.

He doesn't even blink, holding Moth in the intensity of his gaze. This is how they speak when words won't come, when Moth's emotions are so turbulent that he's incapable of voicing them.

'We've got a bed,' Gabe whispers finally, with a slight jerk of his head. 'You got a preference on what side you take?'

They had never slept in a bed together, only huddled under floorboards or spooned on a cold, hard floor with only the comfort of a straw mattress if they were lucky. Gehenna is all dark stone and frigid chill, its walls etched in misery and misdeeds. V's house in contrast is a fever dream of colour and lavishness and serenity.

'No preference,' Moth answers, his hand snaking around Gabe's waist.

Their bodies meet in an embrace that is both tender and unashamedly passionate. They will make their love and then he'll ask Moth again as they bask in the afterglow.

Gabe winds his fingers through Moth's hair, presses gentle kisses against the jawline his finger had so recently traced.

A groan from Moth as he arches his neck, offering Gabe his throat: the ultimate mark of trust for a vampire.

Their worlds tilt into one of their own making.

This place might be totally over the top but it's *safe*, and that fact lights the embers of their passion.

Moth grabs a handful of Gabe's hair, pulling them apart for a moment. He gazes into the navy-blue of his lover's eyes, the long lashes dark against the pale skin, letting his need build until it's a chorus of fire in his belly.

His hand drops, practised fingers unzipping, that moment where his palm meets the soft, supple flesh of Gabe's lower belly, coarse hair between his fingers and then the beauty that is Gabe growing in his grasp.

A rip of fabric as Moth tears away the cloth surrounding what he needs.

He falls to his knees and buries his face against Gabe's groin, his hand still holding what is unbelievably his.

A smear of pre-cum against his fingertips. Moth grins, and the grin is pure lust and darkness. He tilts his head and looks up at Gabe through a fall of hair, sees the bliss etched upon his face.

'Don't stop.'

The breathless plea reaches Moth's ears and it's the sweetest fucking music he's ever heard.

'You like this?' He runs his tongue over the tip of Gabe's cock, salt exploding in his mouth, licks it like he's enjoying an ice-cream cone, knows the constant touch-and-leave is one of Gabe's ultimate triggers.

Gabe's fingers tangle in his hair and Moth's own moan leaves his lips.

His hand drifts to the inside of Gabe's thighs... he lets his fingers travel up a well-known path, lets them delve into the soft skin behind Gabe's balls.

Moth's mouth does what it's meant to do when it isn't ripping out the throat on his next meal: he takes Gabe fully, rejoicing in the pressure against the sides of his throat as Gabe pushes his hips forwards.

And then the slow dance of give and take, of wet sounds filling the ancient room, of passion building and sweat-slicked skin. Gabe's cry of release echoes around the room, his fingers tightening in Moth's hair to the point where Moth absorbs the pain and allows himself to fall into it as he swallows Gabe's gift.

And then the quiet as Moth laps each precious drop, a last inhalation of that special place before Gabe drops to his knees and takes Moth in his arms.

And for these cherished moments nothing else matters.

9 / NIGHT 1

V COULD HAVE WARNED ME...

Éric says, 'Gabriel and Moth have been gone awhile. Let's go check on your luggage and take it to the rooms. Okay?'

Teal smiles, the light in his eyes dimming ever-so-slightly, but only because he feels compelled to put down the book he had selected. He hopes Gabe and Moth have talked things through, that Gabe has been able to turn Moth's damper down, that he and Éric won't interrupt their time alone: time that is always hard for them to come by.

But Teal is a guest in this house, and his genteel nature comes to the surface. He defers to his host, and moves to replace the book in its empty spot on the shelf.

Éric tilts his head, watching Teal in curiosity. V would be *super fucking impressed* at the way Teal is handling these antique books: with pinnacle respect and care. He stops Teal a fraction of a second before the book snuggles into place, and lays a gentle hand on his shoulder.

'Teal... it's okay... you can take the book with you to your room. You can take any books you want. Our house is your house.'

Éric tucks his next words away. He and Vauquelin discussed Teal's love of books before the boys' arrival, and they've already planned to send Teal home with a carton of whichever ones he would like.

That must remain a surprise.

Teal's eyes return to their brightest illumination as he smiles, hugging the book tightly against his chest, and Éric once again finds himself mesmerised.

Where's that light coming from?

A warmth surges in Éric's chest, and he parts his lips. A question is dying to emerge, but his shyness stifles it. He hears Vauquelin's voice whispering in his ear: *you have much to learn...* so he'll be patient. But so far all he knows is that these boys are pure magic.

Even Moth, damn him!

'I'm sorry for staring, Teal. Your eyes are just...' he heaves out a deep sigh... 'they're so beautiful. I hope you'll tell me about them while you're here.'

'It's a long story,' Teal says softly. 'I'm...' he pauses and bites the edge of his lip, 'very different.'

As Teal speaks, Éric realises he already doesn't want the boys to ever leave, despite the conflicts... but at some point, they will. They'll go home, back to the UK, and it will just be him and V again.

The thought pulls the corners of his lips down.

Another sigh.

Éric shakes it off.

'Okay, luggage. Ready? Got your book?'

'Yes,' Teal says, patting the cover. 'This one will be perfect.'

Éric peeks at the spine. 'What did you choose?'

'*Crime and Punishment*. I haven't read this one, yet, and I've always wanted to.'

Damn, Éric thinks, scrunching up his face and nodding.

A little serious, but okay.

They hop down the stairs, and in the foyer, their bags have been brought in and arranged neatly.

Even the sight of the baggage brings Éric down.

It means this is temporary.

Can't they all just stay here forever?

Éric leans against the doors to the salon. He can hear the elders talking — V, Flynn, and Clove — their voices are low and hushed. He remains there a moment, ear pressed against the gilded wood, waiting for Vauquelin to sense his presence, to send him a message… but there's nothing.

Éric has a lot of questions about Clove, but that will come later, when he can be alone with V. Clove intimidated the fuck out of him earlier, and he's going to have to unpack that.

He purses his lips and crosses back to Teal.

'I think we can manage these by ourselves, yeah?'

Teal nods and Éric, with a lop-sided grin, hops over the bags, heaving the handles up on two. He nudges the third with his foot.

'Can you get this one?'

Teal takes charge of the last suitcase, clasping the book to his chest.

He still can't quite believe that he's in a place this beautiful.

Outside the door to the room Gabriel had chosen, Éric and Teal bring the bags to a stop with a dull thunk that reverberates across the herringboned wooden floor.

Éric scratches the door with his fingernails, the ancient French way of knocking that V had taught him. It's so elegant, so discreet, yet also slightly naughty. Éric adores it and had adopted it immediately after their arrival in Paris. He may never hard-knock again.

Behind the door, Moth swears.

Jeans are raised, limbs untangled, mouths are wiped.

'Come in,' Gabe says.

The knob twists and the door creaks open.

Éric saunters in, Teal close behind, but halts when he sees them — Teal slams into his back.

Éric instinctively thrusts out an arm to keep Teal from stumbling.

Moth and Gabriel look... *like they've been up to something.*
Éric's nostrils flare.
He tilts his head toward the ceiling, still sniffing.
Gabriel and Moth look at each other out of the corners of their eyes, and when Éric turns his back, rotating around the room, Moth mouths, '*What the fuck?*'
Gabriel shrugs.
For God's sake, be civil.
'Teal, Gabriel thought you might like this room,' Éric says with great authority, walking toward the jib door, looking back over his shoulder at Gabriel and Moth with narrowed eyes. 'Want to bring your bag in here?'
Something is going on, and Teal can't quite put his finger on it: but given everything else that has happened tonight, he isn't surprised. He grabs his bag from the hallway and rolls it across the floor, disappearing into the anteroom.
'I love it, Gabe!' Teal's voice echoes from beyond the door.
He promptly shuts it behind him, and all three occupants of the other room know that Teal will lose himself in his very own privacy and his love for the book he had chosen.
Éric raises his arms over his head, digging his hands into his hair, and leans back hard against the wall. His hands fall to his hips.
'What the FUCK, you guys? Spill it.'
'What the fuck are *you* talking about?' Moth says. Gabriel grabs his wrist.
'Do you think I can't smell it?'
'Smell what, exactly?' Gabriel asks.
Éric's breath quickens, and his chest begins to heave.
'You're gonna make me say it, aren't you?' A snarl curls his lip. 'I smell *cum.*'
'Éric,' Gabriel begins, knitting his fingers into Moth's. 'You know Moth

and I are together. You teased me with privacy and our own room. Did you really think we wouldn't take advantage of that?'

'Of course not!' Éric says, hands back in his hair. 'I wanted you to! But how? How did you come?'

Gabriel and Moth share an absolute incredulous look.

'Erm... the *usual* way?'

Éric's eyes widen.

All of a sudden the phrase *existential crisis* pops into his mind.

Had Vauquelin *lied* to him?

Are these guys even actual vampires?

WHAT THE FUCK IS GOING ON?

He clasps his hands over his ears, growling.

Now it's Gabriel and Moth's turn to wonder what exactly the fuck is going on.

Éric slinks down the wall until he's sitting on the floor.

Moth bursts out laughing. 'You can't fucking *come*? Is that what you're trying to tell us?'

Éric leaps up, lunging at Moth — but this time, Gabriel has enough time to manoeuvre between them. He keeps them each at an arm's length. And turns to Éric.

'Éric, why don't you tell us what this is about? It seems there's a great misunderstanding here.'

Éric wilts, despite the fact that Moth is still drilling him with a sarcastic grin. He brusquely brushes Gabriel's arm aside and collapses in a chair, burying his face in his hands.

He scratches his head wildly, bouncing his curls all about, and emits a loud 'ARRRRGGGGHHHH!' before turning his face back up to the boys.

This is fucking *mortifying*. How can he even say it? But he has to.

'Vauquelin and I can't ejaculate. He told me no vampires can. I had my last one the night I was turned.' He drops his eyes. 'Okay, last two, if I'm honest. FUCK. I never thought I'd encounter that scent again. I'm sorry. But seriously... what the fuck? How come you guys can do it?'

Gabriel frowns. 'I don't know. We had no idea this was unique to us.'

Éric stands and wanders out of the room like a ghost, closing the door quietly behind him.

He feels faint.

He falls back against the wall.

What fucking time is it?

A million fucking things have happened tonight, in just a few short hours, and his brain is *mutilated*.

All night long, he's been the last to know anything.

He's taken in so much.

Too much.

V could have warned me...

He careens down the stairs and, when he reaches the landing, he looks up over his shoulder.

There's only silence above: the boys haven't followed him.

He strides over to the salon doors and hesitates a moment, filling his lungs with air.

He shouldn't interrupt the elders.

Don't do it. It isn't right.

Then again, is anything he's been through tonight right?

Is Vauquelin punishing him for something?

But for what?

10 / NIGHT 1:

THIS IS ALL VERY NEW FOR ME

Éric lifts both fists and bangs on the doors.

They fly open, and behind them, arms outstretched on the edges, is Vauquelin, his face on fire, long raven waves swinging in a wild frame around his face.

In another time, another place, Éric might actually care about pissing Vauquelin off.

But here, now, he puffs his chest out and says...

« *Au lit. Maintenant. Pas de questions.* »†

And he says it with his index finger in V's face.

Vauquelin regards Éric coolly. Lips closed, he drags his tongue along his front teeth. Éric has placed him in an awkward position with Clove and Flynn: his equals... his friends.

'Éric... do you dare assume Clove and Flynn do not understand French, not to mention the expression upon your face?' He hikes a very serious eyebrow. 'Did you truly think it was a *bonne idée*‡ to order me about in front of master vampires?'

Éric wilts as his eyes fill with blood tears... his lips begin to quiver.

'V, please,' he whispers. 'It's been a really rough night. Can't we please

---
†- BED. NOW. NO QUESTIONS.
‡- GOOD IDEA

just go to bed? I'm begging you.'

Vauquelin takes Éric in his arms and strokes his back.

Remorse subdues him. It was just a little show... he has nothing to prove to Clove or Flynn, but he must admit his beloved deserves some explanations.

He whispers in Éric's ear: '*Bien-aimé*, we are all tired. Take me to bed, and I will answer all your questions. But first, let us escort our esteemed guests to their chambers. They deserve this, do they not, as they have not yet seen where they will sleep?'

Éric drops his chin. 'Of course they do.' He turns to the others and bows in sincerity, a hand over his chest, just as V had taught him. He raises his head to meet their eyes. 'Please accept my apologies, Clove, Flynn. This is all very new for me.'

Vauquelin's heart palpitates. He watches his beloved's turmoil, admires the tumbling of chocolate curls across his forehead... one of the first things that had made him fall in love with this beautiful boy.

My dark angel.

The agitation from Éric is a tangible thing.

It fills the air of the salon with its own burning heat.

Clove wonders what has occurred to affect Éric like this. He nods towards the young vampire to show him no offence is taken.

Éric's shoulders cave further. He feels a foot shorter under Clove's gaze.

Vauquelin turns to the other masters.

'Flynn, we have prepared private quarters for you on the second floor, across from Clove's. I took it as a given he would prefer to be in the one closest to the boys.'

Flynn raises his hand and he laughs softly.

'No slight intended, Vauquelin, but I'd prefer to be out of the firing line.' He casts his gaze upwards. 'I'll take the carriage house at the rear. Keeps me close but not too close.' He loosens his tie and flicks the top button of his shirt open… his bag is still in the boot of the car.

Abject horror settles across Vauquelin's face and he gasps, bringing a hand to his chest. The carriage house is dusty, unused since before Vauquelin first left Paris for the United States: over one hundred years ago.

'But… it is unfit… I would never have presumed.'

A mind-whisper in the direction of his beloved, accompanied by a jerk of his chin.

Clean sheets, bien-aimé.

Vauquelin disapproves of Flynn staying in the carriage house, but if this is what he wishes, at least he will have an unsullied place to lay his head.

Éric peels away and rushes up the stairs, returning shortly with a stack of soft, purple bed linens, a down pillow, and a silken duvet. He hefts them into a confounded Flynn's arms.

A low whistle spills from Flynn's lips.

'Five star luxury.'

He nods his thanks towards Éric then turns to Vauquelin.

'A bit of dust won't kill me, so don't concern yourself about that. Besides, I like to be on the outside looking in, gives me ample opportunity to snuff out any unwelcome guests.' He grins, the tips of his fangs glinting in the candlelight.

Éric's gaze travels across the three masters.

They're all tall and intimidating. They're elders, vampires made hundreds of years ago: V was turned at thirty, and Clove seems to be around that same age — but when Éric lands on Flynn, it hits him.

Holy shit … he's like … my age?

Flynn's dark hair is short and cut in a modern style. It confuses Éric. If he was made way back when, then why isn't it long like the others? As these revelations settle in his head, he finds himself locked in Flynn's green-eyed gaze, and it makes him feel just that much more unworthy.

Jesus Christ, he thinks. *They're all fucking gorgeous.*

He's still a little stung by what had just happened, compounded by V ordering him around like a lapdog, but as he watches the three of them, all those thoughts evaporate.

Damn.

Vauquelin cocks a brow at Éric... his beloved's mind is an open book. No doubt the others have interpreted Éric's bewildered expression.

'I'll say goodnight, gentlemen.' Flynn dips his head towards Clove and Vauquelin. He pauses in the doorway as Éric's gaze has followed him there. A smirk touches his lips and as he leaves he turns and meets the young vampire's wide-eyed stare.

Staying in the carriage house is definitely the best decision.

There are fireworks building here.

He can sense it.

'*Bonsoir,*† Flynn. And I thank you again for delivering them all safely.' Vauquelin points to the second floor. 'Shall we?'

Clove and Vauquelin begin their ascent and Vauquelin lingers, glancing to his left — Éric is not beside him where he should be. He halts on a step and looks behind his shoulder.

Éric is a few steps back, crestfallen, his chin on his chest, trudging one heavy foot after another.

Vauquelin inclines his head, and holds out his arm.

'My love... how could I go upstairs to bed without you by my side? As we do every morning?'

Éric's crooked grin creases his face, though he doesn't meet Vauquelin's gaze. He hurries up the steps and tucks himself under his lover's arm, snuggling into his steady grasp.

Vauquelin stops at the top landing, rubbing his Éric's shoulder blade, and turns to face to Clove.

'I believe you should find your room sufficient. If not, we are at the end

---

†- GOOD NIGHT

of the hall,' he says, nodding towards his own bedchamber. He releases Éric for a moment. His beloved falls back obediently, and Vauquelin again clasps Clove's elbows, looking deep into his eyes.

'I am grateful for your presence, Clove. More than you may ever know.'

And with that he bids *adieu*[†] to the other master, reclaiming his beloved and guiding him in the opposite direction.

[†] FAREWELL

11 / NIGHT 1:

IT IS ALWAYS MOTH

Clove closes the door and surveys his room for the first time.

It is exactly as he envisaged — only more *Vauquelin*.

The heaviness of the velvet draperies, the over-abundance of candle sconces, the walls covered in not just one, but a whole host of sumptuous oil paintings. His lips curl into a smile as he crosses to the bed, the embroidered hangings enclosing the impressive wooden frame.

He cannot remember the last time he slept in a bed with all of its comforts; he can only imagine the delight of his boys. Not once have they ever complained about Gehenna's lack of basic necessities, of bathing in ice-cold rivers, of the chill that seeps through the ancient stones in winter and bites bone-deep.

They do not complain because they have the one thing that is of utmost importance. They have safety, and they have each other.

He can indulge them in some luxury during this visit.

They have earned it with every fibre of their being.

Clove sits on the edge of the deep mattress and kicks off the dress shoes that look so wrong. It is not only his boys that feel displaced in their attire. He lies on his back and studies the canopy, a riot of crimson and gold threads interwoven into lavish fleur-de-lys.

Éric's distraught face swims across his mind's eye.

What had happened to upset him so much?

Moth.

That is the name that punches through his thoughts.

It is always Moth.

But Gabriel would not let things go too far.

Moth may be an uncontrollable lit fuse most of the time, but one word from Gabriel in a certain tone of voice, and Moth will bend the knee, tamping down his fury to a level his first-born called Seethe.

No, something else has occurred.

He sighs and steeples his hands against his lips, lets the tension of the journey slip away.

They are here.

They are sheltered within these ancient walls.

Anything else will be dealt with when light gives way to the ever-present darkness waiting in the wings.

12 / NIGHT 1:

LA PETITE MORT
{ THE LITTLE DEATH }

Vauquelin twists the knobs, his fingers tightening on them a moment. He looks back down the passage, and seeing that Clove has vanished into his room, he grasps Éric by the jaw and backs him in through the doors, kicking them closed behind him as he pries Éric's lips apart with his own, drowning him in kisses as he urges him toward the bed.

Éric shoves him back, almost making him stumble.

Vauquelin's eyes flash with anger. 'What is this?' He splays his hands.

Éric sits on the side of the bed, hugging himself, rocking slowly.

'What's *this*?' he asks. 'Do you have *any idea* what you did to me tonight? You threw me to the fucking sharks!' He rises from the bed and begins pacing, cradling his elbows. 'If you knew all this stuff about them and you didn't tell me, you're a fucking monster!'

Vauquelin strides to Éric, tries to embrace him, but Éric is on fire and he thrusts V's arms down.

'Why couldn't you prepare me a little? I thought they would be kind of like me, young vampires who don't know much about anything! But they're not! They're fucking haunted and magic and I'm NOTHING! It's like you brought them here to show me just how unextraordinary I am.' Éric crumples beside the bed, bumping his back down the mattress. 'And you lied to me.'

Vauquelin panics. His eyes could not possibly widen more.

'How do you mean? I did not lie to you! I realise that there is much you do not know about them, but I do not know all, either! What is this about? What has happened?'

'V... first off, Moth fucking hates me and I don't know why. We've almost been in two fights since they arrived. And then...' Éric's chest heaves again.

The sight of Éric in this state worries Vauquelin to no end. He has not seen Éric in such distress since the night Oliver betrayed Vauquelin's time-slips. 'Éric... you must tell me. I will rectify anything that could disturb you so. I promised you I would never lie to you. I gave you my word.'

Éric can't look at Vauquelin.

He hiccups... finally he chokes the words out.

'I walked into Gabriel and Moth's room after they were... alone.' At last Éric lifts his swollen, blood-drenched eyes to Vauquelin. 'You told me vampires can't ejaculate... we could never make each other come. You filled my mind with so many sweet words when we met. I think you fucking *lied to me*. I could smell it, Vauquelin. In their room.'

Vauquelin bristles at Éric calling him by his given name.

Since the night Éric chose to call him V, he has never once called him by anything else.

He reaches for Éric's hand and his beloved promptly snatches it back.

Vauquelin draws in a sharp breath. He sinks to the floor in front of Éric.

'What are you telling me, exactly?'

'Moth ridiculed me... they can fucking come. It filled the air of the room. So why can't we?'

Vauquelin settles back against the side of the bed next to Éric, his eyes darting madly.

Can this be true?

His mind sinks into the trenches of his deepest history.

He drapes an arm around Éric's knees for support, hoping his beloved will be his anchor so that he will not disappear into his depths.

Éric melts into him.

He knows when V needs him. And he needs him too.

The night of his turning, when he was forced to take his sham bride, Vauquelin could not climax. He gave up, from raw exhaustion.

His only other vampire lover was Clément.

Neither of them climaxed.

So many men, so many women have taken the sting out of his endless, empty nights.

Now he feels quite the idiot.

He has only recently acquired the library of vampire lore... he had always assumed it was the nature of the revenant, purely biological: so that their monstrous nature might not reproduce, except through blood.

He turns to Éric and covers his mouth with his hand, a sullen expression overtaking his face.

Éric's eyes widen. 'What?'

Vauquelin curls his fingers into themselves, fidgeting them in his lap, avoiding his beloved's pointed gaze. His words are quiet, sullen.

'I must confess I was unaware of their... ability. This must be our heritage, unique to our bloodline, my love. I can think of no other justification.'

His mind immediately shifts to the nights before Éric was turned... the many times he swallowed the delectable results of Éric's humanity, the very essence of Éric that he will never taste again. The same essence of himself, the flavour of which Éric will never know.

The one night he was human again, in his inordinately fucked-up timeline, Vauquelin felt the viscosity of his ejaculate as he smeared it across the flat plane of his stomach. He can still recall the scent, its fecund spice perfuming the air, can still see the way it webbed between his fingers in the sunlight from the open windows.

He will never forget it.

Himself.

Just as Éric encountered it tonight, found it forbidden to him while others revelled in it… now his beloved's overwhelming melancholy makes sense.

Without hesitation Vauquelin unbuttons Éric's trousers, slides the zipper down… he rests a strong hand on Éric's shoulder, informing him he is not to move, and their eyes meet. Vauquelin looks at his hand dipping into the depths below Éric's fly, probing deeper and deeper, as his beloved expectantly parts his legs.

A quiet whimper escapes Éric's lips.

Do you still love me? Vauquelin asks.

You know I do, Éric replies, and his eyelids grow heavy.

Vauquelin places his hands on either side of his beloved's hips and in one fell swoop sweeps his trousers to his ankles. He unties Éric's boots, kissing his knees whilst he tosses the shoes across the floor along with his black trousers, and then urges him up, heaving both their bodies to the surface of the bed.

He lifts Éric's shirt with his nose and kisses down his favourite trail — the one he had fortuitously preserved the night of Éric's turning. He arrives at his beloved's cock, ebbing the beautiful foreskin back with gentle fingers, worshipping its hidden jewel with his lips… and then he releases it, looking up.

Vauquelin peels off his clothing, slow and deliberate.

He tears apart the centre of Éric's shirt, sending the buttons flying god-knows-where. Now they are in the state Vauquelin prefers: skin to skin. He caresses his way from Éric's collar bone back down to his cock, and gives it a teasing lick — and then he grasps his beloved's hips and flips him over, hoisting those hips into the air.

A brief pause, leaving Éric suspended in expectation as he retrieves a glass jar from the night stand. The metal lid clangs across the parquet floor, piercing the silence of the room, and from the corner of his eye Vauquelin catches Éric flinch. When it comes to a stop, a sucking sound is all that can be heard as he extracts lanolin-streaked fingers from the jar before moving them to open Éric.

While he works his lover to blossom for him, Vauquelin traces a fingertip from the nape of Éric's neck down his spine, until his fingers meet again.

And then Vauquelin takes himself in his hands and impales Éric.

He grips Éric's hipbone with his right hand, his shoulder with his left. Éric is on his knees, just as Vauquelin had been the night they met. He wants to give Éric what Éric had given him... only then, neither of them knew that he was giving Vauquelin the only orgasm he will ever know.

Yet it won't be the same — because *they* are no longer the same as they were when fate delivered them to one another. He mimics his memory of Éric moving in his body for the first time — slow, unsure — and then a frenzy takes over. His love for Éric, for being inside Éric's body, for being joined to him in this way, compels him.

Beneath him, Éric bites his lip. He looks back over his shoulder, watches V labouring into his body, and his mind incinerates. Éric drops his chin to his chest, curving his hips to crest with the pulsating rhythms of Vauquelin's thrusts.

V brings his hand to Éric's abdomen. He leans into Éric, his stomach in arc with Éric's spine, and he slows. Their bodies are in tune like a fine instrument. He pauses a moment, as deep as he can get. Their balls nestle. This is the closest they can ever come to being one.

They collapse like a house of cards onto the mattress.

V is crushing Éric, Éric's body is wholly filled by V, *owned*.

And right this second Éric wants to die... because this would be the *very best* way to die.

But V fills Éric even more. V's fingers pry his mouth open, even while he resumes moving inside him like the slow movement of a symphony… V's fingers dig into his throat, choking him, and Éric bites. Blood flows into his mouth like melted chocolate, and he does die for a fraction of a second.

La petite mort. The little death.

They both die for each other.

And they will do it again and again, every morning, for as many dawns as there are to come.

Éric comes back with a gasp, with a vengeance.

He wants to *live*.

He does not want this miracle to ever end, but it does.

It wanes.

Vauquelin cannot spill anything across his back, nor can Éric release anything from himself or feel it drape down his hand like heavy cream.

Instead, Vauquelin withdraws and they cling to one another, blood sweat glistening on their skins.

Éric's body is empty, so resolutely empty without V inside it.

Fangs sink into necks and they drink it up, greedily gulping hard, becoming drunk on the only essence they can give.

Now they take one another's jaws in their hands.

Their eyes drown in the same sea, and there is no doubt there.

They both plunge in.

Vauquelin parts his lips.

Éric susses the words before they emerge.

He brings a finger up to shush V.

Don't. I know.

Éric cradles Vauquelin's head in his arms.

This is their way.

This is all they need.

They can only find it within one another.

And then they surrender to their sleep.

13 / NIGHT 1:

A SHARP TWINGE OF ANGUISH

'Are you going to tell me what's eating you up?'

Gabe lays with his arm around Moth's shoulders, together in this ancient bed, together in V's palatial home. He can't quite work out how he feels, whether he's happy to be here away from the dour gloom of Gehenna, or whether he'd rather be back there where everything is so familiar.

It will be an adventure, Gabriel. But an adventure that will test you. Clove's words, from before they left, drift across his senses.

Beside him, Moth tenses like a compressed spring, and Gabe tries to take that tension into himself. For all of their delicious interlude earlier Moth is still strung out, but at least he's not at exploding point. His antagonism towards Éric seems excessive and he desperately wants to get to the bottom of it before it turns into its own monster.

He pulls Moth closer, offers his neck for comfort if Moth wishes to take a mouthful, but his lover simply lowers his head into the curve between Gabe's ear and shoulder, his cool breath whispering against Gabe's skin.

They are naked, the discomforting clothes they had travelled in discarded on the floor.

Gabe lets his fingers trace the topography of Moth's spine, lets them sweep across his lover's slender back from hip to hip before coming to rest in the curved hollow of the small of his back, the place where flesh rises again into the swell of youthful buttocks. And Moth shivers, not in lust but in the pure joy of touching. It's the most intimate of experiences.

Gabe presses his face into Moth's mussed up hair and inhales the strange floral scent of shampoo. Clove had insisted they find a place to shower before their journey and Elijah had sourced a house in the middle of nowhere where the owners were away.

It was the most surreal experience after years at Gehenna; hot water and cleansing lotions, soft towels and electric light.

He thinks about that and then Éric's distraught expression after his bombshell confession. A sharp twinge of anguish settles in his gut, but dawn has broken outside the heavily-draped windows and his eyelids flutter closed as he follows Moth into the clutches of the death sleep.

14 / NIGHT 2:
DEATH LOVES HIM

Gabe opens his eyes: for a millisecond the strangeness of his surroundings propels him into a seated position — his lips draw back on his fangs.

A vampire's instinct overrules everything else.

He finds Moth curled into a pillow, one hand over his face as he always sleeps. Even now this image still has the most profound effect on Gabe. It touches him soul-deep and he reaches out to trail his fingers across Moth's cheek. His skin is cold, he's still cocooned in the death sleep, his heart as still as a stone.

Gabe has no right to pray, and he doesn't believe in the presence of an almighty God... but every dawn before they fall he sends a wish spiralling into the darkness they call home, asking that Moth be kept safe.

He pulls the bed curtains apart and pads across the floor, gently opening the jib door set into the wall. A smile travels from his lips to his eyes as he finds Teal wrapped in the huge silk comforter, an open book on the pillow beside him.

The darkness here has a different feel. A tingle spreads across the back of Gabe's neck and for a moment the richness of soft earth after a rainstorm drifts across his senses.

The witch in Teal never really sleeps. It watches over him and he's certain it's because of Devlin, the witch boy who gave up his life so Teal could live. Gabe is never quite sure if part of Devlin stayed with

Teal, just like the flickering light of the last fireflies — the souls of two persecuted vampires — because, really, no one could ever want to willingly leave his bright-eyed brother.

Gabe closes the door softly and hangs his head for a moment.

Death loves him.

It follows him, reaches out tendrils to those he loves, curls into his shadow, an ever-present wraith.

Come to me.

The mind-touch blazes into him and he's already at the door, going to Clove, before he realises that prowling naked along the hallway when he's a guest probably isn't the acceptable thing to do.

He opens the nearest suitcase and yanks out the closest item: an old pair of light blue jeans, ripped at the knees, the stitching unravelling, old blood staining the thin fabric. He knows he should get rid of them: it's not as if they can't acquire new things every night they go out to hunt, but this is the last pair of jeans that connect him to being human. He was wearing these the night he died, the night he was reborn.

He can't explain why he still feels the need to keep them, but it's a reminder that he wasn't always Gabriel Davenport, heir to the necromancer's awful legacy, he was the baby who was hunted by a demon, a child brought up in a house of love and respect, a house — and its occupants — that shaped him into the human Clove saw fit to bless with his ancient blood.

Gabe pulls on these cherished jeans, because he can. They fit him like a glove, hang low on his hips. There's a fuckton of rules out there and if he's breaking any by keeping a piece of his past he doesn't give a damn.

His head is full of teeming thoughts, of then and now and what is to come, as he opens the door to the hallway and finds Éric only a few steps away.

Éric's hair is still wet from the shower: dark ringlets cling to his face. He was just about to head downstairs when he heard the boys' door open.

Seeing Gabriel standing there is a little surreal. Actually *every*thing that happened last night is replaying through his head on a hallucinatory repeat. There's still so much to decipher.

V is taking a bath. Who knows, he might be in there for hours — but Éric hopes not. He has no clue what their plans are for the night, and the prospect of having to talk to Moth looms over him like a black cloud. He's not sure he can handle him alone again and he'd like V to be there next time.

He saunters over and hikes an approving eyebrow, flicking his eyes over Gabriel's bare chest. He leans to the right slightly, peering behind. The room is dark behind Gabriel, and Éric can't see Moth, *thank god*.

It's way too fucking early for that.

'Well, good evening. Did you run out of clothes already?' He laughs. 'I hope you guys slept well. It's always weird the first night in a new place.'

'Hey.' Gabe decides that he may as well embrace his half-naked state. It's not as if he can fade into the wallpaper. But a little acknowledgement won't go amiss. 'Apologies for my uncovered state. I was just on my way to see Clove.'

He sees relief wash over Éric's face after realising Gabe is alone, then the weirdness of his host's words finally sink in.

'We slept like we always do, although whether that's well or not we can never tell.' He lets a small grin play on his lips to show Éric that he isn't being testy. 'Moth always comes out of his death sleep later than me so you can relax a bit longer.'

Death sleep? These boys are just full of fucking surprises.

'What are you talking about?' Éric mutters.

Gabe feels his brows lift and once more he's in unfamiliar territory.

'The death sleep. Where we all end up when the sun starts to rise.'

Éric is looking at him like Gabe has grown two heads.

'Where our hearts stop beating. Clinically dead. Or more dead than we actually are.'

He stops before his mouth adds any more ridiculous detail.

Éric's fingers begin to tremble. He knows his and V's hearts don't beat while they sleep, but they can wake. When Éric was first turned he'd had horrifying nightmares, and V would wake and comfort him. He pictures the boys in this death sleep Gabriel just described — beautiful little corpses, with the promise that comes as a blessing of their darkness: that they will rise. But these words won't come to his lips so he just stands there, staring at Gabriel with a blank expression.

'That doesn't happen to us. This is wild.' Éric whispers, 'How can we be so different? I don't understand it.'

'Fuck.' The expletive drops from Gabe's lips as ice-cold realisation dawns. 'It's a bloodline thing. Whoever turns us gives us their own unique traits.' His eyes widen. 'I didn't know that we could be so different either.'

'An unfortunate gap in your education, Gabriel.'

Clove's voice in the gloom of the hallway has Gabe spinning around.

Fuck, fuck, fuck. Clove called me and I didn't go.

Another apology forms on his tongue but fades as his gaze alights on his maker's face. There's no recrimination there, just a mild amusement at catching his first-born in what could be called a compromising position.

Éric blurts, 'I have to grab something downstairs. See you later,' and flits down the steps like a startled gazelle.

Gabe has only just woken but already the edges of his known world are slipping. Instead of launching into an admission of guilt he keeps his silence, waiting for Clove to continue.

Clove comes to him, and it is this, rather than his words, which make the blood pound in Gabe's ears. He should be the one going to Clove, out of respect, out of devotion.

He lifts his chin before Clove can do it for him and a cool palm comes to rest against his cheek.

'I believe the full explanation should come when Vauquelin is present.'

The tension Gabe is carrying melts away into Clove's touch. It's always like this. Clove has the ability to soothe away any jagged edges, to settle the disquiet in Gabe's mind. He knows his maker wants him to bloom, to question and to forge his own life, but he's always grateful for this safe port in any storm he manages to unleash.

He's only just aware of Éric's footsteps racing down the stairs and knows he's not the only one adrift in disorientating waters.

15 / NIGHT 2:

NONE OF YOU CAN SEE IT

Vauquelin emerges from the bedchamber and finds the hallways smothered in silence, empty of his guests.

He knows exactly where Éric will be.

A wry smile twists his lips — he had hoped he had sufficiently worn Éric out this morning, at least enough to still his beleaguered thoughts... yet Éric had spent a restless day, tossing and turning. He had risen early, highly unusual for him, and showered while Vauquelin still slept.

A muted din increases in volume as Vauquelin approaches a room off the former larder, the heavy doors scarcely capable of containing the thumping music Éric is blasting in his lair. Vauquelin knocks his forehead gently against the doors. When the music is this loud, it can mean only one thing: Éric is in distress, and he disappears into his own world when this happens.

He knows Éric will not hear him knock, so he opens the doors and walks right in.

Éric is stretched out on a sofa, his foot twitching to the rhythm, his hands folded behind his head. His body jerks when he notices V standing there, and he aims the remote at his speakers, killing the sound.

'Sorry, V... was it too loud?'

'No, my love.' Vauquelin, more than anyone else, understands Éric's need for solitude.

But they have guests who have taken a long — and potentially risky — journey for them all to be together, and this is not the time for it.

'Where are the boys? Have you greeted them tonight?'

'I saw Gabriel in the hall. Did you know they all go into death sleep?'

'Yes...' Vauquelin replies quietly.

Éric sighs and looks at the ceiling. He bites the inside of his cheek to prevent himself from being snarky to V. It isn't fair to be mad at him — did he expect V to give him a fucking *manual* for dealing with the boys?

Éric has been a brat... he knows it.

V knows it, too.

Éric can tell by the way he's looking at him right now.

'I'm really sorry, V,' he says. 'I haven't handled things very well. I promise I'll do better.'

But then his stomach drops when he thinks of Moth.

He's still *super fucking embarrassed* about what happened when he walked in on them last night. It was none of his business.

'I think it is time we were all together,' Vauquelin says. 'We are going to the salon. Clove and the boys should be there in a few moments. Come, *bien-aimé*.'†

Éric takes Vauquelin's hand as they amble through the salon doors. He crosses and draws the curtains back, because it has begun to rain: heavy, fattened drops cascade down the windows, seeping soft wafts of petrichor though the sills. Éric leans his cheek against the cool glass while V lights the fireplace.

What a perfect night, Éric thinks.

It's his favourite kind.

It hardly ever rains in L.A.

He's brimming over with love right now, and he desperately hopes it's enough to keep him and Moth from locking horns again.

---
†- BELOVED

The salon doors sweep open and Clove strides in, followed by Gabe and Moth, flanking Teal. They have shed their stiff, formal clothes and are all clothed in black: jeans, T-shirts, boots — although Clove wears a loose shirt tucked into his belt.

Only once had Clove let his boys lead him. That time was at Gehenna when they brought Teal to the necromancer. That repellent event was *their* choice, and even though the pain had seared through Clove's bones he had not stopped them because Teal had accepted his fate.

'Vauquelin.' Clove holds out his arms and inclines his head as Vauquelin rises to his feet. 'Your hospitality is unrivalled. My grateful thanks.'

He turns to the young vampire standing by the window.

'Éric, we have not yet become acquainted. I wish to remedy that. Come and sit with me.'

He does not mention Éric's abrupt interruption last night, his disrespect towards his maker. That is not Clove's place.

Teal settles himself on an emerald green silk couch and Moth and Gabe go to stand behind it. There's a serious air about Gabe, a certain tightness in his jaw. Moth is silent, his gaze fixed on the floor because he'd rather be anywhere else but here. Gabe has had *words* and they still sting.

Éric looks to V for a soothing glance, a small gesture... anything at all... but he's already on the other side of the room in a chair, his legs crossed, his concentration devoted to rolling a cigarette.

Éric realises he's on display, and that's something he fucking despises.

Always has.

But he doesn't want to dishonour V again. He won't.

He peels himself away from the window and slips into the spot next to Clove on the settee.

Another apology hovers in his throat but he already apologised last night, and Clove's expression implies that grovelling isn't exactly an admirable quality.

'Clove, I hope you...' he gets tongue-tied. Everything in his head sounds stupid. 'I hope you know how happy Vauquelin and I are that you're all here.'

He cuts a glance at V, who gives him a long wink as he takes a massive drag off his cigarette.

Moth mutters two words that definitely begin with F and Y.

Gabe immediately shoots a Look and Moth presses his lips together, although there's a smirk across one edge.

Although Clove's attention is firmly fixed on Éric, he does not miss Moth's snarky muttering. A small line creases his brow. He will intervene if Moth does not tow the line. It has been a while since he felt the need to supersede Gabriel's authority and he knows it will not be a palatable experience for either of them.

'It is the greatest honour to stay with Vauquelin and yourself.' His eyes soften and he fixes Éric in place with their intensity. 'I believe you must have been an extraordinary human for Vauquelin to have chosen you. And I believe you will be an extraordinary vampire, albeit one that may take a while longer to find his feet.' This last is said with a smile.

The weight of Vauquelin's gaze, watching him from across the room as he takes another draw of his cigarette, settles on his shoulders like a favourite blanket.

Vauquelin closes his eyes at Clove's statement and his heart reverberates. He is well aware that Clove never speaks without measuring his thoughts: or else they would never emerge. His fellow master's approval of Éric is of utmost importance. Now he can only hope that Éric will accept those words and believe them himself: which will be a challenge.

Éric, for his part, can scarcely believe Clove is speaking to him this way. A strange sensation bleeds across his senses. No one — with the exception of V — has ever taken him this seriously.

'Thank you, Clove,' he whispers. He can feel it crawling around in his chest. It always, always happens when he gets this emotional.

Don't you dare fucking cry... not now.

He sniffles.

Oh god... NO. No way. Moth would crucify me.

That thought alone is enough to bolster him.

He relaxes his back, leaning into the settee.

Vauquelin sits on the armrest next to Éric.

'Many questions have arisen between Éric and the boys, Clove. Perhaps it is time we answered them.'

'I happened upon Gabriel and Éric earlier. They were discussing the differences in bloodlines which they knew nothing about.' Clove looks across to Gabriel. 'Come to me.'

In a few short strides his first-born is there before him, kneeling on the floor as Clove is sitting: a mark of respect. A warm glow touches his heart.

'I have been remiss in my education on certain points and for this I apologise. I assumed wrongly that Elijah had informed you all and that is an unfortunate oversight.'

He reaches out, places a hand on Gabriel's shoulder. 'You know now that bloodlines all carry their own unique fingerprint. Mine to you contains the death sleep, single fangs, the ability to walk upon the Bloodvyne, and to ejaculate as you did when human.'

Gabriel meets his gaze and something else passes between them. The darkness in their blood is a shared symphony. Clove did not mention what else runs in his bloodline. It is, perhaps, too early to drop that particular bombshell. Éric has enough to absorb and it is unfair to burden him further.

Vauquelin cringes at Clove having to discuss such an intimate subject, and he swallows his own regret — for he had not known about this prior to Éric's revelation. Nevertheless, he has lived it with since his turning. He had long ago accepted it, adapted to it in his own way. Éric is the one who truly suffers from this reality. But it is something he has lived with since his turning. He had long ago accepted it, adapted to it in his own way. Éric is the one who truly suffers from this reality.

He squeezes Éric's shoulder, and Éric brings his hand up, lacing their fingers together.

Well, that was fucking awkward, Éric thinks. He wishes he could blend right into the upholstery and disappear.

There's another question trapped in the messy tangle of Éric's thoughts, but it's for V. And it can only be asked when they're alone.

The atmosphere of the room is charged with excruciating silence.

Éric takes great pains to avoid looking in Moth's direction, even going so far as to twist his torso toward Clove, so that not a centimetre of Mothness enters his viewpoint.

He leans into V, and the masters exchange glances.

Vauquelin is reminded of the war years, and the eerie stillness that follows an air raid siren: there is no way of knowing just when the shells will begin to fall, but one is assured of their impact.

Communicating with Clove silently seems disrespectful to Éric... he'd prefer they walk into another room. He should have spoken to Clove alone before this gathering tonight. He has half a mind to suggest they all go out into the city — or have some blood sources brought in — but he would never offer this in front of the boys without first consulting Clove.

Regardless, going out or bringing in some kills would only be a brief respite. Something must be done about Éric and Moth or the remainder of this visit will grow further fraught with tension, and Vauquelin wants Clove and the boys to stay as long as possible.

The voice that breaks the silence is a surprise to everyone gathered in the salon, including its owner. It's a gentle voice that prefers to stay mute, and it's this fact alone that gives it such power in the thick, gauche hush.

'But isn't it our unique differences that shape us?'

All eyes wheel to Teal and he finds himself in an unaccustomed spotlight. One thing he knows is that hovering quietly on the outskirts of conversations gives him the ability to see what others miss as they tumble in the whirlpool of the attention centre. He hasn't missed a thing since they arrived and he's absorbed each fragment, fully conscious that the ticking time bomb between Moth and Éric could very well cut their visit short. And he desperately doesn't want to leave.

There is so much he needs to see.

He sweeps his hair out of his eyes and continues. 'What we see as failings can be strengths. We,' he gestures to his brothers and Clove, 'all fall under the death sleep as dawn breaks. It's something we have no control over. That leaves us vulnerable.' He takes a breath and turns to face Vauquelin and Éric. 'Your bloodline can wake in the daylight hours. If there is a threat you're much more able to confront it.'

He looks to Clove now, unsure if he's said too much.

A barely perceptible nod gives Teal permission to carry on.

Gabe comes to sit by him, interlocking his fingers with Teal's.

'I guess what I'm trying to say is that we need to accept what is different about us, even if we don't like it, or want to rage against it.' Now his gaze is fixed on Éric but it's gentle, without a shred of judgement.

Teal closes his eyes for a moment — he can do this.

He *has* to do this.

'My bloodline isn't pure at all.' A small shrug as his lips try to form the words. Gabe's fingers tighten, and now Moth is on his knees before him, those bicoloured eyes blazing with such fierce protectiveness that it gives Teal the strength to say what he knows he must. 'I am vampire, but there's something else. I'm part witch too.'

One could hear a pin drop in the expansive salon.

Éric's fingers rise to tweak his silver ear hoops… he's mesmerised by the entrancing, flickering lights in the blue-green of the quiet vampire's eyes…

he had known something was incredibly different about Teal, but *this* possibility had never crossed his mind. V's fingers sink softly into his hair and Éric flinches before burrowing into his lover's comforting touch.

Just a few short years ago, Éric hadn't even believed vampires existed: now he is one. And before he was vampire, he was already different — he had been all his life.

It was something he had had to accept about himself in order to stay alive. He found solace in a tiny world of his own making, and then V came along and made that world infinitely wider. Despite tucking Éric under his dark wings and stealing the sunshine, Vauquelin had filled his soul with a more encompassing kind of light. He'll never have to fear staying alive again — because he is bathed in love and acceptance.

He is immortal, his love is forever.

And now Éric, with Teal's powerful words sinking into his psyche, can see that this gathering is the greatest gift Vauquelin has given him. He can see that maybe he *is* extraordinary, like Clove said, because V would never have chosen him, would never have pledged his love for all eternity... V would not have gifted him all this wonder and magic had he not believed Éric was worthy of receiving it.

Teal's revelation, of being part witch, suddenly seems as believable as Teal being blond, or the fact that Éric has learned to speak French.

Éric *is* different, they all are, and he is a part of this unique gathering. The world may never know about them, and this beautiful poison that they all share, but at last Éric is beginning to understand: the world doesn't deserve to know about them.

Maybe they are all here together because they are the only ones that can understand each other. His heart expands, brimming over with serenity.

Éric sinks to the ground and scoots over to sit in front of Gabriel and Teal, folding his hands in his lap. He's ultra-aware of the proximity of Moth but pushes this awkwardness away... because what he has to say to Teal is more important.

Vauquelin tilts his head, focussing on Éric. His beloved's understanding radiates from his soul and touches his own. Maybe, at last, Éric can see himself as something *more than*.

'Teal, I don't have the right words now... my brain is a little muddled tonight. But I already knew you were something special. I'm lucky just to be sitting here at your feet, knowing that I know you.'

Éric is severely in Moth's space. In fact, he's barely an inch or two away and he wants to elbow him away from Teal, but a glance from Gabe leaves him rooted to the spot.

Don't you dare, the glance says, and Moth swallows the fury burning in his throat. None of them understand how he feels, even Gabe, and it's this that is peeling his heart into shreds. He *wants* to tell Gabe, yet his reasons sound so childish, and he knows he should just bury them — but Moth has never worked like that.

What you see is what you get.

No one can ever accuse him of secrecy.

The way Éric is gazing up at Teal and the heartfelt tremble in his words is turning Moth inside out — part of him is happy that Éric is appreciating how amazing Teal is, but another part, the much larger part, is so insanely jealous that his eyes start to sting and he turns away as his throat closes up.

Teal's reply to Éric floats past him.

'I'm just me... a little messed up at the edges, but then we all are.'

Movement from the corner of Moth's eye as Teal takes Éric's hand.

And the dam breaks. Waves of molten lava bubble up from his core and he's caught in the flow, helpless and terrified of what he might do.

Teal's eyes widen as Moth lunges for Éric.

Moth knows his fangs are bared, which is probably the worst sin he can commit in a room full of vampires — and he's ready to strike and be damned for the consequences, when he finds himself flying backwards.

His feet scrabble for grip but the hand on his collar is as firm as iron.

Fuck. Fuck. Fuck.

This is Clove and there's no coming back from whatever punishment is decided for him...

Moth is a maelstrom of conflicting emotions and he can't get a handle on any of them. *What if Clove banishes me? How can I exist without Gabe and Teal?*

The cry that comes from his throat is a cry of absolute terror.

His back is slammed against a wall, so hard that the paintings twitch, but it's not Clove's eyes he's looking into, it's Gabe's — and the pain within them takes every ounce of fight out of Moth's body.

Everyone is on their feet.

All eyes are on Moth.

Vauquelin steps behind Éric, enfolding him in his arms, placing his hand over Éric's heart. His eyes have gone deep dark blue, and a vicious verdigris vein erupts across his forehead. As much as he adores the young vampires standing before him, as much as he loves and respects the master vampire at his side, he will not tolerate danger aimed at his most precious one. He had given up too much for the privilege of holding him.

His breath comes hard and fast.

He silently says to Éric: *Not a word. I am here. I am always here.* Beneath his grip, Éric's body trembles. His beloved's knees buckle, but Vauquelin will not let him fall.

He steels his embrace.

Again silence envelops the salon but this time it is the silence of absolute shock.

Clove goes to Vauquelin. Clove's jaw is set so tight that his fangs ache in his gums. What Moth has done is almost unforgivable.

'My sincere apologies for this condemnable outburst, Master Vauquelin.' He uses the deferential term to try to soothe the savage waters Moth has left in his wake. 'He will be punished.'

Teal sits on the couch, frozen in place, his arms wrapped around his body. *How did it all go wrong so quickly?* He had tried to be kind, to open up to Éric, to let him know that he isn't alone in his uniqueness, and now it's all ruined. Numbness seeps through his limbs.

Gabe feels the fight ooze out of Moth but it's too late. All eyes are glued to them both and how Gabe conducts himself now will shape this visit and everyone's memories of it.

'Tell me,' he says, and he winces at the coldness in his voice. 'Tell me what's wrong and why you wanted to attack Éric. In. His. Home.' He punctuates the last three words to amplify their importance.

Moth meets his gaze and what Gabe sees ices his heart. The stubborn tilt of his chin. The tight lips. The shadows in those mismatched eyes.

Moth's shields are slammed shut.

Gabe rests his brow against Moth's and closes his eyes.

Tears burn behind them but he cannot cry, not here.

Please, please, tell me. You're crucifying me here.

Silence.

Gabe waits a few moments, swallows the lump in his throat. He doesn't want to hand his authority over to Clove but what else can he do?

He turns...

Moth's hand snakes out and grabs his wrist.

I'm so fucking scared.

The mind-touch sears against Gabe's mind, the emotion behind it almost too powerful to absorb.

Tell me. We can do anything together.

He takes Moth's hand and places a kiss against the palm.

A minute, I need a fucking minute.

Gabe stands back and gives his lover space.

He sends a mind-touch to Clove.

Please, just a little more time.

Because he knows Clove is seconds away from taking the matter into his own hands and that can only end badly for Moth.

Moth paces to the window where the rain batters against the glass.

He wishes he could slip outside and lose himself on the wet midnight streets, to run away from what he has set in motion. His cheeks burn, his heartbeat pulses in his ears. He feels alone even though his brothers are in the same room.

'It's just...' he pauses and rakes his fingers through his hair, trying to stop the tremble in his words. 'Can't any of you see it? Am I the only one?' His voice raises an octave and the sound echoes around the room.

Gabe's expression says he wants to sweep him up in his arms and fuck off out of here, but he knows that can only be a dream. Moth *has* to confess this now even though he's sure it can't save his skin, only condemn him further.

He can't look at Éric, although Éric's gaze is laser focused in his direction. *Everyone* is looking at him.

Could I run?

The thought hits him as adrenaline quicksilvers through his veins, and then a small laugh catches in his throat.

Who the fuck am I kidding?

There's two master vampires here, plus Gabe.

No, he has to say it.

He *has* to say it now otherwise he's going to break down and cry.

No one has answered his question, so he ploughs ahead, aware that once the words leave his lips he can't swallow them back down. One beseeching glance towards Gabe as he begs him to understand.

'None of you can see it.' He shakes his head, lets his hair fall over his brow. Tries to hide his distress. 'None of you can see that Éric is supremely fucking special.' His voice rises again but this time it's the heat of anger that laces it. 'He's the one, the golden boy.'

Moth hates himself for using the term he once applied to Gabe.

'He's the one who got to choose. None of us had that, not even you, Gabe.' Moth's lips are so dry he feels like they're going to crack open. 'Éric got to choose the darkness and that's why I hate him.'

Éric collapses on the settee. There it is — the confirmation that Moth really does hate him. His lungs refuse to take in air. He begins to wonder if he'll ever breathe again.

Vauquelin brings a fist to his lips, cutting his glance to Clove. He cannot interpret Clove's expression. None of them expected to end up at such a crossroads.

Moth's revelation smothers him, replaying itself over and over in his mind. He cannot bring himself to look at the young vampire, though Moth's stature is significantly muted from the fever-heights he had reached just minutes ago.

Vauquelin had known the very night he met Éric that he needed him… and that only having him forever would do. He recalls what he had said to Éric that day, after he had stayed awake agonising over his intentions as he watched the human Éric sleep.

He *did* give Éric a choice. He was explicit in defining the ghastly confines of the life of a revenant.

And then he set him free, hoping against hope that he would return.

But now, in the context of Moth's startling accusations, Vauquelin considers that perhaps he had not been honest enough. That he had sold Éric dirty goods, or promised him a dark life of adventure that turned into a bloody fucking nightmare when Vauquelin disappeared into a time-slip and left him on his own.

Rarely has Vauquelin felt so raw: Moth has once again cracked through his unbreakable shell, and he fears that what remains of his soul is exposed for all in this room to see.

You are so selfish.

The voices have not returned since Vauquelin terminated his maker, Yvain — they rattle his already-shredded nerves.

You have ruined Éric, stolen his life in the guise of giving him a choice. Now look at him. Everyone knows what you have done.

He has been staring at his beloved for all of these thoughts, his eyes back to their icy pale blue, widened in panic... and Éric has heard every single one of them.

Éric's head begins to quake.

There have been a few times when Vauquelin thought Éric might leave him — this is one of those times. He has tried Éric's patience too often, though he would never be intentionally cruel to him: yet Éric always comes back, always forgives him.

He fears he has gone too far, and what was supposed to be a beautiful gathering of his most-loved beings has gone to hell.

He wants to flee. But that is not an option..

'We will leave immediately if that is your wish, Vauquelin,' Clove says. But he does not want to leave like this. He cannot leave this trail of destruction.

No... Vauquelin speaks directly to Clove's mind. No one else.

That would be the end of everything. Please. Please do not —

But it is Éric who speaks next, startling everyone.

'Moth, you're wrong. I didn't choose darkness. I chose Vauquelin.'

'It's the same fucking thing.' Most of the fight has left Moth but he can't fully back down. He's crossed the line and he can't go back.

Éric blinks rapidly at Moth.

All this vitriol and they haven't even had the chance to have a normal conversation. They know *nothing* about one another. Éric wishes they were alone, that the entire fucking room wasn't waiting to hear what he'll say next, but V is crumbling and now it's time to stand up for him.

There are a million thoughts flooding his mind right now. Would Moth like to know Éric almost took his own life six months before he met V? Éric would never tell him, because even V doesn't know about that.

Would he like to know Éric had never known a love like he has with V?

There's a lot Éric would like to ask Moth, and even to tell him... but they aren't there yet. Maybe they'll never get there, though he suspects they have more in common than Moth thinks.

'Moth, listen... it's clear you don't really know the truth about me. I would have told you a lot already if you had given me a chance. Can't you imagine doing something just for love? I would have done anything to be with Vauquelin. It made no difference to me that he's vampire. If marrying his darkness was what it took, then fine... that's what I fucking chose. But then he was gone for *four fucking years*!' Éric plunges his hands into his hair. 'I was on my own. I had nobody... *nobody*! I thought he was never coming back, but you know what? I'd still choose the darkness he gave me, even if he couldn't find his way back, because I had him for a little while. It was all worth it and I'd fucking do it again. So you can hate me all you want, but that man right there' — he flings an arm toward V — 'is the only thing I care about in this world, and if you burned this entire fucking palace down right now neither of us would care. Because none of it matters except for us.' Éric stomps across the floor and wraps his arms around V's waist, resting his chin on his shoulder and glaring at Moth.

Éric's words wash over Moth and he wants to incinerate them because they're coming from Éric's mouth, but some of those words have arrow tips and right now they are lodged in his heart.

Can't you imagine doing something just for love?

He glances to Gabe, who is watching him with such a fierce love in his eyes despite the fucking awful confession Moth has just made. He looks to Teal, crumpled on the couch, and knows his bright-eyed brother is weighed down because he thinks he's responsible for this fucking mess

— Moth's heart cracks open. He doesn't look at Clove. He can't bear to. Because he's let Clove down and he knows that Clove is a fragment away from wiping the floor with him for everyone to see, but has stalled to give Éric a chance to speak.

'I've done things for love.' Moth finally finds his voice. 'No matter how much you think that's impossible.' He thinks about the time he was on the run with Gabe and Teal, when every night might have been their last, of being frozen and starving but too scared to go out and hunt. He thinks about Emron D'Grey — Moth's eyes close and he can almost smell his own flesh burning — he thinks about losing Gabe and finding him again, of watching Teal die because they had no choice.

And he can't voice any of this — so he just stares at Éric and keeps his runaway mouth shut, because that's as close to an apology as he can get.

Gabe is only a few feet away and he so desperately wants to go to him for comfort, but he doesn't deserve it. Not after what he's done.

He takes a breath, tilts his chin up, and prepares for the missiles to fall.

Vauquelin turns to his fellow master, mystified by both of their levels of self-restraint on this night. Neither of them had expected this.

'With your permission, Clove, I would like an audience with young Moth. Alone, if you will allow it.' He hoists an index finger to hush Éric.

Moth opens his mouth to protest but fear crawls up his throat, leaving him mute. He doesn't want to be alone with Vauquelin, can't bear to hear the words that will be fired in his direction. Vauquelin will skin him alive for what he has done to Éric.

But then Clove strides towards him and all bets are off. He tenses as Clove's shadow falls over him.

'You *will* go, Moth, and you *will* be courteous. You must learn that there are always consequences to your actions. And after Vauquelin has finished with you, an apology — a true apology — to Éric will be required. Now go.'

As Clove dismisses him Moth risks an upward glance. What he sees nearly makes his legs give way.

'You have disappointed me, Moth. I thought you knew better.'

Moth stares straight ahead as he forces his jellified legs to walk towards Vauquelin. He wants the ground to open up and swallow him whole.

Vauquelin embraces Éric, whispering, 'Do not worry, my love,' as he kisses him behind his ear.

Éric is struggling to keep his tears at bay: Vauquelin knows that expression. Éric's sensitivity undoes him, every time. It is one of his beloved's most endearing qualities. But now he knows Éric will not leave him. Before Éric's speech, Vauquelin would have been unable to let him out of his sight in this situation, even for a moment.

I will not be long.

He inclines his head to Clove and crosses to Moth, taking him brusquely by the elbow.

Moth's shoulders slump in resignation and he allows Vauquelin to lead him out of the room. The doors come to a gentle close behind them, and then they are gone.

16 / NIGHT 2:

LOVE AND HATE AND CHOICE

Through the noiseless passageways, Vauquelin doesn't say a word: and this frightens Moth more than anything. He can deal with anger because he just throws it back — *not this time, Moth, not with a master vampire* — but this solid silence fills his throat and he can't breathe. They stop in front of the door to the catacombs and then Moth begins to quiver.

He's going to fucking kill me!

All he can think is that Clove has given him a death sentence.

Vauquelin releases Moth's arm only to retrieve the key, and clasps it again to drive Moth into the yawning black cavern beyond the door. They walk deep into the catacombs, deeper than Éric had taken them, and mercifully their steps continue past the ominous acid pit.

Moth can imagine Vauquelin opening the hatch and tossing him right in. Part of him knows he fucking deserves it for the disrespect he's shown.

But instead, Vauquelin points to two wooden wine crates, and they sit.

Vauquelin splays his knees, leaning his elbows on them, and drags his hands down his face before steepling them on his lips.

'Moth, Moth, Moth. What are we to do with all this fire in your belly?'

Moth glues his gaze to his boots, fixates on a scuff mark on one toe.

Vauquelin is fully aware that his silence is more painful than words could ever be.

And then, when Moth thinks he can't stand it a second longer, Vauquelin speaks.

'Do you know why you are all here?'

'No, I fucking don't. Clove made us come.' Moth's words feel like they are pasted to the back of his tongue.

'I had rather hoped you and I could be friends, Moth. In fact, after our last meeting, I thought that might be the case. I once believed you and I were cut from the same cloth. But now I see that I was wrong. You do not understand the pain you so easily dispense. Even to Gabriel. Can you not see that you hurt everyone around you?'

This is worse than Vauquelin's anger.

This is like the tip of a dagger probing into Moth's flesh, each word laced with poison. He's just seen what his outburst did to those he loves, and he doesn't think he'll ever forget Gabe's heartfelt plea — or the look of anguish on Teal's face. There's nothing he can say so he just looks up at Vauquelin through a fall of hair.

Vauquelin continues. 'Moth. I know the story of what you have suffered. It is unspeakable. You deserved none of this. But one's adversities do not make one superior to others. Would it satisfy you if I had taken Éric by force, if he were here because I could not control myself? If I had not given him a choice, would you then hate him so? He would not love me… he would hate me, and I would not truly love him. What Éric and I have together, this is not the same.'

Vauquelin's words pummel into Moth and the burning misery inside him is so strong that all he hears is *love* and *hate* and *choice*. They all tumble together and for a moment he's back in the early nights of Gabe's turning… and he's looking at this new Chosen One sitting by Clove's side with purebred blood pumping through his veins. Moth feels, with a heartsick pang, the acid-laced hate he had for Gabe then, the way it ate him up night after night. Gabe didn't deserve that. Just as Éric doesn't deserve what Moth flung at him. He hangs his head.

Vauquelin rises and begins to pace.

Moth also stands, praying that's the end of this miserable fucking lecture.

'Moth, sit. I am not finished. You will know when I am ready to release you.'

Moth's knees buckle and he sits because he has no other option.

'You have been inordinately disrespectful since you set foot in my house. It is not my place to admonish you for your behaviour... that is Clove's right, and I shall not contradict him. But Moth...' Now Vauquelin sits and faces him once more. He takes Moth's jaw in his hand and forces the young vampire to look him in the eye. 'You hurt *me* tonight, not just Éric. You made me question something that before this night I believed was written in stone. Do you know how many vampires I have created in eight hundred years?'

Moth shakes his head, the pressure of Vauquelin's fingers bruising his skin. He grabs hold of the pain and clings on because otherwise he fears he might drown.

Vauquelin holds up four long fingers.

'Only two of them remain alive and one is in the salon. I would like you to think about the significance of that for a moment. Yes, I gave Éric a choice. I broke all the revenant edicts for him... I told him I was vampire the night we met. Even so he chose to stay with me for four nights, fully aware I could kill him in a heartbeat. And then I exiled him. He returned to me, knowing *everything* that would happen to him, all that he must surrender from his humanity. With all of my darkness firmly in his hands, still he made his decision to join me. I have never been so honest with another individual in my entire existence. I was offered no alternative. None of us were... but you know as well as I that when you love another, you will do anything for them. Moth... meeting you and your brothers changed my life. And *you* changed it most of all.'

Now Moth's eyes widen as Vauquelin's last words sink in.

How could he have changed anything?

'I don't understand.' At last his voice appears and this time he doesn't care that his words tremble.

'So of course I do not wish to kill you.'

Fuck! He had dropped his shield and Vauquelin heard him.

'You must not realise it, Moth, but I love you. And I love Gabriel, Teal, and Clove. That is why you are here. I wanted us all to be together... so that you could meet Éric. I have never loved another as I love him. I wanted all my loves under one roof. But you have made things quite difficult for us all, Moth. Éric may have more human years than you, but he lacks your experience. Simply because he has not suffered as you have, you must never assume he has not known torment of his own. You could have given him a chance.'

'I...' Moth's breath leaves his lips in a shaky exhale.

All of his emotions are tangled up in a huge ball of panic and remorse and he wants nothing more than to flee and hide somewhere so he can lick his wounds. But he knows that this time he has gone too far. And even Gabe can't save him. No, this fucked-up mess is all his fault and he has to own it, no matter how much his own bloody-mindedness is screaming at him to rebel. 'I... I was wrong.'

It's all Moth can manage but he prays that it's enough for now.

'It is important to me that Éric sees the magnificent love you have with Gabriel. I purposefully did not tell him about this before you arrived, because he must see this as something we share in common, something that is quite natural. He is American, Moth, and he grew up being ridiculed for the way he is. Do you think this is fair? Is there anything shameful in the way we love?'

This question catches Moth in a tender place. He has never thought loving Gabe was wrong, not for one instant. There are a fuckton of things he feels guilty about but what he has with Gabe has always felt *right*.

'There is no fucking shame.' Moth tilts his chin up and for the first time his words have an unshakable strength.

'Éric has many stories he could share with you if you will listen. But they are his, not mine, and I shall not tell you now. It is my greatest hope that you will speak with him.'

Talking to Éric is something Moth doesn't want to do but he can't spend the whole of this visit avoiding him. He brings his curled fingers to his mouth and closes his eyes for a moment to stop the sting of tears.

If there even is more of this fucking visit after tonight.

He nods his compliance to Vauquelin.

'Had I never met you, Moth, I would never have met Éric, and I would have been unable to open my heart to him. I had never seen anything like what you share with Clove and your brothers. You may not understand how extraordinary this is. It profoundly affected me... I wanted it for myself. That is why I left Gehenna so soon: my heart was too full, I could not bear it a moment longer. A month later Éric came into my life like a gift from the universe. I did not believe myself worthy of him... still I do not. And you made me question that further tonight, that perhaps I had destroyed him. But had you not called me on the mat years ago you would never have seen me again — because I would be back in the seventeenth century. I was so close to finding the way. But I will tell you a secret, Moth, and you must promise not to confide this to Teal and Gabriel.'

'Why would you tell me a secret?' Moth asks.

He's not sure if this is some kind of test he has to pass before Vauquelin lets him go, and if he doesn't answer right he'll be locked up down here forever.

'Because you have done something they will never understand.'

Moth panics. His heart leaps into his throat.

What the fuck is Vauquelin referring to?

'Does Clove know?'

'Clove knows everything important about me, Moth. It was a requisite for your visit here. More than *you* will ever know. What I want to tell you is that after Éric and I were together for only a few months, I experienced a time-slip. He was lost to me, left here in this cold, cavernous house all alone, with very little education. I had prepared for this possibility, and he had orders to go to Gehenna, to your family. I need not tell you he did not go. He was too frightened to leave. He was forced to fend for himself. For me, my time-slip was ninety days. For Éric, it was four years. I do not know whether you understood the severity of this when he told you just now. You were so angry. I know how it is to have only blood in your ears, Moth. Sometimes it veils the truth.'

Four years? Moth hasn't had time to unpack all of Éric's words yet, but he remembers that part… and the burning loneliness in Éric's eyes as he hurled his anger towards him. He tries to imagine four years without Gabe. Without Teal. With only his own company. He knows he would have gone quietly insane. Or maybe he would have trashed this fucking over-the-top house and gone to live here in the catacombs.

'While I was away, I learned that my time-slips were executed by blood sacrifice. This is the secret, what you must tell no one. Do I have your word?'

This is really happening. A master vampire is trusting him with a secret. Moth's head loops like a rollercoaster, and he has to bite down on his lower lip with one fang to bring himself back into focus. He nods, solemnly.

'I killed my oldest friend, my brother, my progeny — because it was the only way I could return to Éric, to this time. Now I have burned the papers that held that curse. I no longer wish to return to my past because I belong here, with him. I never want to be apart from him again. So now you know the depths of my love for Éric. And the reason I tell you this is that you, perhaps more so than the others, know what desperate lengths a vampire will go to to survive, to stay alive so that he might again see the one who owns his heart.'

Vauquelin reaches out to stroke Moth's hair: he knows full well Moth hates being touched (at least by him), but he does it anyway.

Moth wants to pull away but he's frozen into place, the synapses in his brain blasting in all directions like a rogue firework, Vauquelin's confession riding on each spark. He understands soul-deep what Vauquelin has just told him so he consents to the intimacy, his eyes drawn towards Vauquelin's face and the earnest expression in those ice-blue eyes.

'Words are capable of dealing a mortal blow, Moth. Please remember that often you cannot reclaim them, nor can you resurrect the one you have impaled. I have one last thing to say, and then you may return to the others.'

The room starts to spin — Moth reaches out and grasps Vauquelin's arm. The battlefield he has left in the salon has so many fucking casualties, and he's not sure if what he has done is past redemption.

'You were not given a choice. You were thrust into this existence. The hand you were dealt was cruel, to say the least. But when you return to the salon, I insist that you go straight to Gabriel. Look at no one else until you reach him. Take him in your arms.' Vauquelin stands and extends a hand toward the entrance to the catacombs. 'And when you look at him, think about this: had you not been turned, you would never have known those eyes.'

17 / NIGHT 2:

FUCKING EGGSHELLS, GABRIEL?

Moth follows Vauquelin out of the catacombs, both retracing their steps to the salon. There are no more words to say. Moth's breath hitches in his throat; part of him wondered if he'd ever set foot in the hallway again. He remembers Teal telling him about a book he had read about a vampire who had done something awful. That vampire had been stripped and nailed to a wall by a master, left there to slowly starve to death as others passed by and watched his slow desiccation.

He's well aware that could be him... that he's got off lightly. But Vauquelin's words have flayed the skin from his bones and left him wide open, the bruised places he tries so hard to defend exposed and bleeding.

The salon doors open and Clove stands by them, his steady gaze falling on Moth. Vauquelin goes to Clove's side, places his hand on Clove's arm, and Moth wants to wither away because maybe then this torment will fade with him.

Even though Éric and Teal are sitting side by side on the couch and he has to pass them to get to Gabe, he swallows the jealousy that wants to rise. He only has eyes for Gabe, who stands by the window, his head turned towards the rain-laden night. Gabe wheels around and his expression brightens. Gone is the mask of shock and now there's only the soft swell of relief etched on his face.

Moth throws himself at Gabe, his hands grabbing hold of his lover's face. He does what Vauquelin has instructed him to do: he just looks into the navy-blue depths and his heart cracks open again, for what he might have lost. Tears stream down his face but he doesn't care, there's only him and Gabe in this moment.

'I'm so fucking sorry,' he whispers as Gabe's lips smooth away his tears. 'I lost it. And I hurt you.' His voice fractures.

Now it's Gabe's turn to cup his hands around Moth's face. The sobering reality of Moth's vulnerability spears through his chest and guts him open from sternum to belly. He starts to tremble and he can't stop.

It's okay. I've got you. This will be over soon.

Gabe's words wash against his mind.

I've fucking messed up everything.

And then Gabe's lips are on his and the kiss is so tender: because Gabe knows he's exposed and open and only hanging on by a thread.

A hand gently touches Moth's shoulder. Teal is there and Gabe pulls him into the embrace. This, this is what Moth exists for, this brotherhood and passionate love, this unbreakable bond they all share. This unquenchable connection even when Moth fucks it up as badly as he's just done.

He glances back over his shoulder and sees Éric with his elbows on his knees and his head in his hands, alone.

But not for long. Vauquelin strides across the room and sinks at Éric's feet, astonishing everyone in the room. He drops his cheek to Éric's knees. No one is prepared to see a master bow to his own progeny. Vauquelin would never let other vampires — besides these — see him so submissive. They are all raw now... all of them have laid themselves bare, and he can fathom no reason to hold back.

Vauquelin wants nothing more than to whisk Éric upstairs, to have him alone and give Éric all of himself, to show his grief for what has transpired. This is not the time for that, and his vulnerability has deposited an ache in his heart. He rises, kisses the top of Éric's head and careens across the floor to a cabinet — he pours a generous glass of wine, downs it immediately, and pours another.

'I'll have one too, please,' Éric says.

Vauquelin holds out the bottle, a silent offer to any of the others who might need its solace.

The boys look at him like he's offered them some strange, alien food. Clove simply shakes his head.

Soon, they will all need blood. But for now, the wine will have to suffice. Vauquelin's nerves are shredded, and the second glass knits them back together sip by sip.

He perches on the armrest next to Éric, passing him a goblet with a smile, his eyes full of relief that the lightning storm of this evening seems to have subsided. Their thoughts entangle like a fast growing vine until they are unintelligible, and they come to a rest in an unornamented *I love you.*

The remainder of their words for each other will come later, when they are alone.

Gabe takes Moth's hand and walks towards where Vauquelin and Éric are sitting. He can feel the reluctant drag of Moth's feet but knows he won't rebel... not this time, not after everything that has happened.

The weight of Clove's gaze settles upon him.

Teal drifts across to a shelf of books set into an alcove and pulls one of the gilt-etched spines towards him. He checks the title and settles himself in an ornately carved armchair at the edge of the salon. He is both part of the room and on the outskirts, his preferred place, but Moth's outburst has left him anxious. He chews the edge of his thumbnail, keeping one eye on what is about to unfold: praying that this even keel will prevail.

Gabe stops in front of Vauquelin and bows his head. He turns to Éric, whose fingers have tightened around the goblet stem.

'Éric.' Gabe steels himself and locks Éric in a gaze he hopes the young vampire won't want to wriggle out of. But both Vauquelin and Éric are seated and it feels wrong that he and Moth are standing. Gabe drops to his knees and pulls Moth down with him.

'I know nothing I can say will take away the hurt you've endured tonight and I can't form the words to say how sorry I am. You have been nothing but kind and gracious.'

Moth is in an alternate dimension now and Gabe's words, that sound so much like Clove that he thinks he must be tripping, fade in and out like an out-of-tune radio.

Mentally he's already on his feet, racing along the hallway and out into the night.

'Moth has something he'd like to say.' Gabe's fingers tighten. 'Isn't that right, Moth?'

It's not any kind of right, but Moth is all out of options.

'I might have been a bit over the top earlier.' He cuts his gaze to Éric, who is looking at him like Moth is about to eat him alive.

In his peripheral vision Vauquelin arches a dark eyebrow.

'What I said was just me mouthing off.' He stares at the floor, finds some saliva to coat his tongue — which feels like a fucking dried husk of meat. 'I do that. A lot.' He shrugs and raises his head again, gritting his teeth as he prepares himself for Éric's full condemnation.

Éric closes his eyes.

Fuck.

He isn't ready to do this... not now, not in front of everyone.

V's hand snakes behind his neck, and Éric appreciates the grasp of his lover's formidable fingers, now enclasping his shoulder and giving him just the strength he needs for this moment that has come far too soon.

'Moth.' He takes a quick swig of the wine but it goes down wrong, and he coughs and splutters.

Seriously? Ugh!

He wipes his mouth with the back of his hand and starts again.

'Hey. If anyone can understand that, it's me. I'm like the *king* of sticking my foot in my mouth. Just ask him,' he says, side-eyeing V with his crooked smile. 'Anyway, it's me who should apologise. I started it and I kept on pushing your buttons. I'm so sorry... I wish things hadn't gone this way. I wish we could start over, but I know we can't. What's done is done.'

There's so much more he wants to say, but he won't.

Not here.

Moth catches his jaw before it falls open.

He hadn't expected this. He watches Éric's face, waiting for him to morph into fury, but all he can see is openness and honesty.

The monster inside him tells him this is all a front.

No, fuck it, no!

He pushes it back down into its nest.

'Moth, I'd like you to go and talk to Éric alone.' Gabe is unsure if he's opening up the biggest sinkhole in history but he knows Moth is too vulnerable with all these eyes upon him.

'Is that okay with you, Éric?'

Then he turns to Vauquelin, inwardly wincing, as he should have asked him first.

'As long as that's fine with you, V?'

Éric sucks in his breath, jerking his head toward V and slowly back to Gabriel. He narrows his eyes.

'What did you just call him?'

Gabe holds his hands up. What the hell had he just said?

He replays it and can't find anything wrong.

Vauquelin bites his lip. Another omission.

He will feel Éric's wrath again.

'Éric, when I first met Gabriel, I offered this initial to him,' he says quietly. 'This happened long before I met you. He has my permission to use it.'

'But...' Éric thrusts his chin out. He thought *he* was the first one to call Vauquelin "V". His jaw tightens as he thinks back to their first night in Paris, and Vauquelin's strange reaction when he called him that.

Vauquelin is kind of a mouthful, Éric had said.

An irrational thought blazes the edges of his mind.

Did V and Gabriel — no no no no. No way.

That's fucking stupid. UGH!!!

Beside him, Vauquelin sways his head back, his lips parted, his brows drawn together in an expression of utter mortification.

Éric! Mon dieu,† *do you truly believe me capable of such depravity?*

Éric gawps. *No, no, V... my head is just so fucked up right now. I'm sorry.*

When he's agitated, he forgets that V can hear his every thought, should he care to wander inside Éric's muddled brain. He shakes his head violently.

Okay. Okay. Okay.

This is not a big deal. It isn't. It's a fucking letter. Get over it.

Éric puffs out his cheeks.

'Wow. Okay. I just thought that was my own thing, but that's cool. I guess.' He shoots a look at Vauquelin over the top of his wine goblet as he sucks the last of it down. He stands, places the glass on the table, and shoves his hands in his pockets. 'Come on, Moth. Let's do this.'

As Moth reluctantly gets to his feet, giving Gabe one last long look like an animal being led off for slaughter, Gabe turns to Vauquelin.

'Fuck,' he says softly, as Moth follows Éric out of the salon, 'I had no idea. I'm so sorry. Of course I won't use it again.'

Vauquelin purses his lips, looking at Gabriel from beneath his brows.

'He will survive this. I do not wish for you to stop calling me V, Gabriel. If anything, this gathering has revealed that we all have quite a lot to explain to one another.' He glances at Teal, content and far away in his

---

†- MY GOD

book. 'I have had little time to speak with you. But I hope you have been happy here, despite the — shall we say, volatile circumstances.'

Gabe grimaces but there's a touch of humour there. 'Living with Moth is the ultimate volatile circumstance.' He pauses and graces V with an easy smile. 'But even I thought he'd gone too far tonight. He needs this alone time with Éric. They have to get whatever is in their systems out. We can't all spend this visit walking on fucking eggshells.'

Clove comes to join them, his hands resting on the back of the couch.

'Fucking eggshells, Gabriel?' He cocks an eyebrow in Gabe's direction. 'A succinct turn of phrase.'

He has stayed back and watched yet more madness unfold, but Gabriel has handled it well. What his first-born doesn't know is that this visit is the first part of his education outside of Gehenna, and his diplomacy so far has been exemplary.

Clove compares that with Moth's unbridled outbursts and a wry smile touches his lips. He has always known that there is balance in everything and his boys are showing him that this is now the absolute truth.

Vauquelin sends a thought to Clove: *Have we lost our minds in coordinating this visit?* He delivers this with a wistful smile, knowing that despite the relentless horn-locking, all the boys needed this. And he and Clove have benefited from it as well.

Our minds were lost when they wound their way against our hearts.

Once upon a time Clove would not have admitted to this, yet it is a fact he now wakes with each and every evening. But the price of any love is commensurate pain, and Clove would move heaven and earth to keep that pain from ever touching his boys or Vauquelin and Éric.

Deep inside him the shadows coil, begging for release. He closes the door on their predatory faces.

18 / NIGHT 2:

BAIT HIM WITH YOUR LOOKS

They stand a moment outside the salon doors.

Éric considers suggesting they just go their separate ways. Moth can do whatever the fuck it is he does, and he can go smash some virtual cars and blast some ear-splitting music, and then they'll meet back in the salon and act like everything is just fine and fucking dandy now.

But they can't do that, and he knows it.

There will be questions... everyone will want proof that they fucking sorted this shit out.

'It stopped raining. Wanna go outside?' Éric asks. 'I might crawl out of my fucking skin if I have to stay in this house a minute longer.'

Éric's words are not what Moth is expecting. He has bolstered up his shattered walls, ready for whatever Éric feels fit to hurl at him now that they're alone.

'Sure. Why not? This place makes me feel like the past threw up all over it.' His lips draw back in a slight grimace. *That's right, Moth, build bridges by insulting where Éric lives. Nice move.* But now that Éric has mentioned it he can't wait for fresh air to touch his skin.

'Cool. Let's go to the back garden. You haven't seen it yet. Or we could — ' he clamps his mouth shut. He had started to tell Moth that, from the balcony on the third floor, you can view beautiful patterns and swirls in the sculpted shrubbery that forms the maze-like paths throughout the expanse of the gardens. Éric often goes up there and leans over the iron railings, sniffing the air that smells so elegantly superior to L.A. air, looking down over the artful landscape beneath him... still in denial that he fucking lives in *Paris*. On the ground it's not as impressive.

Whatever... he's pretty sure Moth wouldn't care about all that stuff.

At the back door, he grabs two coats from the mounted brass pegs. They've come this far — he doesn't want to make Moth go all the way back upstairs for one.

He hopes it fits.

But then he shrugs into his own and opens the back door.

Beyond them, a walled expanse of gravel walkways, finely-chiselled greenery carving out paths, peppered by triangular topiary trees — above their heads the slate, mansard rooftops of Paris slant down toward them, assuring them of their safety within Vauquelin's ancient walls.

In the centre is a large fountain, with red uplights dancing across the rising and falling water. There's an odd silence about the garden, despite it being in the middle of the city.

'Pretty, crazy, huh? Vauquelin never does anything half-assed. It's so extra and completely ridiculous, but I love it.'

Moth runs his fingers down the butter-soft leather of the coat he's pulled on. The inside is trimmed with some close-fitting fleece, and the springy down is soft against his bare arms.

'Nothing's too good for you, Éric.' It's not meant in any derogatory way: he's just stating a fact. 'There's zero luxuries at Gehenna. Most of the time we go out without coats even in the middle of winter, and then Clove or Elijah hauls us over the coals when we get back. *"You must remember to fit in. Do not give people a reason to remember you."* He does a passable imitation of Clove, and then freaks out in case Éric tells him when they go back in.

The water from the fountain splashes against his skin, and, in a sudden fit of Crazy, he dunks his whole head into the water. It's freezing cold and he comes up spluttering but it's just what he needs to clear his head.

Fuck, Éric will think I have a screw well and truly loose.

Éric laughs, covering his mouth.

'If you wanted to go swimming, you should have said so. There's a pool inside. You guys haven't even seen the rest of the house yet. I guess the tour got cut short, thanks to us.' He sits on a stone bench and pats the open spot next to him.

'I never had anything like this, Moth,' Éric whispers. 'Sometimes my life seems so surreal. I can't believe any of this is true most of the time.'

'You have a pool?' Moth's voice climbs an octave.

Just how much money does Vauquelin have?

He doesn't need to ask if the pool is heated.

'I raise you a river. A fucking cold river. Ball-shrinking fucking cold.' He starts to laugh, then catches it and looks away. 'Gabe came from money. I don't know about Teal. I didn't.' He keeps his reply short, a myriad of emotions running rampant in his veins. It's been a fucking long night already. And he's starving, even though they fed last night before Flynn picked them up. Whenever he unleashes his mouth the fallout always feeds the flames of his hunger.

'Me either,' Éric says, his voice quiet. 'You must think I'm a spoiled fucking brat. Or a gold-digger.' His jaw muscles begin to twitch.

Moth turns back to face Éric and studies his profile.

He's fucking beautiful, kinda exotic.

'Yeah, you probably are. The first one anyway.' He looks down at his feet for a moment, thinking about Vauquelin's words back in the catacombs. 'But we didn't get to choose the life we had before. Luck of the fucking draw. Guess we were all out of luck.' He pauses again, shakes the water from his hair onto the ground. 'But I wouldn't change it, what we have now.'

'Zero regrets. I wasn't kidding earlier when I said you could burn this place down and it wouldn't make a difference. None of it matters. I mean, don't take me seriously and *actually* burn it down, okay, but all I care about is V. I'd live in a cardboard box with him and be perfectly happy. I doubt he'd say the same thing though!'

'You asking me if I have matches in my pocket?' Moth lets his soaking hair hang over his eyes and peers through it to study Éric again. He keeps his face deadly serious.

Éric probes his tongue with the tips of his fangs.

Please let him be fucking joking.

Now he wonders if he should laugh or not... because the thought of Moth literally burning their house down isn't that hard to imagine.

He inhales sharply.

'Actually, do you? Because I'm dying for a fucking cigarette. V won't let me smoke in front of you guys.'

Moth delves into his jeans pocket and then stops.

'All out of matches...' A grin forms at the side of his mouth then disappears as he utters the word, 'sorry.'

Relief washes over Éric. He's fluent in sarcasm. He can handle this.

'No worries. I got it.' Éric takes a leather pouch out of his jacket pocket and lights up. If it bothers Moth, too bad. He really needs it after everything that went down tonight. His nerves are fucking *shot*.

'You smoke?' Moth inwardly grimaces at the obvious question. 'I know Vauquelin does and he drinks. Clove doesn't do either so I guess we've never thought about it. Maybe it's a fucking bloodline thing again?'

As soon as the words drop Moth wants to snatch them back. This isn't how he wants things to go, reminding Éric that he can't fucking come.

Another nice move, Moth. He's no good at small talk.

'Yeah, sometimes. It's kind of how V and I met. I chased him down outside a bar in Los Angeles and asked him for one. I ended up in his bed that night and I never wanted to leave. So there. I begged for the fucking darkness, okay? And the rest is history.' He exhales, politely blowing the smoke out of the side of his mouth, away from Moth.

This is so weird.

'Hey. Can I ask you a personal question?'

Moth immediately wants to disappear into the greenery, but he's trying fucking hard tonight — so he just pastes what he hopes is a smile on his lips. 'Sure thing.'

Éric taps the cigarette end on the armrest to ash it and focusses on it as a question forms.

'Did you always know you liked boys? Before Gabriel, obviously.'

Éric never has a chance to talk to other guys like this.

He isn't wasting this opportunity.

Moth's eyes widen slightly. 'I always knew I liked boys. I wasn't ever attracted to girls, even when all the other boys were egging each other on.' He pauses and grabs the cigarette from Éric and takes a long draw. The smoke scorches his lungs and he coughs and splutters as he hands it back. 'That's fucking nasty.'

Éric laughs. 'I know, it's super fucking gross but I can't stop. Besides, it's not like it's gonna kill me or anything, right?' He delivers his crooked grin and takes another big drag.

Moth collects his thoughts before continuing. 'Gabe and I didn't have a good start. I hated him at first, which probably meant I loved him and didn't know it.'

He's not sure why he feels the need to explain more, but everyone inside will be clamouring for details later... so he's going to serve them up on a silver platter.

Look how fucking unMoth I'm being.

'So, do you like girls, too?' Moth throws back another personal question. He still feels as wound-up as a coiled spring, but some of the links have started to slacken.

'Only as friends. I like being around women, but I've never slept with one. I kissed a few. That was a joke. No question about it... definitely gay.' Éric leans down and stubs the cigarette out in the gravel. He takes a deep breath. 'Vauquelin has been with lots of women. But I don't really like to think about that.' He has no idea why he said this out loud... and to Moth, of all people? 'Umm... it'd be best if you didn't tell him I mentioned that, please.'

Moth's head starts to reel.

What is it with fucking secrets tonight and people trusting me with them?

He wonders if the house really is some kind of alternate dimension.

'I never had much to do with girls, even when I was human. I was always the kid no one wanted to play with and I was pretty much resigned to that.' He thinks back to Before then shoves it away behind its trapdoor. 'Gabe used to live with a girl... a woman I mean.' *Fuck, I'm never quite sure when a girl passes into womanhood.* 'She was a paranormal researcher, could see ghosts and call them to her. Olivia helped us when we were on the run in Westport Quay, helped us defeat the demon who was hunting Gabe...' He stops suddenly, aware that this must sound fucking deranged.

A swath of emotions swirls across Éric's face.

What the actual fuck?

There's so much to unroll in Moth's words: he doesn't even know where to begin.

He hoists a palm.

'Dude. Tonight I learned that Teal is part witch and now you've unloaded ghosts and demons on me. I literally have zero idea how to process all that, I'll be honest. I'm gonna need the full story. But like... maybe not tonight.'

Éric wonders how long they've been outside. The passage of time is still an ethereal concept to him. He looks up to the sky, trying to determine it by the position of the moon, but it's still cloudy and the moon is obscured.

There are so many questions he wants to ask, and now there are demons in the fray. But he turns to Moth, and all he can say is, 'I'm really sorry about how things went down. There's so much more to you than I imagined. You probably fucking hate it here, and I don't blame you. But...' Éric grows tongue-tied again.

He's said too much.

He should have just kept it simple.

Still, something has changed.

At least maybe this means Moth won't rip his throat out.

Moth watches Éric as a jumble of words spill from his lips.

There doesn't seem to have been a right time to answer his questions and now Éric's laid the whole 'sorry' thing out on the slab again. He backtracks the conversation.

'The whole demon thing is Gabe's story to tell. It was fucking freaky. But if it hadn't happened, I wouldn't have met him... so I count it as a good thing.' He looks out into the darkness of the garden as his stomach clenches. He *really* needs to feed. Otherwise he's going to say something he severely regrets.

'And it's just gone eleven. I saw you look up at the sky. Gabe and Teal and me all have a kind of built-in clock because we don't have any other way to tell the time where we live.' He shrugs.

And at Éric's heartfelt expression of regret his words dry up on his tongue. He wipes away a few droplets of water from his cheeks, chews over his confession before he sets it free.

'I don't hate it here.'

There, he's said it: an admittance he never thought he would utter. And here's another one hot on its heels. 'And I don't hate you, not really.' He meets Éric's gaze and tries to keep a certain amount of indifference in his eyes but Éric is looking at him weirdly so he drops the mask.

'I'm fucking starving. Want to hunt?'

Éric tamps down a frisson of panic.

V and Clove will fucking kill us if we go out.

He pats his pocket nervously, and relaxes when he feels the hard length of the Opinel inside.

This morning, before they went to sleep, V mentioned having something brought in for them all: but there's no way Éric can resist this adventure.

'Fuck yeah. Let's go.'

They scale the back wall easily and drop down into a narrow cobblestone alleyway. The last thing Moth expected to happen tonight was to be hunting with only Éric but he decides to roll with it, because this night has been wired to the max already — so what's one more act of rebellion?

Éric twists the sleeve of Moth's jacket in his fist.

'I have to confess something. I've never done this before, not on the streets. We always lure them into the house and kill them there. The acid pit. Get it?' His voice is tense, his words delivered with a punch.

Moth takes a deep breath. *Fuck.* Another thing he hadn't expected. His head starts to reel again and part of him wonders if they should just go back.

'Don't worry.' He turns and Éric is a shadow at his side. 'Clove just told me I couldn't go out alone, so we're not breaking any rules.' He grins. 'And besides... they wanted us to get on, right?'

Éric's stomach drops. Even though he was on his own for four years, Vauquelin's lessons reverberate in his ears like the final notes of a symphony. While V was away, Éric became the master of vampire takeout, ordering delivery from restaurants all over Paris: only it was the drivers that were his main course, not whatever was in the boxes they brought. And they've never, ever killed outside the walls of the house. Not even once.

Under no circumstances leave a body.

There are cameras everywhere.

Never, ever kill on the streets.

Éric brings his fingers to his lips.

The fact that Éric has never hunted outside before is running through Moth's veins like a drug-laced cocktail. *Fuck.* Vampires are born to hunt. Éric has never lived!

Éric gnaws on a cuticle.

This is so wrong.

He should say no. But right at this moment, he wants nothing more than to run out into the night.

He may never have a chance like this again: it's a brass ring.

Too bad it's with Moth.

So he grabs it.

'We can't disappoint them now, can we?' Éric grins. 'But you have to tell me what to do. I'm freaking the fuck out.'

'Okay.' The adrenaline in Moth's bloodstream is sparking like a live wire. 'When I go out to hunt with Gabe or Teal we use one of us as bait. Usually Teal because he looks so fucking innocent. But I'm not putting you in that situation so we'll just have to play it differently.'

Moth sends a hurried mind-touch to Gabe.

Gone out to hunt. Do not tell!

This is just a simple trip: they'll be there and back in less than half an hour.

At the end of the alley raucous laughter comes from a bar at the corner of the opposite street. Moth scans for any vampire danger and finds none.

Éric turns to Moth with a dazzling, full-fang smile. He hasn't had so much fun in ages.

And he certainly didn't expect to be having it with Moth!

'Fuck.' The expletive spills from Moth's lips. His eyes are fixed on Éric's mouth: or rather, his fucking fangs. Instead of a single curved canine, Éric sports two deadly tips on both sides. 'You came out tops when fangs were handed out.'

His memory smugly reminds him that Clove mentioned this back in the salon, but actually seeing them messes with his head a little.

Éric works his jaw side-to-side, running the tip of his tongue across his fangs. His brow crinkles as he recalls Gabriel's similar reaction — there it is, back in the forefront: yet *another* difference. It's not like he spends a lot of time thinking about fangs, unless they're sinking into someone and drawing blood ... especially when they're sunk into V.

A lascivious grin settles on his face at the same moment a black velvet shiver runs up his spine.

Always protect yourself from all sides, my love.

Éric's smile morphs into a twisted frown.

'Moth... we can't kill them. We'll get as much as we need and I'll take care of the rest.'

'We can't kill them?' Moth opens his mouth to ask why, then decides that he doesn't want the trouble of having to dump the victim in the river or wherever else they can find. This is a city, not the remote moorland he hunts on with his brothers.

'Okay.' He's not sure what Éric means but right now his hunger is a feral beast in his belly and he can't be bothered asking.

'Yeah, no. There are fucking foot cops everywhere in Paris. Just look around... it's too dangerous. That's why we have the pit. ... duh.' He cocks a brow.

'Come on.' Moth grabs Éric's sleeve and they dash across the road.

A car speeds around the corner and barely misses them — the driver blares his horn. Moth flips him the bird, then drags Éric down the alleyway behind the bar. There are human heartbeats down here.

'It's a couple... at least it looks like it from here,' Éric says. 'What do we do? I'm following your lead.'

The men are half-hidden at the other side of a huge waste disposal bin. Remnants of cardboard boxes and empty bottles litter the rain-slicked ground. Moth pulls Éric behind him and signals to follow as they advance in the shadow of the alley wall.

Raised voices now and one of the men curses in French, a heated exchange: the other storms away. The retreating heartbeat makes Moth grimace. He was hoping they could feed from two. He's starving, but what about Éric? How well can Éric control his hunger?

If they take too much...

But only one means it will be so much easier to take him down. He can feel Éric's excitement... it's palpable, and it's driving Moth towards the edge of the cliff they're about to jump from.

'Call him to you,' he says, and his grin is tinged with an untamed shadow. 'Bait him with your looks.'

'Oh, fuck,' Éric huffs, raking a hand through his hair. *I am so dead.* 'Come on. I need you to pretend you like me for a minute.' He takes Moth by the wrist and they walk toward the man, Éric swinging their hands between them.

Thank god no one back at the house can see the two of us right now, walking this way, Éric thinks. *Everybody's jaws would be on the floor, and they'd never let us live it down.*

Moth is catapulted back to the yard in Westport Quay where Gabe and he pretended to make out to lure their victim behind the containers. That was the night they couldn't wake Teal and then he'd gone missing... and the shock of Éric grabbing his hand is riding on the back of all these pulsating memories...

« Hé, matou ! » Éric jerks his chin up, raising his voice just enough to get the man to look at them. « Tu as perdu ton mec ? Veux-tu nous embrasser ? »†

Éric lifts his and Moth's hands to his lips and plants a gentle kiss on their clasped fingertips.

---

†- HEY, TOMCAT! LOST YOUR BOYFRIEND? WANT TO KISS US?

Moth watches this unfold like he's an onlooker, not part of the whole fever dream scene.

Éric just kissed my fingers!

He withers inside.

They stop in front of the man and he looks them up and down, an approving smile creeping across the corners of his mouth.

« *Ah, deux minets... c'est ma nuit de chance !* »† he growls.

'Go on, Moth... give him a kiss,' Éric says in English, keeping his eyes firmly on the man.

Moth shoots a glare in Éric's direction, but he's already latched mentally onto the beating heart inches away from him. It's singing its siren song and he's powerless to resist. And now that beat is starting to race as the man's excitement rises.

Moth can't risk a stun blow to the temple. The man is too tall and any botched attempt would leave Éric open for attack. He has no idea if their next meal is carrying a knife. And if Éric gets hurt, Moth might as well throw himself in the Seine: because there's no way he's getting out of that one alive.

So he swallows his disgust at the drool oozing from the side of the man's mouth, and graces him with an easy smile. He reaches up and strokes his fingers along the man's sweat-slicked throat, then digs those same fingers into the bundle of nerves behind his ear. It's a swift, sharp move and the man's expression goes from expectation to surprise. He crumples at their feet, his eyes glazing over. Moth follows it with a precisely-placed blow against the man's left temple.

Éric watches in morbid fascination.

He quickly extracts the Opinel and points the blade out.

'Just in case.'

'We've got about two minutes before he starts to know what's going on,'

---

†- AH, TWO TWINKS... IT'S MY LUCKY NIGHT!

Moth says, dragging their prey behind the waste disposal bin. 'Do you want his wrist or his neck?'

'I want you to take the most, Moth. I'll just have a little bit. I'm okay. You're not. Go for the neck.'

Moth doesn't need telling twice, but as he lowers his mouth to the warm flesh beneath him he scans the alleyway again. Feeding is a very intimate act for a vampire — he suddenly realises that he's leaving himself wide open for Éric to study him. But the need in his belly is too strong. His fangs break through the skin and the first hot rush of blood coats his tongue. His eyes dart to Éric's as his world tips into a rush of perfect crimson.

'I'll keep watch til you're done... don't worry.' Éric stands vigilantly, subtly casting his gaze to and fro across the alley. He stops as often as he can to glimpse Moth's ecstatic feeding.

Just a little drink.

At the back of Moth's mind he's counting down until he has to pull away.

He doesn't want just a little drink, but what he wants tonight has been severely upended too many fucking times. He tears himself away, blood dripping down his chin.

When he rises, Éric sinks to his knees and lifts the man's wrist, syphoning out a swallow that tastes better than any other human blood he's ever had on his tongue, and he knows the reason for its exquisite spice is that he's having it out here in the wild — with Moth. He tilts his head back and takes a deep breath, filling his lungs with rainy Parisian air, and then he smacks his lips.

'Okay. Let me just heal him up and we'll be on our way.'

'Wait. Is that all you need?' Moth's jaw drops open in surprise. 'Hold on.' His brow creases. 'What do you mean heal him up?'

The new blood he has taken a little too quickly makes his head spin.

Or maybe it's Éric's words.

Shit. More discoveries.

'Yeah, I'm good. Vauquelin and I only drink once a week. We fed the night before you guys got here. Watch.'

Éric swipes a fingertip over the bite marks he just made, and draws his hand over Moth's damage. The gory wounds wrinkle and smooth themselves before their eyes.

'You're learning a lot more about V's bloodline tonight, I guess. Let's get the hell outta here.'

'Fuck. That's pretty impressive.'

Moth takes a last look at the man's now unblemished flesh, scans the alleyway again and beckons Éric to his side as they retrace their steps.

A light drizzle has started to fall and he lifts his face to its kiss. The fresh blood thrums in his veins and he wants to run and climb and howl his authority into the night.

But he has to get Éric home.

And then they have to sneak back in somehow.

'You know I didn't really mean for you to kiss that guy, right?' Éric says. 'I mean, not the kind of kiss *he* was thinking of.'

'That guy was *so* not my type.' Moth grimaces at the thought of actually kissing him. He's still amazed that Éric took so little blood. 'You didn't take enough to keep a mosquito alive.'

Éric shrugs. He didn't need any blood tonight. He just wanted a taste and god, was it good. It's kinda beautiful right now walking in the rain with Moth, with adrenaline spicing his veins... it might even be worth the tongue-lashing he'll surely get from V if he finds out. But what amazes him even more is that he's having a good time with MOTH.

Their footsteps shuffle across the ancient cobblestones, and for just a moment, Éric is weighed down by the full brunt of his immortality. It bolsters him. He loves Paris... his adopted city has wormed its way into his blood, and his and V's treads will meander across her streets for centuries to come. Who knows what it'll be like in the future? It sends yet *another* spike exploding through his veinery, because he'll get to see everything that lies ahead of him. Things he doesn't even know about yet.

Fucking magic, this life I've been given.

But back to reality.

To now.

He looks down at Moth, sucks in his breath.

And he halts.

'What's wrong?' Moth immediately flicks his tongue, a wave of panic unfurling its wings.

Did I fucking miss a danger?

'Nothing... it's cool. It's just —' Éric feels like a landmine has detonated in his brain.

With all the glacial cracking that has happened tonight, this long fucking night that won't seem to end, Éric had somehow managed to forget that Moth, Gabriel, and Teal are frozen in time. They hadn't even finished growing when they were turned.

And now, for the very first time, he understands the significance of Vauquelin asking him a certain question: *Are you happy with your age?*

He locks Moth in his gaze.

Moth's brow creases.

Okay this is weird. Really fucking weird.

Moth is looking at him like he's on a microscope slide.

When Éric first met the boys he thought they were so young... but now he knows they *aren't!*

This is how they will be forever, and so will Éric be. He could live to be three hundred and forty-seven and he'll still be twenty-four.

I am thirty. I will always be thirty, Vauquelin said to him on the night they met.

At that instant, the reality of eternity settles its way into Éric's bones.

The choice.

The topic that was such a tipping point at the sour beginning of this long, bizarre night… now he understands why the choice he was given is so profound.

Éric wilts.

And he feels incredibly fucking childish. The things that had made him jealous about these boys… suddenly he can see them with clarity and he sends a silent *thanks* to V. Because now he knows why he was sent away in the first place.

But he's here on the streets of Paris with Moth, and he can't betray himself. He once thought he was so good at keeping himself hidden, but these boys have a way of peering through his façade. They've all proven that.

So he throws his shoulders back.

Back to Moth, and to right now.

Fucking MOTH!

'Anyway, so the healing thing… you and Gabriel get to come and I get to heal victims. Really fucking sweet deal. I'll trade with you anytime,' Éric says, his voice dripping with sarcasm as he watches Moth out of the corner of his eyes.

Moth can feel Éric's gaze on him as they walk, and he inwardly winces at the subject Éric has just brought up.

'That's a fucking tough deal you got there.' He shoves his hands into the pockets of his borrowed coat and his tongue flickers out.

This time, he lets Éric see.

'This is my thing,' he says as Éric's eyes widen. 'I can taste things, tell when other vampires are near.'

'Wait, what? Please do it again.'

Moth flicks it out once more, holds it there for a moment.

Éric leans toward Moth, captivated.

He sticks his own tongue out... he gets nothing.

And again Moth is catapulted back, this time to the night in Westport Quay when Gabe had done almost exactly the same thing.

'Damn... wow!' Éric says. 'My mind is kind of blown by our differences. You'd think vampires would be the same way. I don't understand it, but it's super cool, yeah? Like maybe it was meant for us to be together. We'd be fucking invincible with all our unusual skills.'

They scale back up the wall, and Éric stops Moth before he hops over the edge.

'You know they're gonna kill us. We've gotta sneak in really quietly. Just follow me and I'll take you into my game lair. It's the most logical place for them to find us.'

After they leap down, landing gracefully on the manicured lawn, Éric opens the back door, just a crack — listening for any sounds of life. The house is quiet... everyone must still be in the salon.

'It's through here,' he whispers, tiptoeing through the larder and down a dark hallway.

Éric grasps Moth's elbow and squires him into his private room... it's outfitted in a unique mashup of centuries. A flat screen hangs on the butter-yellow wall above a fireplace, flanked by a dozen skateboard decks interspersed with band posters — all of this is flanked by gilded mortises and seventeenth-century panelling. No big deal. Éric flicks on a table lamp before making a mad dash to the television and firing up the game system.

He thrusts a controller into a bewildered Moth's hands and pulls him down onto the sofa.

'Start shooting.'

Deafening music fills the room as he takes up a remote in his other hand and hits play.

Once again Éric feels very exposed.

He's showing Moth a part of his life that no one else has seen besides V.

But it's just part of their cover-up... right?

Yeah, that's it, he tells himself.

Moth's mind is blown.

Éric has his own gaming lair?

His eyes flick over the huge television screen, the wall-mounted speakers, the games stacked haphazardly on the floor.

The controller in his hand is nothing like the one he had in his mortal life and he stares at it like it's a rocket science test paper. At the corners of his vision the skate decks loom, mounted on the wall like fucking works of art. *In another life...*

Éric is lounged back, his gaze fixed on the video game, his fingers twitching expertly. The lights cast flickering shadows over his face.

And then the doors to the gaming room open — Moth gathers his wits and presses a few buttons.

This *is* a fucking alternate dimension, but he has new blood heating his skin and he's kinda broken a few rules: so despite the horror of what happened earlier, he counts it as a win.

Éric drapes a long leg over the armrest, firing away, and looks calmly over his shoulder to gaze upon Vauquelin and Clove, Gabriel at their side.

'Oh. Hey, guys. What's up?'

19 / NIGHT 2:

HELL IS KINDA MY DEFAULT

Vauquelin's nostrils flare.

There is an odd scent in this room, one he had certainly not expected. He strides across the floor, his shoes registering decisive thunks across the parquet. He seizes the remote from the table in front of Moth and Éric: he powers everything down, subduing the raucous noise into silence.

He looks down his nose at his beloved, who sinks deeper and deeper into the sofa, and robotically transfers the gaze to Moth.

'Where have the two of you gone tonight?'

Clove joins his fellow master. He knows full well that Moth has fed. It is obvious from the flush of colour to his skin and the plumpness of his lips. But something has changed between these two young vampires.

'Moth,' he begins and his voice is like a shard of ice. 'I believe you have something to say?'

Moth cowers in the corner of the sofa.

Fuck, fuck, fuck. Clove *knows.*

Not that that's any surprise. Suddenly, his little outing with Éric seems like the worst idea he's ever had.

Éric squirms under Vauquelin's blistering scrutiny. In his memory, V has never *once* looked at him this way: like he's disappointed. It makes him want to puke — or run. Instead, he forces words to his tongue.

'We just went for a walk.' His eyes dart from V to Clove: he doesn't dare look back to Gabriel. The last thing he needs is *another* set of daggers coming his way. 'You wanted us to get along. We had to remove ourselves from everything that happened inside and that's how we chose to do it.'

Gabe steps forward. He can feel Moth's rising panic and Éric is obviously sinking into the same mire.

'It was okay,' he says. He tries to keep his voice level. 'I was scanning for them. They were never in any danger.' He won't let Moth take the fall for this by himself, not when Gabe knew he had taken Éric onto the streets.

Clove turns to him and the expression on his face strips Gabe to the bone. He meets that gaze with his chin up.

Yes, I knew.

Éric hugs himself, clasping his elbows.

What's going on here? How did Gabriel know they were out? He looks at Moth, and a flash of anger washes over his face. Had he told Gabriel somehow? But when? It's kind of a little betrayal, like something has been taken away from the slight miracle that had occurred tonight: the miracle of them truly getting along. Which is what everyone wanted in the first fucking place — so what are they all so upset about? GOD!

Moth takes a deep breath but he's so panicked that his throat closes up. There is no fucking way he can crawl out of this one even with the benefit of his big mouth. This was all his idea. He'd been the one to suggest going out to hunt. When Éric said that he'd never hunted outside, Moth should have taken that as the huge fucking red flag it was and hauled him back over the garden wall.

It's clear that Clove and Vauquelin have already decided he's the bad guy, so it's up to him to take the flak. Maybe, just maybe, he'll live to see another night.

'It was me,' Moth says, lounging back in the sofa corner. He pastes what he hopes is an expression of defiance on his face, even though all he wants to do is crawl into a hole. 'I told him to come hunt with me.'

'No!' Éric stomps across the room. 'Everyone needs to calm the fuck down. Listen to me...' and he adds, prudently: 'please. This has been a really tough couple of nights. It makes my brain shut down just trying to sort all of the thoughts that are swirling in my head. I want everyone to think about this... if Moth and I hadn't gone out together tonight, you'd probably find that we still weren't speaking to each other. But fucking look at us! Come on!'

He intentionally avoids looking at V: instead, he stares at the wall, and thus he can't see his maker's face — hovering somewhere on a treacherous edge between terror and relief.

Gabe goes to stand behind the sofa between Moth and Éric. He has no idea what happened on their hunt: that will be for Moth and him to unpack when they're alone. What he's very grateful for is that Moth hasn't ripped Éric's throat out and brought back the pieces like a fucking gun dog.

'Nothing bad has happened.' He appeals to both Clove and V. 'I know they shouldn't have sneaked out. That was wrong. But can't you sense all the tension has gone?'

Éric shoots a glance at Moth. His eyelids grow heavy.

All I wanted was for us to be friends.

We were so close.

And now it's all gone to hell.

Moth's eyes widen.

Fuck, that was Éric's mind-touch.

Moth hadn't realised his shields were so shot.

He sends his own in reply.

Hell is kinda my default. It's okay, we can work this out.

He prays that that's true.

Both sets of vampire eyes go into saucer mode.

Éric hears Moth loud and clear.

Prior to this moment he's only heard Vauquelin's silent voice, and the sensation blazes through his brain cells like a lit match.

He doesn't know how much more he can take, but at least it's another special thing he has with Moth now. He would never have expected this.

Fuck... I wouldn't have expected anything *that happened tonight.*

Clove stands by Vauquelin. He is well aware of the mind conversation between Éric and Moth but he stays silent. Although he is furious with Moth for possibly putting Éric in danger, he needs to see how this all plays out. This is Vauquelin's home. Clove will not sully these rooms by launching into a vilification first. Even if Moth does deserve it.

The intensity radiating off of the masters standing behind them trips down Éric's back like a knuckled fist. He turns to face them, and he walks straight to Vauquelin.

He curls his fingers around his maker's neck.

Are you mad at me?

No, bien-aimé...[†] I am only grateful you are safe.

Éric drops to his knees in front of Clove.

'Clove, forgive me. Please don't punish Moth. We're equally guilty. We just did the best we could... what felt right at the moment. I promise we were careful.' His chin falls to his chest.

Clove looks to Vauquelin. He is not used to these levels of displayed emotions — unless, of course, one counts Moth. He places his hand on Éric's shoulder and urges him to stand.

'You do not belong on your knees in front of me, Éric. But your gesture of humility touches my heart.'

Vauquelin opens his arms and Éric immediately folds himself into them.

Clove cuts his gaze to Gabriel.

'What do you think we should do?' He knows this will test his first-born

---

[†] - BELOVED

to the extremes, but Gabriel will not grow without compression.

Gabe's world yawns open, threatening to swallow him whole.

He's caught between his love for Moth and the weight of his bloodline, but what he says will reverberate through the rest of this visit. He finds a shred of courage amidst the turmoil in his mind and straightens his spine.

'Moth and Éric aren't fledglings. They knew what they were doing, weighed up the odds and decided that this was right. For them. And we can't haul them over the coals for that.'

Éric turns his head a fraction. Moth is straight in his gaze: he winks.

You're right. I think we're gonna be okay.

Gabe sees the wink. It's outlined in blazing technicolour, a spear of blinding light across his eyes. *What the fuck has happened between them?* Moth had thrown such hate towards Éric earlier and now they seem as thick as thieves. A stab of jealousy pierces his heart and his lips tighten. He knows he shouldn't, but a mind-touch bursts out of him and drills into Éric's thoughts.

Is there something we should talk about?

It's an innocent enough question but each word has a barbed point.

Éric slackens into V's embrace. His mind is being pummelled by thoughts that are not his own, as if his mind isn't full enough already — and this one is clearly Gabriel's.

Fuck. That unmistakable voice.

There are so many explanations forthcoming, because he and Moth are in the red right now.

'Gabriel... I think we should have a word in the hallway.'

He doesn't look behind him. He's kind of done at this point. He wants everything out in the open. He thinks back to a moment with Moth... only a little while ago, though it seems like decades now.

Moth took charge.

Éric loved that.

He flings open the doors and extends a hand outward.

'Gabriel. Please?'

Gabe marches past Clove and Vauquelin.

'With your permission.' But his words are only tossed in his wake.

This bitter feeling refuses to back down and right now it's curdling in his veins, spreading its poison. It's been such a fucked up night and he's exhausted by all of it. He doesn't even glance back at Moth as he strides through the salon doors.

And then he's out in the cooler air of the hallway. He hates where his mind is going. He trusts Moth with his life, is secure in the love that they have — he's never had a reason to doubt him, but he can't tamp down the red veil threatening to descend.

'What happened? Tell me.' His voice is hard.

Gone is the Gabe from when he first introduced himself to Éric.

And inside his veins the shadows dance.

'Gabriel. There's some crucial information missing here. I can imagine how this looks from the outside. But maybe there's something you don't understand about me and Vauquelin. He's not just my maker, or my lover. We made a vow... he gave me his name. We might as well be married. I was never unfaithful to him when he vanished into the past, not even when I started to believe he was never coming back. He was gone for *four fucking years*. Do you think I'd break that? For *anyone*? Nothing would be worth breaking the honour that we have for each other. We don't share each other. And I know you have that with Moth, so why can't you just trust him? Why can't you think that maybe, just maybe, Moth could share a tiny part of himself with another person and have something that is just his alone? Being in a relationship with someone doesn't mean that you own them and every single thought in their head.' Éric slams his back against the wall. 'Believe me, I get possessive too. I have *major* issues. I'm fucking jealous as hell... I don't even like anyone *looking* at Vauquelin! But I don't *own* him.

I just get to be his most special person. What more could I ask of him?'

Gabe lets Éric's words wash over him and nearly every single word is something that could have come from his own mouth. His head starts to spin as blood rushes through his veins. In his mind's eye it is thick and black and wanting, and he's glad that Éric has the bit between his teeth and isn't giving him a chance to reply.

A memory spears him: he's in the tower at Gehenna, Sasha's heart grasped in his hand. There is blood, so much blood. And then Moth forcing Gabe to look at him — *Fight it, damn you!* — Moth's fist connecting with his jaw, this boy he loves so much standing before the dark, hissing shadows, as Gabe fought with every inch of his being to break free of the darkness.

The jealousy that had come from nowhere dissipates and his shoulders slump. His vision starts to tunnel and he has to reach out and steady himself against the wall. A jumble of voices sound in his head, a whispering, an urging, and he has to fight to keep them at bay. They want to crawl up his throat, seep into his mind and seed their corruption. And he knows that if he lets that happen, he is lost.

He's barely aware of the lair doors flying open and then Clove's arms are around him.

'Breathe, Gabriel. Focus. Look at me.'

Gabe lets himself sink into his maker's arms.

He wants to curl up and never come up for air.

Éric's heart lurches at the sight of Gabriel wilting against Clove, and the reality of his big speech crawls through his marrow like a spider.

It takes a minute for it to settle.

Where the hell did those words even come from?

But as they hang in the heavy, remaining silence, he realises he has spoken his truth.

Does Vauquelin even know all this?

I know, my love. I know.

As V's words run through Éric's veins, as his dark blood embraces him — his knees buckle. He knew that first morning he woke up in Vauquelin's bed in Los Angeles that V had shown him magic: but the past few nights have delivered too much of it at once.

The revenant life opens before him like a black hole, hurling its mysteries at him faster than he can catch them. It's infinite. Yet tonight, he's grateful that V kept the boys' secrets, has left their alchemy in chapters for Éric to uncover like he's reading a book. Their eyes meet, and Vauquelin recognises his beloved's newfound understanding.

And that is how Éric knows they will all survive this crisis, that they will all be able to come together again without barbs.

Éric lengthens his spine, extending himself to his full height that is almost the same as Vauquelin's, drags a finger down the divot above Vauquelin's lips. He sinks both his hands into V's hair, bringing their bodies as close as they can be in front of others. Their lips meet like magnets, their tongues enfold. Éric pulls back and their eyes speak the words they cannot utter aloud in front of anyone else.

At this moment, no one else exists. It is only them.

It will always only be them.

It's Moth's cry of alarm that brings Gabe back to the present. He lets Moth drag him from Clove's arms and then Moth's mouth is against his and there's wetness pressed against his cheek: because Moth is crying.

Clove exchanges a look with Vauquelin.

I believe we should retire. The boys have experienced an emotional night and they will need space to process everything.

He sends this to Vauquelin although his eyes convey his thoughts. This night has changed them all in profound ways none of them expected.

A door opens at the end of the hallway and Teal slips through. He goes to Moth and Gabe, huddled on the floor together, and kneels between them — taking each of their hands in his. Distress is etched across his face.

He felt the darkness expand as he sat in the silence of the library, heard the whisperings in the still night air. Of course, this moment had to come, when Gabe's legacy reared its serpent's head and tried to bite him. It is part of his brother, a part that hibernates, and the witch in Teal can sometimes see this darkness coiled deep within Gabe, seemingly dormant:but it always has one eye open.

The weight of Clove's gaze settles on Teal and he turns.

A moment passes between them, a moment in this ancient hallway of gilt and marble and opulent richness.

The fireflies in Teal's eyes are, for this moment, a beacon.

A light he will burn forever to guide his brothers home.

20 / NIGHT 2:

IF YOU MUST WANDER...

It is Éric who closes their doors behind them.

He confronts his lover: their last kiss was an unfinished sentence.

Vauquelin is the em dash.

He slips an arm around Éric's waist... an ellipsis.

Did you drink the entirety of a stranger's blood on the street

A question mark.

Absolutely not — just a sip

Period.

Relief washes over Vauquelin.

Éric is unharmed.

He is home, he is safe.

Vauquelin traces Éric's collarbone with his nose, bringing it up his neck to breathe in his slightly-altered scent, awash with the outdoors — he joins their lips together so that he might die a moment in his beloved's kiss. As he will do any chance he has for eternity.

He still carries the damage from his final time-slip and their forced separation: yet he must let Éric spread his wings, lest he risk losing him again. If something dreadful were to happen to Éric, if he were to leave him, it would mean the end of Vauquelin.

Éric still doesn't know what happened between Vauquelin and Moth in the catacombs.

And Vauquelin doesn't know exactly what he and Moth did, either.

The unknowing is a parentheses, and neither of them reveal what is contained in between.

But Vauquelin had heard Éric's words in the hallway, and Éric is right: sometimes we have things that belong to just ourselves. It doesn't diminish the other.

Éric hefts his sweater over his head, flinging it to the floor, and grasps Vauquelin's shoulder, authoritatively unbuttoning V's shirt and travelling his hand down.

I need your skin against mine, Éric pleads.

Vauquelin sheds his shirt, drops his trousers to his ankles. He kicks them to the side. He was already barefoot.

Their chests meet.

Éric takes Vauquelin's jaw in his hands, drives his tongue past V's fangs... they swallow the coppery drops of their merging blood, the sweetest flavour either of them have ever known.

He backs V up against the gilded wall and flips him around, his hand held fast against V's neck, his other fingers tripping down his maker's spine. No one else would ever be able to do this to Vauquelin.

Only Éric, and he knows it.

He *knows* V is inviting him to possess him.

Vauquelin yields to every blow of Éric's frustration from the past two nights. But as he takes Éric's thrusts, arching his hips back to let his lover fill him, his hands gripping ancient mouldings, Vauquelin understands that he has everything he ever wanted.

He surrenders to Éric, laying himself bare as he only could to a certain extent in front of the others, as Éric's cock pulses inside him, thrusting across his inner map that only Éric can navigate: or ever will.

He wilts and careens to the bed.

Éric follows him.

He spoons into Vauquelin, kisses his shoulder. His hips are still thrusting, still wanting, and Vauquelin's body finds its voice. He faces Éric, throttling him — and Éric snuggles into his death grip.

Just like he did their first morning.

Vauquelin devours Éric with kisses, relishes their tongues battling.

He rolls his shoulders, his fingers still gripping Éric's windpipe — but Éric undoes him with that crooked smile and a whisper that brightens the darkness of the room: 'I love you so much.'

Éric draws his knees back and Vauquelin sinks into him.

Their bodies rock together like a ship on the stormy swells of a deep sea.

Their eyes never leave one another.

Éric brings a hand up to cradle Vauquelin's head.

He drowns in the depths of V's love — he blissfully disappears beneath its turbulent waves.

And as the sun rises, before he drifts off to sleep, with Vauquelin nestled against him, breathing softly against his neck, it dawns on Éric that he no longer envies Gabriel and Moth.

His eyes close.

His breath slows... Vauquelin's hand comes to a rest over his heart like a blanket, and he knits their fingers together.

'Please, *bien-aimé*. If you must wander, always return to me as you did tonight,' Vauquelin whispers.

'I told you a long time ago... I never want to be where you aren't. I'll always be here with you, V. Always...' Éric whispers back.

They have this.

It is all they need.

Their hearts whisper into stillness.

21 / NIGHT 2:
YOU ARE IMMORTAL... NOT INFALLIBLE

Clove leads his boys up the curving marble staircase. They all pause for a moment and he rests his hand in the small of Gabriel's back.

'Come with me.'

He sees the yearning look pass between Gabriel and Moth, the connection joining them pulsing with its own heartbeat.

'I will not keep you for long, Gabriel.'

Clove glances to Teal.

'Take Moth into your chambers and stay with him.'

He does not need to add this last part, for Teal will not leave his brother alone: not with what has transpired on this long, disquieting night.

Gabriel follows Clove into his room and Clove lights a candle on the nightstand. They both watch as the small light bravely stands against the darkness.

'I'm sorry I didn't tell you about Moth and Éric going out,' Gabriel begins, but Clove hushes him with a raised hand.

He goes to his first-born and tilts Gabriel's chin with one long finger, looks deep into his eyes, finds his truth.

'You did what you thought was right,' Clove says, and he gentles his tone. Gabriel has dealt with too many emotions tonight and Clove knows he is hollowed out. 'I can never fault you for that. But despite everything,'

Clove shakes his head, and the gesture really says *Moth*. 'I am exceedingly proud of the way you carried yourself tonight.'

Moisture builds in Gabriel's eyes but he forces it back.

'But what about the jealousy? I let the darkness take a hold of me.'

His voice trails off as he berates himself inwardly.

'Hush,' Clove says and bends to press a kiss to his first-born's brow. 'You are immortal, Gabriel, not infallible. Now, go to Moth, and hold him close.'

Clove opens the door and beckons Gabriel through to the hallway beyond. There is so much more he would like to say but for now this is enough. Gabriel knows he is loved, that he has Clove's blessing.

Clove watches as the boy he saved, the boy he gave life to, pauses at the door to his chamber. Two sets of dark eyes meet, a nod between them, before Clove closes the door.

22 / NIGHT 2:

THIS ISN'T ABOUT HUNGER

Moth and Teal are sitting on the bed as Gabe enters. Teal rises and goes to him and Gabe sinks into his brother's embrace. Teal's fingers tangle in his hair, clasp the back of his neck, and there's safety there.

'It's okay,' Teal whispers. 'I'm with you.'

A rush of warmth floods Gabe's veins. He pulls away slightly and meets Teal's ocean gaze.

'Jeez, you two, get a room.'

Moth's voice interrupts them and Gabe laughs. He feels his muscles relax for the first time in what seems like hours.

'You wish.' Teal delivers his own throwaway remark and Moth pretends to faint, the back of his hand sweeping his brow.

Teal slips behind the jib door and now Gabe and Moth are alone.

They watch each other for a moment and then Gabe strides across to the bed and gathers Moth into his arms.

He holds him tight, a little too tight.

'Crushing me,' Moth yelps, and Gabe loosens his grip, taking Moth's hands in his own. Their eyes meet.

'What a fucking night.' Moth delivers the mother of all understatements. His eyes drop to the elaborate stitching on the silk coverlet. 'I...' he tries to find words to express how he feels.

'Stop.' Gabe presses a finger to Moth's lips. 'I let an unwarranted emotion get the better of me. I could blame everything that's happened tonight, but I'll own the fact that for one instant I thought you'd messed around with Éric... and I let that stupidity take me over.'

'Me and Éric? You're kidding, right?' Moth can see the anguish written in Gabe's eyes and he hates the fact that he's responsible for it, even if he didn't do anything wrong. 'Éric would rather die than let my dirty mouth touch his.' Moth pauses. 'Although he did kiss my fingers.'

Gabe's eyes widen.

'No, not like that. We were play-acting on a mark, and we fed. Then Éric did this fucked up thing where he healed the fang bites with his fucking fingers... oh...' That's the last word Moth utters before Gabe's lips are on his and they both collapse onto the bed.

The time for words is over.

Gabe rips off his own T-shirt and helps Moth tear his away. Then fingers are on jean zips and boots and palpable need builds in the ancient chamber. The candles flicker in their sconces as the draught from two boys in urgent disrobement catches the flames.

Skin against skin at last and they both groan. Gabe winds his fingers into Moth's hair, urges him to arch his head back, plunges his fangs into that column of perfect pale flesh. A whimper from Moth as he raises his hips in ecstasy.

Gabe savours each precious mouthful as if it's fine wine.

He isn't hungry.

This isn't about hunger.

It's about need, about connection: of pushing back the awful fear when V marched Moth away, that maybe Moth's punishment would be more than he could bear, more than Gabe could bear.

Gabe doesn't try to force himself into Moth's mind. Moth will tell him what happened between him and Éric, between him and V, when and if he is ever ready. Éric's words about possession, about ownership come back to him.

'Fuck Éric,' Moth whispers, as if he knows — and Gabe breaks free, his mouth smeared with Moth's blood. Then a grin touches Moth's lips, a salacious grin, and they both know that that is what is happening right now in another room.

'Turn over,' Gabe says, his voice husky with need, and Moth complies, his stomach clenching. He buries his head in the ridiculous amount of pillows, presses his hips against the kiss of silk because he needs to fuck and his cock demands, but Gabe is taking charge tonight.

The sound of a drawer opening and Moth begins to turn his head.

'No,' Gabe says, and pushes it back down.

There's a noise Moth can't quite work out and then Gabe's hands are on his shoulders. They feel different, more silky, and Moth shivers. Fingers trail down his spine. It's a slow journey and those fingers know exactly where to stop, where Moth's muscles are always tight.

He winds his fingers into the coverlet, his eyes screwed up, and he wants to drown in the sensations coursing through his body.

Now Gabe's hands reach the base of his spine and they fan out, following the curve of his buttocks. Moth holds his breath.

'Please,' he whimpers.

Please, fuck me. Please show me that I'm worthy even when I hurt you.

Strong fingers dig into his flesh. They knead and pull and just when he thinks he can't bear it anymore, Gabe spreads him apart. A moment where Moth knows Gabe is gazing at the place that gives them both so much pleasure. The moment holds and Moth is pretty sure he's going to come into this fucking antique coverlet if Gabe doesn't do something.

A breath of cool air and then he screams as Gabe runs his tongue across the pucker in his flesh. Moth is spread again, wider still, and now that tongue is delving, delving, and Moth's fists rip the stitching apart.

Gabe tastes and licks and tastes again and Moth is undone to a fragment of himself.

Movement as Gabe rises and Moth wants to beg him to continue — that noise again, and then Gabe's silken fingers find where his mouth left off and he plunges two deep into Moth, begins the slow dance of thrust and retreat.

Moth doesn't know whether he wants to arch his hips back or push forward. He lets his body decide, rising to his knees and pushing his body back against Gabe's onslaught, sweat coating his skin.

Moth is as open as he's ever been and he'll take as much as Gabe can give if that's what he wants.

One last, long delve and Gabe pulls his fingers free. His hands go to Moth's hips and Moth knows what's coming next. He bites into the coverlet, rips it with his fangs as he hangs on the razor's edge.

And then Gabe takes him in one long, deep thrust. Moth's world disintegrates into a cacophony of dazzling light and sound — only the sound is his own voice, pleading and cursing.

He is impaled on Gabe, not just in flesh but in spirit. They move as one, and Moth gives himself completely. Their dance is both brutal and tender and Moth bleeds but he relishes the pain.

Gabe pulls out and the emptiness is a cavern in Moth's soul. His fingers plunge again and then retreat, and then he yanks Moth's head back and rams those fingers into Moth's mouth so he can taste the very core of himself.

Gabe keeps his fingers there and Moth bites down to bone as Gabe thrusts into him again. Fireworks in Moth's mind as Gabe reaches his climax, as Moth feels the ejaculation erupt: they both hang in the sweet, dark fist of rapture. A few final thrusts then Gabe withdraws and collapses onto his back.

He pulls Moth close and finds his willing mouth. Their kiss is as deep as the ocean, their love as bottomless as time.

There is no need for any words: their coupling spoke for them. Filled with desire and devotion, underscored by need and the bliss of ecstatic pain, it is the tablet on which they write their lives upon.

Moth closes his eyes and winds his body against Gabe's. He's throbbing inside and he wants to hang onto this feeling and never let it go.

A kiss to his brow, a mouth curling into a smile.

'What?' he manages to mumble, although dawn is close and his eyelids are heavy.

'You taste fucking delicious.'

Moth's stomach clenches again and he presses his hips closer to Gabe's. They fit against each other like pieces of a puzzle. He knows exactly what Gabe means.

'Dirty boy,' he whispers and bites his lip, before he falls into the deep black maw of the death sleep.

23 / NIGHT 3:

ABOUT THAT LABEL...

The sun begins its *coucher*,[†] the night drapes its violet silk across the city. Six kilometres from Vauquelin's house, the Eiffel Tower illuminates for the first time this night, inspiring a hushed cry of delight from the tourists clustered around its base.

Tucked safely behind ancient walls, seven pairs of vampire eyes open.

In truth, six.

One still sleeps.

Vauquelin rises on a shoulder and gazes down upon his dark angel.

Éric may no longer be a fledgling, yet still he sleeps hard. His arm is arced around his head, the fingers of one hand curled into a fist.

Vauquelin nestles into him and sighs, wondering what dreams are murmuring in Éric's mind.

So much has happened to his beloved in the span of two nights... he has many lessons yet to learn. He has grown... this he knows.

Vauquelin fervently wishes this for him: provided Éric does not flourish beyond his grasp.

He had missed so much of his beloved's early revenant life.

But Éric said something monumental to Gabriel last night, something

---
[†] - BEDTIME

that had not been meant for Vauquelin's ears. The phrase hovers on the edge of his consciousness, like a trapped bird that flaps madly against a window, desperate to return to the outdoors.

'Éric,' he whispers.

On any other night, he would never attempt to wake him.

A grunt.

An *annoyed* grunt.

Éric rolls onto his stomach and buries his head under a pillow.

After last night's emotional hurricane, Vauquelin cannot begrudge him wanting to sleep longer. So he knits his fingers behind his head, linking their ankles together.

Vauquelin has never had an appreciation for labels.

The love he has for Éric needs no definition: it simply *is*, as indisputable in its existence as spilled blood is crimson.

It cannot be categorised, particularly in one of such human invention, so tied to human social constraints.

But then he reminds himself that, between the two of them, Éric is vastly closer to his humanity than Vauquelin will ever be again. He cannot drive Éric's observations... he must let Éric become who he is as vampire, in an authentic manner.

Just as Vauquelin had done, only he had always been alone.

Éric is not the only one having new experiences courtesy of this extraordinary visit.

His eyes close and he drifts off again, killing time until the moment Éric comes back to life.

But it is Vauquelin who bursts into consciousness again when he realises Éric is straddling him, their faces inches apart: so close that Vauquelin can simply pucker his lips to kiss him — which he does.

'I never wake up before you,' Éric says.

'I have been awake for hours. Just waiting for you,' Vauquelin says, with a grin.

'Liar,' Éric says, and then a skirmish begins, punctuated by their laughter and playful punches. Éric pulls the duvet over their heads, and they settle into soft kisses.

Vauquelin grips Éric's jaw, bringing him to stillness.

'You said something about us last night. To Gabriel,' he says.

Éric swallows. 'You heard everything, didn't you?'

'Yes. Perhaps it was unjust of me to listen. It was a private conversation between the two of you.'

'It wasn't anything I wouldn't say to your face.'

'But is this truly how you think of us? We are not married, Éric. This is such a very human term. I must admit it was strange to my ears.'

'Not exactly... what would we do, go to a courthouse or a church? V... Gabriel and I are both young. I had to say something so I could explain us to him in a way that made sense. But it makes sense to me, too. I don't even know where that came from. When it was out in the air, I knew it was true.'

Vauquelin begins to tremble.

No other being has ever held such a passionate sway over him.

Lightning flashes of his recent displays of humility — and his shameless subservience to Éric — illuminate his brain. He had shown them all the depths of his adoration, and he had done it without the slightest trace of shame. He will likely do it again — because now he has dropped his façade for Clove and the boys.

Now he is free.

Éric's fingertips dance across his chest, light as a feather.

'You did make a vow to me, at Évreux. Actually, I kind of dragged it out of you,' Éric grimaces. 'But you never once asked me if I was faithful while you were gone. Didn't you ever wonder?'

Vauquelin sucks in his breath.

He has never admitted to Éric that yes, he had wondered — wondered about it so much he thought he might be ill. But it is true: he never asked. Vauquelin convinced himself of what he wanted to believe.

He lifts a hand, dips it into his beloved's curls, the curls that never cease to spellbind his heart.

Éric is so beautiful.

And while he was away, Éric was alone for four years: he was out on the streets of Paris, living his life, choosing to put himself on display in front of cameras. To throw himself into the arenas of human temptation. There is no doubt in his mind that many who encountered Éric then had been captivated by his beauty, had attempted to take him into their beds.

Now it's Éric's turn to listen in.

'I told you in the letter... after Vauquelin, no one comes close.'

He lowers his face to V's, brushes their lips together.

'I'm starting to think you don't believe that yourself.'

Vauquelin turns his head to the side.

He does not, in fact, believe it.

He still does not believe he deserves this, any of it.

But this is not the time to ponder the complexities of their love... there are others in the house, others that expect his presence.

Blood desire agitates the edges of his veins.

Soon, they will have to make arrangements.

For now, Éric will have to do.

Vauquelin urges Éric onto his back, flings the duvet behind them.

He runs a finger down his favourite trail, and he sinks his teeth into Éric's thigh.

Éric groans with pleasure, writhing his hips.

And then he halts his movement.

'Did you ever sleep with Clove?' Éric whispers. 'Come on... you can tell me. I promise I won't be mad.'

'What?' Vauquelin jerks his head up: a thin line of blood cascades down his chin. He furrows his brow. 'No!'

He cannot fathom this question. Surely Éric would understand, based on Clove's humiliating explanation to them all in the salon, that if it were so Vauquelin would have already uncovered this truth. But no. Clearly, his beloved has not done the maths.

A devilish smile from Éric. 'Okay. But you thought about it. I can tell.'

'Who would *not* think about it? Look at him! But that was a long time ago... it was B.E.'

'Huh?'

'Before Éric.'

Éric looks down and away, suppressing a small smile.

A vampire blush.

'Well... all I can say is I wouldn't blame you if you had. *Whew.*'

'It was not from lack of trying. The man has an iron will. We could both walk into his chamber naked right now and he would not blink.'

'There must be something really dark in his past if he could resist you.'

'There is much more to Clove than meets the eye. He is a stronger vampire than I will ever be. Were it not for him and the boys, I would not have been in any condition to be with you. I was a disaster when I went to visit them.'

Éric snorts.

'Come on, V, face it... you're *still* a disaster. ow ow ow!'

24 / NIGHT 3:

YOU SAVED HIM

As Clove exits his chamber, all is quiet in the room occupied by the boys. That is a good sign. He doubts they are still sleeping, not at this hour, but they need some time alone after the emotional upheaval of last night.

His hair is damp from the shower — a luxury he is unaccustomed to, but is making full use of — and he wears black jeans and a burgundy silk shirt, courtesy of Flynn. The garments feel odd against his skin, but this trip is all about taking everyone out of the zone they are accustomed to so they may learn: and he is part of that.

At the head of the staircase he hears a door open on another hallway and he pauses. The sound of a door latch catching, and his host appears in the corridor.

Vauquelin stops when he sees Clove.

A moment of embarrassment catches in his throat — he has not been an exemplary master vampire on this visit.

But somehow he knows Clove will not denigrate him, will not fault him for exposing this other side of himself.

Vauquelin approaches his esteemed guest.

'Good evening, Clove.'

He prevents himself from surveying his peer. He would prefer to call

Clove his friend, his *copain*:† only he is not convinced that is the correct definition for their kinship.

Though he masks his reaction he is overcome by this vision of Clove, so vastly different from how he had known him in Gehenna. Here they are, gathered in Paris, which a few years past Vauquelin would never have predicted: and in very different circumstances.

Clove, by his generosity to Vauquelin on his visit to England — and by welcoming him into his covert world, designed to protect three young vampire boys — had effectively incinerated the French vampire's perceptions of revenancy.

There is still a pilot light for Clove in Vauquelin's memory, ignited the night they met — such a light cannot be extinguished. Vauquelin is not a mere man: he is vampire, flesh and blood and bone, and he can conceive of no harm in admiring the quietly smouldering, *ancién*‡ beauty of Clove.

Vauquelin will never stop worshipping beautiful things.

It is a crucial part of his genetic makeup.

And now they stand facing each other.

Clove arches a dark brow in greeting. 'Vauquelin.' He extends one hand and clasps Vauquelin's arm.

Vauquelin cannot allow his eyes to leave Clove's face, no matter how much he would enjoy the sight of Clove's fingers digging into his flesh. Their profound pressure is quite enough.

'I am grateful we have this time to talk amongst ourselves. It has been a little overwhelming for our charges and it has been necessary to look after their interests first.' He meets Vauquelin's ice-blue gaze. 'Shall we discuss the need for sustenance? I know you and Éric do not feed as often as my boys require. They can leave and take what they need from the streets, if you prefer that?'

---

†- FRIEND
‡- ANCIENT

Vauquelin exhales at last.

'I know safety is your utmost concern. If you will accompany me, I would like to show you how Éric and I manage for ourselves. Please.' He gestures towards the stairs, and they walk in silence to the catacombs entrance.

Once inside Vauquelin ignites two torches, passing one to Clove. This is a most appropriate environment for two immemorial vampires: no light except that of fire, the shadowy darkness their natural home... surrounded by ancient stone walls.

Here, there is comfort.

Here, they can be their true archaic selves, without the folly of youth to temper their topics of conversation.

Clove surveys the dank, hidden chamber beneath this magnificent house. He holds the torch high and for a moment he is back in the lair of the necromancer asking him to spare his boys.

But he pushes this imagery away.

This is not that time. This is not that place.

He wonders why Vauquelin has brought him here. Then a smile touches his lips. This is a supremely private place. Here they can talk.

'I thought you might appreciate this most of all, Clove,' Vauquelin says, returning his smile. He walks deeper into the caverns, illuminating the bones. 'The collection began in 1668. The second 1668, I should clarify. The first one began in Los Angeles, in 2000. Sadly, it no longer exists. I do not know its fate.' He waves the torch to another, less populated area. 'This is Éric's collection, which he began the night of my final time-slip.'

Clove casts his gaze over the stacks of ancient bones, the skulls with their hollow eyes facing towards him. He is not easily impressed, but he allows himself to appreciate the magnitude of this macabre collection. He turns to the smaller stack and a small sigh escapes his lips.

'I wish things could have been different for Éric when you were swept away. There is, and there will always be, a place for him at Gehenna. I do not like to think of him alone in these vast hallways.'

'Your generosity toward Éric gives me more comfort than I could ever express, but you know this. I only wish he had heeded my advice to come to you at once. Yet, despite his occasional...' — and here Vauquelin permits himself a rueful grin — 'wilfulness, I am proud of how he developed in my absence.'

Clove does not speak of what Vauquelin had to do to return to Éric, but the coffin is in his peripheral vision.

Vauquelin's chest caves as he realises the coffin, though it is pushed to the furthest edges of the chamber, is visible.

Vauquelin approaches it, inhaling sharply.

'Olivier, my brother, lies here... and I must confess. I know not what I would encounter were I to open this coffin.'

It is none too easy to forget Clove's inheritance, the darkness that clutches his heart... the same legacy runs through Gabriel's veins. The unspeakable tragedy of their bloodline, which is also their glory.

He panics: surely Clove does not think he would ask — his heart stops a moment, and he turns to face his fellow master.

There is a long moment between them. And, at last, Clove speaks.

'When this grim birthright passed to me I vowed that I would never use it. That I would never raise the dead, for they have earned their rest. I locked it deep inside and it will reside there, for all time. I cannot risk this passing to Gabriel. Do you understand?'

Vauquelin sinks to a wine crate, the same one he sat upon for Moth's lecture. The majority of his and Clove's existences has been spent under the wings of darkness, Death an ever-present shadow: part and parcel of their nature. They have ushered untold numbers of humans into the black clutch of Death, severing them from the mortal coil in order that they themselves could live.

Yet despite their similarities, Clove and Vauquelin have trod across their centuries on very different paths.

Vauquelin knows he is spoiled. Were one to describe him as such to his face, he would not argue. His entire life, human and immortal, has been smothered in privilege. Yet there have been times, since his first meeting with Clove, that he felt himself unworthy of taking in the same air as Clove. This is one of those times.

How could their struggles possibly compare?

Vauquelin had an insidious maker: a frivolous vampire who might as well have been a puppeteer, but Clove's maker was the Necromancer.

And now Vauquelin is the caretaker of the French vampire lore. He knows that a vast, gaping depth of darkness could open a vortex and swallow them all.

He does understand Clove's statement — and on a deeper, cellular level, he senses how close to the bone the shadows can come. With his final time-slip, they had severed the lines between him and his beloved. And they follow far too closely on the heels of Gabriel and Clove.

Vauquelin will never surrender any of them — he will fight for them with his own life. With his chin on his chest, he looks up to Clove through heavy-lidded eyes.

'I do, Clove. I do. All I would ask of you, my friend, is your guidance. I did not expect this conversation, nor did I bring you to the catacombs with any intention other than to discuss our charges. In truth, the coffin's very existence has been buried in my subconscious along with my detestable act, until you noticed it now.' He stands and begins to pace, lacing his hands on the crown of his head. 'I was in despair the night of Olivier's demise. The time-slip, the separation from Éric, knowing the sinister act required of me so that I might be reunited with him. I could not bear to destroy Olivier. All bodies go into my acid pit. Yet I could not do it for him.'

Clove watches the struggle Vauquelin is suffering. Turmoil rakes its dark claws through Vauquelin's heart, its tendrils tormenting his thoughts. Clove can only imagine the horror of having to destroy one progeny to return to another.

His gaze flicks to the coffin and the darkness within him strains against its leash. Something inside calls to him, a weak and plaintive cry for salvation. He could lay his hands upon this ravaged wreck and raise it from the dead. But he will not. Still, the desperation within the coffin is a palpable thing and he turns to Vauquelin.

'I could aid you, if you wish.' He adds no more.

Vauquelin takes Clove's meaning — it writhes into his soul. He knows that Clove will not touch his brother. That this is not what Clove is offering.

He had struggled over what his intentions were by keeping his old friend here. No restoration of their past affinity would be possible — for all was lost in his reclamation of Olivier's life, and Vauquelin will never return to his past.

Yet the sting of Olivier's harsh words on their last night together — his spewing of hatred toward Vauquelin's professed eternal love for another male — still pierces his heart as cruelly as when they had left Olivier's lips.

At once, it all becomes clear.

Vauquelin heaves open the hatch to the pit, turning his head against the merciless fist of the acid.

He had dreaded this moment.

He had not known whether or not it would come.

Olivier had been left in suspended terror, frozen in a hell that was not of his own making.

Vauquelin grasps a brass handle, dragging the coffin a few metres closer to the pit.

Clove recognises the horrific agony written across Vauquelin's face. He has seen it many times on other faces… far more often than he would like.

Vauquelin pauses and looks across his shoulder to Clove, a calming, steadfast presence, his face half-obscured by shadows and half-illuminated by the golden glow of the torch held aloft in his hand.

'Clove... you saved him. Centuries ago, when you were in Paris. And that is why I came to seek you in the first place... for I never thanked you.'

Serenity eases its way into Vauquelin's soul, and he realises now that he would never have been able to do this were Clove not here with him now.

Clove remembers that night clearly, as he remembers all of his nights. He has never stood back when weaker vampires suffer at the hands of persecutors. He recalls the night Teal came into his life.

He takes two steps forward to close the gap between himself and Vauquelin but he dares not go further — for the shadows that coil against his bones have awoken and are demanding to be fed.

But he feels the need to bolster Vauquelin's courage.

'This is the right thing to do, Vauquelin. Every vampire, no matter what sins he committed in his immortal life, deserves to rest in whatever peace awaits.' He wants to press his hand to Vauquelin's shoulder but he cannot, not when Vauquelin's touch remains on the coffin.

Blood tears fill Vauquelin's eyes and he blinks them away, nodding at Clove. The words in his heart need not be spoken. His gratitude for his friend's strength is evident by his feet moving forward, by his determined acceptance of this surprising turn of events.

He eases the coffin to a rest at the edge of the pit.

He looks up to Clove once more and hoists the palm of his free hand: Vauquelin does not wish him to be harmed by the toxic bath that lies beneath them.

Clove retreats a little, although his eyes do not leave Vauquelin's. Anguish is etched against Vauquelin's face, and Clove wishes he could absorb some of that pain to make this task less horrifying.

Vauquelin rests the heels of his hands atop the coffin: he cannot bear to lay eyes on what might be inside. He has no concept of the state in which he would find Olivier's corpse. He unlocks the lid and casts it aside, fixing his gaze on the ceiling as he hefts the coffin's contents into the pit. His fingers are white-knuckled as they grip the brass handles on the side.

A hideous sizzle overtakes the silence of the room as Vauquelin ducks behind the scant protection of the black wooden coffin, and yet still the acid splashes its way upward and onto the exposed skin of his hands.

He scrambles backward, his spine colliding with the wooden shelf behind, agitating its bones and sending them a'clatter.

He sucks air in through his teeth, cradling his burning fingers between his knees. His skin swiftly reinvents itself and erases his agony along with it, though he does not believe he deserves the rapid evacuation of such crucial pain.

It darts from his hands into his heart like a thief in the night, and his back arches. Then there is only silence.

There is only himself and Clove.

Olivier's bones rise to the surface, demanding their attention.

Clove kicks the hatch to close it, to take the repulsive imagery away from Vauquelin's sight. The unmistakable scent of healing flesh fills the air as blistered skin regenerates. Clove crosses to his fellow master's side, places his hand on the trembling shoulder. Utter dejection vibrates from Vauquelin's frame.

Then he does something he has not done apart from with his boys. He disregards his history from the times he took lovers. That was merely lust, not comfort. Clove pulls Vauquelin towards him and holds him close, lets his strength pass from one master to another.

'It is done.'

Vauquelin ebbs under the seas of Clove's solace.

25 / NIGHT 3:

THE COFFIN IS EMPTY

Teal strides along the hallway with Gabe and Moth flanking him.

It is their default whenever they are together, even though Teal doesn't really need protecting anymore. He's purposely not brought his book so he can join in with whatever his brothers and Éric decide is fun entertainment. Already he misses the smell of the ink on the yellowed pages. Unlike Moth and Gabe he doesn't remember any of his mortal life — but he knows, instinctively, that books formed a pivotal foundation.

A little earlier Éric's slightly muffled voice had come from outside the door to their room.

'Heading to my lair, guys! Come find me if...' and then Éric had taken a breath, 'if you want to hang out.'

Now their footsteps echo on the marble floor leading to that room.

Teal stops just before the double doors. His fingers rise to his lips.

'Haven't you noticed?' he says.

Moth looks around, his gaze flicks to the chandeliers strung in a perfect line along the ceiling. They are unlit, but the crystal beads are aflame with the reflection of the flickering candles set upon every surface.

'Noticed what?' Moth says. 'That we're literally drowning in shiny stuff?'

Teal glances across to Gabe.

'That's not what Teal means,' Gabe says softly.

But he doesn't carry on, and a warm glow of happiness spreads through Teal's core. Gabe is letting him take centre stage.

'There are no mirrors,' Teal says. 'Anywhere.'

Gabe pushes open the doors to the game lair and Teal's discovery tucks itself inside three vampire minds.

Éric nods as they enter and pauses the annihilation on the screen. He's lounged back on the sofa with one leg sprawled over the arm, a controller clutched in his hand.

'Hey,' he says and licks his lips. It's a nervous gesture after the events of last night where world shattering words had pierced them all.

'So when do we get to fucking hunt?' Moth asks.

He's not irritated with Éric, not yet… it's just better to get the most important details out there.

Éric places the controller on the table and sighs.

Hunt? That's now how he and V usually refer to it, and come to think of it, it's not how they do things.

'Why? I'm sure V and Clove will figure something out for us.'

'Figure something out for us?' Moth blinks. He side eyes Éric.

Are you messing with me?

Gabe is tuned into Moth's radar. He needs to act fast before this all dissolves into another *incident*. And fuck knows they don't need another one of those. He smiles, goes to the sofa and leans towards Éric. His words are lost in a tangle of curls.

Éric's eyes grow wide and then a burst of laughter falls from his lips.

'Glad you found it. Yell if you ever, you know, need a refill. We've literally got an unlimited supply.'

Éric directs his crooked grin at Moth, still standing by Teal's side, and Teal holds his breath. He's unsure of how Moth will handle being back in Éric's company. They have built bridges but Moth has a habit of burning his down.

Moth hangs his thumbs on the belt loops of his jeans.

He studies Éric from under a fall of hair.

'Yeah, about that.' His voice is soft and sultry, his mismatched eyes never leaving Éric's face.

'No doubt it made the —' *Don't say it, don't say it...* Éric swallows his next words: *the pounding you took from Gabriel a little sweeter*. If he's learned anything about Moth, it's to stop shooting first and asking questions later. Regardless, the lascivious expression on Éric's face makes it unequivocally clear what he left unspoken, and he hikes an eyebrow.

The atmosphere in the room compresses.

Gabe's eyes flick to Teal with an unspoken message.

Hold him back if you have to.

'What I mean is, I guess you guys figured out that you'll never wanna do it without that stuff ever again.'

Moth has been ridiculously laid back since they woke, and Gabe knows their intense coupling just before dawn is a huge part of his unruffled attitude.

'That stuff is fucking magic.' Moth grins, showing the tips of his fangs, and the room exhales. He goes to the stack of games on the floor and flops down, his fingers tracing the spines.

Éric says, 'I know, right?' He glances up to Gabriel and offers him a fist bump, and a small bud of joy blooms within Teal.

Maybe, just maybe, they will get to stay now.

Teal really likes Éric and wants some time alone with him to talk. But he will wait his turn. Teal doesn't mind hovering on the outskirts: it gives him a chance to gaze at the paintings, to imagine the artist, brush in hand, creating something that will exist for centuries. There is immortality on these walls and within these walls. To Teal it is a perfect union.

He basks in this awareness whilst his brothers talk to Éric, and when the seismic shift hits him it takes the breath from his lungs.

The catacombs. Something is happening in the catacombs.

The toxic stench of acid invades his nostrils and he instinctively covers his face with his hands. A momentary blast of agony against his palms.

His brothers rush to his side and he's caught in Moth's anxious embrace, Gabe's concerned face fading in and out of focus.

Éric is on his feet, a wave of terror and confusion emanating from him.

'What's wrong with him?' He fidgets the controller he still has clutched in his hands, unsure how to help.

Gabe's eyes flick to the doors and moments later Clove strides in.

He crosses to Éric and clasps his shoulder.

'Go to Vauquelin. The coffin is empty.'

A crash as Éric's hands lose their strength. The controller falls, sending shattered plastic pieces flying across the wooden floor.

To Éric, this all happens in slow motion, and his blood thrums in his ears. He stands frozen for a few seconds until his heartbeat doubles in time.

V.

Éric races past them and Teal wants to comfort him, but for now all that is left is the witch in his blood murmuring its song of knowledge.

26 / NIGHT 3:

THE FUTURE... PAVED WITH BLACK SILK VELVET

Éric fumbles the doorknob to the catacombs. His hands are shaking so violently he can hardly get it to open. He pauses inside the entrance only long enough to reach for a torch.

There's one still lit — Clove must have left it.

For him.

Thank you, Clove: a silent whisper of gratitude as he waves the torch left and right, the heat off its flame scorching his cheeks and sucking up the scant oxygen of the subterranean cavern.

It illuminates his lover: crumpled in the black depths, huddled against the bone shelves in a vertical foetal position.

Vauquelin extends a desperate hand to Éric.

Éric places the torch on the stone floor, caresses V's hair.

'Tell me how it happened, my love.'

Vauquelin can only point.

Éric takes up the torch, twisting on his heels, and he sees the open coffin — lid cast to the side, the hatch of the pit firmly closed.

He turns his head slowly back, and finds the explanation written all over Vauquelin's face.

Éric brings his forehead to V's: he lands a tender kiss.

The despair radiating from Vauquelin's heart is a killing blow —

or it would be if they were mortal.

But V needs him now, and Éric lengthens his spine.

'I did not anticipate this turn of events... not this night... or possibly ever,' Vauquelin whispers.

'I know, *bien-aimé*,' Éric whispers. 'I know.'

Vauquelin lifts his chin.

Éric has never addressed him so.

It is his own special name for Éric in French: *my beloved*.

Now it belongs to both of them.

He stands and lifts Vauquelin up, placing an arm about his waist, and drops the torch in the extinguishing vessel by the door. He locks up, and they walk slowly upstairs to their bedchamber.

Éric knows the boys are fucking *starving*, even though he and Moth had gone out last night. They had all been discussing it in the lair, just before Teal freaked out — and then Clove stormed in with a *very* intense look on his face, beckoning to him.

He understood in an instant something was seriously wrong with Vauquelin, and he's the only one who can help him now.

Éric guides V into their bathroom and runs a bath. He removes his own clothes first, balling them up and pitching them in the corner (one of his many bad habits that V overlooks), and then he undresses V.

They are both clean... they have only been awake for an hour.

This has another purpose.

Éric steps into the tub, and V follows.

He wraps his arms around V, cradles his head in his arms... their skins find comfort in this proximity of one another.

It's feral, animalistic.

Water has always been Vauquelin's comfort, the place he runs to when he needs its warmth to soothe his cold soul, and Éric, blood of his blood, craves it too.

Éric gently turns him around so that he can embrace him from behind, and they sink down together.

Like the night V turned him, Éric gives his lover all his safety, his promise that he will never let him go, that he will be there waiting at the bottom to lift him back up… that he'll be on the other side. He nestles their cheeks together, keeps V afloat in the water. The tub is so long they can fully stretch their tall limbs out. He cups the arch of V's foot with the high arch of his own.

For the longest portion of his human life Éric always hated his feet.

In his dreaded gym classes, when the other boys saw more of him than he would have liked — especially as he was trying so hard not to look at them — they made fun of his girly feet, his high arches, his long toes.

Now he knows why he has these feet. So that his arch could nest with Vauquelin's equally long, equally high feminine arch, at this exact moment in time.

He was made for this man.

No… he corrects himself.

For this *vampire*.

If only he had known that so long ago… the waiting would have been easier. But everything he endured was necessary, so that he would be ready to meet Vauquelin. He can see that clearly now, as he holds Vauquelin in his arms… that V saw all of this in him their bizarre first morning together, when Éric said there was nothing special about himself. He didn't understand it then, but now he fucking *gets it*. V knew Éric belonged with him — it was Éric who lacked the capacity to believe it, not then.

Now he does.

Éric tilts his head to the side, brushing V's black, black hair away from his forehead, so that he might see his closed, contented eyes.

He kisses V's temples.

He sighs — a deep, soul-replenishing sigh — and watches V's chest heave and compress with his own.

This.

This is all he ever wanted.

They stay in the water until it chills, and Éric pulls the plug.

They stand, their slippery bodies quivering against one another.

'Are you okay?' Éric whispers.

Vauquelin encircles Éric's waist with a decisive arm, drawing their torsos together. They are not aroused: this is not that. But still, their cocks leap when they are this close.

Something has changed in Vauquelin tonight — Éric can sense it.

There's an endpaper, marbled in blood, the closing of a chapter that had been left unfinished before the boys arrived. It was a 'to be continued,' and Clove was there to give Vauquelin the strength to turn the last page. Now it is done and they can move forward.

There has been so much talk of choice.

Of love, of hate.

Vauquelin made his choice the night he met Éric.

And then his life unravelled yet again.

He had not yet healed...

Until tonight.

Olivier was the last thread tying Vauquelin to that dreadful moment when he thought he failed to master the secrets of his time-slips and would never see Éric again.

And then a thought punches Vauquelin like a fist to his stomach: he craters and slumps to the floor, clasping his abdomen.

He glances up toward his beloved: he finds so much despair on his face that Vauquelin cannot bear it.

He tilts his head and beckons Éric to join him.

He kisses Éric's forehead, whispering, *I will be alright, my love... shhh... just give me a moment...*

A bridge forms in Vauquelin's mind.

Had he not been forced to relive his life...

Had he not turned Olivier...

Had Maeve not rejected him...

Had he not been determined to shut the door on his future...

Had he not met Clove and the boys...

He would never have met Éric.

Turning Olivier in his second timeline was the key to it all: had Vauquelin not turned him, he would have had no progeny to sacrifice — he would have been unable to return to Éric.

The diabolical spell responsible for his time travel has been destroyed.

He can never go back, nor would he.

Not now.

Vauquelin lifts his chin, drowns in the depths of his beloved's concerned expression. It may have taken centuries for him to gain the capacity to understand, but Éric is his destiny... he is the reason he has been so fragile in front of Clove and his boys. They are part of this. And — though Vauquelin is unsure how the rest of them feel — they are the closest he will ever come to knowing a family.

He compresses his lips between his fingers.

Even Olivier could not give him that... because Vauquelin had withheld his truth from everyone once he became vampire in his first timeline. Olivier never knew him as well as Éric does now: just as Éric does not know him as well as Olivier did. An unfortunate fallacy of Vauquelin's improbable, fractured timelines.

He takes Éric's chin in his hands, and for a moment his beloved trembles beneath his grasp.

Vauquelin has unmasked himself during this visit.

And it is all because of Éric, of this immense love that frightens him.

He has displayed it to everyone under this roof: his vulnerability had been beyond his control. Everything that has happened unfolded between them all, collectively and individually, precisely as it was ordained to do... Moth and Éric, Éric and Gabriel, Gabriel and Moth... Vauquelin and Clove. Flynn. And Teal, the eloquent voice of ethereal sanity just when they all needed him the most. His quiet, powerful words are taken for granted far too often.

So much grace... there could be no other way.

Vauquelin's strength replenishes within his bones even as blood tears well in his eyes.

His hands quiver, yet he has never felt so invincible as he does now looking into Éric's eyes — the only one who has ever dared to truly understand him.

Their future unfurls in his imagination like an endless highway, paved with black silk velvet. But now...

Maybe he *has* earned this beauty.

He kisses Éric's forehead.

'Let us go to Clove and the boys. We owe them a great debt, *bien-aimé*.'

He locks Éric's eyes into his own, ensuring that Éric has captured his meaning. He does not need to hear Éric's reply, because it hovers in both their thoughts, waltzing in perfect unison.

We owe them everything.

27 / NIGHT 3:

I AM STARVING

A stunned silence follows in the wake of Éric's panicked flight from the game lair to the catacombs.

Gabe leads Teal over to the sofa and makes him sit.

Moth collapses by his side.

'Fuck it, Teal... what happened?' Moth's face is bleached-bone white, concern etched deep within his eyes.

Gabe knows what he's thinking.

This is exactly what engulfed Teal in Westport Quay when the White Witch penetrated his thoughts. They've had years of calm at Gehenna, and this, coming right out of the blue, is a gut-punch.

Teal holds his hands up. 'I'm okay.' He waves them in front of his face. 'I *am* okay,' he repeats. 'This isn't like before.'

Gabe sits back on his heels and blows out a breath. He glances across to Clove, who motions with a fluid spread of his fingers.

Do not worry.

Relief surges through Gabe's chest. His mind was already ricocheting off into the realms of telling Clove they had to leave — that if *something* else had found them, they couldn't put V and Éric in danger.

And he doesn't want to leave. Not now.

He's fast forming a connection with Éric: something Moth hasn't said anything about. But Gabe knows Moth is still reeling after the events of last night when he exploded so catastrophically. He might not outwardly show it, but he's been quieter and more receptive: well, as receptive as Moth can get in a strange environment.

Gabe reaches across and pushes the hair out of Moth's eyes.

'Just when we were hoping for some fun, eh?'

He's talking about the set-up Éric has, the chance for them all to kick back and relax. For once he just wants to be Gabe, not Clove's pure-bred fledgling with all the connotations that carries. Not that he can't relax at Gehenna, but this place is different. He can't quite put his finger on it.

'Fun, Gabriel?' Clove's voice is as smooth as oil on water. His arched brow says the rest. That brow can communicate numerous things and Gabe narrows his eyes to catch its meaning. And then a smile breaks on his lips, a smile with more than a hint of darkness.

That brow says *let us hunt.*

'What about Vauquelin and Éric? We can't just leave.' This from Teal, who has pressed his fingers to Moth's lips to stop any more fussing.

Moth doesn't do *Fuss*.

But Teal is the exception to everything in Moth's book.

'I believe you fed last night, Moth.' It isn't an admonishment from Clove, merely a fact.

'Yeah, but it was quick and I was too bothered about Éric tripping over those fucking fancy boots he wears and getting us both into trouble. I fed but it wasn't satisfying.'

Every vampire knows that there are two types of feeding: the quick, grab-what-you-can-and-leave snack, and the long, luxurious feast of a throat opened and waiting — the chance to savour the nectar as it slips down your throat.

Moth had the equivalent of a late-night kebab after a long drinking session. It hit the spot, but left the nastiest of aftertastes.

'Teal?' Moth says, and Gabe knows Moth is thinking again about Westport Quay, where Teal's appetite had all but disappeared as he hung in the White Witch's clutches.

Teal bites his lip and hangs his head, his blond hair hiding his face. Then his chin lifts and he looks Moth right in the eye. That ocean gaze darkens, as though this is deep water, unnavigable water.

'I am *starving*.'

There's something slightly unpredictable about Teal when he needs to feed. Gabe has always wondered if it's because his bright-eyed brother is so calm and easy-going most of the time, and when the blood lust screams its need Teal becomes the antithesis of his usual self. He remembers the girl they found in the car in the woods when they were hiding out in the abandoned mansion, recalls the way Teal fed. They were all starving, but Teal had almost worshipped the stream of blood gushing from her slit wrist, before tearing into her flesh with brutal abandon.

'Gabe.' Moth's voice cuts into his thoughts along with a roll of those bicoloured eyes. 'I'm not waiting all fucking night for Éric to decide what shirt to wear. Can't we go now?'

Clove does not want to discuss what happened in the catacombs: he suspects that his words to Éric have made them all aware, but this is a traumatic event in Vauquelin's life — if he wishes to tell the story, he will.

I know.

A mind-touch reaches him.

From Teal.

I knew something was alive down there on the first night.

Clove does not question this knowledge. It is part of who Teal is. Part of the witch that swims in his vampire blood.

This visit has already delivered more than its fair share of upset and upheaval, but underneath it all he can feel the tendrils of an unshakeable connection unfurling, creeping feelers ready to ensnare them all.

Together they will be — Clove shakes his head: he does not care for the term — a transitory coterie the likes of which has not been seen for centuries.

He will do his level best to make sure this morsel does not find its way to the Bloodvyne. He has no need for vampire fawning and midnight adoration. All he requires is under this roof, apart from some of Vauquelin's immoderate choices in furnishings.

Gabriel comes to him as Teal takes Moth across to a painting of Paris in the eighteenth century. Moth pretends to drag his feet and Teal digs Moth in the ribs with his elbow.

Clove watches them. He is — he examines his emotions — fulfilled. It is a strange emotion after years of treading the dark highway in his own solitary way. Gabriel tucks himself against his side: something he has not done for a very long time, for Gabriel is growing, learning, becoming the vampire he is meant to be.

The coffin. Gabriel's mind-touch drifts across Clove's senses.

But for just this moment, as Moth and Teal play, Clove pulls his firstborn closer.

'What you said the other night, Gabriel...' He pauses as that questioning navy-blue gaze rises to meet his own. 'I believe those fucking eggshells are dust in the wind.'

A laugh bursts from Gabriel's throat and Moth and Teal look across.

'This feels right,' Gabriel says softly. 'I don't know how long it will last but we'll feast on every second.'

Clove nods as a smile curls on his lips. From the hallway comes the sound of footsteps. And just before the doors open, Clove presses a kiss to Gabriel's brow.

This is our night. Let us make it bleed.

'Hi,' Éric says, flopping down on the sofa as if nothing happened. Everyone's staring at him. He knows they expect him to say something, but it's V who needs to tell them: if Clove hasn't already.

Vauquelin's voice comes low and soft from the threshold.

'Clove, a word, please.'

Clove goes to Vauquelin's side as Gabriel joins Éric on the sofa.

Vauquelin seems extremely balanced for a vampire that has just sent his catatonic progeny into a pit of acid.

Their eyes meet.

Vauquelin draws the doors to the lair closed, silencing the chatter of the boys. A dark fold of fabric is draped over his arm.

'Before you ask... I assure you I am fine. I am honour-bound to you for many reasons, not the least being what you facilitated this night, and for sending Éric to console me. There is more I would like to say to you, but not in front of the boys. In the meantime, I thought perhaps you and I could do something for them. So that as they walk in Paris tonight, there may be no doubt amongst the public as to who watches over our most precious ones.'

He raises the fabric, presenting it to Clove. It is a black velvet, post-revolution frock coat, circa 1790, studded with ebony seed beads, sewn into elaborate patterns on either side of the lapels and the cuffs.

It was the most understated coat in Vauquelin's armoire. Vauquelin knows Clove does not crave attention, does not seek eyes upon himself. But they were both alive at the time this coat was made, and as they will be appearing together out-of-doors for the first time, Vauquelin hopes that they might slip into their ancient selves together.

That they might show their connection.

There are four very modern young vampires accompanying them tonight: it will make the most exquisite contrast.

A scarlet frock coat of the same era adorns Vauquelin's back, albeit considerably flashier, the cuffs fringed in ivory lace. On his legs: skintight, black leather trousers, chosen by Éric. He grins at Clove.

'Do you accept this challenge?'

Clove pauses as he collects his thoughts. He does not remember the last time someone offered him a gift, even if this one is merely borrowed. He reaches out, his fingers trailing over the silken surface of the fabric.

'A challenge, Vauquelin?' He returns not quite a grin but a warm smile. 'I accept a challenge when the positives outweigh the risk. And this is not a risk. This,' he pauses again, 'is a beautiful garment.' Their eyes meet and the meaning behind the gift is clear. 'Consider your challenge accepted.'

Vauquelin laughs — *si libérateur !*[†] *After such a heavy evening!* — and holds the coat up so that Clove can slip into its arms.

He opens the doors and they come to a stop in the centre of the room.

Éric gawps, elbowing Gabriel in the ribs. He whispers *fuck* under his breath, and then, a little louder, 'God... just look at them.'

Gabe has to fight to keep his jaw shut. He's never seen Clove in anything like this but Éric is right: *fuck,* he looks magnificent. They *both* look magnificent. Gooseflesh rises on his arms.

He knows Clove and V never met centuries ago, but they look *so* right together. He turns and looks over his shoulder at Moth and Teal.

They don't need to speak to show their approval.

It's written all over their faces.

Vauquelin and Clove have turned away to talk to Moth and Teal. Éric nudges Gabriel again, whispering, 'I never saw this part of V until we came to France. You know we met in Los Angeles, right? He fits in so well there... but Paris is where I finally understood him. The history. Here, he just seems *correct.*'

'I've always thought Clove looked timeless,' Gabe says, 'like he could fit in anywhere, but still look like his own person. Does that even make sense?' He shrugs and shakes his head, but the gesture is one of amazement. 'Talk about having to live up to a legend.' He's not too sure if he's expressing

---

[†] - HOW LIBERATING!

himself right, but hopes Éric can grab the gist of it.

'Yeah, no, it totally makes sense. It's the same with V. But my favourite thing is to mix up his eras. All of them at once. That's when he truly blows me away.'

Now Éric's eyes are starry as he blatantly stares at Vauquelin.

Damn.

His heart revs in his chest.

It's one of the moments when he can't believe V belongs to him.

But as Éric watches Vauquelin, who's smiling, speaking warmly to Teal and explaining details about the painting that has captured Teal's delight, he's filled with joy: because V will be okay (Éric knows he can't fake it), and they have *friends*. More than that, but he doesn't know how to define it yet... he just feels so fucking fantastic right now — they're all together, no one's in a bad mood.

And they're going out!

He can't wait to see what the rest of the night holds.

Gabe has been watching Éric, and although he hasn't picked up on his thoughts (he could, but he won't... that's an invasion of privacy), Éric is positively glowing with the kind of elation that causes its own energy. Gabe basks in its potency. It sizzles against his skin, heightening his own excitement at what the coming night has to offer.

'Hey,' he says, to bring Éric back down off the cloud he's floating on. 'There's one more thing.'

Éric doesn't tear his eyes off of V until he feels Gabe's sharp knee knock against his. He knocks him right back, grinning. 'What?'

Benevolence washes over Gabe. He lets it settle to test its *rightness* before continuing. 'My name. You can call me Gabe.'

Éric smiles, big and full, exposing his teeth — he doesn't often smile like this when he isn't alone with V, and it gives him a strange buzz.

He brings his fist to his mouth.

Gabe. Wow.

In a different place, he would totally hug Gabe right now, but things are too good with Moth.

There's no way he's gonna risk fucking that up.

Instead, he just says, 'Cool,' and offers Gabe a fistbump.

He stands and stretches, running his palms down his chest.

'So... are we ready, or what?'

28 / NIGHT 3:
WE CAN SHOW HIM WHAT WE ARE

It is Friday night in the City of Light... the City of Love.

They slip out onto the boulevard, six figures more at home in the shadows: but tonight they do not shirk away from the golden illumination of the street lamps. They embrace it, the glow turning their skin to a shade of pure moonlight, at least for the elders of this immortal band bound by blood and the dark gift that will sweep them into the future as their bodies preserve the past.

Along alleyways, slick with rain, and out onto narrow side streets.

The tourist throng grows heavier as they walk (Moth with Teal, his mesmerising eyes covered by sunglasses, Éric with Gabe and Vauquelin with Clove), for this is Paris and she never sleeps. Out onto tree-lined boulevards, the garish lights of shops and bars spilling out into the darkness.

People stop and stare, move out of their way, because there is *something* about this group that makes the hairs rise in the napes of their necks. But still they look, because predators are beautiful: nature designed them that way.

'Are you okay?' Moth bumps his shoulder against Teal's.

He still hasn't forgotten the haunted expression that washed over Teal in the game lair. He hasn't forgotten Westport Quay. Its legacy still coats his memories with poison. And he won't let them drift back to the tower and that fuck-awful tree. He won't let them destroy this night.

He slips his arm through Teal's and two men whistle their approval as they emerge from a bar.

Even though Moth hates being centre stage, the energy in this city is sizzling in his veins. He stops and cups his hands against Teal's cool cheeks, lifts the sunglasses and looks into those ocean eyes, then presses a long kiss to his lips. The corners of Teal's mouth quirk into a smile and that smile lights up Moth's world like a beacon.

'Whoa,' Éric says and glances at Gabe. 'Did I just see that?' A nervous agitation sweeps over him. He doesn't want anything to spoil this night. He wants it to go on forever.

'It's cool,' Gabe replies, drawing his bottom lip into his mouth. 'You might have guessed we're all really close.' He sees Éric's eyes widen and quickly adds more. 'Not like *that*. Teal is...' He pauses then because it's hard to find the words to explain what their relationship is with Teal, how they can be so inseparable and share some physical attraction but that it never morphs into anything sexual.

That's Teal's story to tell.

Éric inclines his head, glances again to Moth and Teal who have continued their lead, arm in arm.

'You guys blow my fucking mind, Gabe.' His voice hangs on the last word and he looks down, kicking a stone into the gutter. It's the first time he's used that name and he loves the feel of it on his tongue. His eyes track the stone's movement and his mind follows it straight into that gutter.

Oof, he thinks. *Do not even go there.* He shoves his hands in his pockets and flings his head back.

'I FUCKING LOVE PARIS!' he shouts to the sky.

Clove watches as all this unfolds. He is ever vigilant but there is nothing in the air that suggests there is any danger lurking on this auspicious night. Unless, of course, you count themselves; they are all most able to paint the streets with scarlet.

Vauquelin directs them from Clove's side, both of them resplendent in ancient frock coats, the adornments catching the lights as they pass by the treasure-trove windows of tourist delights.

'This night, Clove... I sense it is a momentous one, one which will burrow into our bloodstreams. I will keep it close for it has opened doors for me I never thought possible.'

A breath of wind brings the scent of sandalwood and vetiver. Vauquelin's scent. Clove breathes it in. He understands how trauma can unfurl into enlightenment. The truth of it walks before him, beside Éric, the love of Vauquelin's immortal life. Fate is often cruel to vampires but in this case, she has smiled upon them all.

A figure up ahead, leaning against a lance-shaped lamp post, dressed in tight ripped jeans and a leather jacket over a black shirt, his hands stuffed into his pockets. As they draw near he raises his head, a fedora hat shielding his eyes. The barest nod of acknowledgement to Clove and Vauquelin from Flynn — who has followed them to be an extra set of eyes and other more vigilant senses.

'We are blessed,' Vauquelin says.

Clove can only murmur his agreement.

Their promenade has brought them to the entrance of The Louvre, looming above them in ancient majesty: once the home of the kings of France, now a sanctuary for many of the world's masterpieces. There are countless less-tourist-plagued museums in the city, but Vauquelin does not want Teal to miss this opportunity.

It is their first stop, less than two kilometres from Vauquelin's house. Night tickets have been procured: still, they only have a few hours before the museum closes.

He turns his head and wrinkles his nose at the Pyramid — in his opinion, it is merely a modern architectural blight: but Gabe and Moth are enthralled by it. Éric, on the other hand, seems to be enthralled merely by the proximity of Gabe, Moth, and Teal.

This is precisely what Éric needs, Vauquelin thinks.

Éric does not crave friendship... he is content alone. But having young friends near his human age, especially young, male, vampire friends — two of whom also happen to be in a relationship — is the best gift: one Éric had not known he needed.

Vauquelin adores the boundless joy he receives from seeing them interact, but he worries for Éric's emotional state when the time comes for them to return to Gehenna. In truth, he worries for his own as well.

But he and Éric will make the journey to England, to repay this visit.

It must happen.

'We will all stay together.' Clove's unquestionable authority. 'The museum is vast and we do not have the luxury of time.'

Before leaving the house, they had quickly scanned The Louvre website for current exhibitions and closures: Éric had pulled Gabe and Moth aside and secretly proposed they give *all* the Louvre time to Teal. They agreed without argument — it was to be Teal's event.

The few hours they have in the museum are largely spent lifting Teal's jaw off his chest: all of them are infected with Teal's unadulterated rapture. Instead of the art, Éric studies V and Clove, whispering together in front of an ancient, larger-than-life painting. They look like they could both step into the craqueleured oil and disappear, instantly resuming their earlier roles in their pasts.

For a flash, Éric wishes they *could* do it, but only if he could jump in right behind them — that he could have been with V right from the beginning and their years of knowing each other could be measureless, even though he doesn't belong there. He'll never be a part of V's hundreds of years of existence before he was even born and thinking of it drowns him in inexplicable dread.

But V *had* gone back.

The thought twists Éric's stomach into knots: it wasn't that long ago that V had stepped back into his true history, and when he returned he smelled like the inside of this museum — cold and ancient and marble-like, almost as if Éric shouldn't touch him, or a guard would come and slap his hand away: the implication being *this is not yours to touch*.

V pledged that it's no longer possible, but Éric has his doubts.

A chill hardens his body, despite the heavy jacket he's wearing.

Suddenly he can't wait to get the fuck out of this mausoleum and get back on the street. He looks to Gabe and Moth sitting next to him.

They're close, their hands are touching. They're fucking gorgeous and he loves looking at them, loves hearing their English accents in his ears. Somehow it's like he has little brothers now... but he could never tell them this. Their brotherhood is different, special... it's their very own thing, with Teal. He tucks this feeling away and smiles at them.

Moth says, 'Why don't you take a fucking picture, Éric?'

He has no idea why he just said that. Maybe it's because he wants, in some small way, to have some documentation of this night, which he knows is fucking crazy: because it will always be with him.

'Fine, I fucking will.' Éric whips his phone out of his pocket and turns his back to them, snapping a selfie.

And then it is time to go... the museum lights dim briefly, and staff have begun urging the patrons toward the exits.

Vauquelin and Clove each have a hand on Teal's shoulders, as if they must prop him up because his heart has gotten too full and heavy.

Teal holds his sunglasses in his hands as the crowd has dwindled to a trickle. His ocean eyes shine, not just with the golden sparks of light but with unshed tears. He half wishes he could stay here forever, become a ghost to haunt these rooms when all have gone, to wander and stare and weep at the evocative immortality of art.

Flynn walks behind them. It's a very long time since he's been out in public view with such a group of exceptional vampires. He has a job to do, a job he takes extremely seriously, but this gathering reminds him of the earliest days of his revenancy and the streets of the French Quarter in New Orleans, where bands of vampires prowled the night, when they hunted in plain view.

Times have changed but this, this night is a kiss in the dark from a stranger, and just as enthralling. The energy buzzing from the boys vibrates against the delicate skin of his inner ear.

A fragment of a Rimbaud poem rises and the perfection of it catches in his throat.

Il entend battre leurs cils sombres dans des parfums
Silence: et leurs doigts, électrifiés et doux.[†]

Éric stands and kisses Vauquelin, who pulls them together and returns the kiss with a hand on the small of Éric's back.

In Vauquelin's not-so-distant past, two men could not have done this in public without causing an outcry. Éric does not know that shame — or perhaps it is only that he simply does not care what others think — and Vauquelin gratefully rides the waves of Éric's youthful irreverence.

He is in love with each of the vampires who surround him tonight, the young and the ancient, and with one in particular: that is an altogether different level of love. In all their veins flows immortal blood, the exquisitely cursed *sang*[‡] which consecrates their union in this place and time.

During this visit Vauquelin has been the purest version of himself he has ever been in his interminable life, excepting when he is alone with Éric.

It had been his perpetual, classical technique to disdain the company

---

[†]- HE HEARS THEIR DARK LASHES BEATING IN PERFUMED
SILENCE: AND THEIR FINGERS, ELECTRIFIED AND SWEET
[‡]- BLOOD

of others, revenant or no. His journey to Clove and the boys at Gehenna opened his eyes, his heart... and their presence, with him and Éric now, has cemented this in his spirit.

They emerge once again into the petrichor-fragranced air of Paris.

It is 22.00.

The remainder of the night hours and all the streets of the city lie open to them. They all inhale the crisp, autumn air, taking it into their lungs in greedy, feral sips, and they are intoxicated by possibility.

Vauquelin studies this gathering, and a devilish grin spreads his lips as he encircles Éric's neck with an arm.

'Now we seek the ones whose luck has run out... we will end their mortal suffering, and they will repay us in crimson.'

Moth bounces on his toes as he stands by Gabe and Teal. The moments before they set out on the hunt always fill him with a crazy energy. If this were an ordinary night, they would already have started off on their own. Clove trusts them implicitly but tonight — he glances at Éric as he leans against Vauquelin. Moth grinds his back teeth together. It's not like he doesn't want them here: part of him, a part that doesn't seem like him at all, fucking loves that they're all here together. He'll unpick the tangled knots of this later.

Éric meets his gaze and Moth finds a grin creeping onto his lips.

Should he ask?

Fuck it, he's going to.

'Éric can tag along with us, if he wants?'

The force of Gabe's astonished gaze settles and his grin spreads wider. Another thing he fucking loves is surprising Gabe. He lets his hair fall over his brow and peers through it, settles his weight on one hip in a casual pose.

We can show him what we are. What we were made to do.

Gabe can't keep the smile off his own lips but he turns to Clove and Vauquelin as Moth expects him to do.

'Will you let Éric hunt with us, V?'

A sudden silence descends as the wind drops, as the gravity of that question digs its fingers into Vauquelin's flesh. His immediate reaction is an emphatic NO. This is the first night he has brought his beloved out onto the streets to hunt with others. He is wary of the eyes of mortals upon them: even though Flynn is at their backs, constantly scanning for danger.

He *needs* to trust. He *does* trust. But this may be a request for which he cannot give his consent. Éric gazes up at him with hopeful, adoring eyes and Gabriel expects an answer.

'I do not believe that Éric is ready for such an adventure,' Vauquelin says, and as soon as the words leave his lips he sees hope wither in Éric's eyes like a wilted blossom.

'He hunted with me and he was fine.' This from Moth as he stands by Gabriel's side.

Vauquelin sighs.

It is *always* Moth.

But he remembers that if it were not for Moth's intervention at Gehenna, Éric would not be with him now.

Vauquelin is torn. He looks to Clove for his sage advice.

'My boys have exceptional experience in this matter. Éric will be well looked after.' Vauquelin does not miss the way Clove's dark eyes flick to Gabriel with the most pointed message. 'But this is your decision to make, Vauquelin, and they will accept whatever it is with good grace.'

Moth barely stops himself heaving out an exasperated sigh. He doesn't really understand why this is such a big fucking deal. He directs his attention to Teal because if he doesn't he might just explode from waiting too long.

Teal is quiet but there's an aura of complete contentment surrounding him. Moth has no idea why looking at statues with no arms, and paintings of dead people donned up in their fucking finery, makes Teal react as he does… but he won't deny his bright-eyed brother anything.

'Earth to Teal.' He snaps his fingers in front of Teal's face but there isn't a morsel of aggression in the gesture.

And *still* Vauquelin is fucking silent after Clove's words.

Vauquelin turns his face away from Éric so that only Clove can see his expression of fluctuating uncertainty. His mind-touch to Clove stutters in his mind: he can scarcely believe his own admission.

I will allow it… on the condition that Flynn will tail them.

A single nod from Clove, and Flynn moves toward the boys.

'Wait… what's going on? V… are you actually letting me go?' Éric asks. He doesn't realise that Flynn's appearance next to them means they're to have a fucking *babysitter*. He looks to Moth — whose face is the answer.

'Really?' Moth turns to Clove with his hands held aloft. He's this close to adding something else he can't come back from, when Gabe grabs his arm and drags him to the mouth of the alleyway.

Gabe doesn't like the idea of a babysitter either… but if that's the concession they have to make, he'll roll with it.

Now Éric understands. His chest begins to heave and he's unsure what emotions are boiling in his mind, but he keeps his lips tight. He crosses to V and takes his elbow, urging him away from the others… he could say this silently, but he needs V to understand something.

'V. I love you, but I'm not your fledgling,' he whispers. 'Not anymore. I'm your *partner*. I know I still have a lot to learn, but don't treat me like a child. Not in front of them. Please… you have to trust me.'

Vauquelin has yet to fully absorb the trauma of their separation. There are still mornings he wakes in a fevered panic, terrified that Éric will be missing. But he cannot deny it — Éric is right. They cannot continue this way, and Éric deserves to live his life. Vauquelin cannot smother him. He must allow Éric his own choices, lest he risk waking and finding Éric gone for a very different reason than the robbery of a time-slip.

He swallows hard, taking Éric's jaw in his hand.

'Forgive me, *bien-aimé*... I have been unjust to you. Go, but please be safe. And — ' he locks his mind tight, sucking the thought down with a deep breath: *defer to Gabriel*.

It would just be more of the same, another blatant display of mistrust.

Éric smiles. 'And what?'

'And I adore you.' Vauquelin kisses the tip of Éric's nose and gives him a gentle shove toward the boys, and then he turns his back to all of them, buries his face in his hands for a brief moment. He cannot bear to watch Éric walk away.

What am I sending him into?

The boys disappear into the black maw of the alleyway, and when Clove turns Flynn is gone. Clove does not assume he has trailed after the boys, especially after Vauquelin's heartfelt speech to Éric. But one thing Clove knows about Flynn is that he is astute. He will not make himself known, for that will undermine the trust he has forged with his boys: but he also knows that Gabriel is aware of Vauquelin's struggle... how difficult it was for him to release Éric into the night.

The streets of Paris will never be the same after this quartet of vampires have slaked their thirsts.

But now it is the master vampire by his side that needs his attention.

'I understand your trauma with this decision, Vauquelin. But I believe Éric will return to you a wiser vampire. My boys will guide him and treat him as one of their own. He will have the thrill of the hunt in his blood.' Clove pauses and inclines his head. The wind whips a strand of hair across his face and he sweeps it away. 'And you will reap the benefits later.' He laughs then, a soft sound, dissolving into the night. 'I know what lays on the nightstands in all your bedrooms.'

'Is that so?' Vauquelin cocks a dark brow and bites his lip.

This means that Éric has been generous in ensuring Gabriel and Moth have access to this magical elixir. He shivers at the mere thought of the lanolin on Éric's body, and archives this vision.

Later.

Clove, as always, is correct... and his unexpected levity is a tender balm to Vauquelin's dismal mood. It is a milestone in their relationship: they have never spoken so informally. The humour defuses the gravity, and it is needed — he and Clove will be alone on the streets, at least for a little while, and Vauquelin wants their time together to be amicable. Yet he must admit one last dark thought, and he can only hope it will not alter what has just been forged.

If I lose him again, I am finished.

He closes his mind to Clove for the subtext of this thought: *I have had more than my share of existence. If there is to come a night when I must face living forever without Éric, I will make my exit from the world.*

Clove locks his gaze with Vauquelin. There is no doubt of the meaning behind those harrowing words.

'You will not lose him, Vauquelin. The affinity you have with Éric is something that will resound through the centuries.'

He does not add the observation he once told Gabriel, that sometimes lovers are torn apart, or grow apart, that steadfast bonds can melt away like snow. He will not add this to Vauquelin's burden.

Their shared gaze requires no definition: they both know all too well that when love's cruel arrow aims at the heart, it rarely misses — and if the barb is removed it might prove fatal.

Clove grasps Vauquelin's elbow, lets him feel the strength in his fingers. 'But now I believe it is our turn to haunt the streets of this City of Lights.'

They move under the golden glow of an ornate lamp post, two tall dark figures caught in a Parisian moment. And their eyes meet again.

'Will you hunt with me, Vauquelin?'

With Éric off on his own night adventures with the boys, there is no one else walking the earth that Vauquelin would rather hunt with.

His irises metamorphose into their darkest blue.

His heart fills with bestial need.

They are vampire: they own this night.

Now, all his thoughts turn to hot blood — blood that he will consume with Clove. He dashes his tongue across his lips and their feet begin to move — their eyes are alert to any movement, any sign that the perfect throat will make itself known to them.

29 / NIGHT 3:

THE BLOODY LITTLE PROPHETS — PLUS ONE

Éric is hot on the heels of Moth, Gabe and Teal.

Blood pounds in his ears and he's still reeling after his exchange with V. Whatever he'd imagined from this night, feeding without him wasn't on his scorecard. Yet as he watches how these three almost melt into the shadows, stepping in and out of the gloom, their faces raised to the night, a thrill sweeps through him.

Gabe is in the lead with Moth close behind. Éric knows that Moth's tongue will be flicking in and out as he tastes the darkness, and this seems so fucking intimate that his stomach clenches.

He catches up to Teal and the others slow, Gabe's hand raised before him. It's a signal and they all stop dead in their tracks. All Éric can hear is his own rapid heartbeat as it thunders behind his rib cage.

There's a club up ahead on the corner, a cacophony of blazing light and raucous sound. People mill around its doors, lean against the garish pink exterior walls, smoke hand-rolled cigarettes.

Gabe gestures to Teal, and before Éric can take a breath Teal has drifted past Gabe and Moth, his hands thrust into his jacket pockets, aviator sunglasses on his eyes.

He pauses for a moment, lowers his head and ruffles his blond hair so it falls around his face in a come-to-bed invitation.

A sudden streak of fear hits Éric hard in the gut.
Why aren't Gabe and Moth going with him?
He steps forward, but Moth catches his arm — and that mismatched gaze sears into him, followed by a mind-touch that doesn't try to be gentle.
This is how we work. Learn and fucking live a little.
Teal stands opposite the door to the club.
Anyone exiting has a clear view of this beautiful boy, bathed in the light that spills from this den of human indulgence.
He has the pose polished to perfection, his thumbs through the belt loops of his jeans, the relaxed lean against the wall as cool as the night air surrounding him. He looks like he was born to do this. The fact that his eyes are hidden behind dark glasses gives him an air of mystery, a delectable tender parcel just waiting to be unwrapped.
He waits.
Moth and Gabe are about twenty feet away, pretending to be deep in conversation… but Éric can sense they're tuned into Teal like he's the only radio station in hell.
'Éric.' Gabe beckons him over. 'You up to play a little?'
He catches his jaw before it falls open.
Am I? I have no fucking clue.
Gabe takes this as a yes, and leans closer.
He's torn between wanting to keep Éric safe and letting him have the freedom he's never had.
'I want you to go to Teal and act like you're propositioning him. I need attention on him so that the jackals start sniffing around.'
Éric's mouth goes dry as a desert. For a split-second, he has major regrets about coming. The thought of hunting on the streets had been intoxicating him all night — he could think of little else. Now, seeing lovely, ethereal Teal placed out in the field: it overwhelms him. It's too fucking real, and he wonders if it's too late to run back to V.

He feels so alone, even with Gabe and Moth right there next to him. Jealousy floods his stomach. He's too soft, he's not like them. He *wants* to be like them. But he knows he isn't.

Then the thirst hits him, hard and fast, and he can smell it as it burrows into his veins — there's so much blood right there in front of him, just waiting to be tapped, and Teal is leaning up against the wall like a hot little meal ticket.

Éric jerks when a hand grazes his arm. He doesn't know if it's Gabe or Moth and he doesn't have time to care. He shakes it off and his feet propel him in Teal's direction.

He extends his arm, planting his palm on the wall next to Teal's head, and brings his lips down to Teal's ear.

« *Salut, chaton* , »† he whispers. 'The boys said we should play. Are you ready to play with me?' He tilts Teal's chin up and licks it.

Teal arches his head back, exposing his pale throat. It's an invitation for Éric to carry on with their game. Teal has honed these skills from hours of watching his brothers in the dark, of listening to their cries of pleasure flutter out into the night... but his own sexuality is a complicated beast. Still, he doesn't mind Éric's touch, just like he doesn't mind when Gabe or Moth hold him.

He knows they have an audience now. He can feel the weight of their hungry eyes. His hand slips around Éric's waist and pulls him in tight. A soft moan falls from his slightly parted lips.

Éric plants his other palm on the wall, and he sniffs Teal's cheek, exhales cool breath on his neck.

Teal's skin is so soft...

FUCK. *Fuckfuckfuck!*

What is going on, and how long is he supposed to keep doing this?

Because he's having some Very Conflicting Thoughts right now.

---

†- HI, LITTLE CAT

'Don't be afraid,' he whispers, swallowing hard, 'it's just a game...' — although he can't tell whether he's reassuring Teal or himself.

But if Gabe and Moth don't do something soon, he isn't sure he can keep this up without crossing a line.

Near the club entrance Gabe watches from the shadows, aware of every movement going on around him. He signals to Moth, who peels off into the darkness.

Two men watch from the doorway.

Gabe flicks his gaze over them.

Early twenties. Slim built. Dressed in clothes they don't feel too comfortable in. Gabe instinctively knows that this is new to them and their pounding heartbeats are a backdrop to their building excitement.

Gabe can smell their heated blood pumping through their veins. His eyes half close and he smiles to himself, a smile made of darkness and hunger, forged in death, reborn to this life that he wouldn't change if he was offered a gold-plated return key to his human existence.

These two will do... but he doesn't think they'll approach Teal.

He'll need to change his plan.

He saunters over to them, opens the door to his own seduction.

They watch him. They lick their lips.

Oh yes... they want what he can give.

And he *will* give it, but on his own terms.

« *Veux-tu nous regarder ?* »[†] he says, cutting straight to the quick. He rubs his fingers together indicating cash.

Éric jerks his head at hearing Gabe speak French, but he's drawn straight back to Teal like a magnet. He's lost all sense of anyone else around them... the noise of the bar dissipates and all he can hear is his and Teal's breaths.

If only he knew that Gabe is about to set everything in motion... that he's assuming his own role in the game.

[†] - WANT TO WATCH US?

One of the guys pulls out a wallet and peels off a thick wad of Euros.

Gabe can smell the desperation prickling through their pores. Maybe they're questioning their own sexuality, or maybe they're just out for a night of something a little risqué.

He pretends to flick through the notes as their aroused scent curls into his nostrils, and he has to fight to keep his lips drawn over his fangs. He can see Teal and Éric in his peripheral vision and wonders how Éric is coping with the situation Gabe flung him into.

A little more. He sends the touch to Teal.

Gabe doesn't want these men to get cold feet; he wants their hot blood on his tongue and his fangs in their flesh. And then Moth brushes against his thoughts as clearly as if he's standing at Gabe's shoulder.

I found somewhere. It's fucking perfect. Has Éric died yet?

Teal knows that the next stage of their plan is about to unfold, but Gabe has asked for a little more... so he will give it.

He stands on tiptoe and brushes a lock of hair out of Éric's eyes. The dark curl winds around his fingers. He brings that same hand down to caress Éric's cheekbone, trailing his fingertips lower until they meet the curve of slightly parted lips. Neon light winks from the silver hoops adorning Éric's lobes.

Then he slides his thumb between those lips.

Éric closes his eyes... his mouth seals around Teal's thumb, his tongue makes an arc across the soft pad of flesh there.

His shoulders crater as a live current travels down his throat, exploding in his stomach like a cluster of furious butterflies. Their hips are too close: he's just become hyper-focussed on that fact and he lurches backward, his face bewildered and confused.

It was only supposed to be a game... so why does it seem like it isn't all of a sudden?

He's startled when Teal slips a hand into his, and he stares down for a few seconds before allowing himself to meet Teal's gaze.

Teal whispers, 'You did great. Now, onto the real fun.'

Éric flips his back to the wall and leans his head against Teal's, panting, blinking wildly.

A barely perceptible nod from Gabe and they follow him with the two guys he's picked out from the crowd, the poor unfortunates who won't see another dawn. Teal feels bad for being part of a situation Éric didn't feel wholly comfortable in, but it has worked its magic like all Gabe's plans do. The men think they're going to stand back and watch, maybe pleasure themselves at the same time.

Teal isn't sure what it is about sex that makes men act like they do. He's not really even sure why Gabe and Moth can't keep their hands off each other, but he appreciates beauty and his brothers have that in droves.

He's always been different, and becoming vampire didn't change that. There's witch blood in his veins, firefly lights in his eyes, and a need for connection that doesn't crave the intimacy of a sexual union.

Still, he likes to be held.

Sometimes he wishes he had someone that could do that all the time.

Gabe stops at a darkened door about halfway down the alley. He pushes it open and the dank, sour stench of neglect pours out. Teal can feel Moth waiting in the darkness, can feel his brother's rising hunger as well as he can feel his own.

The men follow Gabe over carpets of broken glass, scatterings of used needles and crumpled foil, stacks of filthy rags that once clothed filthy bodies.

They don't feel threatened. Gabe looks like a kid but acts like a pimp, and Teal isn't much older. Only Éric could be a problem and there are two of them.

A back room beckons, well away from the street, a low-ceiled, grimy-windowed, dejected hulk of a space.

'Okay.' Gabe slips into English and turns to the men.

His lips draw back on his fangs.

There might not be much light, but the men have clocked those razor sharp additions to this kid — and their minds are caught in a freeze frame of petrified shock.

Moth slides from the shadows and blocks the doorway.

And now the men see a predator in his natural environment. It's in the fluid way he moves his body, the way his off-kilter eyes are already stripping away their flesh.

They wheel as one: and just as a shout rises in a throat Gabe is on one of them, slamming his body against the wall and pinning it there like a butterfly on a board.

Moth lunges and grapples the other man to the floor, his arm tight across their prey's throat. His quarry can squirm and fight all he wants — but he'll never break free from a vampire's hold.

It's a death grip.

'You have a preference, Éric?' Gabe asks, as though he's choosing a wine for Sunday lunch.

Éric's heart leaps into his throat and he might as well be suffocating... he clasps his elbows and gasps for breath. Everything that's happened, now punctuated by the muffled cries of these strange men, is fucking with his head. His eyes focus in the dark and he searches for Teal. The instant he locates him he freaks: he's on the verge of hyperventilating, and he jerks his head back to Gabe.

He can barely get his thoughts together, but one stabs its way to the forefront and he blasts it out.

We can't kill them.

He can see the mind-touch land with Gabe. They're all looking at him like he's completely lost it, and maybe he has — Moth's the only one who knows why he said this, but even he's glaring.

'We do what Éric wants.' Gabe complies because he can feel Éric's panic and that's one thing a killing room doesn't need.

Or *not* a killing room in this case.

Moth mutters something under his breath.

The Bloody Little Prophets didn't need a babysitter — they *are* the fucking babysitters!

Anger floods his veins and he presses his arm tighter against the man's windpipe. The body writhes underneath him.

'Éric,' Gabe says. 'Are you ready?'

He still has the guy pinned to the wall and now the stench of urine joins the other nastiness pulsing in this obnoxious room.

A sharp, pained cry as Moth sinks his fangs into a sweat-slicked neck. He's done waiting for permission to feed and he's furious that the thrill of the kill has been taken from him.

But no one said he couldn't fucking drink his fill.

Teal drops to his knees in the filth and pulls the man's wrist to his lips. His fangs slice through the thin, tight skin as easily as a knife through soft butter. And when the warm blood hits the back of his throat a groan of ecstasy drowns in the crimson of his overflowing mouth.

That groan sinks right into Éric's marrow, takes him right back to the wall and Teal's thumb: that sound... he's cratering and he has to reach out.

'Gabe?' His voice is a frantic whisper. 'Please... can you let me drink with you?'

You know why we can't kill them... right? We only kill in the house...

His breath quickens.

He wonders if V can hear him from wherever he is... if he knows what's going on. And surprisingly, he hopes he can. He wants V to know that all he wants is to fucking massacre these guys they found — that he wants to rip their hearts out and soak his face in their blood. But that can't happen, and he's teetering on the edge of oblivion. Gabe is his only lifeline right now, the only one who can keep him from falling into the abyss.

Gabe can sense the turmoil writhing like a serpent inside Éric's chest.

He's been here before, hovering on the edge of darkness, dangling in the grip of its maw, its hunger, its ever increasing need. He understands — more than most — the overpowering temptation to simply give in and fall into its embrace.

He slips his free arm around Éric's shoulder. The human in his grasp has stilled, his eyes wide and unfocussed. His head is turned towards his friend, the friend Moth and Teal are feasting on.

'We drink together and I'll be in your head the whole time. When it's enough you tell me and I'll pull us both out.' Gabe isn't sure if Éric will be strong enough to do that on his own.

Feeding in the wild is a whole different ball game to feeding in the safety of the place you call home.

It changes vampires into the killing machines they are meant to be.

And he's painfully aware that the latter part of what he said to Éric is what he said to Moth the first time they slid into the Bloodvyne.

Instinct heats Éric's blood and he digs his fingers into the man's cheeks. The voice that comes out of him is foreign to his ears, as if someone else is channelling through him.

'Stop fucking looking at me!' He drives his fangs in, only slightly conscious of the fact that Gabe has his mouth clamped to the other side of the guy's neck. The copper hits Éric's tongue and his eyeballs roll back in their sockets. He gulps, he gets stronger with each swallow.

At first the hot blood in Éric's throat erases all his worry, and a calmness settles across his veinery. And then something happens that he'd completely forgotten to worry about, because he's always with V and it's never a problem: he gets hard.

Fresh blood makes him want to fuck.

FUCK!

He brings one hand over his groin, the other to the man's heart. The blood has already dwindled with two vampires feeding: it's almost time. Panic shoots through his consciousness like an arrow, and he's afraid he might die on its poisonous tip.

Just then his gaze lands on Teal, drinking like a little beast: his entire body clenches.

Enough, enough.

Gabe is waiting for the touch and he's purposefully not gone in too deep, not let himself fall into the heady enticement of a beating heart: because he has Éric to look out for, and part of him fears that Moth might be just bloody-minded enough to kill the other man... given that Éric told him he couldn't. *Fuck.* He needs to be in two places at once.

He wraps his mind against Éric's, draws a shield down around them both... and just before he yanks them out, he lets the intimacy of this moment linger for a millisecond.

This is what it's like, Éric. To live in the moment.

A hesitation as he pulls them both back from the crimson precipice, because a connection such as this makes his mind soar into places he could drown in. It's a vampire drug and Gabe knows he's addicted.

He draws his fangs out of the bruised flesh beneath him. Blood drips from his lips as he squeezes Éric's shoulder, and then he stumbles over to Moth and Teal: his veins are alight with scarlet fire.

Live in the moment, Éric thinks.

He places his hands on the dying human's neck, tracing his fingertips across the wounds he and Gabe inflicted. All that remains are messy streaks of coagulating blood. He releases the body, letting it fall to the floor with a cruel thunk, and his soul crashes as he does — he doesn't know why he feels emptier than the man they just drained.

Gabe knows as soon as he leans over Moth and Teal that things have gone to hell very quickly. There is no heartbeat in the chest on the floor.

It's an empty husk.

Moth wipes his hand over his mouth.

'What?' He glares up at Gabe. 'I stopped drinking. Teal stopped drinking. But his heart gave out. I'm not responsible for his fucking weaknesses.'

'It's true,' Teal says. 'He just... he died. We only just pulled out in time.'

Éric turns on his heel.

He trips, flinging an arm out to catch himself on the grimy wall.

His eyes widen.

'What the fuck am I gonna do now?'

He digs his hands into his hair and begins to pace. The walls echo with the sound of his feet crunching and scattering god-knows-what.

Then he halts.

There's nothing he can do now.

Nothing.

Éric squats next to Moth. He's so fucking angry right now that he wants to punch Moth in the face. Instead, he extracts the Opinel. His jaw is set: the muscles in his cheeks are twitching. He opens the blade and takes out his anger on the fang marks Moth made, slashes the wrist where Teal had fed — so violently he almost cuts the guy's fucking hand off.

But as he licks the blade and closes it, Éric realises that he doesn't fucking care about leaving the bodies or concealing his damage.

The violence is coming from somewhere else and he can't identify it.

He tucks the Opinel back into his pocket and sits back on his heels, his hands dangling between his knees.

A million thoughts blast through Éric's mind. He isn't mad at Moth... he's full of blood and despair — his heart hurts and this has never happened after a kill.

Everything has gone wrong, and he's still got a raging boner.

He rises and punches the wall again and again until his fist opens a hole.

« PUTAAAAIN ! »[†]

Moth watches Éric attack the wall. He didn't mean to let the man die. This time it really wasn't his fault, but somehow he's pretty sure Éric will hoist the blame firmly onto his lap. He's quietly impressed at Éric's knife skills, but he's not about to mention that. He doesn't understand why this is all such a big fucking deal.

He glances around the filth-laden floor and his gaze settles on something nestled next to a mouldy half-eaten hamburger. A needle. A slow smile spreads on his face as he reaches across and grabs it. Without a moment of hesitation he plunges it into the crook of the dead guy's elbow.

He's not sure if there's anything of use in it, but by the time this body is discovered the dirty needle will have introduced all kinds of nasty things into what's left of the collapsed veins.

Gabe nods his approval, goes across to Éric, plants himself between the young vampire and the wall, one hand against Éric's chest. He can feel the violent thrashing of Éric's heartbeat.

'We're going now. We're leaving this mess behind. No one can trace it to us. Do *not* beat yourself up about it.'

Éric plunges his fists into his pockets and knocks his forehead against Gabe's. *Thank you.*

Back on the street, Éric searches for a marker to pinpoint their location. They're about three kilometres from the house.

Thinking about being at home with V, where things were so much simpler before these boys came into his life, is making him ache.

Éric rushes ahead and turns around, walking backwards to face the boys. He starts prattling, which is his defence when he's a nervous fucking wreck.

'You guys probably think I'm a total pussy. Even when I was on my own I always brought them to the house. It's just the way V taught me. It has to be all measured and planned out. V never lets anything get out of control.'

[†]- FUCK!

There are hidden words there.

And I don't either.

It's super awkward and he's just fucking babbling, exactly like he did the night he met V. He's done this his whole life and he knows it's a mask. But this time seems a lot worse.

He's desperately grasping for a connection, anything to make it seem like he has a hold on what has transpired. And maybe to deflect from the truth, because...

What the actual fuck happened here tonight?

He's not that upset about the kill, but he can't admit it... not now.

Not even to himself.

Despite the chaos of the night, Éric can't remember ever feeling so free. He isn't used to improvisation on this level. It isn't V's brand of discipline he craves: he's been this way his whole life, but even his own spontaneous moments have their limits.

If he can control everything, nothing (and no one) can hurt him — at least not as bad. Maybe it was the *lack* of control that sent him spiralling.

He cuts his gaze to Teal and looks away just as quickly.

This whole fucking evening has been out of control, he thinks, turning back to walk the normal way.

He's pretty sure Moth's eyes are drilling into his back, confirming that yes, in fact Moth *does* think he's a total fucking pussy. But he tucks his tongue behind his fangs and feels alone and judged once again.

Whatever.

He's used to it.

He blows air through his lips.

They trudge along in silence, and Éric is grateful for it: it gives his brain a little time to settle.

They all have so much to say to each other and no language for it: not yet.

30 / NIGHT 3:

BEAUTY DRESSED IN DEATH

A minute after the quartet leave the alley, another immortal slips into the room where the game was played.

Where the game was lost for one.

Flynn had followed the boys not because Clove told him to, but because he wanted to see them in action. For those who know of the Bloody Little Prophets, the way they hunt together is becoming its own legend.

He had crouched on the roof of a building overlooking the alley and had a bird's eye view of the events that had transpired, cloaking himself in a manner he hadn't used in decades, because below him was Gabriel Davenport and that particular vampire didn't miss a thing.

If Flynn had moved a muscle Gabriel would have sensed it.

Their method of hunting, of trapping, enthralled him: although Éric's confusion and turmoil had been almost palpable. Still, Vauquelin's beloved boy had done well, although it was perhaps better that Vauquelin hadn't been present himself.

Flynn looks down at the dead man at his feet. He looks to the one curled on his side on the floor, his last breaths rasping in his lungs.

Flynn Frenière does not like little ends left open.

They have a nasty habit of reforming into ropes. Into nooses.

He pulls a small item from his pocket, thumbs the metal dial on its side.

A tiny flame bursts to life.

A tiny, courageous flame trying to eat the darkness.

Flynn understands this flame, its need to devour.

He takes a petrol-soaked rag from his pocket, puts the lighter to one corner… and in moments the entire rag is ablaze. He feels the sting of the flame against his fingertips, tosses it to the floor, where it spreads and hisses and swells. The heat envelops him.

The man who is not dead groans softly.

Flynn could pull him out onto the street and leave him there, but he will not risk the chance of of the boys' conquest pouring out his garbled story — even though he doubts any would believe him.

He crouches and grabs a handful of hair and the man opens his eyes, his pupils dilated with fear.

'Just remember,' Flynn tells him. 'Remember as the flames touch your skin, that it would have been much more of a noble end if they had fed until your final heartbeat, if your last memory was of beauty dressed in death.'

He releases the human, sees the realisation dawn, the horror reflected in the fire in his eyes.

And then Flynn turns on his heel and steals out into the night. Smoke clings to his skin and he smiles, settling into a nonchalant walk with his hands in his pockets as the street burns behind him.

31 / NIGHT 3:

THEIR YOUTH, THEIR BOUNTIFUL YOUTH...

Vauquelin and Clove stand with their backs to the mighty museum, the streets of Paris beckoning to them: they are no longer surrounded by the internal walls that have kept them in their proper places as masters.

Vauquelin's body vibrates with the possibilities that lie open to them. There are infinite places he could take Clove, but one calls to him in particular.

They wander, Clove letting Vauquelin guide them, their hands laced behind their backs — two majestic revenants promenading in their perfect environment: ancient souls in an ancient city.

The night is where they belong.

The city is still busy at this dark hour. This quarter is overrun with tourists attempting to blend in with Parisians — yet so obviously *not* from Paris. Laughter pierces the vampires' sensitive ears and they hurry their pace, anxious to move past a bustling café. Such a place is not where they will find their feast.

A few blocks past, Vauquelin comes to a stop.

It is an upscale *parfumière*,[†] closed for the night, very much of modern society, and Clove glances toward him, an inquisitive eyebrow lifted.

'This is our destination, Vauquelin?'

[†] - PERFUMER

He has spent the time in their companionable silence wondering where in this city, that Vauquelin knows so well, their steps will end.

They have not talked about the boys — in particular *one* boy: Éric. Clove does not want this night to be one of distress for the master vampire at his side. For concern to worm its way through his veins and for the tarnish of that worry to spoil this remarkable occasion.

They have both earned what is to come. *Earned.*

Clove lets the meaning behind that word drift across his mind. It is such a definitively mortal word and he contemplates that spending all of his time with young vampires, who still carry the breath of a shadow of their human lives with them, is changing his perspective.

He does not mind this, for vampires must adapt to the modern world... but nothing will change what he really is. This thought he takes and spins it down into the lightless void he conceals within — hungry things dwell there and they tear it to pieces.

Gabriel, Moth and Teal will deliver their own unique brand of death to this fair city. He only hopes Éric will be pulled tight into this mesmerising embrace.

Vauquelin clasps Clove's shoulder.

'In 1668, this was a brothel. These modern glass doors were once wood.' He turns his head to glance at the cobblestone street behind them. 'Can you not hear it? The ghost clatter of the carriage wheels? Mine was stopped, just there.' He points. 'A woman called to me, behind the wooden door that once was. Below this deceptively sinless *parfumière* lie the depths where I first succumbed to darkness.'

Clove arrests the breath that has risen in his throat. He is unused to surprises. In fact, sometimes he thinks that he has lost the capacity for astoundment. But this. He lets the moment settle then mentally grasps it from the air and swallows it whole.

He turns to Vauquelin, one hand on his fellow master's elbow.

'The honour of this knowledge moves me. This is a pivotal part of our existence. Our transformation to vampire. The fact you have chosen to share it I will hold close and treat the awareness with the utmost respect.'

Vauquelin tips his head back, gazing at the sky above... gratitude for this kinship swells in his chest. 'I have yet to bring Éric here. I am unsure whether the significance would register for him. I turned him in a modern house in Los Angeles, the city in which he matured. This is not the same.' He meets Clove's gaze once again. 'Their youth, their bountiful youth... it is humbling. Enlightening. We need them. We cannot do without them.'

Vauquelin's words sink deep into Clove's marrow. Each one is true. He thinks of his boys — of Teal who he had rescued on that heinous beach, of Moth who has single-handedly been the biggest pain in his side, of Gabriel who he had chosen to be his first-born after more than two hundred years of darkness.

'They are the very best part of us.'

Vauquelin closes his eyes.

Clove's utterance is indisputable.

Between the two of them, their progeny is few.

For a moment, Vauquelin indulges himself in pride for his own rebellious nature. It has never been tamed. He disobeyed his maker's orders from the beginning, orders that were given in a dismal cavern far beneath their feet: to create vampires indiscriminately. He waits until Clove's eyes meet his again. He needs not say it aloud.

Neither of them abide by this creed.

'I have often thought about breaking into this building, to confirm whether my portal to hell still exists... yet I have no true desire to see it. You will know my meaning.'

Clove lets the enormity of these words nestle against his mind. He is unused to sharing his deepest thoughts, his aching memories, but the time feels appropriate: so he sheds the skin on his restraint.

'My journey to darkness began behind a tavern in a small fishing village, on the southern coast of England. That night I had been called out in a game of cards.'

He pauses, unfolds the memory one frame at a time.

'I will admit that I cheated. To ease my ire I wandered into the back alleyway where one of the sailors I had slighted lay in wait. I was drunk. He was not. And I did not see the knife that slit me hip to hip.'

He thinks back to the blinding agony of that moment as he held his own slick intestines in his hands, of laughing in the face of a certain death.

'I collapsed onto the ground, heard the rats as they scurried in the gutters. I closed my eyes. And then I knew, I knew without a shadow of a doubt, that something was before me. You know my history, Vauquelin. You know what that something was.'

They have just passed a dim street lamp, and Vauquelin's face grows even more shadowed by this candour they share. It is one thing to answer Éric's many questions, to explain to him the sinister oath of revenancy — Éric's darkness is his own. It is quite another to discuss it with a master, with one whose dark soul is of a similar era.

'These are concepts that we cannot so easily reveal, even to those we trust... those who have felt their way down the same dark corridors. I suspect it is not the same journey for any of us. I think back to Moth's accusations toward Éric, that darkness was an option for him. It is true... none of us sought this. Though, in theory, I was given a choice: become vampire or accept a mortal death. It was offered to me a second time and I did not hesitate, as you well know, despite the brief, beguiling glimpse of the sun...' his voice breaks: '... and my own humanity. Would you have made the same decision?'

Clove considers the importance of this question.

It is like a comet in the sky of his darkness.

'If I had known Gabriel was waiting for me on the other side, in the nebulous mists of the future, unequivocally yes.'

Vauquelin's mind stutters a fraction — the sole reason he had embraced immortality a second time was for the dubious promise of reuniting with his human lover, Maeve. Then, he had no concept of the other plans fate had in store for him. No concept of Éric.

His timelines tangle in his mind like barbed-wire.

But now he knows that he had chosen correctly, for had he not turned Maeve in his second timeline — had things not gone so drastically wrong — his heart would never have settled as it has now, now that it has found its intended owner. All his blackened, blood-drenched history, all his mistakes, all his horror... the heartache... it is all worth it.

Now.

This very moment would not be happening.

He would not be here with Clove. Not like this.

He looks to his dark companion.

Their eyes meet. They bow their heads.

Such wicked, beautiful tunnels within the heart... perhaps none of us may ever chart their expanse, even with the infinite time afforded us.

Certain revenant words cannot be uttered aloud, lest they be strangled by the darkness.

Vauquelin turns his attention back to their agenda, giving the *parfumerie* one last glance for now. They will not hunt here.

They will not carry their newly-forged bond onto sullied ground.

They need a fresh field, one that belongs only to them.

Vauquelin nudges Clove's shoulder.

Doubtless the boys are uncovering this night's bounty. So shall we.

They continue walking, close but not too close... their eyes are on everything and everyone around them.

It is late.

Most humans are asleep.

This is the vampire's golden hour, so to speak.

Vauquelin and Clove together are intimidating: but under the cover of night, especially of night in Paris, they are a vision.

And so it is for the two women who approach them.

They have just emerged from an elegant champagne bar, full of oysters and bravado from bottles of bubbly, and they stop to catch their breaths. Vauquelin and Clove seem to have walked out of their very fantasies, out of the historic French films these women have watched... here stand the princes they had always wanted to meet, the unvoiced reason they had travelled to Paris.

They now know that it is worth taking the time to dream, to hope, for sometimes those dreams come true.

'Ahhhh! Come siete belli, tutti e due! Siete usciti dal set di un film, vero?'[†] the brunette woman asks.

Vauquelin tilts his head at the lilt of Italian... a language that has not crossed his senses in centuries, but is still just as crisp in his memory. He quickly translates this to Clove in a mind-whisper, imperceptibly cutting his gaze back to the woman.

'Un set cinematografico? No, tesoro mio... ci vestiamo sempre così. Ti vedo sorpresa; sei delusa?'[‡] He bows with his hand over his chest.

The brunette blinks, astonished at this man speaking to her in near-flawless Italian. She briefly turns her chin to her blonde companion before addressing Vauquelin once more.

'Allora, sei uscito direttamente dai miei sogni?'[§]

The women both bite their lips, and any restraint they might have held prior to this conversation evaporates.

But certain dreams can morph into nightmares... and even so one will

---

[†] AHHHH! HOW HANDSOME YOU BOTH ARE! YOU MUST HAVE WANDERED FROM A FILM SET, RIGHT?
[‡] A FILM SET? NO, MY DARLING... WE ALWAYS DRESS THIS WAY. I CAN SEE THIS SURPRISES YOU, BUT ARE YOU DISAPPOINTED?
[§] SO, YOU'RE VISITING ME FROM MY DREAMS?

willingly die on the blade of its spell.

Vauquelin and Clove need not look to one another to know their perfect prey has arrived.

They immediately bow, they take the women's hands in theirs — they lift their fingers to their chilled lips, and the women wilt beneath their touch.

Their heads are tilted in disbelief, and only then do Clove and Vauquelin allow their eyes to meet.

It is the thrill of the hunt in its most primal form. Their prey does not sense any danger — they are does in the forest where the wolves are dressed in lace. The women are captivated: and, after all… what could go wrong when they are in public view?

The hands that hold theirs are ice cold, but this is a seasonably chilly night for autumn in this city.

These men are so charming, so respectful.

The women do not see the wolves behind the smiles.

Clove leans in and whispers an endearment. It is in English but this does not matter to the woman. She hears the unasked question in the sultry lilt of his voice, tamps down the prickling in the nape of her neck, and slips her hand into Clove's.

Vauquelin resorts to his tried-and-true method.

He pulls the woman against his chest, drags the slightest tip of his nose up her neck.

She shivers beneath him.

His hand wanders as his tongue darts behind her ear.

Her body unthaws, relaxing into compliance: and then he knows he has prevailed. He backs her up to a wall, delves his tongue between her willing lips. He withdraws, bringing their shoulders apart, leaving her breathless.

Their hips are compressed — his desire is evident.

He draws a hand up between her legs: she is wearing trousers, but his thumb instinctively knows the precise spot where she will come undone.

He presses there, holding tight against her as he tilts her chin up and drowns her again with his dark kiss.

This time, he bites.

His daggers sink into the warm flesh of her tongue... the metallic magic courses through his mouth, and from here there is no turning back.

A scream erupts in her throat and Vauquelin turns the length of her hair in his fist like a noose. He pulls his hand back until her eyes meet his.

Silence.

His fangs pop the skin on her neck and Vauquelin surrenders to the nectar of her blood gliding down his throat.

The last time he hunted on the streets was in Los Angeles.

But this is not desperation as it was then: this is pure sport.

Her blood flows into his body and his cock fills his trousers.

It happens every time.

He withdraws his blood-drenched fangs and looks to Clove, bringing his hand down to his groin.

He misses Éric.

This is not how his bloodlust is fulfilled of late.

Clove's method of seduction is quieter though no less effective. He is aware of every move Vauquelin makes, aware of the noises emerging from Vauquelin's throat, aware of the sweet scent of arousal from the woman.

But the quarry pressed against him is nervous, less accommodating — and he knows he must tread gently. He nuzzles against her neck, lets his hair fall over her face. She reaches up to grasp it, winds her fingers into its ebony length, unaware that she is holding Death in her hands. His fingers trail casually up and down her sides, never veering towards her breasts, never travelling beyond her hips. He runs his tongue over her collar bone, tastes her salt sweat explode on his tongue. He waits for the moment, waits for that perfect moment as his lips dance across her throat, bestowing butterfly kisses against the trembling hollow.

Her heartbeat is a wild beast calling him home and he hones into its cadence.

The moment comes.

She arches her back, presses her hips to his — his fangs slice into the perfect curve of her neck and her blood hits the back of his throat.

And she orgasms beneath him.

He drinks. He drinks with the night air of Paris caressing his skin.

And then Vauquelin's fingers lace into his.

A lifted eyebrow.

An unspoken creed.

Vauquelin pulls Clove toward him, and they pass one another like ships in the night, their bodies grazing as they switch, as they find the unlocked spots on their victims.

They draw out their remaining sweetness, letting the blood trickle down their throats.

Their victims crumple beneath them, empty rag dolls, and Vauquelin and Clove turn to face one another.

Vauquelin curls his fingers around Clove's neck: he digs in.

Their eyes are locked.

Blood graces their lips.

Their words are silent, but they both understand.

They move apart.

Vauquelin folds his hands in front of him.

Since they set off on their own he has been focussed on his primitive connection to Clove... he has sent his modern, revenant restraints screaming to the dark sky above them: the women are dead.

What shall we do with them?

Clove can still feel the pressure of Vauquelin's fingers against his neck and the new blood thrumming through his veins only accentuates that sensation. He brings himself back to the moment, to the task in hand.

'How far are we from your house?' Clove asks. 'I believe you have the perfect disposal point there.'

He has already discounted the possibility of dumping the bodies in the Seine. They may be discovered quickly and the ensuing police and medical attention would raise too many questions.

'We cannot possibly carry them back to the house. It would be too suspicious.'

'I did not mention carrying,' Clove says.

His lips quirk into a slight smile as he draws a phone from his pocket. He looks at the modern slab of technology in his palm and feels the desire to toss it into the river.

This was a suggestion from Flynn.

That they not rely completely on mind-touches.

Vauquelin smirks as he leans against the wall and crosses his ankles, drinking in the fanciful vision of Clove in his ancient coat, a vampire of the ages... with a phone. In truth neither of them look quite correct with such a modern implement, though Vauquelin cultivates a centuries-long love affair with gadgetry and inventions. With his customary scrutiny — thumb on his chin, a forefinger draped across his upper lip — he watches Clove make the call.

Clove swipes for Flynn's number and brings the phone up to his face. The dial tone rings twice, and then Flynn's voice vibrates against his ear.

'Bring the car,' Clove says. 'Rue de Sainte-Honoré.'

He slips the phone back into his pocket and scans the alleyway.

The night soundtrack of Paris goes on around them, but no one knows of the deaths in their midst.

The passage of time can be cruel to the vampire. They cannot so easily adapt. They do not belong in this world, and yet their improbable lifespans often force them to accept the changes human society demands.

Technology can be used in their favour, as a means of survival.

In this case, Clove's simple call to Flynn will solve their corpse problem in a matter of minutes.

Vauquelin sinks on his haunches next to one of the victims, drawing her head against his shoulder while they wait for Flynn to arrive. A disguise, should someone pass. She will appear drunk — which, according to the odour of alcohol rising from her cooling lips, she was — not dead.

Her debauched blood is a live wire along his senses, and for a moment he is ashamed. Clove seems unaffected. This must be another difference in their bloodlines... and it had never occurred to him to confess this to Clove. He had dismissed his customary vigilance tonight, had not conducted his usual test: to suss unaltered sustenance. He had been caught up in the moment, and now he is slightly *grisé*.[†] With his bloodline, he cannot get drunk from drinking wine or spirits... but by consuming intoxicated human blood, most definitely. He is not obliterated, merely diminished. Ever-so-slightly. He draws a hand over his jaw before speaking, and attempts to regain his composure.

A mask.

Just for this moment, when they are both in a compromising situation.

Clove tilts his head, an imperceptible movement to any mortal eye, but enough that his gaze tracks over his fellow master. He glimpses what Vauquelin is trying so hard to disguise, but he will not comment, he simply secures the knowledge. It may be a discussion point for a later evening, or it may stay within his memories: a frozen fruit that has no need to thaw.

'Not quite as glorious as it used to be, is it Clove? Hunting with wild abandon, appeasing our black thirst without fear of consequence? This is one of the primary reasons I longed to return to my past. Now the only direction for me is forward. Thus the catacombs.' He lifts his gaze to Clove but his mind is on Éric. 'This is not a complaint. I fear our

---

[†]- GREY AROUND THE GILLS; BUZZED

adventure tonight is turning me madly nostalgic.'

'Nostalgia has its own rewards. But we must not dwell on it for long, lest it tries to drag us down into its depths.'

The fresh blood in Clove's veins sings to him. It is the same song, the same indisputable high whispering his name with every single death through the centuries. He will never tire of its call. He cannot, even if he desires it. Because of Gabriel.

His thoughts turn to his first-born and the brothers by his side, turn to Éric shedding the skin of his naïveté out on the streets. And he wants them all safely under Vauquelin's roof.

Two men approach from the opposite direction.

The scent of cigarette smoke filters against Clove's senses.

It is possible they will walk past but Clove will not take any chances.

Turn around. The touch he sends is not gentle: it is sharp and brutal, an undeniable twist of an inferior mind.

Headlights splice the darkness and a car pulls up at the mouth of the alleyway. The driver cuts the engine and the lights die instantly. A soft rain starts to fall.

Clove glances up, sees the delicate droplets caught in the glow from a street lamp. He absorbs the moment and tucks it away: a fragment of peace in the aftermath of death.

Flynn steps out from the driver's side and the boot of the car rises. He comes to them, two tarpaulins slung over his arm. They do not speak, but as they pass each other Clove inhales. The acrid stench of smoke.

It appears Flynn has had his own adventure.

'They're all fine,' Flynn says, as he crouches and expertly wraps the bodies in the tarpaulins — as though he is rolling slabs of meat for the oven. In a way, he is.

The air crisps and Vauquelin drinks it in greedy gulps, such tension melting from his shoulders as even their feast could not release: not even the mellow intoxication of the blood he had consumed could tame it, as it had faithfully done in his past. He has been struggling without success all night to dismiss Éric from his thoughts, to devote all his attention to Clove. He has done his level best, but he cannot show his defeat to the other masters in his presence. Not in this moment.

Vauquelin rests a hand on Flynn's shoulder. He opens his mouth but the words of gratitude he has for this esteemed vampire are greater than he can conjure. *Thank you.*

As Flynn drops the bodies in the boot and closes the lid, a conundrum creases his brow. He has to tell Clove and Vauquelin what happened, yet he doesn't want to spoil what the boys have done.

Because it was a joy to behold.

He waits until Vauquelin and Clove are in the car, and they are speeding back along the streets, to add to his story.

'They're all fine but it didn't go quite as Gabe planned, so he had to switch things up. He handled it.' Flynn looks in the rear view mirror and meets Clove's dark gaze. 'They all handled it.'

To Vauquelin's ears, all this sounds like danger, exactly what he feared. The tentative peace he had achieved evaporates in this instant.

He grips the armrest until his knuckles whiten and gazes out the passenger window, desperate to conceal his emotions from the others. This evening with Clove was priceless: but what will he have paid for it in kind?

The car rolls to a stop at his gates, and he melts back into the leather seats as Flynn engages the remote.

Vauquelin's phone vibrates in his pocket, and he extracts it with a trembling hand.

we're almost home 🖤

2 more blocks

Vauquelin's fingers scatter across the screen in reply as he directs Flynn to drive through the porte cochère to the back of the house:

> we have just arrived.
> bring the boys down below xx

Vauquelin's unease vibrates on the air, a dull energy Clove can taste.
Come to me. A mind-touch to Gabriel.
He needs to know what has occurred, if Éric had been in any danger.
Éric wants us to go down into the catacombs, comes the instant reply.
Clove's lips tighten. This is not a good place for Vauquelin so soon after Olivier's demise. And this is Gabriel making Clove aware of the possibility of added distress.

The car comes to a halt behind the house and the masters pass through the back door. Clove and Flynn hover at the entrance to the catacombs, because Vauquelin is already on his knees, extracting the key to the ominous door. He rises and turns to Flynn and Clove.

'Please... I need a half hour alone. The boys should be here shortly. I have instructed Éric to bring them down.' He closes the door firmly behind him and lights a torch.

There is an unfinished task here, one that must receive its rightful closure.

☥☥☥

Vauquelin catapults open the hatch, exposing the noxious depths of the acid pit.

Olivier's bones have sunk to the bottom, no longer so buoyant after many hours in the acid. He refuses to let these bones mingle with inferior ones pulled from the street.

He extracts them solemnly, placing them on the ledge of the pit one immaculate bone by one, until they dry: the acid evaporates quickly, expelling its malignant gases into the dank atmosphere. There is an empty shelf, away from the others, where Vauquelin arranges them in their own sacred space. The skull is last. He holds it in his hands a moment, placing a kiss to its forehead before depositing it on its solitary stack.

He has already grieved, time and time again.

He bounds up the cold stone steps and hangs the torch before greeting the others. His face is grim, but now all of his loves are gathered in front of him. They have made a triumphant return... they are all in one piece.

Joy overwrites his gloom.

'These are going exactly where?' asks Flynn.

The tarpaulin-wrapped corpses lay at his feet.

Gabe moves to Clove's side, sees the questioning raised eyebrow — and knows he has a lot of explaining to do.

Moth stands by the wall, leaning against it, his head bowed.

A weird kind of energy pulses from him.

Gabe knows it's because of the kill, what happened in that room, the death that shouldn't-have-been but was what Moth really wanted. Moth in conflict is like a lit fuse.

'Hey,' Gabe says as he turns to Éric. 'A pretty wild night, yes?'

Now it's up to Éric to define 'wild.'

Vauquelin reaches out to touch Éric's hair, anxious to hear about his adventures... but Éric calmly moves his hand away.

Later.

Vauquelin's face falls.

'Yeah, you could definitely say that,' Éric replies, his voice colourless. He side-eyes the bodies and dashes down into the catacombs, leaving Vauquelin slack-jawed at the entry.

Gabe goes to Moth's side and leans his weight against his lover.

He's purposefully invading Moth's space which is kinda like poking a scorpion... but he doesn't need Moth to sink into a pit of his own brooding thoughts.

'Don't sweat the small stuff,' Gabe says. He slides a hand around the back of Moth's neck, the skin warm against his fingers.

They both know he's talking about the way things panned out.

Moth's mood alarms Vauquelin. He wonders if this signals the end of the tenuous bond he and Éric had forged, or if something far more sinister had occurred. Regardless, the boys are all subdued: he had expected them to return full of *joie de vivre*,[†] their hearts pumping hot, hard-won blood.

'Flynn, may I ask you to take the bodies downstairs, leave them by the pit? And take Moth and Teal with you, please. We will join you shortly.'

Moth reluctantly tramps after Flynn who has hoisted both bodies over his shoulders. Teal follows like a wraith.

Now Gabe is left standing before Clove and V and the air crackles between them all. He doesn't wait for the questions, launching into his own account.

'Yes, it didn't go as planned.' He lifts his chin. If there is blame here he will shoulder it. 'We played it out as we always do. Éric joined in.' He glances at V, who looks like he has a million questions swarming on his tongue. 'He did great. But then our prey started to have second thoughts and there was no fucking way I was losing them, so Teal had to dial it up.' He doesn't explain the details. 'We took them to an abandoned house. We fed. Éric did his healing thing. But then,' he takes a small breath, 'the one Moth and Teal were on died.' He holds up his hands before V can pin him to the wall with those ice-blue eyes. 'The guy died because his heart gave out, not because they had taken too much. Éric went to work on him with the Opinel. Moth added his own touch. And then we ran.'

There: it's out.

[†] THE JOY OF LIVING

He waits.

Vauquelin does not look at Clove, nor does he attempt to hide his thoughts... he strides to Gabriel and takes his shoulders in a firm grip, locking their gazes.

'Gabriel. I will not doubt the truth of what you have told us. You are the sole reason I believed Éric would be safe tonight. You have returned him to me... that is all I could have asked. Still, I sense something significant has happened to Éric, and I suspect he will only admit it to me. I do not know if he has revealed it to you and I shall not inquire. Now, we must attend to our spoils. The sun will rise soon.'

Vauquelin releases Gabriel, finally permitting himself to look at Clove. He still does not know Clove's assessment of the events that transpired... even so, he extends a hand toward the catacombs.

Some of the tension unwinds from Gabe's muscles.

Éric has been his prime concern tonight.

He only hopes he isn't too scarred by what occurred.

Down in the dusty, subterranean depths Éric is seated on the stone floor, well away from the others. His back is against his own shelf. He refuses to look at anyone: he fidgets with a rib bone, twirling it between his fingers.

Vauquelin's concern deepens.

He had intended for the boys to witness the acid eat their victims' flesh away: but his mind is gone, probing Éric's which is locked away from him, silent as a vault.

He unrolls the tarpaulins, exposing the corpses, looking again to his beloved.

Éric drags an indifferent gaze across the bodies, purposely avoiding V's scrutiny, and returns to working the bone in his grasp.

The temperature in the catacombs drops.

Something is wrong, very wrong — it skitters across all of their senses.

Gabe and Moth drift to Teal's side, Moth's brooding mood forgotten in the face of a possible backlash. Gabe is acutely aware of Teal's withdrawal into himself since they returned.

Clove's focus is on his fellow master. The turbulence is palpable as it builds inside Vauquelin's chest. Gabriel's unfolding of the night's events niggles away at his mind. The atmosphere should not be like this — there is a pressure building like a volcano waiting to blow, and for once it is not emanating from Moth.

Vauquelin crosses to Éric, crouches down in front of him. Again he reaches out to touch Éric's hair — this time Éric lets him, but still he will not look up. Vauquelin squeezes Éric's shoulder and stands, turning to face the others.

'Perhaps under the circumstances we should leave the bodies for now. I believe Éric and I will retire.'

He offers Éric his hand, hefting him up.

'As you wish.' Clove motions to his boys, and leads the way back up the catacomb steps.

They pause in the hallway but Éric and Vauquelin do not follow them.

Flynn drifts into the shadows but not before his steady gaze meets Clove's. An arch of his brow and slightly pursed lips tell Clove all he needs to know. The night has been fractured.

Vauquelin drapes an arm around Éric's shoulders and begins ascending the stairs. He relaxes when he feels Éric lean into him.

Something has disturbed his beloved and he aims to uncover it as soon as possible. He perches the torch above the extinguisher.

Éric stiffens when they hear voices outside the door.

He needs to be alone, hopefully with Vauquelin.

He isn't in the mood for anyone else.

✝✝✝

'What kind of fucked up thing is going on?' Moth shrugs.

Éric had been acting... well, pretty much like Moth.

He's not sure whether to be impressed or supremely hacked off.

Gabe grabs his arm and the pointed glance he gives would wither a lesser vampire. But Moth isn't stupid.

He shuts his mouth.

Clove ushers them to the foot of the staircase.

At some point Teal has drifted ahead.

This fact lies like the tip of a thorn in Clove's mind.

'Vauquelin and Éric need their privacy. I suggest you stay close to your chambers for a while.'

They climb the stairs in silence and Clove leaves them with a small nudge of pressure against Gabriel's back.

It says *I am proud of you.*

As Gabe and Moth enter their room, Teal stands by their bed, his shoulders slumped. He's been a fraction of himself since they came into the house.

'You okay?' Gabe goes to him with Moth by his side.

Teal turns, his eyes searching their faces.

He isn't sure what he's going through, his emotions are too tangled — but he knows what he needs.

'Hold me,' he says, his voice soft in the pre-dawn air.

Gabe pulls him into a close embrace, and Teal lets himself fall into the rising heat from his brother's skin.

Moth's hands find the tight muscles in his shoulders and Teal floats in the sheer beauty of the moment.

It is enough.

32 / NIGHT 3:

JUST LET ME D⊙ IT

Éric stops outside the entrance to their bedchamber and casts a sidelong glance down the length of the hallway. His lips are sealed tight — he hasn't uttered a single word since they left the catacombs.

'The others have gone to their rest,' Vauquelin whispers, answering Éric's unspoken question.

Éric flops down on the floor, untying his boots and flinging them to the left side of the doors. They hit the wall with a thunk, inspiring hiked eyebrows from V. Éric ignores this. He peels off his socks and stands, dropping his trousers and boxers in one fell swoop... he lifts his jumper from the waist, bringing it over his head. He balls it up and this, too, is flung to the floor. He blows his hair out of his eyes and stands upright, as still and naked as a Greek sculpture.

Now it is Vauquelin's turn to cast his gaze down the corridor, concerned one of the others might see his beloved *en déshabillé*.† There is no need for worry — the house is quiet. Nevertheless he opens the doors and Éric careens inside. Vauquelin closes them, leaning against them with his hands behind his back.

He will not pressure Éric.

---

†- UNDRESSED

His beloved's anguish, whatever enkindled it, is apparent in the dark circles beneath his eyes, in the curvature of his spine, in the dimming of his light. He seems to have made himself smaller, and when Éric is in this state Vauquelin knows he is beating himself up.

He will return the favour of silence if that is what Éric wishes now, will wait for him to speak when the words rise to the surface: just as Éric had done for him when he miraculously re-emerged from his time-slip.

V beelines for the bathroom, and from behind the door, Éric can hear the creaking of the brass faucets. Water rumbles through the house's antiquated pipes.

'No. Turn it off. Please.' Éric's voice echoes into the candlelit bathroom.

'I always take a bath after we feed. You know this.'

'Not tonight... please, V.'

Vauquelin glances down to Éric's hand clasping his wrist, and looks back up with only his eyes, a pastiche of intrigue and confusion settling on his face.

Vauquelin is a creature of habit: many of which he has nurtured for centuries. And as most of his life has been spent alone, there has seldom been any other being to criticise him or point out his foibles. But then came Éric and his youthful candour, his buoyant nature, his insatiable curiosity... his lack of shame in asking for what he wants — all of these are qualities Vauquelin adores in his beloved.

He labours to keep his mind open, to censure himself when he senses he is being too rigid: because Éric brings him infinite delights.

But climbing into his bed unbathed is one of his *bêtes noires*,[†] high on the list with shod feet on his duvet or furniture. It is one of the habits — or even requirements — from which he refuses to back down.

After his adventures tonight Éric is dirty and dishevelled... his hair is a mess, his curls askew in savage tangles, a black smudge smeared across his

---

[†] - A PHOBIA, USUALLY IRRATIONAL OR OBSESSIVE

cheekbone. There's no telling what unsanitary filth he's been wallowing in.

The two of them are perpetually clean: normally this is not something Éric minds. He loves the aroma of V fresh from a bath, his alabaster skin fragranced with vétiver soap and his hair scented with sandalwood — Éric can get hard just thinking about it.

By now, Éric knows all of V's hot buttons. He's fully aware this is one of them. He can see it in Vauquelin's slightly narrowed eyes, in the tightness of his lips.

Whatever.

Tonight, Éric wants them both as unclean as he is now.

He wants to fuck all his frustrations out on Vauquelin until they stink of each other, until their foulness matches his state of mind.

Then maybe, he can talk. *Maybe.*

'Get over yourself,' he says. His voice is paved with gravel. 'We can change the sheets.' Éric tilts his chin down. He forces his crooked smile, albeit half-hearted, and bites the corner of his lip.

When a lock of dark curls falls over Éric's brow, catching on his lashes, Vauquelin knows he will not want to miss whatever it is that storms in his mind tonight.

He shuts off the faucets and allows his young lover to lead him back into the bedchamber, thoroughly seduced by Éric's audacity.

Éric wants to bury his face between Vauquelin's legs, wants to inhale every swarthy scent their bodies have generated as they all walked for kilometres across the city.

Before he left with the boys, he had been watching V all night, admiring the long, slender lines of his body, looking at him through a different lens: because the boys and Clove were with them, and they were all on foot. V moves differently when he walks in Paris... like a sultry cheetah.

It was a treat: when V and Éric go out alone they're always in the car.

Vauquelin has been acting a little peculiar since their guests arrived. Éric knows V isn't quite himself when others are around, yet he's shown them sides of his personality that only Éric sees. Sides of him Éric is pretty sure even Oliver had never seen.

The only other vampires Éric had ever met — besides Clove, Flynn, Gabe, Moth, and Teal — were Olivier and Céline. Éric doesn't expect they'll ever see her again. He had really liked her when they met... but she abandoned him along with Olivier.

It's usually just the two of them, and both are content with this.

They have everything they need in each other.

But tonight, walking in the city with this new crew, Éric witnessed a different Vauquelin. All that talk of making humans pay in crimson?

Oof.

Something had changed in V after the earlier incident in the catacombs.

The old V is back, the confident one that whisked him up the Hollywood Hills in an open-topped Ferrari and blew his mind.

And then Éric left him to go off with the boys, and something had changed in him, too. Something feral had come to life inside him and it scares him.

On the walk to the Louvre, Éric flitted back and forth between walking hand-in-hand with his magnificent lover, blatantly kissing him under old, iron lampposts... running ahead and leaving him to stroll with Clove while he hip-bumped Gabriel and playfully slugged Moth on the shoulders, ending with an arm around Teal's shoulders as they stopped in front of the hallowed museum with their night tickets.

Up until the time they left, it had been a *really fucking good night*. He thought it would only get better. And it did... until...

V hadn't wanted Éric to go because V despises hunting on the streets... he thinks it's too dangerous with all the cops and the drugs and the cameras... he's had enough of all that.

Éric understands V's reasons... he really does.

But something else happened tonight: something neither of them had expected.

When they all got home Éric was so relieved when V said to leave the bodies. No one was fucking interested in hanging around and talking about how badass the acid pit is, especially not Éric.

He desperately wants to get laid but he isn't sure he deserves it after everything that unfolded. He could barely make it upstairs, with the new blood flowing in his veins and the way he had gotten it still smouldering in his brain.

Éric knows he's being weird with V, despite all his lusty hot-bloodedness, despite thinking about slamming V against the wall the second they got into the bedchamber, grinding his hips into him... because Vauquelin had wanted to take a fucking *bath*.

But he gave in!

A small victory — at least Éric won *something* tonight, and now his face is buried in the crook of Vauquelin's leg. That soft, soft spot where his thigh meets his hip: Éric drags his tongue along the ridge, his right hand around V's knee and V's cock like a mast in his left. His hand undulates... he doesn't even have to think about it. He knows the veins on that cock like he knows his own name. Their knottiness against his fingers makes his own twitch, and he's a little drunk from the blood.

But really it's V's scent that intoxicates him, not the blood. V smells like himself, like sandalwood and vétiver: but he also smells swampy, slightly damp from the friction of his thighs, from his cock and balls clinging to his leg.

V never wears underwear.

They didn't exist when he grew up as a human and he never acquired an appreciation for them.

Éric had watched him adjusting himself at intervals, and sometimes V would look directly at him when he did it — that certainly didn't help anything.

And now Éric reaps the rewards of Vauquelin having walked around Paris all night long.

It's everything he hoped it would be.

He smells like a fucking hothouse, like flowers and dirt and sweat, and if Éric *could* come, he would have already exploded.

Instead he attempts to flip V onto his stomach.

But this is where Vauquelin draws the line. He knows what Éric wants to do.

'No,' he growls. He cannot allow it.

Éric isn't in the mood for this. Not now.

'Fine,' he says, and he plants his hands on the back of Vauquelin's thighs, sliding them up to the bends of his knees, and traps him there.

When did I get so strong?

Where is this aggression coming from?

Well... he has a pretty fucking good idea where it's coming from, but he pushes this to the back of his mind and, dropping his lopsided grin, exposes two fangs. It works every time.

He wields this fail-safe skill of seduction against Vauquelin and drags his tongue down V's cock, slurping one of his balls into his mouth.

Vauquelin sinks his head into the pillows, burying his face in hands.

There was a time when he would have lost this forever.

He has it now, it is back in his clutches, and he would be foolish to not let it do whatever it wants.

Éric works his tongue further and further down.

And then he freezes.

His face and hands are coated with the scent of Vauquelin.

Please... Éric lets his silent command (or longing or even a mere wish) hang in the air.

Just let me do it.

Vauquelin is a little unnerved by Éric's intensity tonight, but he knows his beloved is struggling on the edges of his unnamed darkness and desperately trying to set himself free.

Vauquelin will walk on the black verge with Éric as long as his beloved needs him… he will hold onto Éric, refusing to let it swallow him whole.

So Vauquelin surrenders and permits Éric to take what he needs.

He turns over… he backs up into Éric's face.

He lets himself be opened by Éric's tongue, writhes under his beloved's wet lips.

Éric digs his fingers into Vauquelin's buttocks, plunges his tongue… he brings his head back, momentarily dizzied by getting exactly what he had wanted.

But then Éric bites the inside of his cheek, whimpers as a trickle of blood slides down his throat — he spreads V, lapping him up, bringing his hand between V's legs to stroke him as fast as he's licking. He doesn't want to stop but there's so much more he wants.

Éric shuffles across the enormous bed and knocks a candlestick over in his frenzy. The flame dies on the rug and Éric doesn't even care that he'll have to clean up that wax tomorrow night.

Now the room is completely dark.

He almost topples the nightstand as he ferrets the blessed tub out of the drawer, and now his hot hands are slathering V's cock with lanolin.

Ummmmmmph.

Vauquelin sniffs Éric's face. It is besmirched by their mingled pungency — the incidental perfume of their outdoor escapades, their blood sweat, their pheromones.

Vampires find their release in myriad other delights, V had told Éric the night of his turning.

The meaning of this, in the context of tonight, sets Éric's spirits aflame.

He takes a strand of V's hair into his mouth. He bites down on it, he yanks. He grips V's face with his delightfully dirty fingers.

This is the most hypnotic fragrance Vauquelin has ever beheld. He courses his nose across Éric's face, up, down, across... he drags their tongues together, he drinks down the taste of himself which he did not want tonight, which now he cannot live without.

Éric straddles V — he reaches behind his back, arching his hips, and settles down on his lover's cock. He braces himself on the carved wood of the headboard so that V might punish him, send him into another world.

Instead V brings their faces together once more, he kisses him... and then he plunges his thumb into Éric's mouth.

Éric's eyes bulge.

Just like that he's back in front of the bar and it's Teal's thumb.

He freezes in place: all his guilt sparks in his stomach like a trail of gunpowder about to detonate.

His body trembles.

Vauquelin recoils. This is a touch they have shared often...

The expression of shock on Éric's face baffles him and he tilts his head, drawing his shoulders back.

'V...' Éric whispers. His face is crinkled with pain. He clings to V's hand and manoeuvres himself onto his back.

Vauquelin brings Éric's leg over his shoulder and slips an oiled hand into his beloved. He fucks Éric slowly with his fingers, he curls them inside him over and over until Éric is a quivering mess beneath him.

'V... please — '

Vauquelin drives his cock back into Éric as far as it will go. He extends his spine, bracing the small of Éric's back, and sways his beloved's body side to side. Vauquelin's hips begin to arc and he hefts Éric up so their chests touch. He draws all over Éric's face with his fingertips, lets him breathe in what they have alchemised. He pulls Éric's lower lip down and bites it. His tongue chases the blood as it runs down Éric's chin.

Vauquelin slows his brutal thrusts. A sigh escapes as he gazes upon Éric beneath him. He backs out, leaving only the tip of himself inside, and Éric whispers no no no not yet, bringing a hand to Vauquelin's chest to check his heartbeat, desperately hoping to stay awake a little longer.

Éric still needs more.

Vauquelin can never refuse him.

He clasps Éric's jaw, he sinks and breathes his blood-warmed breath on Éric's neck... he rises and arches his back, bringing his hands to Éric's ankles. He thrusts into his beauty, over and over again, casting his gaze across his beloved's smooth, pearlescent skin.

And then the sun rises.

It invokes the theft of their breaths, it slows their hearts.

Vauquelin collapses like a swan onto Éric's chest, dropping kisses along his jawline.

Éric's cock is trapped between them: he is still impaled by Vauquelin.

Vauquelin withdraws and Éric cries out. He slithers down Éric's torso and takes his beloved into his mouth, worships his cock's denouement... its softness, its majesty even in stillness. He covers it with his hand, and they succumb as they are.

Éric's words never surfaced.

Vauquelin's heart has already stopped.

Still he has no idea what happened to Éric tonight.

And Éric, his own heart slowing in his chest, looks down the length of their entangled bodies, at V's raven hair fanning out on his abdomen: they are dirty toppled statues, felled by the rising of the sun.

I've never seen such a beautiful sight in my life, he sighs, just before the black folds of sleep smother him back into silence.

33 / NIGHT 3:

DISCIPLES OF THE NIGHT

Something is wrong.

Gabe feels it settle against his bones, that searing touch he knows he can't ignore. They are lying on the antique coverlet, Teal sandwiched in between him and Moth, the heavy bed curtains sealing them off from the rest of the world.

It's not that unusual for them to touch Teal, but it's usually done as they pass him seated against one of the arches in Gehenna's many cloisters — moonlight streaming through the battlements, bathing Teal's hair in silver. Gabe can see it now: Teal with a book in his lap — they rest a hand on his shoulder, Teal raises his own and they intertwine fingers.

But the moment is soon gone.

They embrace before each dawn and curl up together, three slight forms lost in the arms of the death sleep. Frequently though, Moth and Gabe have their own needs, and Teal is always in tune with their energies. Without fail he slips away to give them their privacy.

Tonight Teal is pressed tight against Gabe's chest, Moth spooning behind his bright-eyed brother. Moth's arm encircles Teal's waist and Gabe's fingers entwine with Moth's. They are one, these Bloody Little Prophets, harbingers of death, disciples of the night.

Teal didn't grace them with one of his bashful smiles and pull away, slip into his room to lose himself in his beloved words.

No... this time he clings onto him, his fingers wound into the fabric of Gabe's T-shirt. Over Teal's shoulder Gabe locks eyes with Moth and there's no need for a mind-touch, because their eyes say it all.

Something is wrong.

They've gone through too much together not to heed the warning. All thoughts of ripping Moth's clothes off and pinning him against the silk wallpaper lay in a tangle at Gabe's feet. It's a disorientating sensation with the new blood surging through his veins and the heat from Moth's skin calling his name.

Gabe replays the night's events.

When did it go wrong?

He doesn't mean what happened in the filthy room with the men.

When did something happen to tip Teal into this desperate need for closeness?

And then it hits him, a solid jackhammer blow of realisation that sends a shooting pain through his skull.

It was Éric.

Or rather, it was Éric *with* Teal.

Gabe had pushed them both too far in his own stubborn desire not to lose their meal tickets.

'Fuck.' The word falls from his lips and he screws his eyes up tight. He expects Moth to come back with one of his salacious quips, but when he opens his eyes Moth has already fallen into his dark slumber.

The impending dawn crushes against his senses, but he forces himself back from its brink for just a little bit longer.

This is all his fault. When he hunts with his brothers they have their own invisible thread of connection, of knowing what to do, of trusting Gabe to get them out of situations that go wrong — like tonight.

Trust.

That's the word that blinds Gabe with its blazing intensity.

Gabe had taken Éric out on the streets for his first real taste of hunting, and he'd egotistically assumed Éric would trust him just like Teal and Moth. Would understand how they manipulated the night and made it bow down before them.

But how could he? He barely knows them.

And now something has happened to make Teal feel vulnerable.

To make Éric act as if he wanted to crawl out of his own skin.

You fucked it up, Gabe. You really fucked it up.

That is the last thought tumbling through his mind before he topples into the black maw of oblivion.

34 / NIGHT 4:

I'VE RUINED EVERYTHING

Éric is burrowed into the sofa in his game lair, his chin on his knees, arms wrapped around his shins, frantically crashing cars into walls and inflicting virtual damage all over the streets of Los Angeles. He hadn't bothered closing the door all the way — his ear buds are in because he didn't necessarily want his normal volume to rouse the entire house.

He's so focussed on the game that he doesn't notice the hand on the edge of the door, opening it slightly to better assess the room's occupants — or more importantly, to determine who is *not* present in the room.

But it's only him.

Gabe has left Teal and Moth curled up together on the bed. He woke early, just as the sun sank below the rooftops of Paris. And as soon as he inhaled his first breath, he knew what he had to do.

This is why he is here, standing in the doorway, and he takes the opportunity to watch Éric for a few moments. The way Éric's jaw is set tight, the way the tension cords the muscles in his neck: Gabe recognises all these signs because Moth does the very same thing when something is eating him up inside. The guilt from last night swarms over him again. He feels it like a palpable load in the centre of his chest.

He steps further into the room and closes the door behind him. Éric probably doesn't want to be disturbed but he desperately needs to speak to him. To apologise for pushing him too far when he wasn't ready, when he didn't understand how they hunted.

Éric rockets off the sofa when Gabe's gentle hand touches his shoulder from behind: he fumbles the controller in his hands — narrowly saving it from crashing to the wooden floor — and yanks his ear buds out, tucking them into his shirt pocket.

'Holy fucking shit, Gabe! You could have at least walked in front of me, or something! SHIT.' He drops back onto the sofa, falling hard against the backrest. His heart thrashes his rib cage.

Gabe sinks down beside Éric. He has all these words queued up in his throat, all the explanations about why he acted like he did. But he simply locks his gaze with Éric's and lets the bitter swell of trepidation flood onto his tongue.

'Éric, don't say anything. Let me get this out.' He bows his head for a moment. 'Last night.' He pauses, hears the silence of the room hammering against his ears. 'I put you in a situation I shouldn't have. And I'm so fucking sorry.'

Éric looks away from Gabe's face — it's too open. He isn't sure he's ready to do this. He doesn't even know what he wants to say! Instead he stares at the flaming car still burning on the screen, and it's like watching his brain.

'I don't know what you're talking about.' He swallows hard. 'What situation?'

'You're going to make me say it, aren't you?' Gabe grimaces. He's well aware that he deserves every ounce of the feeling happily dragging its nails over his tender, exposed places. 'The situation with Teal. I told you to proposition him, and then I told Teal to turn up the dial because I could sense the guys were getting edgy and I didn't want to lose them.'

He hopes that Éric doesn't need any more details.

Éric lifts the silver necklace he always wears to his lips, absentmindedly gnawing on its medallion. The whole scene plays over in his mind again, engulfing him like a tsunami.

How can he even process this? To *Gabe?* He briefly considers just running out the front door and never coming back.

'I just thought I was doing what you told me to do... but something happened to me. I don't think you should be the one apologising, Gabe. I think...' At last Éric allows himself to turn and face him. 'I shouldn't have felt the way I did. I don't know what came over me. Fuck, this makes me sick.' He cups a palm over his mouth and buries his other hand in his hair... his knees jump in frenetic bounces.

Okay, what the hell is Éric thinking? A dozen thoughts take flight in Gabe's head. His eyes widen as Teal's behaviour suddenly starts to make sense. His stomach totters on the edge of freefall.

Is Éric saying what I think he's saying?

'You mean you had feelings for Teal?'

It's a softly spoken sentence but it sits like a landmine on his tongue.

Éric stops bouncing and purses his lips.

That feral beast is sticking a claw into his guts right now, and it's telling him to lie. To just suck it all back in, and make up something that is so far from the truth he won't have to face it. But he knows he can't.

'I already told you how things are with V and me. But you trusted me with Teal, and I just... I fucking blew it. I wanted to kiss him and not in a game sort of way. It's fucking tearing me apart, and I haven't even told V. I crossed a line... not just with Teal but with myself. I have never, ever done anything like this before, Gabe, I swear. I didn't know that what Teal was doing with me would send me where it did.' He launches himself up and turns his back to Gabe so that he might catch his breath, lacing his fingers on his head, swerving to face him again. 'I've ruined everything, maybe even with V.'

This is so much worse than Gabe could have envisaged. Éric's words punch into him over and over again, and he feels each blow, the impact sending his mind spiralling. This is what had pushed Teal over the edge. And now Éric is drowning in the kind of guilt that only vampires can feel — because every emotion, when the dark blood runs in your veins, is an amplified version of its mortal equivalent.

He imagines himself in the same position. How would he cope with feeling like he'd cheated on Moth?

It guts him open and for a moment he can't form any coherent thoughts.

'Fuck.' This is a hellscape of his own making and he's not sure how he'll crawl out of it, how he'll manage to fix all the things he's broken.

Somehow he forces himself to his feet and goes to Éric. He reaches out and grabs Éric's arm, needing him to listen.

'If there's ruin here it's all down to me, and I think I've fucked up everything.'

'No, Gabe. This is all on me,' Éric says, keeping his voice low. The topic is humiliating enough without imagining anyone overhearing this. 'You weren't with us. You don't know exactly what happened. Okay, fine, so you told Teal to turn it up a notch. I get that. But I wasn't expecting him to do what he did. I didn't even know he had it in him. I don't think I'm making it up when I tell you that there was a lot fucking more than a game happening between us.'

Gabe doesn't want to tell Éric about Teal, but he has to.

'Teal spent the day in our bed. And not like what you're probably thinking. He just wanted us to hold him. I knew something was off but I never fucking imagined it was what you've just told me.' He runs his hands through his hair. 'Teal isn't like us. He's different.'

Éric walks backward, suddenly needing to put some space between them. Now he knows Teal is upset too. It's like he's at the top of a thrill ride, and he isn't prepared for the drop: but it's coming.

Oh yeah, it's coming.

'I know he is. I know, okay?' A low growl of pure frustration rumbles in his throat. 'Are you not hearing what I'm trying to say? I probably fucking ruined him, because I took things too far.'

'You need to talk to him, Éric. The rest of his story isn't mine to tell. But I will say this. Moth and I would walk into the sun for Teal. To know that he's suffering like this is fucking destroying me.' Gabe's voice breaks. 'And I hate that you're suffering too. We always hunt like we did last night, with Teal as bait, we always have. It works for us and I didn't think when I dragged you into that. I was very wrong. I don't expect you ever to forgive me, but I will do everything I can to mend what I ripped apart.'

Éric studies Gabe... their newly-forged kinship is ebbing at his feet, and it terrifies him. They worked hard for this. And Éric is still convinced he's the one to blame... nothing Gabe just said erases his misery. Or his guilt.

'I just don't want you to hate me, Gabe,' he whispers. 'I don't think I could stand it.'

'Hate you?' Gabe tries to pull his shattered thoughts together.

He half-expected Éric to come at him all guns blaring and he would have taken that gladly. But this, this tears him apart even more.

'How could I hate you, Éric?'

He wants to close the gap between them but Éric has purposefully removed himself and Gabe cannot cross that line.

There's a tightness in his throat, as though all of this is throttling him: and he lets a strangled gasp leave his lips.

Éric inhales that gasp, and releases it with a revelation of his own.

'Because at some point I wasn't acting anymore. And I have no fucking clue how to process all this, Gabe. I mean... what'll happen when V finds out? Because you know he will.' Éric hugs himself.

Why is this room so fucking cold all of a sudden? He strides over to the fireplace and violently hurls logs into the grate, setting them aflame.

This fucking sucks.

He shuts the television off and collapses back down on the sofa. He lights a cigarette, staring into the hearth. V explicitly said he didn't want him smoking in front of the boys but he's beyond caring at this point. He ejects the smoke from his first drag along with a massive sigh.

Part of Gabe wants to exit the room and go to Moth, to comfort Teal, but he can't leave Éric like this. But maybe Éric just wants him to fuck off out of here.

He goes across to the sofa and sinks down. His eyes start to water from the cigarette smoke and he swipes at them angrily.

'V will understand,' he says softly. He prays that's true. 'And before you come at me with your "why the hell would he?" I'll tell you. V will understand because he's a master vampire and he loves you. V will understand because who couldn't be in that situation and not feel something for Teal? He's fucking beautiful. Don't sit here and let yourself get eaten up with guilt, Éric, don't let yourself drown in that despair, go to V and tell him why you're hurting. And if you need me to tell him my part in it, call me, and I'll be there. If V wants to be angry he can be angry at me.'

Éric stubs the cigarette out in a crystal ashtray, focussing his attention on the dying flame and the culminating ashes.

But he still doesn't have an explanation.

He doesn't even know what's going on, except that he feels extremely, *extremely* fucked up.

'Gabe...' he whispers, turning his trembling chin toward him, 'I just hope everything you're saying is true. I want to believe you, I promise. But there's something else I can't get past. I'm older than Teal... I should have been able to control myself.' His chin falls to his chest.

The understanding hits Gabe between the eyes. Éric is flaying himself because he's worried that he's taken advantage of Teal's youth, his innocence.

'Éric,' he says softly. He waits until Éric meets his gaze. 'Teal is the eldest of us. He was vampire five years before me. He's been vampire for twelve years.'

Éric's eyes widen. There've been more than a few occasions during this visit that have set his mind stuttering, but this one... he does the math. That puts him and Teal at roughly the same human age — but Teal has many more vampire years on him.

The *choice*.

Maybe Teal didn't have a choice either.

But they're all here now, regardless of the circumstances.

His mind swirls, and again he's reminded of V asking him if he was happy with his age.

At the time that question hadn't meant much to him, because who *wouldn't* want to be twenty four forever? But the reality of this settles on his skin like mist. A little bit of Éric's light returns, but he can't smile.

Not tonight.

He's still got so much work to do, so many words to find.

Not just for V and Teal, but for himself.

'This helps. I can't even tell you how much. And I guess this means that maybe Moth won't kill me... at least not for this?' At last Éric laughs, a tentative laugh that takes some of the chill out of the room.

Gabe lets a grin touch his lips. Relief washes over him. Okay, perhaps he still has bridges to build, but if Éric will talk to V maybe that will take away the guilt burdening Éric's shoulders.

The whole vampire age thing fucks with his head too.

'I like you, Éric,' he says. 'I *really* like you. And I know Teal and Moth feel the same, even if Moth would never admit it in a hundred years. We all got off on a shaky start.' He grimaces, then laughs. 'A fucking minefield of a shaky start, and I think it says a lot about all of us that we're not rocking in a corner by now.'

'Oh my god, that's a fucking understatement if I've ever heard one! And I really, really like you, too, Gabe.'

Éric stands and holds out a hand to lift Gabe up. He's been waiting for a moment like this and it's weird that this is the one, but whatever — he's gonna do it anyway.

He pulls Gabe to his chest and sways him in a hug.

Gabe grins as Éric's arms enfold him. This feels *right*. This feels like they've turned over a new page in understanding each other.

He buries the worry about Teal and lives in the moment.

35 / NIGHT 4:

THE DOULEUR EXQUISE OF THE VAMPIRE
{ EXQUISITE PAIN }

With every step Éric takes away from the game lair — each one bringing him closer to having to come clean on this with V — the confidence he had gained from his conversation with Gabe flakes away. He had left Gabe at the second-floor landing.

'Gabe... thanks for talking me down off the cliff. See you later, okay?'

Even as the words fell from his lips, he knew he was still teetering on the edge. And now he's walking with leaden feet down the opposite corridor.

By the time he reaches the doors to their bedchamber V's potent energy begins to pulse in his chest like an electrical current, and the last bit of his nerve all but evaporates.

He knows V will continue to not pressure him.

That's how they've always been with each other.

They are patient... they wait for the other to talk.

If Éric spills, it will be his choice.

But he can't keep this in a moment longer — it won't get any easier.

He opens the doors, and V isn't in the room. The bed is stripped: a fresh set of sheets awaits, folded on the naked mattress.

Éric notices the wax stain out of the corner of his eye and rushes to it.

He drops to his knees and pries it up from the rug with his fingernails.

It isn't as bad as he imagined: it comes off in almost one solid piece.

Whew.

He sticks his head through the door to the bath: V isn't there, either, but the room is still humid, like a sauna, and V's scent hangs on the steam. He sniffs it and smiles.

Éric wheels around and finds himself face to face with a half-naked vampire, a towel knotted loosely around his waist.

V inclines his head. 'There you are, *bien-aimé.*'

Éric throws himself into V's arms.

'I'm sorry about last night.' He leans back, searching V's face, not sure what he's apologising for. *Everything?*

'I, on the other hand, am not,' V says, a devilish smile curling his lips. He ducks into the bathroom and re-emerges draped in a banyan.

'I liked your other outfit much better,' Éric says.

Vauquelin is delighted to hear the return of his beloved's humour — his mood has shifted somewhat closer to his normal exuberant state, though shadows remain behind his eyes. Still, he does not ask.

Éric wishes the bed was made, that he could curl up under the blankets next to V and just let it all out... but it would take too long to put clean sheets on the massive mattress and what he has to say is nipping at his tongue.

He takes V's hand and leads him to the anteroom, a room with no windows, which is mostly their closet but large enough to hold a daybed. And this he sinks onto with V, falling back into the silky down pillows.

'V...' Éric swallows hard, doubting whether he can actually go through with this.

Just stop fucking around and tell him. Okay, okay, okay. Whew.

'I got in a tough spot last night and I didn't handle it very well.'

Éric exhales, turning away from V's panicked expression.

'I, uh... I kind of had a very sexual moment with Teal.'

The run-together words burst from his throat before he even has a chance to think about it. He braces himself, gnawing his fingertips.

He can't lie to V — if he tries, V will know.

Of *course* he'll know.

He waits for V to rain wrath upon him, and he deserves it. After all the grief he had given V about his past, demanding fidelity. Now look! He bends at the waist on the edge of the bed, thinking he might hurl across the floor.

But V is just sitting there watching him with that impenetrable gaze, the one Éric still can't always decipher. V is so calm that it frightens Éric to his core. He sucks in his breath.

'Did you, now?' Vauquelin finally asks, lacing his hands behind his neck. 'Why did you allow this?'

Still, V's expression eludes Éric. He swallows repeatedly to keep the nausea at bay.

'Last night we were using Teal as bait, and I was supposed to act like I was coming onto him. It was just part of the game, but then... something else kind of happened.'

'I see... it just *kind of* happened.'

A sudden camera-flash blinds Éric for a minute.

Teal's cheek against his: the crush of their hip bones, the electricity. All the confusion comes rushing back and a bead of blood sweat trickles down his temple. He whisks it away and drops his gaze to the floor. If a portal could open up and take him straight to hell, Éric would jump in without question.

He's a fucking sinner!

'Well,' he pants, 'not exactly. We were supposed to just *pretend* like I was seducing Teal, and somehow it... didn't feel like we were pretending anymore.' He bites his lip.

Oof. Did it ever not feel like pretending, he thinks, closing his eyes.

Vauquelin regards Éric coolly.

It is all he can do to remain serious, to make Éric believe he is angry, because he knows Éric expects him to be.

Last night was the evidence.

But he is not angry — he is bewildered.

Teal?

He must buy some time to process this.

'Go and put the sheets on the bed, *bien-aimé.*'

Éric does not hesitate and Vauquelin has yet to see him move so swiftly.

When the jib door closes, Vauquelin twists the crown of his hair into a knot. He pulls it back until it stings his scalp. He had half-expected *some* sort of sexually-charged conflict with four young, male vampires running safe and free in the house. He and Clove had not discussed it prior to the boys' arrival — Vauquelin had seen no need. He just had not anticipated this *particular* scenario to be the cause of Éric's distress when they returned last night.

Éric has been vampire for only five years. The boys may look like teenagers, but they are far more experienced than he. Their visit is a vital lesson in many ways.

Vauquelin lies back on the narrow bed, resting his head on his elbow.

Dread takes his heart into its clutches. What had he done, agreeing to let Éric out into the wild? He must face this head-on. He opens the jib door slowly to find Éric in their freshly-made bed with the duvet over his head.

'Where were Moth and Gabriel while you two were... occupied?' Vauquelin demands.

Éric drops the blanket and thrusts his chin out with an exasperated sigh.

'I wasn't exactly paying attention, V, but they were scoping out the scene. Moth found the abandoned house.'

Vauquelin's worst fear manifests: that he had taken Éric too young.

The deafening vortex of the hundreds of years between them rings in his ears... it renders him weak and he braces himself on the edge of the bed.

'Have you tired of me so quickly then, my love?' Vauquelin asks.

Éric gasps. 'Oh my god, V, no! It wasn't like that. I swear it.'

Vauquelin pulls Éric's face to his and kisses him deeply.

'But did you enjoy it, being so close to Teal?' Vauquelin whispers.

Éric is so freaked out he pulls away, breathless.

Enjoy? Éric cocks an eyebrow. That word is such a poor choice that it erases his mind for a second. Sometimes the way V says things is confusing and ancient and very French, and Éric has to pause and reinterpret.

But were you flung into a cauterising pool of hellish self-torture? Yeah, that's way more accurate.

'You're scaring the shit out of me right now,' Éric murmurs. 'I don't even know what to say.'

'Just answer the question. Honestly.'

Éric's heart quickens. He's pretty sure V is about to end him.

At last he breathes out, 'I don't think *enjoy* is the right way to say it. It changed something in me, okay? I've never done anything like that before... and with another vampire, obviously not.'

'I must know... just how far did this go, Éric?'

V's meaning writhes into Éric... he vaults out of bed and begins pacing.

'OH NO! No, no, no, no no. V, I love you! I would never... but Teal...' He returns to the bedside and drags a hand through his hair, a desperately puzzled expression ravaging his face.

'Hush. I am not mad.'

'Well, you have a fine fucking way of showing it!' Éric crawls across Vauquelin's hips and clamours back under the duvet, folding his arms in a huff. 'I'm SO FUCKING CONFUSED right now.'

'Have you talked to Teal since?'

'No. Only Gabe. But I'd like to talk with Teal... if he'll even speak to me, that is.'

'Has this experience altered your love for me?' Vauquelin whispers.

He cannot bear to look at Éric now, and turns his face to the wall.

V's despair writhes into Éric's veins and he crumples onto his lover's — his *maker's* — chest.

'Absolutely not! You're my everything!'

'Éric... you must realise I anticipated something like this happening. I adore each and every one of the vampires who sleep under our roof. Do you think I would invite anyone I did not trust and respect to be here with us, in our sacred space?'

'No. I know you wouldn't.'

'I would never. They are like family, Éric, perhaps the only family we will ever have. Events have passed that have bonded us all for eternity. This is a lesson, *bien-aimé*. When you felt betrayed by my past relationships, I told you jealousy is unbecoming in a vampire. You remember this, no?'

'Of course I do.'

Vauquelin swallows hard.

Jealousy. *La jalousie.*

He swats that green fairy away.

Seldom has it touched him throughout his long existence: he had steeled himself against its touch, had ceased to doubt he would encounter it again — but here it is, pummeling his heart with its punishing wings.

'It is true, but only within reason. If this had occurred with a stranger it would have crushed me, and I would have destroyed whoever dared to lay hands upon you. I will always know if you are lying to me, and you will know the same from me. Our shared blood will always deliver the truth. I hope I am being quite clear.'

Éric's Adam's apple bobs in his throat.

'I absolutely understand that. V, no one else has ever turned my eye. But something enormous happened between me and him last night... I don't know if I can explain it.'

Vauquelin is aware his beloved has experienced true magic — he can see it etched beneath the shadows on Éric's face. He is not happy to witness it, to see Éric embrace the *douleur exquise*† of the vampire.

'There is no need for explanation, my love. I hope this reminds you that you still have much to learn. They are all extraordinary, yet Teal carries a beauty of his own. Quite unique, different from the others. I am not surprised that you felt this powerful draw to him. And now, perhaps, you understand that though you and I may be devoted to one another, we are not bulletproof when it comes to exceptional beauty of flesh and mind.'

Revelation brightens Éric's face.

Vauquelin continues. 'The night I spent with the four of them in England, at their home in Gehenna… it altered my existence. I desperately wanted what they had. It was the only event that could have prepared me for you. So no, I would never begrudge you loving them. I want you to love them as much as I do.'

'Did you know they're all older than they look?' As soon as the words leave his mouth, Éric scrunches his face.

What a stupid fucking question!

And now V is looking at him funny.

Fucking great.

'I knew. Look at me,' Vauquelin says, stretching his arms wide. 'For our entire existence, Éric, this will never change. In fifty years, a thousand… however long we are granted to walk the earth under Death's shadow, we will be the same. And so will they.'

It's yet another reason, Éric realises, that he still has so much to navigate in the labyrinthine life of the vampire. He's mystified, spirited away by V's bombshells.

'But why couldn't you just tell me all this before they came here?'

'Some things cannot be so easily explained, my love, only experienced

---

†- EXQUISITE PAIN, THE PAIN OF MISSING SOMEONE

for oneself. Only then can you believe.'

Éric gazes into the fireplace.

'V... I thought this would be the end of us. I thought you would never want me again. Because I did the very thing I asked you not to do.'

'The only thing I will ever ask is that you never take your love from me and give it to another. That would devastate me. But did this occur? Must we separate now?' Vauquelin's voice breaks and he clutches the small of Éric's back. He lost Éric once before. He cannot bear it again.

'Oh, V, no.' Éric draws against him. 'God, I love you so much. It consumes me. I thought I broke everything, but I could never lie to you.' He bursts into tears, heaving great sobs against Vauquelin's chest.

'My love, my love...' Vauquelin draws Éric's chin up so that their eyes meet. 'The boys' presence is my gift to you. I could not bear to share you with someone I did not love and trust. I trust them all with my soul, and yours. Yet had I known your heart was on the line...'

He cannot say the remainder of his words. Without seeking permission, Vauquelin plunges his fangs into Éric's neck. He withdraws after a moment, whispering, his voice heavy with his beloved's blood.

'You are mine, and I am yours. No one must ever change that. I would not surrender you so easily.'

Vauquelin sighs. His heart hurts for his beloved — for though Éric has chased *le sang*† in nightclubs like a champion, he has never encountered a Teal: and there will never be another like him.

He cradles Éric's head and kisses his brow.

'I cannot fault you, *mon cher*.‡ But I have sheltered you too much. I can see this now. Think back on the many nights we have play-acted ourselves, when we seduced humans into our house. The vampire will do what he must to secure the blood. These acts will not always make one proud.'

---
†- THE BLOOD
‡- MY DARLING

They lie in silence for a while, Éric curled against V, their bodies curved into a question mark.

It is always Éric who breaks their silences, and this time it is a whisper.

'After everything you said, I have to ask. Were you with anyone while you were away?' Right now all he wants is for V to have sinned too, to somehow even things out.

Vauquelin draws his mind closed tightly.

Éric has heard the key events of his rambling history: but after Vauquelin's return from his final time-slip, he omitted a crucial fact. He had encountered a former lover... Clément, who very nearly derailed his second existence. There has never been an appropriate time to discuss it, though Vauquelin was faithful. He had refused to even utter Éric's name in Clément's presence.

His desire to return to the present — and Éric — dictated his every move. Now, the mere thought of it makes him quiver, for he has always promised Éric the truth and this particular juncture is not the time.

Tonight, he will not risk adding another layer to Éric's tormented emotions.

'No, *bien-aimé*. Since you came into my life I want only you. No one else.'

Éric sighs. Even more ammunition to beat himself up with for his lack of self-control.

What if V had said yes? The thought makes his stomach turn, and he rolls over to face the wall. He shouldn't have asked. He's heard enough details about V's past lovers — more than enough to be careful what he wishes for.

'I just can't shake this feeling that I crossed a line with Teal. Gabe said he was in distress last night. If Teal's used to acting like this when they hunt, then I'm responsible for upsetting him!'

Vauquelin promptly spoons him again. 'Éric... only Teal can explain his thoughts. But you, more so than others, will understand that no being owes another an explanation about their life and how they live it.'

There is much more he could say, but he will not.

'Yes,' Éric murmurs. 'I do know that, all too well.'

This is one of the reasons Vauquelin had agonised over turning Éric. When they met, the human Éric had already hidden himself away: he was closeted, never free to show the purest version of himself. Now he is even more inextricably obscured — and by much darker shadows — but he is beginning to discover the myriad sublimities of the vampire.

Vauquelin cannot shield Éric from the thorns of the underworld, no matter how much he desires to keep him safe.

Nor can he tell his beloved to keep his heart closed: for then he would no longer be Éric, his precious one who was temporarily blinded by the haunting light that could only come from Teal.

'By virtue of all I have said, you must promise me you will go to them should you ever need help again. I admire your resilience while I was away, Éric, but by now you must know they are your other home.'

The subtext of V's words registers and turns Éric's veins to ice: all he can take away is there might come a time when V will leave him again. He hopes V's right about them.

'I promise. And I'd help them if they ever needed me, too. But they won't... especially not now, because I fucked everything up.'

Meanwhile, their connection is so fractured that they cannot see they want the same: they only desire comfort from one another, yet their language to reach for it has been muted.

Vauquelin wants nothing more than to join with Éric, to merge their bodies. The primal way he can have faith in their union: the lone way he could once place his trust that Éric could not be taken from his grasp. For when one physically tethers to another's soul... that, he knows, is inextricable.

He senses Éric slipping from his arms, and he cannot contain his terror.

So he dons his cloak of aristocracy, of propriety: his voice grows distant, cold.

'We must dress. We cannot keep the others waiting.'

All their words hover unspoken.

The longer they are stifled the wider the cavern grows.

Vauquelin turns his head in fear.

36 / NIGHT 4:

HE'S A DIFFERENT KIND OF VAMPIRE

Teal wakes to find Moth propped up on one elbow, bicoloured eyes softened with devotion.

'Hey,' Moth says. He leans across and plants a soft kiss on Teal's brow. 'Who do I have to kill for making you feel like this?'

There's a fifty-fifty chance that Moth isn't joking and a surge of love flows through Teal's veins. He stretches his limbs, an odd sense of bewilderment throbbing in his gut.

Why do I feel like I was run over by a truck?

'What happened last night, Teal?'

He turns to meet Moth's gaze, and there's such concern written in his brother's eyes that Teal almost wants to look away. But he doesn't — because this is Moth.

'There was a moment... with Éric.' Teal pauses and fights for the right words. 'When I felt like he wasn't acting.' He grabs Moth's hands and holds them to his chest before Moth goes into freefall. 'He didn't mean it, Moth, it just happened... so I don't want you thinking you need to rage at him. Promise me you won't rage at him?' He squeezes Moth's fingers.

Moth rolls his eyes and a sound of intense frustration leaves his lips. But he would promise Teal anything, so he nods: even though all he wants to do is rip Éric's throat out.

'It just made me feel strange.' Teal lifts a hand and brushes Moth's hair out of his eyes. 'You know how I am, that I don't operate like you and Gabe. I love you both fiercely, but don't *want* you. Not like that.'

'You don't have to say anything. You know we love you. We love all of you.' Moth brings Teal's hand to his lips and kisses the palm. Seeing Teal struggle like this brings out every fucking ounce of his protective instinct.

Moth is caught in Teal's ocean gaze and he allows himself to drown.

But then a shadow emerges from the depths.

'There was a moment when I felt Éric open towards me, when I knew he wasn't playing. It scared me. But a very small part of me wanted to kiss him, just for a second, and then it was gone.'

They're both silent then as the enormity of the words sink in.

Éric's meltdown in the catacombs suddenly makes sense.

'That's a fucking mess,' Moth finally says.

It's all he can manage because his head is *fucking* reeling.

Teal blows a strand of hair from Moth's brow, and the sheer force of the love he has for his brother rises like a flaming phoenix and engulfs him. It's a different kind of love, just like he's a different kind of vampire.

He needs to speak to Éric, to make him see that it wasn't his fault.

But first Teal needs to think. *So much need.* But not in that way.

'I'm going to the library,' he says, rising from the bed. 'Alone.'

He gently adds the last part because Moth might follow him, and he has to have space to clear his thoughts. Before he talks to Éric about the one aspect of himself that he isn't sure he'll ever find the right words for.

The part he doesn't really understand.

37 / NIGHT 4:

I DIDN'T KNOW THE RULES... SO I MADE UP MY OWN

Vauquelin and Éric are halfway down the hall when V halts without warning, tilting his head as he lifts two long fingers to shush Éric.

The complex, sombre tones of a harpsichord weep into the silent corridor from behind the library doors... it is a sound which is embedded in Vauquelin's eternal soundtrack.

The music is Rameau, a piece which lives eternally in Vauquelin's heart, every note imprinted for eternity. The memory steals his breath, roots him to the floor. His arm flies out to grasp Éric's shoulder. His beloved is there: he is solid, corporeal.

Vauquelin is still traumatised by his time-slips: even though they are impossible now, any sudden appearance of a marker from his past sends him reeling, terrifies him that it is happening again. Nevertheless Éric is still by his side — they are both still here, it is the present: he *thinks*.

'Do you hear it?' Vauquelin asks.

He desperately needs Éric's confirmation.

'Yes... the library.' Éric is already freaked out about having to talk to Teal... V's edgy state certainly isn't helping matters. All of a sudden he's hyper-conscious of the fact that his hands are sweaty — he rubs them vigorously up and down his thighs.

A moment of silence at a cadence and the music begins again in earnest.

It has been an age since Vauquelin has heard the instrument come to life in this house... the last was well over a hundred years ago, when he fled back to France with his tail between his legs. Only then it had been Olivier delivering the notes — and the harpsichord was in the master's bedchamber.

They pause outside the doors and Vauquelin leans against them a moment, lost in the refrain. All at once it dawns — the music can only be coming from one source: Teal.

'I think you will know who is at the keyboard now, Éric.'

Éric gulps. Is he ready to face Teal?

He turns to V to get some support but he's already at the bottom of the stairs, and he looks up to Éric with a tender smile. V touches his fingers to his lips, and then he is gone.

Éric stands outside the doors, worrying the bridge of his nose as he listens. A heavy sigh. He lets the notes wind their way into his blood, and imagines that every single pluck is there to empower him. Somehow he finds a shred of strength to lift his fist, and he holds it there a moment before knocking.

The notes scatter away like dead leaves into the air.

Teal waits. He knows it is Éric behind the door, and sitting at this antique keyboard — with the strains of the eighteenth century music still vibrating in his ears — he suddenly wants to begin playing once more. He has no idea how he even knew how to place his fingers on these keys, to coax the song to life again. He just sat down and began, and he doesn't question the how.

Teal keeps his eyes firmly fixed on the door. He doesn't blink as Éric enters and closes it behind him. The space between them seems like a bottomless void and the words they need to say are hanging over the precipice.

He bows his head, strokes his fingers across the ivory keys, depresses them until a sombre chord fills the air.

Then he lifts his gaze to meet Éric's.

Last night Teal had been wearing sunglasses.

Tonight he isn't, and Éric has to look away: the light swimming in Teal's eyes drowns every justification he had been rolling around in his mind as he prepared for — dreaded — seeing Teal again.

He isn't sure he can do this.

He wishes no one had ever learned about what happened with Teal, that he had hidden it away like a postcard and could bring it out from time to time, whenever he needed it — to keep it for himself alone.

Now all the others know and they can't take it back.

But he's positive Teal doesn't feel the same... why would he?

Teal's made out of stardust and he isn't.

Éric has to say something, but he can only whisper it.

'Teal... can you ever forgive me?'

'Forgive.' Teal murmurs the word as though he isn't sure what it means. It worms its way into his heart. 'You didn't do anything wrong.'

His voice breaks and he curls his fingers into his palms.

Can I do this?

Can I lessen Éric's guilt without gutting myself wide open?

He has to. He stands and pushes the bench away, walks towards Éric even though each step is like walking towards Madame Guillotine herself. He stops about four feet away and holds out his hand.

Éric looks at Teal, brings his fingers to his lips like a prayer.

Why did it feel so wrong, then? he wonders.

He whirls and returns to the doors, taking long strides with his eyes squeezed shut. He's lightheaded... he's afraid he might faint.

He pauses for a moment with his hands on the knobs, quaffing air into his lungs before flinging the doors open and sticking his head out into the hallway: he looks left and right, peers down the staircase. There are plenty of minds under this roof that could hear everything they say, but if someone had been purposefully listening outside, Éric knows that no words could come from their mouths.

Luck's on their side: no one's around.

He eases the doors closed again with a quiet snap and leans his forehead against them.

I can't do this... I have to do this.

He returns to Teal, but this time he's the one who reaches for Teal's hand: even though his own is trembling.

He walks them over to a chaise and they sit.

'Yes, Teal. I did. I...' The words are already dying in his throat and he tilts his chin to the ceiling. 'I didn't know the rules. So I made up my own.'

Teal's tongue feels glued to the roof of his mouth. He swallows. There are no rules for the situation they've found themselves in.

'I know what you felt,' he says softly, pressing his lips together. 'It was a shock.' Every emotion in his body is screaming for him to stop, because he's not sure if what he is about to say will make any sense — or will make everything worse.

'It was a shock because I'm different. And I don't feel things like you do.' Tears well in his eyes. 'But just for a moment I did.'

Teal's tears unravel Éric and his breath quickens.

Oh god, oh god... he rocks himself, clasping his elbows.

A realisation washes over Éric and he can't process the irrational reaction that's creeping into his brain now: the way Teal moved last night, that sound in his throat... maybe it didn't mean anything.

Was it all just part of the game?

Éric isn't sure whether he should be relieved or crushed.

But regardless, Teal's explanation breaks his heart a little.

If only I had known, he thinks. *It would have changed everything.*

But then the irrational thought morphs into something else.

'Teal. You probably think that I knew what I was doing, that maybe

I have everything figured out for myself… but I promise you, I don't.'

He stands and walks over to the window, leaning the heel of his hand against it. He can see himself in the glass slightly, but it's filmy because the window is old and wrinkled.

He looks distorted and fucked up, which is totally accurate.

Below are the gardens and Éric wishes they were down there instead, under the night sky like they were last night… maybe things would seem less suffocating and more in focus. Because right now, with Teal only feet away from him and surrounded by these gilded fucking walls, he feels like he's gonna choke.

He sinks onto the window seat and murmurs, 'If you say you think I do things like that all the time, it will absolutely wreck me.'

All he wants right now is for Teal to know how magic it was for him. That it could never have happened with anyone else. But how could he ever say that?

Teal watches the internal struggle battling inside Éric. He knows it all too well, this maelstrom of utter bewilderment, of feeling like the world is toppling you into oblivion. They're much closer in nature than either would like to admit.

'I would never think that about you, Éric. The love you have for Vauquelin is rock solid. Everyone under this roof can feel it.'

He gestures around him and finds a small smile to paste onto his lips. The irony of this happening in the library, his most sacred space, almost overwhelms him.

'And I want you to know that no one thinks badly of you for what happened last night. It's just that…' He pauses before delivering his confession. 'You made me feel something I haven't felt before.'

Teal's meaning sways in Éric's mind.

He folds his hands in his lap and knocks the back of his head against the window. The coldness of the glass seeps into his scalp and it's so, so good because his brain is on fire right now. Everything is just hanging on a string here, and one wrong sentence could make it all unravel.

'I've never been very confident. I know because of the way I act everyone thinks I must be, but if they could see inside my head they'd find a disaster. I don't let people in easily. I know what I like... I mean, what I'm trying to say is... that what happened last night wasn't because I like touching and I want that and everything that goes with it... sometimes, I don't think I can ever get enough. But I only want it with V. No one else. What scared me last night was that I *desperately* wanted someone else — I wanted you, Teal. I didn't have any control... I lost it all in a matter of seconds. I have no idea what to do with that.' He finally peels his gaze from the ceiling and allows himself to look at Teal.

A high-pitched buzzing resounds in Teal's ears.

It was true. He hadn't imagined it.

Éric had felt that same spark, but for Teal it had flared and then extinguished itself in the tears of its own making. He wonders what he would have done if it had kindled to a flame.

Even though vampires are immortal they don't get to make wishes... and maybe how he is is a blessing.

Because he could never have anything with Éric.

He would never tear him apart like that, make him choose, rip what he had with Vauquelin into bloody shreds. He moves to the window, stands by Éric and stares out into the garden.

He closes his eyes, lets his mind spin away, feels the grounding whisper from the trees.

Devlin.

He remembers the witch boy who had died for him, remembers the life Devlin could never have. And Teal smiles although inside his heart is breaking.

'I'm going to tell you something I've never told anyone before.' He takes a breath and it flutters in his chest. He turns to Éric. 'I've never made love to anyone or let them make love to me. I've never even pleasured myself. I'm not just a vampire with witch blood in his veins, I'm...'

He can't voice the last word so he just lets it die.

Time grinds to a halt and Éric's mind vanishes from the room.

He's back in elementary school, he's twelve years old. He's behind a tree, with a girl. She wants to kiss him. All the girls want to kiss him — he's the prettiest boy in the whole school. She does, and he feels nothing. Nothing at all.

He's supposed to want to kiss girls, so why does he just want it to be over so he can bolt? She wants to show him things, she wants him to show her things, too. She touches him, just a light touch, and then her fingertips sneak under his shorts.

He runs. He runs all the way home, even though he was supposed to go back to class. He hides in his room and he doesn't let anyone else touch him for years: not even his grandmother.

And then Eric is fourteen.

His best friend Austin is spending the night. They've been playing Halo 4 until they can barely keep their eyes open any longer. Eric crawls into his twin bed and his friend stretches out on a pallet on the floor. They can't sleep next to each other, obviously: that would be super gay!

But during the night, Eric gets up for a drink of water and Austin's fingers coil around his ankle.

'Come down here, Éric,' he whispers.

Éric obeys, sinks to his knees... and Austin's warm tongue slips into his mouth.

Then he knows.

He really, really wants to be touched.

Like that.

Before that night, Éric thought maybe he would never...

'Teal, I understand. I do. At least I think I do.'

This is so different than when he talked with Moth... then Éric had a certain bravado and he could identify himself with confidence, because he knew Moth clearly wasn't questioning anything. It seems like that conversation was weeks ago, but it was only the night before last... still, long before Éric had let himself come undone at the seams.

'Now I feel even worse, like I took advantage of you. But I don't wish...' He doesn't know if he should say this... but somehow the words tumble out of his mouth. 'I don't wish it hadn't happened, because it was one of the most beautiful things that I've ever experienced in my life, being close to you like that.'

Gabe and Moth have always had Teal's back, have always told him he's beautiful and worthy and fucking special — that last from Moth with his mismatched eyes blazing. But to hear it from someone else's lips, Teal can't quite believe it. It's like someone covered him in sunlight.

Their confessions hang between them and inch by inch, Teal feels it pulling them closer.

'Can I tell you what I do like, Éric?' he whispers.

'You can tell me anything. Anything you want. I'll keep everything that we say to each other safe. Always. Knowing what you *do* like is the hard part.' Despite his gloom, Éric's lopsided smile finds its way to his lips.

Teal reaches for Éric's hand. The fireflies in his eyes have taken flight at his own wonder. Their manic dance pulses like a racing heartbeat.

'I like to be held. Just held tight with no other agenda. It brings me comfort.'

He's not sure if this will scare Éric away after what he's just admitted, but it's important to Teal to be honest. Because they have laid everything on the line here. And nearly burned everything down around them.

Éric pinches his lips.

He wants to ask something… and if Teal says yes, he doesn't know whether he can even handle it. But he *wants* to… he wants so badly to restore the brilliance of that few minutes between them, even though it can never again be like it was last night.

He doesn't want Teal's beauty to be stolen away from him.

So he whispers, 'Could I?'

Teal knows that this is a pivotal moment after all the tender places they've exposed. But he needs Éric to understand this about him. And part of Teal really wants Éric's arms around him again. But this time they will know the limits. This time they will know the rules.

He steps close to Éric and gazes up at him, tentatively lays one palm against Éric's chest. The strong beat of a vampire heart soaks into his hand.

Static sears through Éric's nerves at Teal's touch. He still doesn't know if this is an invitation.

'Are you sure it's okay?' he whispers.

'It's more than okay.' Teal smiles. It's one of the most truthful admissions of his life.

Éric leads Teal to the chaise.

He takes a deep breath.

He would do anything to preserve this, anything at all to keep this grace that has shone on them. He lies back and pulls Teal down with him, wrapping him in his arms, chest to back.

He rests his cheek against Teal's... their heartbeats tap against each other through their shirts. He squeezes Teal closer, encircling their ankles, and breathes Teal in — his golden hair smells like angel wings should.

Now Éric is grateful they're here in the library, the one place in V's house which enchants Teal the most. There's a poetry to him and Teal together like this that could only have taken flight in this room.

He could lie like this with him for infinity.

Teal relaxes into Éric's embrace. It feels different to Moth's, to Gabe's, but it feels good. It feels *right*.

'Thank you,' he whispers, entwining his fingers in Éric's. Curls tickle the nape of his neck. 'Thank you for being here. For understanding. For gifting me that one perfect moment where I felt the connection that Moth and Gabe have.'

He closes his eyes and files the beauty of those ephemeral seconds away, knows he will cherish them forever.

'Thank you for giving me what no one else ever has.'

With his lips, Éric brushes Teal's hair away from his ears.

'Baby...' he whispers. 'I wish I could do this for you all the time. But I can't.'

Éric has never called anyone else baby... never. He always wished someone would call him that, but no one ever did. And the way it came right out of his mouth for Teal astonishes him — like it was patiently waiting just for this moment.

Saying it out loud makes his heart heavy.

So he hides it in his soul instead.

If only I could.

38 / NIGHT 4:

THIS IS WHAT MOTH LIVES FOR

Moth sits in the dark with only a single flickering torch to keep him company. After Teal had left to go to the library — alone, and that still stings — he had an overwhelming need to destroy something. Given that shredding a priceless oil painting or smashing one of Vauquelin's fucking pretentious vases would probably warrant him a place on the streets, he settles for the next best thing.

The corpses from last night lay before him. They stink and he wrinkles his nose. Moth is completely detached from his humanity and the way he's looking at what's left of the two hapless women is akin to someone looking at a joint of meat riddled with maggots.

He didn't ask if he could come down here. He reckons that Vauquelin would say he had the run of the house as long as he treats it with respect.

Respect.

He mulls that word over. It sounds a lot like restriction.

He's still shellshocked about Teal, about his confession that he wanted to kiss Éric. Anger swirls in his gut and he takes hold of a still, cold hand and snaps the wrist.

The sound of the bone breaking echoes around the catacombs.

Moth isn't handling Teal's words very well. He's always thought it would be just him and Gabe and Teal forever: and now, in the space of a few nights, Éric is suddenly the shining star. An image of Éric leaning against the wall, his face close to Teal, sears across his mind.

He kicks the nearest corpse with the toe of his boot, hears the satisfying crack of a rib bone. Then he picks up the limp wrist, twists hard and yanks. Flesh separates from flesh. Tendons hang like string. He hurls the cold, dead lump of what was once a hand into the corner and it thuds against the wall before hitting the floor.

What will I do if Teal says he wants to stay here with Éric?

The thought slices him open and a scream builds in his throat.

'That's never going to happen. You know that, right?'

Moth spins and meets Gabe's level gaze.

Of course Gabe knew where he was.

'Why not?' Moth asks, wiping his blood-smeared hand down his jeans. There's a look on Gabe's face that reminds Moth too much of Clove. He narrows his eyes.

'Because Éric is V's and nothing can tear those two apart. Because Teal is...' Gabe pauses and a shard of pain shadows his eyes. '... Teal. You know how he feels, how his body reacts. There might have been a second or two of attraction for both of them but that doesn't mean Teal and Éric are going to hook up. That would be — '

'Fucked up,' Moth interrupts.

Gabe simply nods.

'So when we go back upstairs you're going to be civil and —'

'I won't kill him. That's all I can promise.' Moth delivers this with a twisted grin and Gabe knows he's lost this particular argument.

'Shall we clean up?' Gabe motions to the corpses.

'I thought guests didn't clean up.' Moth says, looking at him through a fall of hair.

Gabe sucks his bottom lip into his mouth. 'I think we're past the guest stage, don't you?'

He doesn't have to list the major disasters they've all crawled through and somehow come out intact.

Moth shrugs. 'Yeah, I think you're right.' He looks up to the curved ceiling and blinks as a droplet of water hits his brow. He settles his weight on one hip. 'There are better things to do down here.'

'Absolutely not.' Gabe shakes his head. 'V would freak out.'

'You don't think he's fucked Éric down here amongst the bones?'

Gabe opens his mouth to argue. 'Point taken.'

'Talking about points.' Moth pops the button on his jeans. There's a slow smile on his face, the kind of smile Gabe knows is only after one thing.

He'd come down here to talk Moth out of his melancholy, had expected an argument or possibly a stony silence as Moth worked through his feelings. He definitely hadn't expected the kind of offer Moth is laying on the line.

Fuck. What is it about this house that makes everyone in it react like they do? Makes them ride on the devil's back of their heightened emotions?

'Open the pit hatch,' Gabe says. 'I won't fuck with leftovers on the table.'

It's a completely Moth thing to say and the surprise shows in a flash of those mismatched eyes.

'Nicely fucking played, Gabe.' Moth sweeps a parody of a bow.

Gabe bites the edge of his lip. This is a lead up to the main course: a sweet, little entrée they're playing with words and subtle gestures — and it's beginning to drive him wild.

Moth pulls the handle on the hatch and raises it. He shields his face as the pungency of the acid bubbles beneath him.

'Careful.' Gabe is there beside him, and together they drag the two corpses to the edge.

'We slide them in, okay? This stuff is lethal.'

Moth nods and they tip the corpses slightly, then feed them slowly into the acid. It devours the flesh instantly and they both have a moment of incredulous wonder at the perfection of this disposal method.

They lower the hatch into its resting place.

'Fucking Vauquelin.' Moth shakes his head.

Gabe arches a brow.

'Stop it.' Moth grabs a handful of Gabe's hair. 'Stop being like Clove. It's messing with my head.'

Gabe could easily twist out of Moth's grip but he doesn't want to. He kinda likes the sting against his scalp.

'I like you messing with other things.'

His hand falls to Moth's belt and he yanks it open.

After everything that has happened. After the hunt and the kill and the things that went wrong. After holding Teal as he struggled with a barrage of emotions. After talking to Éric and building new bridges.

After all this, Gabe needs a little fun.

He needs a good fuck.

Moth's firm fingers grasp his wrist. Moth leans close, brushes his lips against the shell of Gabe's ear.

'My turn tonight, Gabe.'

The growl in his throat adds another layer to the seduction.

Gabe could argue. He's in the mood to make Moth dance like he did the other night, yet the thought of surrendering is equally delicious. He groans softly and feels Moth's lips curl into a smile against his cheek.

'Take your clothes off for me.' Moth pulls away and walks to the wall.

He settles himself against a shelf, a stack of bones at his back.

He folds his arms.

Gabe closes his eyes and lets himself hover on the edge of submission. Most of the time he's the one who leads, the one who's expected to make the right decisions, the one who protects. But with Moth he can drop his guard, hand the reins across and let him take full control. It's a dizzying experience, intimate in its power — and right now Moth is making full use of the sexual attraction that sparks between them.

Gabe pulls his T-shirt over his head and throws it on the ground, feels the cool air emanating from the stone surrounding them caress his skin.

Moth gestures with his hand.

The rest, Gabe. Slowly.

Even in a mind-touch Gabe can hear the dark honey throbbing in Moth's voice.

Gabe unbuttons his jeans, kicks off his boots. He's not wearing socks or underwear. He was in too much of a hurry to get to Éric.

Was that only a couple of hours ago?

He sways from side to side and the jeans fall low on his hips, exposing a flat, pale stomach and a line of dark hair… Moth's gaze follows that line and now his own jeans are uncomfortably tight.

Moth reaches behind him and pulls a bone from the stack. It's a fibula bone, the top worn to a smooth dome. He taps it against his palm and his eyes darken.

A shaky exhale leaves Gabe's lips and his stomach clenches hard.

'All the way off,' Moth says as he walks across, each tread easy and measured, the slow tap of the bone against his palm like a calculated heartbeat.

Gabe tunes into its call as he lets his jeans puddle to the floor and steps out of them. Being naked in front of Moth when he's fully clothed is blowing his mind. His cock jerks, pre-cum glistening at its tip.

Moth is by his side now and his eyes are devouring Gabe inch by inch, appraising him as if he was a horse at a market.

Which he is. Because Moth is looking for a ride.

Gabe's legs start to tremble, but he can't move because Moth hasn't given him permission. He bites his lip hard, drives a fang through the soft tissue — and before he can taste it Moth's tongue is there lapping like a kitten birthed in hell.

The roughness of Moth's clothes against his bare skin, his lover's palpable need pressing through denim...

Please. Gabe mind-whispers his plea, although what he's pleading for is anyone's guess.

A tongue. A finger. A cock.

Moth pulls away and the expression on his face could make Gabe come just looking at it. The curl of his full lips with the tips of his fangs visible, the hooded lids over those bicoloured eyes, the mussed up hair he wants to wind his fingers in constantly.

Moth runs the tip of the bone down Gabe's chest and Gabe shudders, his eyes half-closed.

This. This is what I live for.

This time with Gabe where they push each other's buttons to the point where neither of them is sure which way is up, or where one flesh becomes another. He licks his lips, tastes Gabe's blood upon them and he smiles.

'On your knees,' he growls. The floor is dirty and littered with tiny fragments of bones. Another layer of pain to add to Gabe's pleasure.

'I said... on your knees.'

Gabe complies: a small cry leaves his lips as the fragments grind into his skin.

Moth unzips his jeans, his eyes never leaving Gabe's face.

He offers his cock.

'Just your mouth. Work me with your fucking mouth.'

And then Gabe's lips are upon him and Moth's cock slides into that sweet, slick cavern. He arches his back and thrusts his hips, and Gabe's throat takes him right to the hilt. The rhythm begins, the slow play of a tongue, the slip of hardened flesh into a willing mouth.

It's a dance they both know the steps to — but not without a hand to encourage. This is a new ballet. Gabe's lips move faster, wet sounds of passion gurgling in his throat. Moth could let himself come right here but he won't... he won't... he grits his teeth.

'Stop.'

The single word echoes around the catacombs.

A groan from Gabe as he lets Moth's cock slip free.

Moth moves behind Gabe. He pushes him onto all fours, kicks his legs further apart. Then runs the tip of the bone along the notches of Gabe's spine, circles the small of his back, taps it against the cleft in that perfect swell of flesh.

Gabe settles himself on his elbows and hangs his head. He knows what's is coming. They both know what's coming.

Moth discards his jeans, runs a hand along his own cock and it jerks. He squeezes the pre-cum into his palm and coats the tip of the bone, then spits against it. His fingers part Gabe's buttocks and his cock jerks again. He lowers his head, lets his saliva drip until it coats that place — that fucking flawless place — he leans in and lets his tongue lap and lap.

Gabe shudders again. His limbs are shaking and he's no longer sure where he ends and Moth begins. He pushes himself back, needing Moth inside him, *needing* to be filled.

And then a slow, hard pressure — he cries out.

Moth rests the tip of the bone against Gabe's puckered star, begins a slow, measured insertion. This is so fucking hot he knows he could explode right now and he has to fight to keep himself under control. The tip of the bone disappears and he lets it rest there, leaning over and grabbing a handful of Gabe's hair.

'How's it feel to be fucked with what's left of a corpse, Gabe?'

But Gabe is lost, flying on the wings of Moth's seduction: he can only gasp, sweat dripping from his face.

Moth releases his grip — reluctantly, Gabe's hair in his fist is one of his favourite things — returns to the bone, inserts it a few inches more.

If Gabe could spread himself any wider he would: his brow is on the filthy floor, his fingers curled into the dirt. There is so much wrong in what Moth is doing but Gabe is a willing participant.

He is fucking damned.

They are *both* fucking damned.

But he wants more. He *wants* it all.

The bone begins its retreat, but now Moth is turning up the dial because he's twisting it slowly as it withdraws... Gabe comes undone and the hill he's been climbing to oblivion suddenly peaks...

Moth yanks the bone away, sees the invitation Gabe is offering, a void waiting to be filled. He drives a fang through his lip, lets his blood pool in his mouth then spits it into that void, following it through with his cock. Gabe screams and it's the most beautiful sound Moth has ever heard. His hands drop to Gabe's hips and he thrusts slow and hard, their flesh slapping together.

This isn't one of their slow, easy, lovemaking sessions. This is lust and power play and need, all fighting to be dominant.

Moth's climax builds: the noises from Gabe's throat are flicking all his fucking buttons into maximum overdrive. His mind cartwheels into the only heaven he'll know as his rhythm intensifies, as Gabe pushes back against him so hard Moth knows he'll have bruises to show... for a little while.

The moment where they both link minds, their bodies sweat-slicked, their blood surging through immortal veins. One final thrust as Moth digs his fingers into Gabe's hips, his cry of release as Gabe trembles beneath him.

They stay like that for a few moments, letting the ecstasy of their coupling swarm over their flesh, letting their racing heartbeats slow, and then Moth takes Gabe in his arms and pulls him close. Those navy-blue eyes aren't quite focussed yet ... Moth winds his limbs around his lover and kisses his hair.

Gabe groans softly and raises his head, the fingers of one hand splayed on Moth's chest.

'Holy fucking shit, Moth.'

Moth's mouth falls open and Gabe grins.

'Éric taught me.'

'Too much?' Moth says, nodding to the discarded bone.

He's impressed by Gabe's profanity, but the fact it came from Éric needles him in a tender place.

'We're going straight to hell, Moth. You know that, right?' Gabe eases himself into a more comfortable position and winces. 'I think you broke me. But fuck, don't ever stop.'

Moth smiles into Gabe's hair as they lay in the glow of the flickering torch with the bones of the dead as their witnesses.

39 / NIGHT 4:
NO ONE EVER EVEN KNEW I LEFT

Éric closes the library doors behind him.

Teal has returned to the keyboard.

The resumed notes soothe Éric's spirits with a balm of peace.

He bumps his spine down the wall outside the doors and, head buried between his knees, listens to Teal play.

Before he met Vauquelin, Éric had never heard music like this. It wasn't a part of his world. The night of Éric's turning, V had played something from his past. It was Éric's first true taste of V's antiquity.

The music affected him on a cellular level.

It calmed him... it was almost as if he'd heard it before.

But how could that be?

How could he ever explain that, how familiar it was?

And here... on a very different sort of night... he can still feel Teal in his arms, and the ancient music emanating behind him from Teal's fingers is embracing him in a very different way.

The morning after their first night together, Éric woke to find V staring at him. His face was so serious, so grave... Éric won't ever forget it.

V had looked so desperate.

No one had ever looked at him that way before.

Now Éric understands how a desperation like that can be born.

Éric had realised, the very first time he saw himself disappear inside Vauquelin's body, that nothing would ever be the same for him again.

But he hadn't understood, not then, the bottomless, magnificent depths of what V was offering him.

Éric knows he's what some people would call hot. There was a time when he was pretty cocky about it. At least he used to feel like he was hot... now he can't even fucking see what he looks like anymore, except in pictures. He stands and starts to walk down the staircase, but with one foot on the first tread he turns back and looks at the library doors.

He sighs.

Somehow his legs get him downstairs, and Teal's music grows fainter with each step down. He doesn't look back again... he can't, or he'll come apart.

In the foyer, he shoves his hands in his back pockets. He looks down the long hallway between the staircases... at the end is his lair. He could go in there and totally just disappear, which sort of sounds appealing right now... but he knows it'll just leave him empty.

He turns his head to the right: Vauquelin and Clove are talking in the salon, their low voices muffled by the ancient wooden doors. He could go join them: they wouldn't mind... they might even be happy to see him. But the thought of going in there and listening to them, possibly having to answer questions — he just can't.

He has no fucking clue where Gabe and Moth have run off to, and he certainly isn't going to chase after them... not now.

The fact is, he doesn't want to see *anyone*.

So he pops in his ear buds. He grabs his phone and he starts other music — loud, pumping, fast, *new* — something that'll set his head straight. He grabs his skateboard and slips out the front door.

He hasn't done this in awhile.

Since V came back, Éric doesn't like being away from him.

But while V was gone, Éric did this all the time.

He kick-flips at the gate and keys in the code, and just like that, he's sailing across the sidewalks of the Rue Malaquais. V's street.

Their street.

He needs to just be himself.

No one could say anything to him right now that wouldn't piss him off, so the best thing to do is this. He squats on the board, he eyeballs the traffic signals... fate is on his side. He surfs right over a crosswalk and when he reaches the other side, he stands upright. He acknowledges the long lines of his body as he flies past ancient buildings, a song about Los Angeles in his ears as he careens past Parisian pedestrians.

He raises his arms to the sky, he feels even taller. He smiles, a big smile, and he doesn't even care if anyone sees his fangs. He tucks them over his bottom lip with pride. V is super fucking uptight about that, but there are so many fake fangs on the marketplace that no one bats an eye. It's like a *trend* now.

He skates across the Pont d'Iéna and ends up on the opposite side of the Seine, in front of the Trocadéro. It's ridiculously fucking crowded and noisy here, with all the tourists and street vendors selling tacky, LED souvenirs. They're blasting music and he can hear it even over his ear buds. He skips down the steps to river level and sits on the deck of his board, right on the banks. It's so much more peaceful here... he can finally hear himself think. Now it's only his music.

Across from him the Eiffel Tower is illuminated.

It'll begin to twinkle in a few more minutes

He doesn't take his eyes off it.

They live on the opposite side of the Seine from the Tower... they can't see it from the house. Éric moves his hips back and forth to the rhythm of the music as he sits on the board, resting his knees on his elbows.

Clove and the boys have been here for *three fucking nights*.

This is only the fourth. Éric's life has changed more in these four nights than he could ever have imagined.

Since he became vampire, he never forgets anything. His mind is an ever-growing repository of memories. But tonight, he wishes he could recall everything V said to him that morning he first woke up in V's temporary bed in the Hollywood Hills... because it was *fucking overwhelming*.

If Vauquelin had told him he turned into a fucking *fly* when the sun rose, he still would have said yes.

Éric once thought Vauquelin was the most beautiful man he'd ever seen. He doubted he would ever see anyone as beautiful... now there's an exception: Teal.

With Clove and the boys here, there's so much beauty under their roof that his senses can hardly fathom it. He thought it would just be an ordinary gathering, like when Olivier and Céline came to Évreux. But while he's thinking about it, that week had seriously fucked him up, too — because that was when he first learned Vauquelin might disappear.

And now Olivier is gone forever.

Éric sinks his head to his knees... it's so fucking heavy with all these thoughts pouring into his brain like concrete.

So many of the things V said to him before... he couldn't have possibly understood it all. And what V said to him earlier tonight really stands out: *some things you have to experience yourself.*

His mind is *blown*.

Fucking obliterated.

A flash from under his arms.

The shimmering lights on the Eiffel Tower.

They twinkle every hour on the hour after sundown — like clockwork.

He raises his chin, he thinks of Teal's eyes.

That's exactly why he came to this spot.

He watches the tower lights trip and sparkle.

And it's another one of those moments where he can't believe he fucking lives in Paris. He can't believe he's fucking vampire: he can't believe fucking Vauquelin exists, and gave him all this.

He can't fucking believe *Teal*.

He can't believe that he's gonna skate right back to the dreamworld he just vacated. He can't believe *anything* right now.

He rises when the tower stops flashing, returning to its normal illumination, and he knows that this is where he is meant to be: that all of the INSANE events of the past few nights are just part of being with Vauquelin.

This is simply how things are.

It's just that he had no idea, because he had been alone for so long after V left... and when he came back, it was just them.

They didn't want anyone else.

They didn't need anyone else.

Now he's skating like he's escaping a fire — he can't get back to the house fast enough: because everything and everyone he needs will be waiting right there.

He skids outside the gates and keys in the code, slipping back in before the gates fully extend.

He edges the front door open a few inches... the house is quiet.

No one ever even knew I left.

He lets his breath calm before he scratches on the doors to the salon.

V will know he's been out...

But it doesn't matter.

Not anymore.

40 / NIGHT 4:

THE TWO OF HEARTS

Clove opens the carriage house doors. He has come to thank Flynn for his help the previous night. A master vampire does not take such assistance for granted, especially when it concerns his boys and Vauquelin and Éric. He ascends the stairs and scratches on the door to Flynn's apartment.

'Come,' says a voice from inside.

Clove pushes the door open and finds Flynn, dressed in faded jeans and a dress shirt, the sleeves rolled up to his elbows, three buttons undone on the shirt front.

Clove arches a brow and Flynn laughs.

'It's not what you think. I don't have time for company here. Your boys keep me busy enough.'

Clove lets a small wry smile curl his lips.

'It was I who needed your help last night with disposal. Your swift aid was very much appreciated.'

Flynn shrugs, alters the leather strap on his watch.

'It's what I signed up for.'

'I recall that you did not sign anything. I asked for your assistance and you gave it. You continue to give it.'

Clove goes to Flynn and grasps his forearm in a gesture of unity.

'I will not forget this, Flynn Frenière, you have my word on that.'

A moment passes between them, a moment borne from respect and trust, both traits a Holy Grail for those who walk the night. Flynn motions to the low wooden table, where a deck of cards lies. He hikes his brow in a perfect imitation of Clove, and Clove laughs.

He is unsure what it is about this place that has teased out such things for himself, but for now he is content to roll with them. When they return to the grim walls of Gehenna, all may be different.

'I am afraid I must decline. Vauquelin asked me to meet him in the salon along with the boys. We are to have an evening all together.'

Flynn crosses to the table and picks up the cards, flicking them expertly in his fingers.

'I sensed how the last one of those went down.' He thumbs the cards again, fans them out and offers them to Clove. 'Choose.'

Of course Flynn felt the emotional turmoil in the house. It must pulse like a living thing, a magnet to immortal intelligence. Flynn will not pry, but he is ever vigilant.

Clove lets his finger hover over the cards and then touches the corner of one. A sharp sting of electricity shoots into his wrist and he grits his teeth.

This does not bode well.

Flynn takes the card and slowly turns it over.

It is the two of hearts.

Then he buries it in the pack as if they had both never seen it.

☦☦☦

And now Clove is walking towards the salon doors, his boots echoing on the marble floor. Vauquelin is not present, so he opens them and enters the room.

A fire has been lit and candles glow on the mantel. A bottle of red wine stands uncorked on a side table with two crystal goblets nearby.

A scene has been set.

Clove settles himself on a couch embroidered with golden crowns and waits for Vauquelin's arrival.

There is turmoil in his boys. He can feel it bubbling under his senses. Gabriel did not come to him when he woke, and it is this small detail that writhes inside Clove's gut. But it is not only Gabriel who concerns Clove. This time his concern is for the vampire with witch blood in his veins.

His concern is for Teal.

Something happened last night between Teal and Éric when they were out on the streets. It was evident from Éric's unnerving behaviour in the catacombs, his fall into despair. Evident in Teal's quiet confusion.

Clove wants to discuss this matter with Vauquelin before the boys arrive. He does not wish another powder keg to explode amongst them. This visit is supremely important to everyone under this roof: but none of them could have foreseen the emotional tatters each night has spawned.

He straightens his spine as Vauquelin's footsteps approach.

This house has centuries of history written into its rafters, its floors... Vauquelin absorbs Clove's energy as it radiates from the other side of the doors. He stretches his arms toward the ceiling and then folds them behind his head, building up strength for what he must say.

His thoughts swirl in an unfathomable ocean... infinite teardrops of emotion. He brings his hands to his throat: gently, so gently. A small amount of grace, of forgiveness for himself. Perhaps he deserves it... perhaps he does not.

When Vauquelin had left his beloved outside the library, he had walked swiftly to remove himself: these are Éric's waters to sail, not his. He had given every ounce of his self-confidence to Éric, and now he slumps against the corridor wall.

Dread swirls in his psyche... he can only hope that they will emerge from this incident unscathed.

And now he stands at the entrance to the salon, knowing that Clove will recognise his dismay — he has no doubt it is written across his face.

It is pointless to attempt to disguise it so he saunters in, tying his hair up into a knot as he enters.

'*Bonsoir*,† Clove.'

He pours a generous glass and sits opposite his fellow master.

Vauquelin's hand trembles as he sets the goblet on the table that separates them. His fingers do not calm until he manages to land a cigarette between his lips and light it.

He stretches his arm across the back of the sofa.

'Something tremendous has happened.'

He wonders if Clove already knows.

Clove presses his lips together. His instincts have never failed him and this is no exception. He straightens his spine and folds his hands on his lap.

'Tremendous, Vauquelin?' Clove studies his fellow master: he is seemingly at ease, despite the fact that every muscle in his body is tensed like a coiled spring. 'In what way?'

Tremendous is a word that encapsulates many meanings. He can neither apply it to the way Éric behaved last night in the catacombs, nor to his own disquiet over Teal.

He thinks back to the previous night, to when he left the catacombs with his boys... to Moth and Gabriel talking quietly amongst themselves about Éric and his odd behaviour. Teal had gone on ahead, but his shoulders were slumped, his energy levels depleted — when they should have been consummate with the fresh blood in his veins.

Vauquelin perches a thumb under his chin and rests his forefinger across his upper lip. 'Éric is in the library with Teal as we speak. How could I say it... there was a moment where their game of the hunt became quite serious.'

---

†- GOOD EVENING

Clove narrows his eyes.

'Was Éric in any danger?'

He had impressed upon Gabriel the importance of keeping Éric safe from any harm. He may have to unleash strong words if that was not the case.

'*Euh*... none that I am aware of. Except perhaps for his heart, which he wears perpetually on his sleeve. Do you understand?'

The English language throttles Vauquelin's tongue as it always does when he is in distress, and he drops a quivering hand to grip the carved wood of the sofa's armrest. He is unsure whether to continue, to spill it all, for he only knows Éric's account... but Clove's displeased expression makes the decision for him.

'Éric and Teal performed as bait for the humans. Their closeness sparked something between them. I will not presume to imagine Teal's thoughts... I only know Éric's. But my beloved is struggling... his emotions have been shipwrecked. This is why they are upstairs together as we speak.'

He splays his knees, exhaling and stubbing the cigarette out in an ashtray with unnecessary violence.

The ever-present nest of shadows inside Clove's gut begins to stir and a chilled finger of ice walks itself down his spine.

'Teal,' he says softly. 'Teal and Éric?'

Clove unfolds his hands. He is unused to the sensation of confusion but he cannot find another name for the perception settling upon his skin.

'Teal is not like other vampires in many ways. I am not talking of the witch blood in his veins or the fireflies in his eyes. He is different in the way he bonds.'

Clove understands it is an immensely difficult burden Teal carries, one that he keeps hidden: because he possibly does not understand it himself. He meets Vauquelin's ice blue eyes.

'Teal does not feel sexual attraction.'

A sharp pang erupts in Vauquelin's chest.

There is a distinct possibility that, upstairs, Éric is hearing this fact from Teal's lips. He allows himself a shred of relief.

Perhaps Teal is shutting Éric down and this cloud will pass quickly so they can all put this wretched turn of events behind them.

The solace is brief, however.

His instincts tell him this storm has only just begun.

'I need not remind you Éric is still close to his human years. He is quite naïve on certain matters of the heart. I wanted so badly to protect him last night... but it never once occurred to me that it was his heart which would need protecting. I have already spoken to him but I worry for them both, and...' Vauquelin walks to the fireplace, stares into the flames. A log falls and crackles, shooting splendorous cinders up the flue. '... myself as well. Perhaps I have allowed him to become too important to me.'

'Do not say that, Vauquelin. He is your heart, your soul... that is not mere importance. He is as necessary as the blood you drink to survive.'

Clove rises and goes to the table, lifts the goblet and takes it to Vauquelin. He presses it into Vauquelin's hand.

'I am not saying Teal does not feel love. He exudes a special kind of love, and for those who bask in its golden glow he is pure sunlight. The connection he has with Gabriel and Moth, I have never seen its like in all my immortal years. Any one who feels that love is supremely blessed.'

Vauquelin closes his eyes as Clove's explanation registers.

Éric had recognised that sunlight: he had gotten too close, and it had cauterised his marrow.

'Though I know Teal the least of the three, I can say without any doubt he is the purest soul I have ever encountered. Still I do not know precisely what occurred between them. I did not wish to pry... or perhaps I did not want to hear it. I told Éric I could not fault him for loving Teal, that I was honoured it was him. I confess I cannot anticipate what the results of their conversation will be.'

This is one instance where Clove wishes he could intrude on Teal's thoughts. But he will not, because that is an invasion of privacy and trust. Teal is under this roof... no harm can befall him, unless it is to his heart.

'We must listen to anything they need to tell us, Vauquelin. We must be there to pick up any shattered pieces.'

Clove lets the supportive weight of his hand rest on Vauquelin's shoulder. It trembles under his touch.

'Can you do that?'

'I shall summon all my strength for this... there is no other option. Let us hope I do not find myself amongst those pieces.'

Come to me. Now.

Clove reaches for Gabriel's mind, adds the final word to make his first-born aware that this is no time for dalliance.

He waits by Vauquelin's side, feels the waves of despair emanating from his fellow master. The affairs of the heart do not care if that heart is an immortal organ: rather, they sharpen their claws at this prized delicacy.

Clove is thankful his own is under lock and key.

Vauquelin follows his fellow master's gaze — those dark eyes focussed on the doors, that strong jaw rigid as a plank. He can only assume that Gabriel has been summoned. Uncustomary heat winds its way through his veins: a disquieting premonition that he is edging closer to a truth he may not wish to learn.

He wants to crumble to the floor.

He wants to scream.

Once, he was confident in Éric's love for him. Now it is unravelling beneath his fingers, and Éric is not here to stop it.

He wants to run upstairs, steal his beloved back into his arms where he belongs. Instead, he extends his spine, spreads his ankles apart, and laces his hands behind his back. He chokes back the tears that want to explode forth. This is not a time for fragility — he must invoke all his ancient authority.

A deep breath and his face turns grim.

The pale blue of his eyes grows as dark as the midnight sky.

☨☨☨

Clove's whisper sears against Gabe's mind as he nestles into Moth's chest. They are still on the catacombs floor, limbs entwined, both lost in the glow of a post-fuck haze. He extracts himself, reaches for his discarded clothes.

'What the hell?'

Moth is up on his feet and pulling on his jeans before his brain has fully registered Gabe's urgency.

'Clove needs me,' Gabe says. 'Now. It's not up for discussion.'

It's been a long time since his maker demanded anything of him, and this realisation opens a fist of dread in Gabe's gut.

He grabs Moth's hand and drags him up the catacombs stairs, not stopping to extinguish the torch or to lock the door.

'Is it Teal?' Moth voices the sour layer of fear lacing Gabe's throat.

They race through the larder and out into a hallway, feet skidding on the marble tile. A flashback of them both sprinting into the repellent bowels of Gehenna — desperate to reach the tower door, desperate to reach Teal before he was plucked away from them forever — spins through his mind.

Gabe scans for Teal and for a moment he can't find him: but then his brother's quiet presence makes itself known.

He's in the library.

It's okay, Gabe tells himself. *That's his favourite place.*

But somehow he knows that it's not okay.

Had Teal talked to Éric?

'Fuck, fuck, fuck.' Gabe grits his teeth as they slide to a halt outside the salon doors. This has all the hallmarks of a situation that wants to burn him alive.

Moth's eyes are wide, his racing breath evident in the rise and fall of his chest.

It'll be blatantly obvious to anyone behind these doors what they've just done. They radiate with the afterglow of their lovemaking, although tonight it was all about fucking — all about Moth surrendering to his base desires, all about Gabe stepping from the pedestal of leadership and the demands of his pure-bred blood.

It was freedom... but what price would they have to pay?

☦☦☦

'Enter.'

It's Clove's voice from within giving them permission, not V's: although Gabe can feel V, too. Can feel his darkness.

He brings Moth's hand to his lips. Their eyes meet.

'I love you,' he whispers, and then he pushes open the doors to the salon.

Clove and V are standing by the fireplace, two dark figures with roaring flames at their backs.

Candles flicker on the mantel in a ghostly erratic dance.

Moth's fingers wind tighter into Gabe's. The master vampires before them look like they're planted at the gates of hell.

Gabe takes a deep breath and, with one sidelong glance to Moth, he releases their hands and strides across to Clove. He bows his head in a gesture of respect, first to V, as their host, and then to Clove as his maker.

He can feel Moth's agitation as it builds: it winds against his own, doubles its intensity until it's a vortex of chaos in his veins.

'Where's Teal?' Moth blurts out. 'Where the fuck is Teal? And where the fuck is Éric?'

At the sound of that name Vauquelin's shoulders stiffen. He sniffs the air, scenting the arrival of his beloved as an animal would know the nearness of its mate.

His silent voice caresses Éric's skin like wet, black silk.

Bien-aimé.

Éric opens the doors.

The energy in the room is akin to a hornet's nest that has been kicked apart. Éric's gaze travels from one pair of distressed vampire eyes to another, coming to a rest on V.

'What's going on?'

His eyes dart quickly around the room once more. One pair in particular is missing.

'Where's...'

He swallows the lump that has arisen in his throat, along with all the joy he had accumulated on his skate — the lights, the freedom — it all vanishes from his psyche as quickly as a candle that has been blown out.

Éric can't bring himself to say Teal's name.

'Do not say his name.'

The words spill from Moth's lips, each syllable drenched in acid. Unbound fury unfolds itself in his gut, the pressure of his veins throbbing against his skin. He grits his teeth although all he wants to do is launch himself at Éric, standing in the doorway like a vision of fucking innocence.

But Moth had promised Teal he wouldn't rage. Right now, all bets are off as to whether he can keep that promise.

Éric's face darkens. Everyone in the room is staring at him, leaving him naked, exposed. They all look so smug, like they're so sure they know what happened: when they don't have a fucking clue.

Éric turns his face, oh so slowly, to Moth.

His lips tighten.

He doesn't attempt to sugar coat the thought he drills toward Moth: *Fuck. Off.*

Moth shakes his head. His lips twist to one side and the red veil descends. 'No.'

Gabe is by his side, curling a hand around his bicep.

'You don't know Éric's side of the story,' Gabe says. 'Give him a chance to speak.'

Moth meets that navy-blue gaze and his chin tilts upwards.

'Since when do you side with the skater boy?'

Éric snorts and rolls his eyes.

Gabe's eyes harden and his grip becomes firmer.

'Since we are guests in this house. Since there are always two sides to a story.'

He understands why Moth is acting up but this isn't helping anyone.

He can feel Clove appraising him, feel V's focussed gaze like a laser beam against his spine.

Éric strides to Vauquelin. He takes V's arm and wraps it around his own waist, leaning back against him. No matter what everyone else in this room is thinking, he knows where he belongs.

Suddenly Éric is terrified that Clove is on the verge of announcing that they're all leaving.

Now.

Or worse — they've hidden Teal away.

They've all decided they won't allow them to see each other ever again.

But even with V's embrace tightening around him, even with V's lips brushing his ear, he digs his fangs into his tongue to stop the question from coming forth.

It doesn't work.

He speaks through gritted teeth.

'Where... is... he?'

Clove's voice spills into the room, dripping with authority.

'Moth. Come here.'

Gabe spins to face his maker.

'I'm handling it.'

He doesn't need Clove to intervene. He opens his mouth to add another sentence, but it's extinguished before it's had a chance to breathe. The look in Clove's eyes tells him everything.

Moth exhales an angry sigh but he knows better than to go against Clove. This isn't a battle he can win, although the fact that he's been made to look like a fucking schoolkid in front of Éric grates along his nerve endings. He crosses the room, his steps anything but hurried. He'll obey — but he'll make sure everyone knows his state of mind.

Vauquelin absorbs the fear oozing from his beloved's body. The fact that Éric had come to him alleviates some of his own. He presses his lips to Éric's neck.

Sois fort, bien-aimé...[†] *keep your shoulders high.*

But he might be speaking to himself, as well. His beloved's eyes are locked on Gabriel: if he is making a silent plea, it is closed to Vauquelin.

Gabe is smarting that Clove felt the need to step in, but at least this frees him up to try to sort the chaos of thoughts spinning around his head. Moth in this mood takes up all of his attention, lest his lava flow spills over, and he can't have another repetition of that catastrophe.

He glances to Éric and sees the intimated appeal written in his eyes.

Is Teal okay? He sends a mind-touch, then realises that they can't all hide the tormented reality of this — they can't all talk in whispers.

He crosses the room and stands in front of Éric and V. The intensity in V's eyes could melt flesh from bone so he fixes his gaze on Éric.

'Is Teal okay? You talked, yes?'

[†]- BE STRONG, BELOVED

Moth bristles behind him. It's not going to take much to flip the lid on Moth's fury.

'He was okay when I left him. I've been gone for a while.' Éric drops his voice to a whisper. 'Why isn't he here, Gabe?' He begins to bounce on his feet and covers his eyes: blood tears are threatening to surface.

Gabe looks away because he knows how close Éric is to breaking down. A log collapses in the hearth and ash scatters into the room.

On the table is a vase of flowers, crimson ranunculus adding their richness to the majesty of the room.

Gabe watches as a petal slowly drifts to the table.

His eyes narrow as another petal falls.

The leaves begin to wither, to crisp, and the flower heads droop as they are drained of life.

And then comes a scratching at the salon doors.

41 / NIGHT 4:

TREADING UNCHARTED WATERS

Éric makes a frantic start for the doors and Vauquelin jerks him back by the wrists. If Éric goes to Teal now, it will make this unfortunate situation worse — for each and every occupant of this room.

'Gabriel, you must be the one to invite Teal to join us,' Vauquelin says, his voice low and severe. Éric fidgets against him. If only he could interpret his beloved's body language... yet Éric's thoughts are a sealed crypt. Vauquelin tightens his hold.

At any other time the honour of V's words would settle against Gabe like a summer breeze. Somehow he finds his voice although his eyes are still fixed on the dying flowers.

'Come in, Teal.' It feels too formal for the boy he's shared his life with these past years. The snort from Moth adds a layer of agreement.

The doors open slowly.

Everyone's eyes are trained upon them.

A slight figure slips in, golden hair mussed around his face.

His eyes are red-rimmed but his jaw is tight.

The flower heads tumble from their stems, become a heap of mouldy offerings.

Gabe swallows the lump threatening to choke all words and reason from his throat.

It's the earth witch legacy from Devlin — although this time, Teal isn't resurrecting nature: he's destroying it.

Teal crosses the room and stands in the centre. He bows his head, rubs the palms of his hands together.

'I'm sorry I'm late. I was... thinking.'

There's a ragged edge to Teal's voice Gabe hasn't heard before.

His heart shatters and he goes to Teal, cups his face in his hands.

'It's okay.'

It's all Gabe can manage.

Éric slumps in V's arms but all he wants to do is run. He thought he'd be able to do this, just look at Teal again and get past it. He looks from the ruined clump of flowers to Teal's reddened eyes. Éric's chest begins to heave and he turns his back to everyone else in the room.

Vauquelin draws a comforting hand up and down Éric's spine, looking at Clove. *I fear we are all treading uncharted waters.*

Clove has watched every moment of the past few minutes, stripping away any cobwebs that may hide the truth. They all know something has happened between Éric and Teal. Something not even master vampires could have foretold.

But no one knows what happened in the library: only the two vampires involved. Clove can feel the brink of their heartbreak.

We are, but we will guide them to a safe port in their storm.

He sends the touch to Vauquelin, who holds a distraught Éric in his arms. Clove is still processing the fact that there was a spark between these young vampires. A spark that should never have been: for Éric is deeply in love with Vauquelin, and Teal... Teal has never shown any tendencies towards this. But Clove knows that sexuality does not follow preconceived rules.

It refuses to sit in little boxes.

It's the earth witch legacy from Devlin — although this time Teal isn't resurrecting nature: he's destroying it.

Teal crosses the room and stands in the centre. He bows his head, rubs the palms of his hands together.

'I'm sorry I'm late. I was... thinking.'

There's a ragged edge to Teal's voice Gabe hasn't heard before.

His heart shatters and he goes to Teal, cups his face in his hands.

'It's okay.'

It's all Gabe can manage.

Éric thought he'd be able to do this, just look at Teal again and get past this. He looks from the ruined clump of flowers to Teal's reddened eyes. Éric's chest begins to heave and he turns his back to everyone in the room. He slumps in V's arms but all he wants to do is run.

Vauquelin draws a comforting hand up and down Éric's spine, looking at Clove.

I fear we are all treading uncharted waters.

Clove has watched every moment of the past few minutes, stripping away any cobwebs that may hide the truth. They all know something has happened between Éric and Teal. Something not even master vampires could have foretold.

But no one knows what happened in the library: only the two vampires involved. Clove can feel the brink of their heartbreak.

We are, but we will guide them to a safe port in their storm.

He sends the touch to Vauquelin, who holds a distraught Éric in his arms. Clove is still processing the fact that there was a spark between these young vampires.

A spark that should never have been: for Éric is deeply in love with Vauquelin, and Teal... Teal has never shown any tendencies towards this. But Clove knows that sexuality does not follow preconceived rules.

It refuses to sit in little boxes.

And this spark does not want to die, even though it has no hope of life.

'Éric. Teal.' He looks from one to the other. 'Can you explain so that we can help you?'

Éric wrenches himself from V's arms and whirls to face the others.

'No! NO. Please, just stop! Isn't it bad enough that you all know about it? We don't *owe* anyone an explanation. Can't you all just let us have this? It doesn't fucking belong to any of you!'

'Éric,' Vauquelin growls through gritted teeth, 'How dare you speak to Clove this way?' He reaches to grasp a handful of Éric's coat but he is a second too late: Éric slips just out of range.

When Éric's temper is unfettered it is difficult to calm him down, and Vauquelin knows he is beyond pacifying his beloved.

He must allow Éric to release his anger.

A blind rage surges in Éric, a desperate determination to protect Teal… he refuses to allow any of them to back Teal into a corner, to force him to admit something he should never be required to share.

Éric has always hated people knowing things about himself that he didn't want them to know. And now it's like both of them are on fucking display and secrets aren't allowed.

What the actual FUCK?

Why does everyone think they're entitled to know every-fucking-thing?

Teal is drowning in the conflict of emotions flooding from Éric and he isn't sure how either of them are keeping this together. He had stayed in the library knowing full well that the others were gathered, that they were all waiting. The fact that he would be the centre of attention only made him want to hide more. But he can't hide forever. It had taken every ounce of his strength to walk to the salon, and in his ears he could hear the heartbeat of the earth. But this only added to his misery.

Devlin had given up everything for him.

Teal rests his brow against Gabe's, Éric's heartfelt words resounding in his ears, in his heart. He'd come here terrified that he would have to unpick every layer of pain and lay it all out for the others to see.

But maybe he doesn't have to: although he's never kept a thing from Gabe and Moth.

He kisses Gabe's cheek and extracts himself from his brother's embrace, somehow walks the few steps to stand in front of Vauquelin and Éric. The fact that Vauquelin hasn't wiped the floor with him is testament to his age, his centuries of wisdom.

But even he must have his limits.

Teal sinks to his knees, looks up at them both.

'I never meant to hurt you. I'm sorry. What happened was something I couldn't control. It won't happen again.' His gaze falls to the floor.

He can only pray that it will be true because he's not sure how he'll be able to deal with the fallout of another emotional grenade.

Éric looks to Vauquelin, and the expression he finds on his lover's face almost tears him apart as much as the vision of Teal kneeling at his feet. He's never once seen V look this way: he has no idea how to decipher it.

Do you trust me?

'Yes,' comes Vauquelin's scarcely audible reply.

Éric firmly believes no one else in this room deserves an explanation. This can't ever be boxed — no box exists which is worthy of containing it.

He holds out a hand and urges Teal to his feet.

He doesn't ask for permission... because he knows this is the last time it will ever happen.

He enfolds Teal in his arms, just holds him tight.

Éric can't contain his tears now.

There's no point in even trying.

They spill into Teal's hair, sullying gold with crimson.

It feels like an eternity passes but it's only a few sweet heartbeats.

When he releases him, he can't allow himself to meet Teal's eyes.

Then he strides out of the room, slamming the doors behind him.

He slides his back down the wall just outside, landing hard on the floor, and unleashes — his chest is racked by sobs.

That's all they fucking get.

Inside the salon you can hear a pin drop. The echoes from the slammed doors have been eaten by the silence. Even Moth is frozen to the spot.

Gabe is the first of them to move, although the action is like swimming through treacle. He's nearly at Teal's side and then Moth barrels into them both — the three Bloody Little Prophets are a tangle of arms and fierce whispers, tight embraces making them one flesh.

Clove goes to Vauquelin, steers his stiff body away from the boys into a more private corner of the salon. He has seen the expression on Vauquelin's face many times, on the faces of his victims as Clove paused in his feeding. It is shock written there, and Vauquelin's next moves will be pivotal in his relationship with Éric.

'It is true what your beloved said, Vauquelin. We are masters and we think we should know everything so that we may protect them. But they do not owe us an explanation. Maybe at some point but not now.'

He goes to the table and pours another goblet of wine and presses it into Vauquelin's trembling hand.

Vauquelin studies them all. His behaviour throughout this visit has been a garish billboard of his vulnerability. Up until this very moment he had not minded, but now there is fear etched across his visage — he cannot control it, and he knows it must alarm the boys to see a master vampire this way. He quaffs the wine, wiping his mouth with the back of his hand, and draws the goblet over his shoulder, aiming to hurl it into the fireplace — but then he remembers himself and places it on the table with a thunk. He collapses onto the sofa and plunges a hand into the ruined flowers, sifting their colourless remains through his fingertips.

From the other side of the room, Teal extracts himself from his brothers' embrace. He's been trying to absorb Éric's pulsing despair but his own is a black mirror.

He goes to Vauquelin and sits by his side, scooping a handful of the dead petals into his fist.

'I don't claim to understand love, not the kind of love you have with Éric, or Gabe has with Moth.' He glances over his shoulder at his brothers. 'But I think I know that love is constantly resurrecting itself because that's how it grows.'

Teal reaches for Vauquelin's hand, lets a few of the petals fall softly into his palm. They are revived, velvet soft and crimson red. He stands, crosses to the salon doors, leaving them ajar on purpose.

Éric doesn't look up so Teal crouches by his side.

'I know this is it for us, but I wanted you to have these.'

Teal opens his hand and lets the remaining petals fall onto Éric's chest.

One lands over his heart and the poignancy nearly undoes him completely. Teal leans close and whispers into Éric's hair, inhales the scent to lock away in his memory.

'My heart is yours.'

Then he gets up and walks away.

Vauquelin chases after Teal, stopping when he sees Éric — but his beloved's eyes are squeezed shut. The sadness enveloping the foyer is as dense and suffocating as fog. He catches Teal by the elbow at the end of the corridor, brushes his lips against his ear... his voice is a honeyed whisper.

'Our existences can be cruel, *mon ange*†... none of us can be faulted for grasping at beauty when we encounter it.'

He briefly clasps Teal's arm and turns on his heel, striding back to his beloved. He reaches down, dipping his hands into Éric's curls.

'Come, *bien-aimé*.'

Éric carefully assembles the petals, placing them in the palm of his hand before he rises... he leans heavily on V as they ascend the stairs, his curved fingers a nest to shelter Teal's fragile gift.

---

†- MY ANGEL

Moth and Gabe are desperate to reach Teal but Clove holds them back.

'Give him space. Teal is going through an intense upheaval of his emotions. I will watch over him. Now, I believe you have a catacombs door to lock.'

Clove sweeps past, leaving them alone in the salon.

'Sweet fucking hell.'

Moth holds his hands up, then clasps them behind his neck. He's having trouble processing what's gone on. If there was something to kill in this room it would have gasped its last breath. He turns to Gabe, standing in the doorway. Gabe's gaze is fixed on the spot on the floor that held Éric only a few minutes ago.

'I fucking *hate* that he's hurting.' He sucks on his bottom lip, worries it with a fang until the taste of copper floods his tongue. 'What can we do, Gabe? Will he be okay?'

Of course Moth means Teal... but maybe a tiny sliver of him means Éric, too. What Éric said about this fucked-up mess only belonging to the two of them has sunk its teeth into his flesh. If he's honest, that sliver is coated with jealousy: he's not sure he ever wants to share Teal with anyone else but Gabe. But he's fucking impressed at Éric's torrent of passion.

He can fully understand that.

He reaches for Gabe's hand, holds it tight as they make their way back down the silent hallway towards the catacombs.

☦☦☦

Clove walks to the bottom of the staircase.

He needs to speak to his fellow master before he takes Éric into their chambers. He rests his hand on the scrolled fretwork of the newel post.

'A moment, Vauquelin, please.'

Vauquelin holds up his index finger.

He continues walking Éric down the hall, whispering, 'I will not be long, my love.'

It is perfect, actually, Clove wanting to speak to him. Éric will need some time to make arrangements for the petals he cradles in his hand like broken butterfly wings.

He leads Éric inside the bedchamber and closes the doors gently behind him. Vauquelin is raw inside... there has scarcely been one solitary second to calculate the emotional damage that has befallen them all these past few nights.

He descends the staircase and leans on the railing next to Clove.

A moment of silence passes between them.

Clove does not want to utter the words on his tongue — but he must.

It is only right after the events in the salon.

'If you wish us to leave, Vauquelin, Flynn can have the car ready in minutes.' He waits.

Vauquelin looks to the high ceiling, dragging a hand down his face. Relief floods every sense in his body... he had been afraid that Clove would announce that they *were* leaving, not providing an option.

He turns his chin, lifting an eyebrow.

'Do you recall what Moth said to me at Gehenna? He accused me of running away, of taking... and I quote... the fucking safest option. I do not think that is ever a good solution for any of us, Clove. I am not prepared for this visit to end, and I know Éric is not either. Though I dare not consider what other upheaval could possibly await us.'

Clove bows his head in a gesture of respect for Vauquelin's words. He did not wish to leave but he had to make this decision Vauquelin's: for they are all under his roof.

And he knows his boys do not want to return to Gehenna yet. They are all growing here: and although their education has been mired in pain, when they eventually depart this dwelling they will be the stronger for it.

'I thank you, Vauquelin.' He smiles, and it is a smile of genuine openness. 'Now, I believe your beloved waits for your arrival in your chambers.'

Vauquelin covers Clove's hand with his own, lifting it just as quickly. So much has transpired since their adventures in the city earlier tonight... they have had no time to bask in their short-lived glory. But they are staying... there will still be an opportunity, he hopes, for him and Clove to speak alone — perhaps with Flynn — without having to deconstruct some newly erupted, youthful tragedy.

'It is I who must thank you, Clove. Though the lessons have been hard, it is not only the boys who are evolving. And I thought I had learned all I needed.' Vauquelin huffs out a laugh. 'Even so, after so many centuries, if one leaves one's heart open as I have, it may still be crushed. I will bid you adieu.'

He walks to his bedchamber with leaden steps.

He does not know the state in which he will find Éric.

He rests a hand on the doorknob, leaning his forehead against the blood-red door, and lifts his finger to scratch.

And then the sweetest sound he could hear at this juncture: Éric's voice speaking his name.

'V, V...'

His beloved's voice grows in intensity as he approaches.

The doors open and Éric flies into his arms.

42 / NIGHT 4:
I WOULD DIE WITHOUT YOU

Éric's face is streaked with blood from his tears... he hadn't washed it away. It's a badge, a gruesome mask reflecting his torment. He leans back to meet V's gaze: his breath catches in his throat and he hiccups as he burrows his head into V's shoulders.

Their time together has been unfortunately pockmarked by tragedy... and in times like this, when the pain has tilted too far in one direction, the strongest rises to carry the other. By now they know how to comfort one another when words will not surface.

Vauquelin brings the duvet back and urges Éric to sit on the edge of the bed. He removes Éric's boots, his socks. He kisses the bridges of his feet, each toe.

In the bathroom, Vauquelin runs a soft cloth under hot water, turning it over and over in his hands until the sting of the heat singes his skin... physical pain to overwrite the unease that writhes within him.

Each thought that riddles Vauquelin's brain seems woefully inadequate of soothing Éric's grief... or his own.

Vauquelin finds Éric on his side of the bed under the duvet, facing him.

He sits next to him and places the hot cloth on his beloved's tear-laden face, absolves it of its bloody horror.

Éric tugs on the top button of Vauquelin's shirt, and V tilts his head.

A question mark.

Éric nods, and Vauquelin removes his shirt.

'Now the rest,' Éric whispers.

Vauquelin obeys and slides under the duvet, suspending it over them both as Éric burrows into him. He is almost afraid to touch Éric, as if he has ascended into some holy realm — and Vauquelin is no longer worthy. He hovers his arm over his beloved until Éric pulls it down, tightening it around his waist.

Éric tucks his head into V's shoulder, clings to him — he can't get close enough.

Vauquelin has been given leave to cradle his love, his treasure.

He caresses Éric's curls with his lips, cautiously tracing his spine with a fingertip.

Tonight, Vauquelin will follow Éric wherever he wants to lead him.

He will assume nothing.

He will ask nothing.

But to his detriment he fails to keep his chaotic thoughts locked away.

'You think I don't love you anymore because of Teal,' Éric whispers against his shoulder.

Vauquelin's eyes widen in the candlelit gloom.

There it is: the thought he had not admitted to even himself.

Éric hoists onto his elbow.

He dials in to the expression on his maker's face, one he had seldom seen since V's triumphant return from the time-slip: a shadow of sadness.

It terrifies Éric, and his hands begin to tremble.

'Why did you bow at my feet in front of everyone when you came back with Moth?' Éric whispers. 'You're a master vampire.'

'Because I have no qualms about showing them what you mean to me, that I would do anything for you. That is how I chose for them to know. Words are often insufficient to convey the meaning of the vampire, Éric.'

Their entire life has been built on a foundation of honesty, established within mere hours of their meeting.

Even so, now Vauquelin cannot confess to his beloved the specific fear which has taken over his mind, and other truths have risen to the surface. Could it be, that in his enthusiasm to introduce Éric to Clove and the boys, he has sacrificed Éric's heart in the process?

Quiet, mystically beautiful, timeless Teal... so vastly different from Vauquelin's boisterous, thoroughly modern boy. He would never have imagined it. At most, conceivably, an irrational attraction to Gabriel or Moth — one which would have been quickly extinguished by either of them.

Vauquelin had underestimated Teal.

He turns his back to Éric.

All he wants is to ask him what happened on the streets and whether the situation escalated in the library, but he will not.

Éric's arm snakes around Vauquelin's hips, and he reaches down to pull him closer.

'By the way, I heard every thought that just went through your head,' Éric whispers.

Vauquelin leaps out of bed and whirls to face him, a splash of anger across his face.

'Yet your thoughts remain closed to me.'

The time for politeness, for respecting boundaries, is over.

He thrusts his chin forward as he grinds his fingers into Éric's shoulders.

'Don't do this, V. Don't ruin it.' Éric slips out of V's grip and out of the bed, backing up against the wall by the fireplace.

Éric's reaction, his hasty retreat, sends Vauquelin's chest heaving... he strides across the floor to him. The vein twists across his forehead like a river on a map.

He narrows his eyes and takes Éric's jaw in his hand, forcing his beloved to look him in the eye.

'Ruin *what*, precisely?'

He cannot allow himself to believe that Éric and Teal shared their bodies past a certain point.

This may be much, much worse than he feared: Éric may be in love.

If it were possible for Vauquelin to grow any paler, he does — because he recognises the absolute terror streaking his beloved's face.

He is being ripped in half.

They both are.

But perhaps Vauquelin is wrong: perhaps things did go further.

He digs his fingers deeper into Éric's jaw, and Éric whimpers.

The whimper sends Vauquelin's mind spiralling down into its darkest recesses — the anger he is pouring into Éric frightens him.

'Don't ruin it by making it so base, Vauquelin,' Éric murmurs, his expression wilting, his voice breaking. 'It's not what you think.'

Vauquelin parts his lips and sharply turns his gaze to the fresco on the ceiling.

The sound of his given name on his beloved's lips stutters his mind — this is the second time Éric has used it since Clove and the boys arrived, and he can only hear it as yet another wedge between them.

V. It is the only way he ever wants Éric to address him.

Vauquelin makes him feel like a stranger… centuries away from himself when Éric says it.

It frightens him.

The second day they spent together in Los Angeles, a sleep-deprived Vauquelin had been gripped by fear as unhinged words spilled out of his mouth — the many unintelligible ones he foraged to try and convince Éric to stay with him. He had been convinced even then that Éric was slipping away from him second by second.

Now that fear has its claws around his throat once more… and he is throttling his beloved. It destroys another piece of his soul (what little is remaining), that he could ever harm Éric this way.

He releases his jaw, translating it into a caress.

'Éric, forgive me... please, forgive me, my love...'

They sink to the floor.

Above them is Vauquelin's majestic second portrait.

Éric will never see how Vauquelin looked as a human man... that portrait is lost to the ages.

Yet here and now, the new and the old melt into one another's arms.

Lips hover against lips, their eyes frantically searching one another's, both unsure how to bridge this cavern that has ruptured between them.

In such times, only silent words will do.

I am so frightened, bien-aimé... I would die without you

He has never admitted this to Éric and now it is too late: Vauquelin cannot take the words back.

He knows his beloved has heard them.

Éric clings to him, he can't get close enough.

You think I wouldn't die without you? I thought I would when you were gone. I don't know how I survived it. I'm just... I've still got so much to learn... I want to know everything... this is part of it

Vauquelin rakes a hand through Éric's hair.

He cannot deny it: not only are there too many centuries between them. Their brief time together was thieved away by a time-slip, all of Éric's early vampire years — and now they have been thrust into a situation neither of them thought they would ever face.

'You didn't want me to go hunt with the boys because you thought I might get hurt. But I did... I got hurt in a very different way, V.' Éric's foot begins to twitch with violence and he brings his fist to his lips to quell the emotions building up in his chest. Vauquelin is scaring him so badly tonight he's amazed he's even able to speak.

But Éric still has so much to learn about the immortal heart: he hasn't earned the capacity to understand Vauquelin's fear, which in the present moment he can only misinterpret as anger.

'*Bien-aimé*. We have an agreement. I will not pressure you. I need not remind you that my love is not a typical love. But if you intend to give your heart to another you must be honest with me... and you must not be afraid.' Vauquelin strokes Éric's cheek and asks a question for which he is unsure he wants to hear the answer.

'Are you in love with Teal?'

This devastating question emerges in a sigh: an anguished sigh, borne from the depths of his ages.

Éric fights for a breath and bites down on the knuckle of his index finger. For the second night in a row, he's afraid Vauquelin will end him.

I will always know if you are lying to me.

His mind flashes to Olivier and the acid pit... his throat desiccates as Vauquelin's voice echoes in his brain... or maybe V is actually speaking right this second. He can't really tell.

But this is so, so huge... the hugest thing that has ever happened to him besides meeting V in the first place... and so he summons the strength to reply out loud as he meets his maker's searing gaze.

'Yes.'

Vauquelin's shoulders sink.

It is as though all of the oxygen has been vacuumed from the room, and all of his language has been stolen from him.

No words arrive to his tongue in French... none in English.

There is much he could offer to soothe his beloved, wisdom gathered across his infinite years, yet his brain is muzzled — and he wonders if he himself is the one who needs soothing.

Éric flutters across another mind-touch.

But not the way I'm in love with you. No one else.

'None of this would have happened if you hadn't turned me.'

'Oh, god.' A strangled sob escapes from Vauquelin's lips and he lurches forward, clasping his hands to his mouth. In Éric's words he hears the sound of his world collapsing down around him. It is the sound of everything he had ever wanted being lost — *again, again, again...*

In seconds Éric's arms are around his waist and Éric is rocking him.

'No, no, V, you didn't let me finish... shh... shh...' Éric swerves around to face V, and takes his maker's trembling face into his hands. 'It came out all wrong. I'm sorry.'

He rains kisses across V's cheeks, his forehead, his lips.

'What I meant was... I never would have known this beautiful pain if I hadn't met you in L.A. All of it. You showed me a glimpse of it when you sent me away, but now I know why you had to. Your time-slip, your absence. The blood. Teal. You made my life extraordinary... I just didn't know that being vampire makes everything hurt so much deeper, or that it would make everything that much more beautiful. But you were right, you never could have explained it to me when I was human... there's no way I would've understood. Now I do.'

Vauquelin staggers out of Éric's grasp and begins to pace.

His breath comes in spurts — his heart stutters.

He has never been quite convinced that he deserves Éric.

He is unworthy.

Perhaps Teal is the one who truly deserves this love, not himself.

His brain continues to betray him, but each erratic step gets a little blood flowing, and he turns to look at his beloved, wide-eyed and crumpled on the floor. He strides at once to Éric and shudders his back down the wall to sit at his side.

Vauquelin recalls Éric's conversation with Gabriel, the one he had overheard: *We don't share each other.*

Has that changed?

Must he share Éric's heart? Can he?

If it is required of him to keep his beauty, he will.

I just want you to hold me, Éric thinks... and then V curves a long leg around his.

I will hold you forever... or as long as you want me to, bien-aimé...

Éric draws in all his breath.

This isn't the first time his maker has said those words.

There's a finiteness to them now that frightens him.

He nestles into V, the greatest love he has ever known.

I just wasn't prepared for Teal.

Nor was I.

Their mind-touches pirouette around one another... they are unsure who said what.

V's arms draw him even closer.

Will you let me keep this other love for Teal in my heart?

Vauquelin traces a fingertip down the unusual muscle of Éric's jaw... a distinctive trail between Éric's chin and his eyes. Then his words return: a last gasp before the sun buries them both under the folds of sleep.

'Yes, *bien-aimé*. You are the one who said it best... there are times when one may keep something that is one's own. I do not control your heart. The fact that I could not keep it safe is proof.'

'You told me you wanted me to love them as much as you do. But Teal...' Éric sighs. 'Now I have to figure out how to live with this ache because I don't think it'll go away anytime soon.'

Vauquelin lifts Éric's chin.

'I do want that, even still with all that has transpired. Éric, Teal is made of magic...' Vauquelin begins, and as those words leave his lips, he turns his gaze to the fireplace.

He loves Clove's boys... he would do anything for them.

The realisation hits him like a fist to the stomach.

'*Bien-aimé*. You may not know this about the boys, and perhaps it is not my place to tell you. Of all of you, only you, Gabriel and Moth know your human lives. Teal does not know who he was before. I remember my life before I was vampire, as you do. Teal is the blessed one, the most authentic one. You and Teal... your souls touched. This ache you own now, it would have been the same for me had you not returned to me in California... and had I been unable to return to you here. I too know this desperation.'

Vauquelin brushes Éric's lips with his own.

'We have infinite life ahead of us, my love,' he whispers. 'This is your first experience of the unfathomable beauty awaiting you, beauty of which you cannot imagine. I am honoured that this happened with you and Teal. I would never have conceived of this turn of events. But I will not ask you to surrender it, Éric... I love you. I only want you to be you. A night may come when you will no longer want me, and I thought perhaps that night had arrived. If I ever dim your light, I will recognise this. I will set you free. Only you... you have given me the most magnificent joy I have ever known.' Vauquelin bows his head, and his hair falls across his face. He is glad of its curtain to obscure his despair. 'All you must do is ask me, my dark angel.'

'You did set me free by bringing them here,' Éric whispers. 'And I still choose you, V.'

Their limbs entangle like a vine, their chests together, their jawbones perfectly nestled.

The last thing Éric remembers is Vauquelin's scent.

The last thing Vauquelin remembers is the winding of Éric's curls in his fingers.

And then their hearts stop.

43 / NIGHT 4:

NEVER LET YOUR LIGHT FADE

Clove expects to find Teal in the library but as with everything on this visit, assumptions are ghosts haunting their nights. He discovers him in the garden by the fountain, staring up at the star-covered sky.

'They understand us, don't they?' Teal says, as Clove approaches.

He has purposefully let his feet crunch on the gravel, but he suspects that Teal would have known anyway.

Earth witch princeling.

Vampire dreamer.

'They, Teal?' Clove goes to Teal's side, offers his presence, his shoulder if it is needed.

'The stars,' Teal answers, his face still uplifted.

Moonlight silvers his hair, coats his pale skin with a pearlescent glow.

A breath catches in Clove's throat.

Teal is exquisitely ethereal.

'They're endless, like we are. They shine when our hearts beat and wane when we fall into the death sleep,' Teal whispers. He closes his eyes.

There are tears nestled in his lashes.

Clove does not wait, he slips his arm around the young vampire's shoulders and pulls him close. Teal winds his fingers into Clove's shirt and Clove tightens his embrace.

'This pain you carry,' Clove whispers, 'We love like no mortal ever will. I cannot tell you that it will fade away but it will lessen.'

Teal lifts his head.

'Have I ruined it?'

He doesn't specify, but he doesn't have to: he means the relationship between Éric and Vauquelin.

'No ruin, Teal. Just a small derailment. But, as you so wisely said in the salon, love is stronger when it is resurrected.'

A moment where Clove senses Teal gathering his strength.

It is a palpable thing: and in the still of the night its beauty is staggering.

Teal turns away and dips his fingers into the bubbling water of the fountain. His next words are lumps of lead in his throat.

'You know about me, don't you?' A smile then but it is filled with such sadness that Clove wants to pull Teal close again and never let him go.

'I do,' he replies softly. 'I've always known.'

'It's...' Teal pauses and a long sigh leaves his lips. 'It's really hard to live with sometimes. I never thought I'd ever experience what it's like for Moth and Gabe, but I did for the briefest of moments. Éric felt it, too. And afterwards, I wanted it all. That's why it messed with my head so much, because I knew I couldn't have it. That what I am wouldn't let me have it.' He meets Clove's gaze with his ocean eyes and the fireflies are as bright as sunlight. 'It made the moment we had something I'll never forget.' His lower lip starts to tremble.

Clove reaches out and draws his fingers across it.

'Never regret what happened, Teal. Keep it safe inside your heart and drink of its beauty when you need to. You are extraordinary in so many ways. Everyone here knows it.'

Teal hangs his head and lets his hair fall over his face.

'You asked Vauquelin if he wanted us to leave, didn't you?'

A slightly raised brow shows Clove's surprise.

'You heard that?'

Teal puffs out his cheeks as he thinks.

'Not exactly. I felt the vibration of the words and pieced them together.'

'There will never be another vampire like you, Teal. Not in an endless span of nights. That is why you were gifted with what you carry, what you might see as a burden... because no one else could bear it with such grace. I have told Gabriel many times that I see in him the master vampire he will become. You, Teal, will be by his side, just as much a master as Gabriel.'

'What about Moth?' Teal asks. A line of concern creases his brow.

Clove tilts Teal's chin up with one finger and allows a wry smile to twist his mouth.

'Moth has the ability to burn the whole vampire world down around him, but if I asked him if he wanted to be a master vampire he would only laugh. Moth does not wish for titles. His only dream is to be by Gabriel's side, by your side, and this I cannot fault him for.'

Clove's gaze travels to the upper floors of the darkened house.

'I believe your brothers are waiting for you, Teal. They will never ask more from you than you want to give. They love you. We all love you.'

He lets his hand trail across Teal's cheek.

'Never let your light fade, Teal.'

Then he turns on his heel and makes his way back to the house.

44 / NIGHT 4:

I'M A LITTLE BIT BROKEN

Gabe lies on the bed with Moth tucked tightly against him.

They have returned to their chambers, even though they have free rein of the rest of this palatial house. Because this is their space and they desperately need the protection of its walls.

Both of them ache to be with Teal.

They feel his trauma as if it's their own.

Moth slips his hand under Gabe's T-shirt, rests his palm across his stomach. But there's no agenda there: just the need to touch skin. Their earlier animalistic joining in the catacombs seems like a lifetime ago.

Clove is with Teal and they must trust his wisdom and his ability to soothe, although every inch of their being wants their brother where he belongs.

With them.

'Sweet fuck,' Moth exclaims.

The frustration in his voice is as heavy as the weight lining Gabe's gut. He was the one to set this in motion and the guilt of it burns at the back of his eyes.

A faint scratching comes at the door and they are both instantly on their feet. Moth peels away into the adjoining bathroom as Gabe yanks open the door.

Teal stands there for a moment, looks down at the parquet wood floor, and then his ocean gaze rises to meet Gabe's.

There's so much swimming in their depths that Gabe is rooted to the spot — haunted pain and confusion, exhaustion and the numb weight of acceptance.

He opens his arms to Teal, and closes the door with his boot.

They don't speak… there's only the understanding of a tight embrace, linked fingers, and the knowledge that here is safety: here is a space to fall into the pit of despair because there are hands to hold onto, reaching into the darkness.

Scented steam curls around the door to the bathroom.

Moth appears, draped in it, and Gabe motions with one hand.

Gently, gently.

Now it's Moth's turn to hold Teal, his hands cupping his brother's face, his lips pressing soft kisses against Teal's brow. It's in these moments that Gabe really sees the connection between them. Moth and Teal walked the night together before Gabe joined their number. They have history together that precedes Gabe's, and because of that their connection is wholly unique. And wholly beautiful.

A fierce protective wave of love washes over Gabe. He would do anything for the two boys standing before him.

Anything? the shadows in his veins whisper.

He wraps his hand around it and crushes it out of existence.

Gabe leads the way into the huge bathroom. Moth has filled the immense bath tub with foaming water and the soft, powdery scent of sweet heliotrope fills the air. It's a luxury they could never before have dreamt of, living as they do in the austere bleakness of Gehenna.

Tonight though… tonight they will worship Teal, take his pain into their own minds, show him their love and never-ending devotion.

Teal's mouth falls open when he sees the bubble-coated water.

The edge of a smile finds the corner of his lips.

'This was the only bath stuff I could find.' Moth shrugs. 'Vauquelin never does anything that's fucking understated.'

For a moment Moth thinks about Éric, but he squashes that image from his mind in case Teal somehow picks up on it.

Moth takes off his clothes and leaves them in a pile, stepping into the waiting water. He grimaces as he lowers himself in.

'Fuck.' He draws the word out, sucks in air through his teeth. 'Now I know what a lobster feels like.'

His comment broadens Teal's smile — and that fact alone makes the sting on Moth's skin a badge of beauty.

Gabe helps Teal undress as Moth dunks his head under the water.

He stays there for a few seconds with the pressure against his ears, opens his mouth... and loosens a silent scream at Teal's distress and his own inadequacy to make things right.

When he emerges, slicking his hair back from his face, Gabe is helping Teal into the water. There's something very vulnerable about Teal, and it's not just his ethereal nakedness: it's as if something has crushed the sap from his stem and now the bloom is wilting.

Moth meets Gabe's eyes. They're both thinking about the petals.

The water level in the bath rises as two bodies move within it. Some splashes over the side, pools on the marble floor. Teal settles against his brother, his back to Moth's chest, Moth's arms around him.

Gabe strips off his own clothes and kneels in the pooled water, his hand trailing lazily in the bubbles. A world away from Gehenna. A world away from a bleak English moor. But a different kind of conflict has found them here, and the casualty has been Teal's heart.

'I'm a little bit broken,' Teal whispers.

It's such a gentle statement, spoken with no malice or desire for pity, but it shatters something in Gabe. He reaches for Teal's hand, draws it out of the water and brings it to his lips.

'You are the best of us,' he says, and then he can't find any more words... so he hangs his head. The lump in his throat is like a cancer, a malignant mass that wants to eat him alive.

So Gabe lets his actions speak. He takes a bottle of scented oil and tips some into his palm. Begins at Teal's toes, moves to his arches, his ankles, travelling up his limbs, cherishing his beloved brother in the way Teal loves the best — with the adoration of touch.

Moth plays with Teal's hair as it floats around his neck, cups handfuls of water to soak the crown and the sides, massages bubbles through its golden length. His fingers trail through each strand, his fingertips kneading circles against Teal's scalp.

Teal sinks into his brothers' care. He came to them tonight with his crushed heart held in his hands, sure that they would comfort him but lacking the words to explain how much the events of the night had decimated his very soul.

But now he knows that he doesn't need to speak for them to understand him. They have witnessed his pain, his plunge into desolation, and they have offered him the comfort of their arms and their never-ending safety. He glances down at Gabe's fingers working their magic, watches as they stroke the muscles along his inner thighs. Teal feels Gabe's hesitation as his fingers climb, meets his brother's gaze, the steam curling the ends of his dark hair. He nods his consent and closes his eyes.

A slight intake of breath as Gabe cups his most intimate area, but Teal's body doesn't react in the way it did with Éric for that one golden moment. He sighs, his breath creating small ripples on the water. He has that moment and no one will ever be able to take it from him.

That is the gift he will carry.

And now Gabe's hands are stroking his hips, his stomach... practised fingers releasing tension everywhere they glide. Along his chest, trailing across his collar bones and down the lengths of his arms to his fingers, kissing each one in turn.

Water caresses his scalp as Moth rinses his hair, his brother's lips against his ear whispering his name over and over.

Gabe's mind brushes against Teal's, with Moth close behind.

Let me in.

And Teal complies, opening himself completely, knowing they can see every thought, every memory if they wanted to.

But they don't.

They find the pulsing ache of his pain, wrap themselves around it, absorb it into themselves as only vampires can. They share it as they have shared everything.

Teal shudders in the water. His skin is alight with Gabe's touch, his nerve endings tingling with pleasure, and Moth's whispered worship of his name is an echo in his ears beating in time with the thrum of his heart. And now his mind is flying, caught in his brothers' embrace.

They spin together into a tunnel of light. Emerge at the other side and fall into velvet darkness. They are not the Bloody Little Prophets in this moment... they are one star exploding through a galaxy, and all is a kaleidoscope of dazzling, coloured light.

It burns through Teal like a blazing comet and he cries out.

It's the closest they can give him to orgasm.

Gabe pulls them all back into the present and Teal opens his eyes, tears streaming down his cheeks.

'One hell of a fucking trip, Gabe.' Moth's words break the silence and he gives a low whistle of appreciation.

The water in the bath is cooling now, the bubbles all but gone.

Gabe reaches behind him and pulls three ridiculously large bath towels from the armoire shelf. He hands one to Teal and one to Moth, and they stand.

Teal's legs tremble beneath him and it's Gabe's hand that steadies him as he climbs out.

It's close to dawn now. It presses against him, its insistent voice crooning in his ear. He wants to thank Gabe, thank Moth, but his voice is gone and he tumbles...

Gabe sweeps Teal into his arms and lays him gently on the bed as Moth pulls the curtains around it, sealing them into their own blessed darkness. He finds Moth's hand as they settle either side of their bright-eyed brother, their joined fingers resting on his hip. And then Moth's hand relaxes as he succumbs to the call of the death sleep, too.

Gabe has a few minutes more.

He cannot voice what has occurred — there's too much emotion involved for even a vampire mind to comprehend.

What he does know is this: they had all come here to establish a bond, to hopefully create a connection that will stand fast through the decades. But what they have birthed in this chaos of turbulent feeling is a beautiful monster with its own heartbeat.

He just prays that it won't eat them all alive.

45 / NIGHT 5:

JUST...
JUST DON'T

When Éric wakes, V is gone.

His shoulders crater when he sees the impression of Vauquelin's absent body in their down-topped mattress: he's bereft of something he didn't get this morning before they fell asleep. He wallows around on the other side of the bed and places one of V's pillows over his face, quaffing its fragrance.

When Éric finally manages to put his feet on the floor a note by the candelabra catches his eye, folded carefully in V's ancient manner:

> *Bien-aimé, I have gone to see Clove and Flynn. We are going out for a while. I know what you are missing right now... I assure you I am missing it too.*
>
> *xx*
> *v*

Éric smiles, biting his lip, and crosses to the dresser.

He places the note in an antique jewellery casket, right next to Teal's petals... he sighs as he closes the lid.

Did everything that happened really happen?

It all seems like a movie.

But it wasn't.

It was real.

He'll have to see the boys, but is he ready? It doesn't matter if he is or isn't... even in this enormous house he can't hide forever. He should probably take a shower, but that'll just prolong the inevitable.

Besides, he smells like V, and he loves it.

Still, he takes his time getting dressed.

He puts on a pair of V's ratty old Levis (they're probably like a hundred years old... at least). V had wanted to throw them away and Éric asked if he could keep them. They've got the perfect holes in the knees, and there's a split below the back pocket. The first time Éric had worn them, V slipped a finger in there, slid it right under his butt cheek.

There's no *way* he's getting rid of these!

He slips his feet into black suede Oxford boots, a pair he bought off the set one night when he was modelling during V's time-slip... and as he laces them up, the events of the past few nights surge in his mind like a tidal wave. He's still alive, V didn't massacre him... he's relatively whole.

Well, as whole as someone can be with a huge notch taken out of their heart. But he'll get there... he hopes.

He ties the boot laces into a bow and pulls the tongue up tight behind them. And when his thumb drags up the leather, a camera flash — the pink wall of a club in the city, pulse-like neon lights, a tilted blond head, shimmering eyes hidden behind sunglasses... another thumb.

Éric's spine arcs.

Just... just don't.

He folds his hands between his knees.

He has to keep doing what he was doing or he'll curl up in a corner.

He takes a deep breath... he turns the cuffs of the jeans into tight little rolls and stands upright. He has no idea why, but he's inspired to ramp up the dial a bit tonight. With the exception of the first night the boys arrived, he hasn't really cared what he was wearing during their visit: until now.

Éric rifles around in Vauquelin's armoire and pulls out one of the ancient linen chemises: the kind with gathers at the shoulders and blousy sleeves. He wriggles into it and tucks the front of it into his jeans, letting the back drape over his backside. He loves knowing this shirt has been on Vauquelin's body.

He lifts the sleeve to his face: it smells good, like the lavender and cedar from the sachets placed here and there to keep destructive moths away. But it holds another odd scent he can't identify. It's just special somehow, like... he thinks on it for a bit.

Well... I don't know. I just love it.

He opens a drawer and runs his fingers over ancient lace: the intricate stitches send pleasing shivers across his skin — as if the fingers of whoever made it, flinging slender thread over thread into artful braids, had made it just for him to touch at this exact moment, centuries into the future.

Éric turns the lace over and over in his fingers.

He's touching V's history.

He suddenly wants it all over him.

He extracts a lace jabot and fixes it around his neck.

Next, he slips his arms into a frock coat... he reaches under the cuffs to pull the bulk of the chemise sleeves into place.

It's black, with scarlet silk lining.

He rolls his shoulders, settling the ancient fabrics onto his body.

V had shown him all his clothes... he explained each era, how to precisely identify the date of each garment. Éric looks down to the exaggeratedly tall cuffs, emblazoned with large silver buttons, and clocks this one at 1695.

Then it hits him like a lightning bolt — he's wearing V's clothes like a leash, and he needs it. NEEDS. He needs this to ground him, to remind him of why he's here in the first place. He needs it for show.

And furthermore, he likes it.

No… likes isn't the right word — he fucking *adores* being smothered in Vauquelin.

He closes the bedchamber doors quietly behind him and stands for a minute with his hands behind his back, resting on the knobs, looking down at his modernly-booted feet. And then another door opens down the corridor.

He jerks his head toward the sound.

☦☦☦

Gabe wakes to find Teal still curled up against him. He lies there for a few minutes, waiting for his brothers to draw their first intake of breath. It's a moment he adores but also one that notches his heartbeat up a gear. He has an irrational fear that one night they might not wake up.

Teal takes a breath first, a deep inhalation that expands his chest. He raises his head, blond hair mussed over his face, smiles up at Gabe like Gabe is pure sunlight.

'You don't have to say anything.' Gabe pre-empts Teal's words.

What happened between them all last night transcends words and he knows that it's bonded them ever tighter, their shared connection blossoming deeper, knitting into the threads of each heart and soul.

A bed spring creaks as Moth stirs.

His arm falls from his face. He stretches out his shoulders, gifts a grin he keeps only for them.

'White is not your fucking colour, Gabe.' Moth nods towards the towel draped around Gabe's lower body. 'You, however,' Moth leans across and ruffles Teal's hair, 'can wear any fucking colour you want.'

Gabe grins as he pushes the bed curtains open, and behind him Teal laughs. The sound courses through Gabe like a warm wind. They both know Moth has settled into accustomed Mothness. It's something normal to cling onto.

They dress together, pulling out piles of clothes from the suitcases. The novelty of choice shakes Gabe a little bit. He's used to sleeping in the clothes he hunts in, the clothes he feeds in.

A flashback from The Manor washes over him, of Ella yelling at him for leaving his clothes all over the floor, and he stops for a moment to recentre himself. She'd never meant it as anything other than a scolding, and he can still hear the Scottish lilt in her voice as she wagged a finger at him.

'The wardrobe, young Gabriel. The clothes go *in* the wardrobe.'

Young Gabriel.

That's what she always called him when her ire was raised.

And now he'll never be anything else.

He swears under his breath and Moth raises his head as he pulls on a pair of faded black jeans.

Their eyes meet.

Gabe never swears like this unless it's warranted.

Teal disappears behind the jib door and Moth bumps his shoulder against Gabe's.

'What's eating you up?'

Moth is never anything but straight to the point, something Gabe loves about him: but this time Gabe shrugs, because he's not sure what he's about to say is actually what is bothering him.

'Just this place. It's bringing out memories, bringing out the best and the worst of us.'

'We could just go out, the three of us?' Moth says. He has a burning desire to kill something, to feel hot blood flooding his throat even though he isn't really hungry.

'We came here to connect,' Gabe says softly, as he glances towards the closed jib door. 'Clove would string us all up if we simply disappeared and left Éric by himself.'

Moth's mismatched eyes darken. 'He has Vauquelin.'

'And that's all he does have, Moth.' Gabe pulls on a plain black T-shirt. 'He has literally no one else in the world. Think about it.'

Moth doesn't want to think about it — but he does.

He promised Teal he wouldn't rage at Éric and he *will* curtail his mouth tonight. He *hopes*.

Teal reappears clutching a book under his arm, and both Gabe and Moth exchange a smile as Gabe opens the door to the hallway.

They saunter down its length, Moth with his arm slung around Teal's shoulders, round the corner, and then they all stop, as one.

46 / NIGHT 5:

« ÉBLOUISSANT »
{ DAZZLING }

Gabe's eyes travel from Éric's face to his feet.

He's dressed in items of clothing that shouldn't go together, but do so in their dissenting clash — their warring of time periods and fabrics. The boots and faded, ripped jeans look like something any of them would wear, but the linen chemise with the gathered neck... the black coat that fits him like a second skin... the crimson lining like a wound reopened... the lace at his throat... Éric looks like he fell from one of V's paintings.

He looks *right*. And he knows it.

Gabe glances down at his own clothes.

'We didn't get the memo on the dress code tonight.' He grins and crosses the space to Éric's side. 'You look fucking amazing.'

This vision definitely warrants the F word. He nearly said *beautiful*, but he's fully aware of the waves of awe and surprise emanating from Teal.

Gabe turns, ready to leash Moth if he launches into derision.

But Moth simply shrugs and tightens his hold on Teal.

'Not bad for a skater boy.'

Moth adds a nod in case his words are taken the wrong way.

There's no chance he'll tell Éric exactly what he thinks — that Éric looks fucking hot, and that Moth would do him in a heartbeat: if he wasn't with Gabe. Not that he likes Éric any more than he did yesterday.

Teal isn't sure where he wants to be right now. On one hand he longs to be curled up in a corner with his book, but on the other he wants to stay here forever just gazing at Éric because he looks — Teal's thoughts stutter as the right word eludes him and he leans closer to Moth.

A small pocket of linen is still tucked into the cuff of Éric's coat. Teal feels an overwhelming desire to stride across and smooth it into place.

'Éric,' he murmurs, « *éblouissant* . »[†]

He isn't sure where the word came from, but it feels right.

It feels like it comes from his heart.

Éric sucks in his lower lip. His hands begin to tremble as Teal's word replays in his mind, and he has to look away. He grasps his elbows to conceal the tremors. This is so much harder than he thought it would be. But the way they're all staring at him makes him wonder about his choices tonight. At first he'd felt like he was wearing armour... that maybe merging V's clothes with his own would've made him stronger. Turns out it's had the opposite effect.

At last he brings his eyes up to meet Teal's, and the air grows heavy between them. Éric's heart begins to palpitate and it makes him cough. He gulps to regain his breath — he wants to imbibe all the beauty radiating from Teal. He mouths 'thank you,' and turns his head again because he has to hide the sadness spreading across his face.

After all the extraordinary events of this gathering, doing anything average seems ridiculous... Éric isn't sure what they're supposed to do now. Just hang out? What? How can anything ever be normal again?

Then an idea strikes him.

Éric begins walking backward, toward the way he came.

There's only one room this way: his and V's enormous bedchamber. The boys haven't seen it... and it's the most beautiful room in the entire fucking house.

---

†- DAZZLING

'There wasn't a dress code, Gabe. Come on.'

Gabe is grateful when something stirs Éric into action. For a few moments he isn't sure if all this is going to descend into an emotional battlefield again, and he knows Teal's heart can't stand that. He follows Éric, glances behind him, sends a mind-touch to his brothers.

It's okay.

He hopes his optimism is grounded in fact.

Moth keeps Teal close by his side. There's no way he's letting him out of his sight tonight. A growl rumbles low in his throat. Gabe is trailing behind Éric like he's the Pied Fucking Piper.

Teal's heart hammers against his ribcage. He's not sure if he can do this, but he has to. He takes a deep breath and tries to find his centre, but all he can unearth is an empty hole — because his centre has been ripped from him. He closes his eyes and feels the beat of firefly wings against his lids.

Éric hesitates a moment with his hands on the doorknobs.

V never specifically said he couldn't bring the boys in here, but it's literally the *epicentre* of Vauquelin.

They'll his the portrait... they'll see their bed.

This might be the worst idea he's ever had.

Fuck it.

He throws the doors wide open and strides in. They pass through a gilded sitting room with a small corner fireplace and through another set of ceiling-high doors, coming to a stop in the middle of the unspeakably enormous main room: below the fresco.

The boys are frozen at the entrance.

'Come on. Don't worry,' Éric says, and for the second time he wonders who he's trying to convince.

Gabe accepts the invitation. He clamps his jaw shut because it wants to fall open at the dazzling opulence in this massive room. Every surface drips with luxury, with extravagance. The fresco, the richness of colour and fabric… just the whole aura of the room is majestic. V is the king here and Éric is his prince. It's like a fairytale. It beats the hell out of the cold, gloom-heavy walls of Gehenna.

A sharp jab of envy catches him in a tender spot and he buries it before it has time to bloom. His gaze comes to rest on the portrait and it's this that unglues his feet from the spot. He can't take his eyes from the vision of V as he was when he was alive.

As he nears the bed he can smell the combined musk of V and Éric. This is a sacred space and Éric has invited them in.

A low whistle leaves his lips.

'Damn, Éric. You win this game.'

Gabe lets his fingers trail across the tassels on the bed curtains, lifts his gaze to the painting again.

'When was this done?'

Moth and Teal haven't moved from the doors. Teal's grip tightens on Moth's arm and when he glances across Teal's lips are pressed so tightly together they've lost all colour.

Moth is half a second away from taking Teal's hand and storming away. But he refuses to retreat. If this is a battle line, he will hold his fire: for now.

Éric startles at Gabe's question. He hadn't really been paying attention… because he'd been staring at Moth and Teal. *When was this… game…* He cringes a little at Gabe's choice of the word *game*.

It has a totally different meaning for him now.

He snaps back into reality.

'Yeah. Okay. Uhhh… the painting.' He clasps his hands and brings his knuckles under his chin. '1668. The second time. You know he was turned twice, right?'

He examines V's portrait with Gabe for a few minutes, then panics when he realises he hadn't made the bed. The boys won't care, but he flips the duvet back into place anyway and arranges the pillows.

It's just something to keep him busy, as he's already noticed Moth glaring at him. Anything to pretend — at least for a minute — that he isn't bothered by Moth touching Teal.

Gabe tilts his head to focus on the detail in the painting. The eyes feel real, as though they're watching them all play out this scene: he finds the phrase he used the other night and a soft noise sounds in his throat... this game of fucking eggshells. He wants to fix this so badly, but isn't sure how. And he's hyper-aware of Moth's suppressed agitation.

This could go wrong so fucking quickly.

But it's Teal who comes to the rescue, who inserts himself into this fractured glass silence. He extracts himself gently from Moth's grip, grazing his fingertips across his brother's wrist, before crossing to the intricately carved armoire. It towers above them in elegant majesty.

He reaches out to touch the incredible detail, and he imagines what it must have been like to create something as beautiful as this, to pour all your love into something you would never own.

His gaze flicks to Éric for a moment and then he looks away.

Éric rushes over but sways when he gets too close to Teal, as though an invisible rope has pulled him back. He turns his head to Moth — he's still drilling Éric with a death glare.

Éric's eyes grow heavy and he turns so he can't see Moth.

He leans against the armoire, idly tracing his index finger over the deep carvings on the wood surface as he whispers to Teal.

'Would you like me to open it?'

As the breath from Éric's words settles on Teal's skin, his fingers start to shake. He clasps his hands in front of him and somehow finds his voice.

'I'd like that very much.'

He keeps his gaze fixed firmly on the key, concentrating on the lines in its elegant scrollwork hilt.

Gabe tears his focus from Teal and Éric. He crosses the room and takes

Moth's hands in his, drawing them up to his chin.

'Moth, look at me.' He keeps his voice gentle.

Moth is struggling because Teal's pain is akin to a wounded heartbeat. Because he blames Éric... when really Éric is a victim of this as well. And when it comes down to it, this is all Gabe's fault.

Moth finally lifts his gaze and as soon as their eyes meet Gabe wants to take all the pain from Moth, too.

'Teal will break if we mess this up. He needs us here to support him, so you have to swallow whatever is driving your fury and keep it bottled, okay?' Gabe kisses Moth's fingers and squeezes them so tightly that his knuckles turn white. 'For Teal, yes?'

For a moment Gabe senses the hesitation, sees the stubborn shield about to rise, and then Moth sighs and crumples a little.

'For Teal,' he says.

Éric turns the key and opens one door. He reaches behind the other and engages a lever, bringing it out to the side. He steps back, resting a hand against the open door, and glances at Gabe and Moth. They're deep in conversation and they aren't paying any attention to him and Teal, so he seizes the opportunity to imagine they're alone for a minute — just so he can watch the wonder in Teal's eyes.

It's a stolen moment, and such moments will be few and far between.

He tilts his head.

'You can touch anything you want, Teal.'

His stomach clenches and he squeezes his eyes shut.

Really bad choice of words.

He didn't mean it that way... it's just that he knows Teal will revere each ancient garment in this cabinet and treat them the way they deserve to be treated.

That V wouldn't mind.

Éric wishes he could be alone with Teal, but the reality is he probably never will be again: he has to accept it. He dreamily watches Teal's fingers caressing the delicate fabrics, hyper-conscious of what little time he has with him. He holds his breath as the minutes fall through this little hourglass... he doesn't want them to end. But then reality kicks in and he turns to the others, waving a hand.

'Come on, guys. Don't you want to see?'

Éric's reverie with Teal snuffs out when Gabe and Moth start toward the armoire and as they get closer, he reminds himself: *he's not yours. You have to let them in.*

Éric's words replay over and over in Teal's head as his fingers find the delights of velvet, satin and silk: *you can touch anything you want, Teal.*

That isn't strictly true. The pain of it hits him between the eyes before the calm voice of logic reminds him that he'll never see the like of such garments again... that he's touching history sewn into each stitch. But still Éric's presence is like a magnet drawing him closer.

He's almost glad when Moth and Gabe arrive beside them.

Almost, but not quite.

He turns to Moth.

'Do not treat these clothes with anything but the utmost respect.'

There's a sharpness edging his voice he hadn't meant.

Moth narrows his eyes.

'Sorry,' Teal whispers.

He turns away and studies the ivy leaf pattern on a vase standing on a side table.

Éric fidgets with the lace jabot on his neck as he watches Teal struggle. He thinks about their time in the library, and how he had wished no one else knew about what happened. But now he does have that postcard, and so does Teal. No one else knows they held each other: no one knows the confessions they made. He lifts the lace to his lips and whispers through it.

'Let's dress up a little and surprise V and Clove when they get back,'

Éric says. 'But what Teal said is true... please be careful. It's an honour to wear these things... they're fragile. Some of them date back to when V was human. Promise me you'll think of it that way. Cool?'

'We all know it's an honour,' Gabe says softly. 'Don't we, Moth?'

He elbows Moth in the ribs.

Moth blows out a breath.

The accompanying eye roll signals his understanding.

'Why don't you choose for us, Éric? Although you and V are taller so it will probably all have to be upper body stuff.'

This could be a way out of the stifling atmosphere that has descended. Gabe hangs onto the wish.

Éric puckers his lips and taps them with a fingertip: his mind is already styling. It's a good distraction — this is his specialty.

He takes out three chemises.

'Start with these.'

Then he turns his back because he really doesn't think he can handle seeing any bare chests right now.

He devotes himself to coats.

A scarlet one for Gabe: watered silk, sprays of dark blue embroidery scrolling across each lapel, twirling around the cuffs like vines.

Damn, he's gonna look so good in that.

He sweeps one coat aside after another.

Moth, Moth, Moth. Nope, nope, nope.

Then he lands on a dark green one. It's velvet and not too fancy... but it's cut like a military coat with dozens of brass buttons down the front and on the cuffs. The lapels are burgundy red.

It's fucking *wild* — it's perfect.

He takes it off the hanger and passes it back over his shoulder.

'Moth, for you.'

His shoulders fall.

He's at the end of the coats and nothing is right for Teal.

At least not in here.

'Hang on,' Éric says, and he disappears behind a jib door into the anteroom/closet. There are more antique things in here, especially the ones Éric and V wear the most.

And Éric knows exactly which one he wants for Teal.

When he locates it, he holds it against his chest for a moment.

He stoops and grabs a wooden box, tucking it under his arm before re-emerging.

He places it on the settee at the foot of the bed.

'Teal,' Éric says, 'could you come over here?'

He wants him a little bit away from Gabe and Moth... just a little.

Teal steals across to Éric. The linen of the chemise feels strange against his skin, but he likes the weight of the natural weft and weave of the fabric. Somehow he's managed to stay upright and focussed whilst Moth and Gabe help each other into their coats — Gabe insists they each play butler and hold the coat open to lessen any chance of splitting the silk linings.

Now they're standing facing each other: Gabe smoothing out the shoulders on Moth's coat, Moth trailing his fingers over the embroidery on Gabe's lapels. They're lost in the moment, in the delight of seeing such unfamiliar but beautiful garments adorning each other.

The chemise slips from Teal's shoulder, exposing an arc of pale skin. He can't take his eyes from Éric's tangle of curls.

Éric hooks a finger over Teal's shoulder but freezes.

'Your shirt,' he stammers, pursing his lips.

He wonders whether he should set it right... or whether it would make him come completely undone.

He's barely holding it together as it is.

'You can fix it,' Teal says, so softly Éric has to strain to hear him.

Truth be told, Teal isn't sure if he can make his limbs do anything at the moment.

'Okay,' Éric whispers, just as softly.

He slides a fingertip beneath the edge of Teal's collar and quickly slips it back into place. But he leaves the back of his hand resting there against Teal's velvety collar bone. Just for a second.

Their eyes meet and they both glance away.

'Turn around now,' Éric whispers. He takes Teal's left hand and slips it through one sleeve, then the right. He walks around Teal to face him, and he feels as though he might turn into a puddle of water.

Teal in rose-petal pink silk.

Silk with millions of little raised petals made of ribbons, scattered across the front and over the cuffs, affixed with silver threads.

Éric sighs.

'One more thing, okay?' He gestures to the settee, and Teal sits.

Éric crouches down at his feet and opens the wooden box.

Teal stares down at the absolute vision of Éric more or less on his knees in front of him, commits the image to his memory to replay in the dark when he's alone.

Éric takes Teal's shoes off.

He curls his fingers around Teal's ankle, gazing up at him through heavy-lidded eyes. A black velvet slipper slides on one foot, and then the other. Éric stops and focusses on his hands resting on Teal's ankles.

He lets himself look into Teal's eyes: but only for a second, because it hurts too much to see them like this.

He says, 'I'll be right back,' and disappears behind the jib door once more. He snaps the door closed and buries his face in his hands.

If the house was burning down around him Teal isn't sure if he would be able to move. He sits here wearing antique pink silk; a garment Éric chose especially for him because of the petals. He stares down at the unfamiliar slippers... but it's the pressure from Éric's fingers he can still feel, burning into his skin.

He glances over his shoulder at Moth and Gabe. They have wandered to the corner, still engrossed in each other, but Gabe catches Teal's gaze and he nods.

They have retreated on purpose to give Teal and Éric a little privacy.

A lump forms in Teal's throat. They are his protectors, even though he doesn't really need them for that anymore — but they understand the power of attraction even if it makes no sense, and they trust him enough to let him walk this line to the very end... the end where he might explode into a burning star.

Teal thought he would be okay tonight, had even imagined Éric and himself laughing and joking, an easy camaraderie replacing this aching need. He thought Éric would have come to his senses after a night with Vauquelin.

But still the thread between them crackles, and if he closes his eyes Teal can see it as a golden thread — exactly what Olivia had called the connection between Teal and his brothers on that fateful night in Westport Quay.

Fate has brought him and Éric together: they will both either die in the flames or soar from the ashes.

In the anteroom Éric knocks his forehead repeatedly against the wall.

Don't cry... do NOT *fucking cry.*

He smothers his face into a bunch of shirts, muting himself, and screams into them.

He sniffles. That scream helped... *a lot.*

He hopes Gabe and Moth didn't hear him, but he's kind of past caring what anyone thinks about all this.

Éric opens the jib door and blows his hair out of his face before he emerges. He locks his gaze into Teal's and stops in the middle of the room, fidgeting with a button on his coat.

'Well... you all look fucking gorgeous and that's all I can say about that.'

Gabe takes Moth's hand and they cross to stand by Éric.

'Hey, something I noticed. You guys don't have a mirror.'

He really wants to see how he looks with Moth by his side, with Teal between them.

He's also giving Teal a moment to collect himself. A moment where Éric's gaze isn't fixed upon him. They both might be trying to hide it but the electricity from them is making the hairs stand up in the nape of Gabe's neck.

Éric gasps. 'Of course we don't... why would we? It's fucking creepy not seeing yourself,' he says, cocking an eyebrow. 'I made V buy me one right after we got here, because I thought maybe I could outsmart it and get a mirror selfie. I didn't believe him, but mirrors don't lie.'

'Whoa.' Moth jerks his head towards Éric. 'What do you mean it's fucking creepy not seeing yourself?' Then the realisation dawns and his jaw falls open. 'You don't have a reflection? Seriously?'

Although Gabe is happy Moth is having a conversation with Éric that doesn't involve too many F words, this one is heading towards dangerous territory.

He interrupts as Moth takes a breath.

'It must be a bloodline thing, yes?' Then his voice trails off at the expression on Éric's face.

Éric's chest begins to heave.

'What? Are you telling me you guys *can*? Un-fucking-believable.'

He rushes to a secretary and fumbles the lid down, extracting a thick photo album: the collection from his and V's only professional photo session. No one else was ever meant to see these images, ever... but he shoves it into Gabe's hands regardless.

'Here you go. The *only* way I know how V and I look standing together.'

Gabe opens the album but it takes him a few seconds to refocus.

V and Éric don't have a reflection? Mind blown.

His fingers skim through the pages as Moth leans in.

Their eyes meet as photo after photo shows Éric and V practically making love to the camera lens. Gabe is surprised his fingertips aren't scorched from the smouldering heat.

Éric careens over to a window and dramatically flings the heavy drapes aside. He hoists the glass panels outward, hanging his head out, gulping the frigid night air into his lungs.

Thank god V agreed to those photos... they're his greatest treasure.

Well, *one* of them.

The other is on the dresser.

He whirls back around to face them.

'Will there ever be an end to these fucking surprises?'

But then something breaks in his chest: he can almost hear it and he starts laughing, so hard he doubles over. He doesn't even know why he's laughing. He stretches back up and Gabe and Moth are looking at him like he's finally lost it.

Teal senses the edge of hysteria in Éric's outburst.

He feels it like the point of a dagger digging into his throat — and if he moves it will slice him open.

These differences in bloodlines... he should have realised there was more to it. He has his own as a precedent.

He turns to Gabe and Moth, Gabe holding the album to his chest.

'Can you give us a minute, please?' The plea vibrates on each syllable.

Moth opens his mouth to argue, but Gabe is already dragging him across the room.

We're in the hallway. We love you.

Gabe's mind-touch reaches Teal as the doors slowly click closed.

47 / NIGHT 5:

FLYING TOO CLOSE TO THE SUN

Now there are only two vampires in this room where Vauquelin makes love to Éric. The *wrongness* of it scorches across Teal's skin but he can't leave Éric in such a fragile state.

He forces himself to his feet, the unfamiliar slippers slowing his steps. But somehow he makes it across to Éric. He stands before him and lifts his chin — Éric is a good six inches taller. His eyes flick to the silver hoops and he's overcome with the need to touch them. His hand lifts but then he curls his fingers into his palm.

'I know it feels like it's too much right now, but these differences are what make us unique. There's beauty in them.'

But there isn't beauty in the one thing Teal can't change.

It's a millstone he will have to carry for eternity.

'How do you do it, Teal? Even with just a couple of words you always make it seem like everything will be okay. You...' Éric drags a hand down his mouth and immediately his shoulders cave. His voice diminishes to a whisper. 'I just don't think there's anything about you that isn't beautiful.'

What he just said to Teal doesn't even come close to what he's feeling right now. But somehow he doesn't believe he needs to spell out what's in his heart, because his instinct tells him Teal already understands...

as if words aren't actually good enough for them.

'Do you want me to go?' Teal asks softly.

They're both treading dangerous waters again and the magnetism between them is making his head spin. He doesn't want to leave but he has to offer. His throat aches. And then he thinks about adding what he told Gabe and Moth last night. But it's too much.

'No... please don't go,' Éric murmurs. He's scared and maybe he should have said yes... but each time he's with Teal he convinces himself it will be the last. 'Not yet.'

Teal wants to rest his hand over Éric's heart and feel its beat thrumming against his fingertips. But Éric doesn't belong to him.

He sighs, hangs his head because his chin is trembling.

If this is so wrong, why is there this sizzling bond between them?

Éric tilts his head slightly to better see Teal's face. He registers the sadness there... his heart begins to convulse so hard it dizzies him.

'Teal... I said you can touch anything you want and I meant it,' he whispers, his voice quavering. 'But maybe you should call them back before we do something we can't undo.'

Teal lifts his head again.

Éric is right.

But he meets Éric's gaze for a precious few seconds, lets his fireflies dance, and hopes they can tell him what his words cannot. Just before he calls to his brothers he finally succumbs to temptation... reaching out, his fingers stroke the space over Éric's heart, the velvet nap of his frock coat almost painful under his fingertips.

An electrical current from Teal's touch travels up Éric's chest and he parts his lips, tilting his head back. He clasps Teal's hand and brings his fingers up to kiss, just for a second... a fragile, fleeting second. He drops Teal's hand and breathes a frantic, whispered command.

'Please call them.'

Now Teal's fingertips prickle with heat, like he's flown too close to the sun — and the pain is an exquisite form of torture.

He takes a step back, stumbles slightly with the unaccustomed footwear. Or is it because the bones in his legs have turned to a jellified mass?

'Gabe,' he calls, but it isn't really a call, more of a hoarse whisper.

But Gabe is ready and the doors swing open. Moth leans against the door frame, his arms crossed. But he isn't saying anything.

And that speaks volumes.

Gabe crosses to Teal and it's all Teal can do not to fall into his embrace.

'Are you okay?' Gabe asks, and then his eyes flick to Éric. 'Are you both okay?'

'I can't answer that, Gabe. I wish I could just say yes, but you know it wouldn't be true,' Éric murmurs, closing the doors to the armoire and twisting the key in the lock. He leans his back against it and stares at Gabe, before daring to turn his gaze to Moth.

Right now he wouldn't mind if Moth just came for him and kicked his ass. It would feel a lot better than the way his heart is shredding itself in his chest. He could probably say one word to make Moth jump him.

But instead Moth is just quietly watching him, and that silence makes him even more nervous.

'We'd better straighten up. V and Clove'll take one look at us and know something's wrong,' Éric says. 'So, Moth... can't you just tell me to fuck off or something? Like anything, honestly, because I'm literally ten seconds away from fucking falling apart here.'

Moth stays by the door because Gabe has told him that he must.

But now Éric is offering a temptation he's not sure he can resist.

He desperately wants to release the pent-up anger scorching his throat and one look at Teal's distraught face has that anger unfurling its fucking wings... but then he looks at Éric.

Really looks at Éric.

And what he sees makes his own heart twist.

He remembers what it felt like when he thought he was going to die. When he could smell his own flesh burning. But the worst part was the thought of losing Gabe. And now Éric has such anguish painted on his face that Moth's anger dies.

He stands straight, meets Gabe's questioning gaze. *Chill.* Walks to where Éric is standing. He reaches out and clasps Éric's shoulder, leans in close and whispers against his ear.

'You don't need me to tell you to fuck off. You're beating yourself up enough. I won't add to that. Clove and Vauquelin will be back soon. You need to pull yourself together, paste that fucking smile on your fucking face.' Moth pauses. He's not used to making speeches. 'I can't fault you for loving Teal... and if he sees something in you that makes him love you back, I guess that's okay.'

Éric gnaws on a fingertip. He hadn't expected anything like this from Moth: not in a million fucking years.

'I have no idea how we're supposed to deal with this, Moth,' Éric says, his voice wilting.

Then he stands tall and walks to the doors.

'If no one minds, I just need to be alone for a little while. Let's all meet in the salon in an hour.'

He unbuttons the front of his ancient coat and shoves his hands in the back pockets of his jeans as he slips out into the corridor.

He doesn't turn around to see if any of them follow.

48 / NIGHT 5:

I DON'T LOVE YOU ANY LESS

The obvious place for Éric to go is his lair but he walks right past it.

He opens the door to the back garden: it's pouring, and as much as he would love letting the rain drench him like so many tears, maybe it could even wash all of this yearning away… getting this outfit wet isn't in the cards. So he turns on his heels and descends into the catacombs.

The heat from the torch detonates across his face and the stairwell illuminates. When he reaches the lower level his foot skids on something hard… he stoops.

A stray bone.

Huh?

He picks it up and replaces it on a shelf.

The catacombs are so dirty… and also creepy as fuck.

It isn't the best place to go given his state of mind, but it's the one area of the house he can hide in right now. He looks around for something to sit on, and his eyes land on the now-empty coffin.

It's back in its original spot, at the furthest end of the catacombs.

Éric hangs the torch on a bracket and stretches out on top of it, lacing his hands behind his head.

He tries to conjure some remorse for Olivier, but he hadn't known him that long… and it was pretty clear V's chosen brother hated his guts.

Nothing comes.

Olivier turned his back on him.

Betrayed him.

It wasn't the first time Éric had felt betrayal... maybe he should be used to it by now, but it still fucking stings.

V meant for Olivier to protect his fledgling.

Me.

He brings his hand to his heart.

Since V sent Olivier to his eternal rest, then backstabbing me must've been reason enough, Éric thinks... *because there's no coming back from that.*

During this gathering Éric has felt the brunt of V's antiquity, even more so than when they'd come to Paris... when he'd seen this house for the first time.

Vauquelin was already an otherworldly creature in Los Angeles. But in France Éric sees him as he is meant to be, as his origins demand.

Clove, the boys, all the secret knowledge that has emerged... it's so overwhelming.

And Teal...

Éric has always found it impossible to love more than one person.

Always.

His mind and his heart gets so full of that one that there isn't room for anyone else. His body never wants anyone else... it's just how he is. He had demanded this, point blank, from V.

So how did he end up here, an ordinary Cali boy lying atop a four-hundred year old coffin in a filthy, subterranean cavern full of bones in Paris, positive his heart isn't big enough to hold all this love?

Like it might explode at any moment?

'I don't love you any less, V,' he whispers into the dark.

He aches with hope that V knows this.

Please let him know.

If only Éric understood that, even from his great distance, Vauquelin senses the black velvet touch of Éric's plea — that it curls into V's soul and warms it... it would take a little edge off his pain.

Éric wonders if he'll ever be able to see Teal again without falling apart.

If he could have anything right now, he'd just want to be close to Teal... to be allowed to hold him in front of the others like it was the most ordinary thing in the world — and that everyone would just be cool with it.

He hates that he has to feel bad about this beautiful gift he's been given. If something is wonderful, how can it be wrong? How can having *more* love be a disgrace when most people are starving for it?

Or maybe he's just being greedy...

Éric's face crumples with confusion.

He has more love than he ever thought possible with V and as it turns out, it still isn't enough.

Éric stands and removes his coat, even though it's chilly down here. He hasn't felt the cold since he became vampire. Coats are just for show, not warmth. He folds it carefully, placing it on top of a wine crate, and lies back down.

He runs a hand under his chemise, pretending it's Teal's hand.

A sharp breath rockets through his lungs and he closes his eyes.

Vauquelin's hands have been all over Éric's body: even inside it.

Éric would know V's touch if he was blindfolded.

He thinks about their first night together, how V had completely opened himself. Éric had only been the giver a handful of times before — he wasn't sure he'd be any good at it.

But it didn't matter because V's body took over. He gave him confidence, a desire Éric had never known before. V let him in, accepted him wholly... and he owned him from that very moment.

Even the mere *thought* of fucking V gets him hard.

He unbuttons the fly of his jeans, spits on his hand and slips it inside — his back immediately arches. This time he imagines it's V's hand, his mouth, himself... and he wishes V were here right now to help him get where he needs to be.

He can't do it by himself: not anymore.

His own hand isn't enough like it was before he was turned.

Éric *would* die without Vauquelin, because he knows V loves him and no one else will ever love him like that again, not the way he does.

You can't give Teal this... he can't give it to you.

This... he thinks, groaning into the cavernous hollows, groans echoing off the bones...

This is why you can't have him.

Éric's blood tears fight their way to the surface and his groans are overwritten with sobs.

He curls his knees to his chin and shivers.

49 / NIGHT 5:

JEWELS OF TRUTH THAT HURT SO MUCH

Gabe closes the doors to V's bedchamber.

The click of the lock settling into place echoes around the hallway, as though the room is relieved that they're no longer in it. He wonders how V will react when he knows they were all in his most private place, let alone what had gone on in there.

He looks towards Moth and Teal, sees Moth take Teal in his arms, press a fierce kiss to his brow. Then Moth sticks his hands in the back pockets of his jeans, the expression on his face one of utter torment.

Gabe hurries across, wanting to pick up the shards of the bombshell that has just exploded amongst them. Maybe he should go to Clove and ask him if they can leave, because every night seems to bring another deeper level of heartache. A muscle twitches in his jaw. He's not sure how much more Teal can take. If Clove says no, Gabe might just take Teal and Moth and leave anyway.

'I just need some time to think,' Teal says softly. 'It's not that I don't want to share, you know I share everything... but my head is reeling and I can't,' his voice breaks. 'I just can't talk about it until it makes sense to me.'

There's a plea on the edge of his last words.

'Promise me you won't go far,' Gabe says, taking Teal's hand in his.

The skin is cold, almost clammy, and a prickle of fear needles his gut.

'I promise I won't leave the confines of the house or the boundary.'

It's all Gabe can ask for, but he still doesn't like the idea of Teal being alone.

'We'll be right here,' Moth says.

His hair falls over his brow as he hangs his head, and Gabe can tell by the way Moth is trembling that he wants to say so much more. No one has discussed what he said to Éric, despite it being a turning point between them both. No one has said anything: because this trauma Teal is going through is so much more important.

'Just call us, okay?' Moth adds, as Teal turns away.

He reaches out a hand but Teal has already gone.

There are no footsteps resounding on the marble tiles.

Teal doesn't want to be found.

Teal puts distance between himself and his brothers as quickly as he can. It's easy in a house as vast as this and he wanders down hallways he has never seen before, peeks around doors into silent rooms. One such room he enters. The drapes are drawn, of course, and there is no fire roaring in the hearth. But it's the emptiness of the space that calls to him. Not emptiness in the way of furnishings — it's still as lavishly appointed as all the other rooms he has seen — but empty of the vibrations of life.

He's still wearing the rose-pink silk coat Éric chose for him, and he runs his fingers gently over the embroidered petals before carefully slipping it off. He folds it and places it on the arm of a chair.

The slippers follow and now he sinks to his knees on the rug before the window, a slight figure with a bowed head wearing an ancient chemise and modern denim jeans. These ones are not new... he brought them with him, and if he inhales he can still smell the scent of cold stone and biting damp: the scent of Gehenna.

He folds his hands in his lap and lets the thoughts tumble from his mind, replaying every fragment from the time in the chamber — right to the point where Éric whispered, '*Please call them.*'

What might have happened if Éric hadn't been so strong?

And therein lies the twisted web of emotions throttling his every thought. He peels away each gossamer layer to find the tender truths hidden within, balanced like morning dew upon a forest web.

These jewels of truth that hurt so much.

He takes that moment with Éric outside the club, where he'd felt the first stirrings of his body: a sensation so alien that it made the breath stutter in his throat. The way Éric's eyes had warmed, the way his lips felt when Teal gently prised them apart with his thumb. He should have stopped then, should have pulled away and erected a shield between them, but he didn't — because for those few precious moments, the burn of desire flooded his veins and he didn't want it to ever stop.

It didn't matter that Éric wasn't his, that he could never be his... Teal just wanted this moment to last and last and never go away.

A tear rolls down his cheek as he takes this fact and lays it out in front of him like an offering to the gods.

But the feeling did wane and for the rest of the night — even during the time they fed — he wished fervently for its return. It would have been so very easy if Éric had brushed this off, if he had even laughed and said it was only part of the game... but it had never been a game. Not for the two vampires out in the spotlight in their first starring roles.

Cue cameras.

Somehow, in that blazing glory of a moment, they had forged a connection that made no sense to them.

No sense to anyone else.

He lets a shuddering exhale of release leave his lips.

You can't have him.

The thought settles as though it came from an outside source, and his mouth twists in confusion.

He returns to the centre of this shimmering, blood-soaked web, a place where there might be an ugliness he doesn't want to face.

And when he digs his fingers into the mire he exposes the one thing he has always shied away from — his own sexuality.

It hadn't mattered when he was with Moth and Gabe.

He loves them for what they are: his brothers, his protectors, and when they're together it's all he wants in the world.

Teal had long ago accepted what he is.

He didn't have to talk about it.

No one pressed him, although he suspected they knew.

They are all close enough that secrets are never secrets for long.

He doesn't remember his mortal life, has no idea if he'd had any kind of relationship then... or if he's just dragged the baggage of what he is into eternity.

He had come to terms with the cold, hard truth that he would never love like Moth and Gabe, never feel desire, never unfurl the wings of his passion.

Until Éric had blazed in like a comet and given him that moment, those exquisite few seconds of sweet deliverance that Teal wanted to drown in.

Maybe it would have been easier if it had lasted, because then Teal would have had a reason for hanging on as if his immortal life depended on it. But it hadn't, at least not the sweet agony of virgin desire. Instead, something else had taken its place: a deep-rooted need to be close to Éric, to be touched by him, to live dancing on his comet's tail.

Because Éric is a burning star and the sparks he throws off scorch anyone who comes too close.

All this Teal lays out in front of him — neat little piles of anguish, all bearing his name.

What could you give him?

And there is the voice of reason he'd been missing, although part of him doesn't appreciate its return. He shivers.

Yes, he could give Éric love: but not the kind of love he needs, not the physical kind, the kind Éric craves.

You can't have him.

'I could pretend,' he whispers.

He hangs his head and a sob breaks in his throat.

But he could never pretend, not for something as pure and honest as sharing your body with another.

And he knows then, as he lays that last fact down, that he has to find a way of being with Éric without this desperate longing that sings in his veins, because it isn't fair to either of them. It isn't fair to Vauquelin, who has been gracious and open despite what the events of the past nights must have done to him. It isn't fair to Gabe and Moth, who had shown him last night what it was to fly because he couldn't do it for himself.

It isn't fair to Clove who trusted him.

You can't have him.

He breaks now and buries his head in his hands, lets the tears fall from the floodgate he'd barricaded them behind. Small cries of distress leave his throat and die on his lips because he doesn't want the others to come running.

This is his pain to bear.

Clove had told them all about the utter despair of a vampire's heart, and Teal had thought he had experienced that at the hands of the necromancer: when he knew he had to die to set his fireflies free.

But this despair is soul deep.

It guts him on an instinctual level, burns him from the inside out. Because he knows that in a different time and different circumstances, Éric would have been his.

He cries until his throat aches and his eyes are raw and swollen.

He cries for what might have been.

He cries for loss in all of its many forms.

As the final sobs quieten he sweeps the figurative piles of hurt into his hands, holds them close to his beating heart, and pads to the hearth. He solemnly lays them in the grate as if he is laying out the dead and then he looks for matches — but there are none on the mantel.

Maybe it's better that they stay like this, discarded in the dark — possibly one day they will burn, although Teal will never know this fact... because he will be hundreds of miles away.

'You can't have him,' he whispers, and as his words spin out into the dark he finally knows the truth, finally understands: even though he knows his heart will never be the same... because sometimes if you love something too much, you have to let it go.

50 / NIGHT 5:
ONLY A SHADOW

I need you.

The thought hits Moth and Gabe simultaneously, and they are at the doors leading from this deserted hallway in a matter of seconds.

Moth pushes open one door, using his shoulder in case it has any notion of sticking. All he can think of is getting to Teal's side.

'Fuck.' The word leaves his lips but this time it's not filled with anger: it's filled with shock.

Teal stands in the centre of the room with the pink jacket folded neatly over his arm, barefoot — the slippers held in one hand. But it's not the clothing that makes Moth's blood ice in his veins: it's Teal himself.

All of the time Moth has known his bright-eyed brother Teal has had an aura about him... something otherworldly, something more than vampire.

But what he sees before him now is a shell. Teal has retreated into himself and his light has dimmed to a fraction of its usual brightness.

'I'm okay,' Teal says as his lips try to form a smile: but it's only a facial movement.

Within half a second both his brothers are by his side and it's Moth who gathers him close first.

'Fuck, Teal. What happened?'

Moth glances around the room but nothing is broken, nothing is out of place. It looks like Teal just sat here and dug his heart out with a spoon. He tightens his grip. Teal's shoulders feel frailer: in fact, he seems like he's only a shadow of what he was.

Gabe had said that if anything else happened Teal would break: and now those fears have come true. Rage boils in Moth's gut and he's an instant away from unleashing that fury on the nearest priceless object.

But this isn't about him and his own issues. This is about Teal.

He glances to Gabe and knows he's feeling exactly the same way.

'Teal,' Gabe begins. He takes Teal's hands in his.

They are frozen, like the hands of a corpse.

'Do you want to leave? This house. Paris. I can get us home.'

Gabe has no idea how he'll accomplish this, but for Teal he would move mountains.

Teal shakes his head. 'No. We can't run away. I have to deal with this.'

There's a rawness to his voice, a tone Gabe has never heard before.

'No,' Gabe says gently. '*We* have to deal with this. You're never on your own, Teal.'

And now there's a smile from Teal — even if it's a muted version of its normal brightness.

'We don't have to go to the fucking salon.' Moth represses the urge to yank the jacket off and toss it into the corner.

He's done with playing dress up.

'Éric will be waiting,' says Teal.

It's all Moth can do not to blow the only fuse he has left.

The fact that Teal is thinking of Éric when he just had his heart ripped out proves that Teal is the very best of them.

They leave the room and negotiate the silent hallways, each step taking them closer to the salon.

Closer to whatever fresh hell awaits.

✝✝✝

Éric bounds up the steps of the catacombs and pauses at the landing, opening the door just a crack... he hangs back, listening for any sign of life nearby, any voices.

The house is as quiet as the bones downstairs: until he drops the massive old skeleton key on the floor and it rings out into the cavernous larder. He replaces it in the panel and leans against the wall. Now that he's out, he isn't sure he can get his feet to move, to go back and face the boys again. But he can't stay here forever.

His boots sound so loud on the floor.

He makes it to the salon and leans his ear against the doors... the silence is eating him up and his blood thrums in his ears. Inside, the vast room is empty... there's no fire going. He stokes it, and his back stiffens when he hears the doors creak open behind him.

Gabe and Moth enter the room with Teal between them, taking up their mantle as his protectors: even though none of them ever thought that would be needed within these walls. They'll be close by his side whatever occurs in this room... and they won't let anyone take what's left of his light.

Éric glares at them when they stop inside the doorway. There's no mistaking the noxious energy coming off of Moth and Gabe.

They've had enough, he thinks. *They probably just want to go home, and how could I blame them?*

Teal is there... he's *right there*. And Éric can't bring himself to look directly at him, even though his presence means everything. He doesn't need to look at him: he just needs him there... but Teal is locked away from him.

His chin quivers and he crumples onto a chaise, covering his mouth with his hand.

There's nothing he can say now.

What's he supposed to do: say hello?

There's nothing he can do... except wait.

So he hugs himself, he sinks into the corner of the chaise.

He starts to say they can sit... but when he looks to their faces again he clamps his jaw and turns to stare into the fireplace.

Maybe he should just jump into it.

It's Moth who breaks the silence.

'Is this what you wanted?' He purposely keeps his tone quiet — because if he lets the anger pour out of him, he'll never be able to claw it back. 'Just look at him.' He slips his arm around Teal's shoulder. 'Look at what you fucking did.'

Éric's brow furrows. If this weren't about Teal, this might be the time that he'd finally go for Moth's throat.

But he isn't angry... he's devastated. Broken.

'Moth, no one wanted this,' he whispers. 'You still don't understand, do you? Maybe you never will.'

Éric's words filter across to Moth. Before he knows what he's doing he's two steps away from Teal, ready to launch his own form of hell on Éric. But Gabe's hand yanks him back.

'Stay with Teal,' he says.

And the way it leaves his lips it's not up for debate.

Gabe knows that if this descends into violence, the aftermath could take decades to rebuild: if that's even possible. He emphasises his words with a pointed look, the one he only uses when he needs Moth to stay his ground.

Clove and V will be back soon, and they need to somehow pull this fucking unholy mess together — or they'll all be grounded indefinitely.

Or worse.

He crosses to the chaise but he doesn't sit. The fact that he's stood here in this eighteenth century jacket with their worlds collapsing around them only amplifies his off-kilter sense of reality.

'I know you didn't want this, Éric,' he says softly. 'And I know you never meant to hurt him.' He pauses, wonders whether he needs to place this next part in a mind-touch, then decides to just roll with it. 'I'm so fucking sorry you're hurting too.'

'I would never hurt him, can't you believe that?' Éric finally allows himself to look at Teal, but he glances away just as quickly. He grasps Gabe's wrist and pulls him down next to him, turning his shoulders: he can't fucking stand having Moth's death glare directed at him, even though it's burning into him regardless. 'I know you blame yourself. But don't. Because I don't think either of us wish it hadn't happened.'

If he could, he'd search Teal's face for confirmation, but he can't — that would finally do him in.

'I don't know why some things happen,' Gabe says, as he stares into the flames. The heat warms his face but the blood inside his veins feels like it's got ice crystals in its flow. Teal's quiet, dignified misery is shredding his resolve.

'Did you know I was hunted by a demon when I was a baby? That it hid in the shadows until I came of age? That it forced itself into my mother?' He's no idea why he needs to voice these memories now. 'I don't know why that happened, but if it hadn't I wouldn't be here now. So I guess what I'm trying to say is that some things happen for a reason, even if at the time they're ripping us apart we've no idea why.' He lowers his voice. 'This moment with Teal. It happened because it was meant to happen.'

Gabe shrugs, wonders if he's just gone off tangent in the most bizarre fucking way.

Éric crosses his legs like V, and this startles him.

He's never done that before. He keeps them crossed though and straightens his back, twitching his foot. There isn't any room in his head right now for what Gabe has said.

'There's so many things I don't know about all of you, Gabe. So many.

It's all meant to be, because if V hadn't come to see you, if he hadn't loved you all, I wouldn't be here now either. So I don't know how, but we have to figure out a way to live with it. Or else none of us will ever see each other again... and I don't want that.'

Suddenly his heart quickens — there's no reason for it. It suffocates him for a second and he flails, bringing his fingers to his lips. Then the reason makes itself known: because Vauquelin and Clove are standing in the entrance.

Vauquelin's knuckles tighten against the doorknob, rising to the surface of his skin.

Éric notices this, even from across the room.

He's on his feet in an instant.

Clove's gaze sweeps across the salon, taking in the sight of his boys and Éric decked in resplendent grandeur: although, unlike the others, Teal is not wearing a frock coat. His breath stalls for a fraction of a second. It is very rare for a moment to surprise Clove.

His gaze lands on Gabriel, the scarlet of his coat against his dark hair, the navy blue of his eyes emphasised by the intricate embroidery.

He is magnificent.

But the beauty of this image quickly turns sour.

Something is wrong. Something is very wrong.

« *Regardez ! C'est renversant !* »[†] Vauquelin begins, clapping his hands on each syllable of that last word as he moves into the centre of the room. He folds his hands behind his back and halts.

'How devastatingly handsome you all look, although it appears you are dressed for war... especially you, Moth. Very fitting given the volatile atmosphere of this room.' He turns to Éric, takes his jaw into his hand. 'But you are the most beautiful of all.'

As he touches Éric, his beloved's melancholy flows into him like blood.

[†] - LOOK AT THIS! STUNNING!

Vauquelin had hoped that the time he and Clove had given the boys might be the opportunity they needed to bridge this fiery rupture: but it has not. In fact, the situation seems to have deteriorated.

He looks down his nose at Gabriel and gives a slight jerk of his head — Gabriel vacates the seat swiftly.

Vauquelin pulls Éric down with him on the chaise. The manner in which his beloved has chosen to dress this night is not lost on him. He hopes it is what he suspects: that Éric has aligned himself with Vauquelin's own history, which in turn is Éric's legacy. However — regardless of the reason — there is a powder keg in this room: and it might detonate at any moment.

Once again, dread splays his heart.

Perhaps Éric and Teal have indeed escalated their bond.

This is not the first time the six of them have gathered under such circumstances. Vauquelin cannot fathom how the light in all these young vampires, light swathed in darkness, had gotten so bright it now burns at a fever pitch, threatening to incinerate them.

Every last one of them.

And the source of it all is Éric and Teal.

'*Bien-aimé*,' Vauquelin whispers. There's a question hanging on his lips. Éric already knows what it is.

'No. I'm not okay, V,' Éric answers in a quiet, quivering voice.

Clove draws his boys close. He knows Vauquelin needs a few moments with Éric and he is grateful for the same with his own charges. But it is Teal who concerns him the most. He lifts Teal's chin with one finger. Clove's brow furrows. Teal's eyes still shine but the level of luminosity has been dimmed to a fraction of their usual iridescent glow. It is the emptiness inside Teal's chest that sends ripples of unease through Clove, as though the young vampire's heart has been ripped from its cavity.

What Clove feared has already happened.

Teal is broken.

And broken vampires are the most dangerous kind.

He should know... he has been there many times in his immortal life.

Clove gathers Teal to his chest, just as he did on that long ago beach with the roar of the ocean at their backs. The time he had picked glass shards from Teal's throat, then wrought his own savage justice on those who had dared to torture a vulnerable young fledgling. But this time Teal's misery isn't physical: it has been carved onto his soul.

'I know I can't have him. I'm trying to let him go.' Teal's fervent whisper soaks into Clove's shirt.

Clove glances towards Vauquelin and Éric deep in conversation, but there's emotional upheaval there, too. The notes of it are a pungent perfume in the air.

It is up to Vauquelin and himself to try to mend these shattered hearts, although he does not know if that is even possible.

Vauquelin turns a pointed gaze to Clove.

Would you entrust me to speak to Teal alone?

Will you entrust me with Éric? Clove returns the question.

I would trust you with his very existence, Vauquelin replies... *and mine*. He brings his hand to his heart, inclines his head in acknowledgement of their bond, which has such ancient roots.

Clove bows his head, echoing Vauquelin's gesture. Their mannerisms may seem antiquated, but at this particular moment they are the most important way they can express the significance of what they are about to do. He strides to Vauquelin's side and grasps his arm. Their eyes meet.

Teal is broken. I do not need to tell you what that could mean.

I have only love to offer him, Vauquelin whispers back.

There is nothing further he must say. Clove continues to honour him by allowing him time with Teal.

Moth watches Gabe's face. It's fixed on both Clove and Vauquelin, his eyes moving from one to the other.

A cold fear clutches Moth's heart.

'What the fuck is going on, Gabe?'

'I don't know,' Gabe replies. 'Their thoughts are cloaked. But I don't like it.'

Clove directs his attention to Éric, but the young vampire refuses to meet his gaze.

In fact, at this particular moment, Éric is trying his level best to melt into the upholstery of the chaise.

'Éric,' Clove says, and there is authority in his voice, but also kindness. 'I believe it is time we talked.'

Panic rips through Éric. His heart jack-knifes in his ribcage — its palpitations pass directly into Vauquelin.

'*Bien-aimé*,' Vauquelin whispers through gritted teeth. He laces their fingers together. 'You must go. It is the only way.'

'No. I won't.'

Vauquelin twists their hands and presses them into Éric's chest.

'Yes. You will. I am not offering you an option. You will go with Clove, and you will go with him now.'

The vein spreads across V's forehead and Éric knows he's done for.

Vauquelin kisses him softly, tangling his fingers in Éric's hair.

You will emerge stronger from this... this I pledge to you.

He stands and turns away from Éric — but Éric grabs his coattail.

'Where are you going?' Éric stammers.

Vauquelin drifts his gaze to Éric's fingers gripping him. He unfolds Éric's fingers one by one and delivers his beloved a withering glare.

Do not try my patience, bien-aimé... I too have a threshold.

Do not forget this.

Vauquelin crosses to Clove's boys, and as he walks he closes his mind to Éric. His beloved will be in the best care: he cannot think of him at this moment, and he releases the gravity with which he had just spoken to him. Now he can only afford to display kindness, for his emotions must be measured only for the most tender vampire in this room.

He does not acknowledge Gabriel or Moth: he places a hand on Teal's shoulder.

'*Mon ange...*† could you permit me to speak with you?' Vauquelin asks in the quietest of his voices, the gentle voice that has always resided within him but makes its appearance for few.

'No!' The word erupts from Moth like a bullet from a gun.

He's seen this coming, has agonised over it while watching Gabe. He doesn't care that it's Vauquelin asking: he only knows that this means Teal will leave their protection and he can't cope with that.

'It's okay.'

Moth wheels to face Gabe.

'What do you mean, it's okay? How can this be fucking okay?'

He directs the heat of his anger towards Gabe now.

Vauquelin turns his chin robotically to Moth, fixes him in his ice-blue gaze.

Silence, Moth.

Moth holds the next words in his mouth. They feel as if they'll poison him if he doesn't spit them out. But Vauquelin's command is ricocheting around his head like a fucking ball in a pinball machine. Moth might be rebellious and wear his heart on his sleeve, but he hasn't got an immortal death wish. He swallows the words. They burn his gullet as they retreat and he replaces them with a glare.

Teal wants to disappear inside himself but he knows that he can't.

He gathers his courage.

'Yes,' he whispers.

He doesn't want to leave the safe confines of his brothers' protection but this is something else he must do, like Éric must speak with Clove.

---

†- MY ANGEL

Teal isn't sure what else he can say, but Vauquelin deserves this time alone with him.

It's the least Teal can do for daring to steal a small piece of Éric away.

He extracts himself from between his brothers and stands, even though his legs, his whole body, feel like they don't belong to him anymore.

'I thank you, Teal... you honour me,' Vauquelin murmurs.

He is quite aware Teal's strength has vanished... he tucks Teal's hand in the crook of his elbow and leads him out of the salon, whispering, 'I will not let you fall.'

He delivers Moth another pointed glare over his shoulder for good measure... and then they are gone.

When the doors snap closed, Éric buries his face in his hands. The stark absence of Teal and V in the room is a vacuum. He can't even begin to imagine what V will say to Teal, but the fact that his maker — his only protector — has left him alone here with the other boys, not to mention Clove, is terrifying.

He drops his hands in his lap and studies them, his chin trembling: and at last he looks up. None of them look pleased with him *at all*.

Before Moth can erupt again, Gabe deliberately blocks Éric from Moth's line of sight.

'Look at me.'

Moth doesn't want to but he does.

Underneath, the fury is still threatening to crest into a tidal wave.

'V won't do anything to hurt Teal,' Gabe says. 'And, for the record, I don't like it any more than you do, but there are rules in this house. Rules vampires live by. V and Clove only want to talk, to offer wisdom...'

Gabe's voice trails off.

Already Teal's absence is a glaring hole in his world.

Éric stands and follows Clove out of the salon, his shoulders slouched as if he's off to the firing squad. Now he knows how Moth felt that night when V dragged him away.

He's pretty sure Clove is going to kill him, and he fucking deserves it.

He's fucked absolutely *everything* up.

He's ruined Teal forever, and if... IF... he survives this meeting with Clove, V will kick him to the curb.

The way he treated him just now is proof.

V has never ordered him around like that.

It's over.

All of it.

51 / NIGHT 5:
HIS NEST OF CASTIGATING DEVILS

Clove leads the way down the shadowy corridor.

Éric lags behind like a scolded puppy. Vauquelin's last words to him were harsh, although Clove understands why. It is sometimes necessary to bestow a stricter form of love. He motions for Éric to walk alongside him and he does not speak for a few moments.

'Tell me, Éric, why do you think I want to talk to you?' He pauses, casts an eye upon a painting of a pale château hung above a marble-topped console table, dripping with gilt detail. 'Alone.'

He adds the last word not as an afterthought but because of its importance.

Éric bites the inside of his cheeks, bites so deeply that his mouth fills with blood. He swallows, hard, and it's like fire sliding down his throat. His lips begin to quiver.

'I can only think you must be disappointed in me. I'm sure I'm not what you were expecting from Vauquelin.'

Éric's anxiety is a living thing pulsing from his skin. Clove could feed from its frenetic energy if he were that kind of vampire.

'I never expect anything, Éric. That way my disappointment is minimal if the outcome is not what my thoughts have conjured up.' He sweeps his hair over one shoulder. 'We are to go to the catacombs. Lead the way.'

Éric swallows hard.

Oh god.

I'm gonna die tonight.

It's not lost on Éric that Clove knows exactly what the catacombs are meant for: but what he doesn't know is that he's taking him straight back to the place of his recent shame... the dirty thoughts he had down there, the things he did to himself. Clove probably senses it or at least has already read his fucking mind.

Éric drags a trembling hand down his face and blows out a breath.

This is his fate and he has to own up to what he's done.

'Okay.'

His feet might as well be encased in stone, but somehow he gets one in front of the other. *Okay... okay... okay.*

He trudges through the unlit corridors with Clove's heavy darkness draping across his back like an iron blanket. He stoops to open the hidden panel and stares at Clove's feet, turning his head slowly up to meet the master's gaze.

He can't run, though that's all he wants to do right now.

Éric inserts the key and stands with his hand on the latch.

This may be the last time he passes through this door — nevertheless, he heaves it open... because there's no other option.

He hands a lit torch to Clove and folds his arms. He doesn't need his own torch to light the way to his end.

His leaden steps continue until he comes to a stop by the pit.

'Why have you paused at this point, Éric?' Clove knows why, but he needs Éric to voice his fear, to crack open whatever shield he is trying to hide behind. He needs raw honesty.

'Because I don't deserve to be here with all of you,' Éric's voice is a broken whimper. He jerks his head toward the pit. 'You should just drop me in there and be done with it.'

'Do you truly believe Vauquelin would have sent you to your death in such a cruel fashion?' Clove moves to Éric's side. It is strange to have another young vampire so close. He inclines his head and studies Éric's profile. Examines it as if it were a marble sculpture, each curve etched from a craftsman's hand. It is not far from the truth. He can see why Vauquelin chose this one, although outward beauty must only be a fragment of Éric's appeal.

Clove has been in this house for five nights and knew by the end of the first one that Éric's youthful effervescence would influence his boys. They are wildly different in some ways, but they share one thing — they are modern vampires and as such they will bond.

An image of Teal touches his senses but he pushes it away. Vauquelin will be kind: he must put Teal out of his mind and focus on Éric.

Éric looks down to the lace at his neck, twists it between his fingers.

'I might've earned it... he's never spoken to me so harshly. So I don't know... maybe he sent you to do his dirty work. It isn't that hard to imagine you also want to punish me for what I've done.'

Clove takes Éric's jaw in his fingers and pulls him close. They are of a similar height but Clove knows his forbidding presence means more than simple inches. His dark eyes drill into Éric's.

'That would be the most dishonourable act, Éric. If I wanted you dead, I would not need to bring you to this place of death to do it. Do you know what resides in my veins?' His voice is soft but each syllable is laced with ice.

Éric gawps. The truth is Clove scares the fuck out of him, and he can't put his finger on the exact reason. He's just so... colossally beautiful and cold and intimidating. An enigma.

He recalls V saying *there is more to Clove than meets the eye...* but V didn't elaborate.

'Vauquelin told me so little about you. He wanted me to discover you all on my own. It doesn't seem like there's enough time in the world for that, not even for immortals. My mind has been like a hurricane since you arrived. When we first met, I told him I was nothing special. I still don't know what he sees in me...' Éric drops his chin to his chest. 'I have nothing to compare with you and the boys.'

Clove motions to the coffin resting in the darkness, empty now of its condemned occupant.

'There,' he says to Éric. 'Sit, and then you will listen.'

Éric does not perceive his own special beauty. How it affects everyone spinning in his orbit. How his boys have been drawn close, then added their own gravitational pull. In the short time they have been here, stars have been formed.

Éric backs up to the coffin, never taking his eyes off Clove, fumbling for its surface behind him — and sits down hard. He splays his knees, gripping the brass handles on the side, and stares at his feet.

He still isn't convinced Clove isn't going to kill him, and nothing he's said so far even comes close to how he really feels. He can't open up all the way. Not yet. He can't bear for Clove to truly see him... though he knows, somehow... that the master is about to unzip his mind and spill its twisted guts all over this filthy floor.

But there's something else writhing in Éric's mind as he fixes his gaze on the wall of bones, pointedly avoiding Clove's scrutiny: and he hopes he can't hear him. He isn't skilled at shielding his thoughts. Despite his own anguish at having to speak with Clove — alone — Éric reminds himself that V has taken Teal away, too... they're together now.

The unknown terror for what may or may not be occurring with Teal upstairs pinches Éric's face with an additional layer of agony.

Is he hurting him?

No, no, no... come ON, *he would never... how could anyone ever hurt Teal?*

Éric covers his face and chokes back the thought.

Clove waits. He watches as Éric struggles with his own inner turmoil, his nest of castigating devils. This is a necessary act. He takes the torch and brings it across to the coffin, wedges it into a cleft in the wall. The flame stutters in a draught and dancing shadows paint this place of bones.

'Look at me.' He rests one booted foot on the coffin lid and his shadow devours Éric's frame.

Éric lifts his chin in fits and starts and when their eyes meet, his shoulders tank. He can barely interpret Vauquelin's almighty vampire expressions, let alone Clove's.

Here it comes. He takes a deep breath.

Clove reaches out and drags a thumb across Éric's cheekbone, and the young vampire flinches beneath his touch.

'How can you say there is nothing special about you, when you own the most precious thing in this house?' He is not sure how Éric will take his next words but they need to be given the space they deserve. 'When you own Teal's heart? He has never entrusted it like this, and I suspect he never will again. That is the measure of how exceptional you are.'

Éric clings to Clove's wrist... a strangled murmur escapes his throat and the dam breaks. Blood tears cascade down his cheeks and he leans on Clove, his body racked by sobs.

'I don't know what to do,' he cries.

This is the honesty Clove needs. He cups his hands around Éric's face, presses a kiss to his brow. Offers him strength.

'Do you love him?'

The word love feels strange on Clove's tongue.

It is not one that spills from his lips often, but this house is brimming with it in so many different ways.

It is this city, he thinks.

It takes a vulnerable heart, delivers a wound that weeps in the night.

'I never thought I would love anyone besides Vauquelin. His love is deeper than I've ever known before. But yes, I love Teal.' The name is sucked back into Éric's throat with a gasp. 'I need him.'

And there they are... truths he hadn't yet spoken aloud.

He hunches down, he shrinks.

He compresses his lips between his fingers and closes his eyes.

There. They. Are.

Clove smooths Éric's curls from his brow.

'I could tell you that you must forget him, that you must pour all of your love and attention into Vauquelin, but I fear that would leave a need in you that would only grow over time. It would become a cancer, eating you from the inside out, and ultimately destroy the love you have with Vauquelin. Hush,' he says as Éric opens his mouth to speak. 'You cannot see it because you are in too deep. I have told Gabriel much the same thing. That sometimes a fracture in an otherwise steadfast bond becomes fodder for the wolves that run in the night. They yearn for the taste of weakness, for any rift they can find. But you know Teal cannot give you what you need in a physical sense. He can only offer the purest form of his love: his need to be simply close to you.'

'I know that,' Éric whispers, 'but don't you understand? I don't expect that from him. All I need is *him*, who he is. I...' He shuts down. He senses he's being backed into a corner and he doesn't want to define this any further. He can't.

Éric spirals a mind-touch. He doesn't know if Clove will hear it, but it doesn't really matter — because it's an admission to himself, as well... which might be more important.

Teal makes me feel complete.

He stands, leans his forehead against the cold, stone wall.

'Why does everyone want to put love into carefully-labelled little packages?' Éric turns to face Clove again. 'Do you think I don't love Vauquelin anymore, or that I want to leave him?'

'I am, perhaps, the wrong vampire to speak to about the intricacies of love. I locked my heart to it a very long time ago, but that does not mean that I do not remember every single time I gave it away.' His gaze flicks to the shadows where a deeper gloom pulsates in one corner. They always find him, these wraiths — he draws them like moths to a flame. He snaps his fingers and it fades but it leaves the taste of despair in his mouth.

'I do not think that you love Vauquelin any less because you love Teal. I do not think that you want to leave him, because it would break both your hearts. And a vampire's love is a precious thing. It is not something to cast aside recklessly. He does not love you any the less, but he is trying to understand. Vauquelin has a jealous heart, but he will do anything for you — because he worships the ground you walk upon, and he has travelled through centuries to find you. That is not something you simply disregard. And vampires have no need of labelled little packages. We love who our hearts are drawn to. We do not belong under the banners mortals throttle themselves with.' He pauses, and the silence in the catacombs is the breath taken before a scream. 'The question is, what do *you* want to do now, Éric?'

Éric is losing the battle against the blood tears, and all that he can give is a guttural sound, the sound that only a tormented soul can emit: *gyuhhhhh*.

He knows what he and Teal want… but there's no doubt in his mind that the others won't let them have it.

'Moth hated me before and he really hates me now. He doesn't think I deserve to breathe the same air as Teal, and maybe he's right.' Éric sits back down on the coffin and buries his head in his arms. 'I don't know what Gabe and Moth think we did. And I don't think they see that this isn't about anything else than we just need to be able to love each other. That's what *we* need. What I want… is for everyone to accept it.' He looks up to Clove again. 'But deep down I don't believe any of you will.'

Éric is still hiding something but Clove will not press him. It will emerge when the time is right. But Éric's openness, the way he has laid his heart on the line, is a tender and beautiful thing.

'Moth is convinced that I hurt Teal somehow. But I would never hurt him! Our souls got tangled. Don't they know that this is killing *both* of us? Neither of us went looking for this.' He squeezes his eyes shut but it doesn't stop the tears. He drags the back of his hand across them.

'Do not worry about Moth. He does not hate you. Distrust is his default, and it is unfortunate that any bond you may have formed with Gabriel and Moth has been damaged by your tenderness towards Teal, and his for you. You must understand that my boys have been through the most traumatic of experiences together. Their love for each other runs deep and Moth sees you as a threat, however misguided that may be.'

Clove crouches before Éric, smooths the tangle of curls from his face. The young vampire's distress is palpable.

'Gabriel understands, but he too has an allegiance to Teal and a need to protect him at all costs. I am going to tell you something now, something that may make the fear in you double in quantity. Do you want to hear my words?'

Éric trembles under Clove's touch. His heart stops beating for a second and he sways, clutching at Clove's jacket cuff. If he wanted to run before, he certainly does now.

'No,' he whispers. 'But I promise I'll listen.'

The silence deepens in the gloom of the catacombs.

The bones will be their witnesses.

'There is a hollowness inside Teal... a desolation that I have only seen a few times in my immortal life. You know that he is different in many ways, that he has witch blood in his veins. He has suffered torments no other vampire ever has. Yet none of us could have known that coming here would be the thing that broke him. He has died before, Éric — and I do not mean his mortal death. He died to free the fireflies that lived within his eyes. I am not going to divulge all of the details. It is a long and painful story, one that I very much hope he can tell you.' Clove takes Éric's hand, traces the lifeline on his palm with one finger. 'But vampires can reach a point where they do not wish to carry on. Where the pain inside them eats away at the very fabric of their being, and the weight of immortality and their own grief becomes too much to bear. That is when they go into the sun, Éric.'

Those words — the thought of V and Teal, the tread of their imperishable souls vanishing from the earth — knock the breath clean out of Éric's lungs.

He hunches over, he gulps for air... he can't get it back.

A multitude of emotions have emerged this week that make Éric realise the danger he was in during V's time-slip. The depths of what he doesn't know, what V has been unable to show him yet, are an abyss... and now Éric is sinking to the bottom.

He finally understands the significance of what he and Vauquelin lost in the time-slip... and why they're all gathered here now. He sees everything that's at stake.

With clarity.

He's about to hit the ground: the pressure of it all is blowing his head apart. But right next to him is a safeguard, a hand up — if he can just accept it.

And so Éric reaches for him.

'Clove... could you just put your arm around me? Please?'

Clove does not hesitate. He draws Éric into his embrace, letting his hair fall over Éric's face to try to shield him from the horrors plaguing his nocturnal world.

Éric melts into him and he soars back up to the surface at once, gulping air into his chest. It's such a contrast to the way V holds him... a vastly different kind of strength.

'I've tried to be something I'm not in front of the boys at times, because I don't know them... but that's never worked for me in the past, and I should know better. Before I was vampire I was just an insecure gay kid in Los Angeles. I never let anyone in. Now my heart is torn apart and it's on display for everyone. I'm smothering in all this and don't always know how to keep my head straight. V told me that Teal doesn't remember how he was before. But as for me, I can't forget it. I was okay while V was gone, and I was okay before Teal. I went out by myself last night and I thought I had gotten a grip on things, but when I came back it was clear I fucking didn't...' He cuts his gaze upward and looks away just as quickly. 'Apologies, Clove... but now I'm not okay all over again. I don't understand all the things the boys have been through, and I'm sure V's struggles have been a lot different than yours. But the one who I've shown my true self is Teal. He's the only one. Why is that?' His face crumples. 'What can I do to fix this? I'd do anything to keep him safe, to make him Teal again. Even if it means we can't be together. Because now that I know he exists, I don't think I could handle the darkness without knowing he's there.'

His spine stiffens beneath Clove's grasp. Vauquelin had said almost the same phrase to Éric their first morning together, when V should have been asleep. Now that he's vampire, Éric understands how tormented Vauquelin must have been to stay awake after sunrise.

He digs his fingers into his thighs.

'Tell me what to do, Monsieur. Please.'

'Why do young vampires assume that masters have the ability to answer all questions?' Clove cups his hands around Éric's face again, lets a smile play on his lips. It slips away quickly at the importance of Éric's plea.

'I will tell you this. I am not prepared to lose Teal. I will not let the despair inside him lead to his final end. It would destroy Gabriel, destroy Moth. And it would destroy you. I do not accept that price. So there is only one alternative.' He rests his brow against Éric's, tries to absorb some of the excruciating pain. 'We must find a way for you and Teal to love one another as you wish to. The final deciding factor in this is Vauquelin. I cannot speak for him. I know his heart is filled with boundless love for you — but I am unsure whether he would let you give a fraction of your love to Teal.'

It is a huge request Éric will ask of Vauquelin. Clove just hopes it is not the attribute that tears them apart.

Éric brings his hands to Clove's neck, lets them rest against the master's cool skin for a few moments before folding them back into his lap.

'I already asked him if I could keep this love for Teal in my heart. He said he would never ask me to surrender it. But that was last night. Now he thinks something more has happened... but it hasn't. Except the pain just grew tenfold.'

He bows his head, knitting and unknitting his fingers over and over again. He doesn't have to tell Clove that he and Teal have never even kissed. That it's nothing like everyone is thinking.

'I wish I had come to you when V slipped, like he wanted me to. Maybe things wouldn't have turned out this way.'

'Wishes are not made for vampires, Éric.' Clove closes his hand over Éric's fingers, feels the pulse of his own heart thrumming through their joined flesh. 'If you had come to me at Gehenna, you and Teal would have made your special connection there instead of inside these gilded walls, and then what would have happened when Vauquelin returned from his time-slip? It is better that it developed this way. If better is the appropriate word.'

Éric's lips part.

Oh my god. It would have. It absolutely fucking would have.

And then he would have been anchorless... he might have lost V forever.

'I need V, too,' Éric breathes. 'I wouldn't be me without him. He keeps my feet on the ground and lets me leave my head in the clouds. I don't have to tell you how much I love him. If I didn't, I wouldn't be vampire... I wouldn't be here now. The love between V and me... it's as soul-deep as with Teal, just in a very different way. Clove, V told me something last night that you probably already know... he said he would die without me. But it would be the same for me. I've been so afraid since the hunt that I destroyed everything. Even though I couldn't have done anything to stop it.'

Éric leans back and studies Clove. This talk has made him stronger, older somehow, like he grew up a little more. He could never have had this exact conversation with V: their hearts are too close. Éric's pain is Vauquelin's pain — and Teal's pain is Clove's.

He slides down to the floor and rests his forehead on Clove's knee.

'Thank you for understanding me... for seeing me.'

Éric's heartfelt words wash over Clove. There is wisdom in this young vampire. Wisdom and a heartbeat filled with courage, filled with love. He rests his hand on the back of Éric's neck, hoping that some of his own strength can filter through and ease his pain.

'You are not a vampire to hide in the shadows, Éric. I see your light. In fact, it is possibly this that drew Teal towards you. His light, his special need for love, was captivated by yours.'

Éric lifts his face, and he smiles so broadly it hurts.

It's the first time he's smiled in nights — at least a smile that isn't tinged with heartbreak.

'The fact that Teal loves me, that he let himself shine on me, is one of the most beautiful things that has ever happened in my life. I don't have to voice the other one. I would do anything to protect him, Clove, anything, even if it meant you would never let me see him again, because we had this... I just hope Gabe and Moth will let me share a tiny part of Teal. I don't want to take him away from them. I love them, too. Even Moth.'

'Gabriel and Moth will come around. I sense the seeds of their understanding, at least on Gabriel's part. Moth is a different matter, but by now you know that Moth is *always* a different matter.' He laughs softly. 'But when Moth loves you he will die for you. That is the truth.'

'I can see that in Moth. He and I have more in common than he'd probably like to admit. None of us had a clue how powerful this gathering would be, did we?'

Éric fiddles with one of the silver buttons on the front of his coat. He's torn: he has a sudden longing to rejoin the others — he thinks Clove has restored him to the point where he needs to be.

He *thinks*.

There's no doubt in his mind that he'll be transformed when he faces them all, thanks to Clove, and they'll all see it — even V.

His fractured heart is knitting back together: its loops re-embrace within and it bolsters him with each passing second. But on the other hand, he wishes (*no, no don't wish*) — he *wants* to stay down here and talk to Clove until sunrise.

'If I had known the emotional fallout of this gathering, I may have asked Flynn to bypass Paris and drive to Orléans. There is a reason he decided to stay in the carriage house.' Clove gifts Éric with an extremely rare gesture — the edge of a grin. 'Now I believe it is time to free ourselves from this macabre place.' He does not add that he wants to return to the salon to see if Vauquelin and Teal have made their way back.

'I don't think I've *ever* spent this much time down here,' Éric says.

He wants to thank Clove again but it doesn't seem right.

Instead, he places his hand in the crook of Clove's elbow.

'I'm ready.'

Clove glances down at Éric's hand. He smiles.

'You are very much Vauquelin's child. When he visited Gehenna he did the same thing to me, which was perturbing at the time. Now it seems like a very normal occurrence. You are not the only one shedding old skin, Éric.'

They pass over the hatch to the pit. Clove closes his hand over Éric's for a few moments.

'Do you still think I want to throw you in?'

Éric's lopsided grin curls his cheek, and he looks down to the pit.

'I guess this means you'll let me live... for now.'

He extinguishes the torch and they leave their shadows and secrets in the capable protection of the bones.

52 / NIGHT 5:

UNSHELTERED WITH HIS HEART IN HIS HANDS

The act of walking Teal up the staircase very nearly undoes Vauquelin. All his ancient strength seems no match for the weight of Teal's sorrow. The tenderest of angels, the sweetest of hearts... Teal is crumbling beneath his arm. So he picks him up. At the library, he opens the doors with one hand and deposits Teal gently onto the sofa nearest the fireplace.

Vauquelin sits beside him, draws Teal's head to his shoulder.

As he studies the otherworldly golden-haired boy, his mind scurries across the myriad thoughts running through. He had promised himself that he would not ask Éric precisely what occurred between them, nor will he ask Teal. But Teal and Éric are both shattered: darkness has replaced Teal's light and Vauquelin must do what he can to restore it.

Last night he felt unworthy to touch Éric, and now the same emotion arises for the broken-hearted young vampire at his side. The persistent magnetism between these two extraordinary boys has shifted them both to a different plane... he can only hope they have not gone beyond his reach. Now, Vauquelin cannot afford such self-centred thoughts: he is here to comfort Teal, to assure him that he will protect him regardless of the circumstances.

All Teal's perceptions are drowning, his senses dragging him to the bottom of a deep, dark well: all his light is lost. Vauquelin is offering such kindness, such gentleness, but Teal knows he has committed the ultimate sin: he has taken a little piece of Éric away.

He hauls his voice from somewhere, forces the words through parched lips.

'Please don't hate me. I never meant for this to happen.'

He glances across the library to the chaise, the one Éric held him upon, the precious moment he wishes he could repeat forever.

'Teal, this word, *hate*... it does not belong on your lips.' The mere sound of it crushes Vauquelin's spirits. 'I have no hate for you, only love. Can you believe me?' He absorbs the guilt coming in relentless waves from Teal: the boy is engulfed in it.

With all that has transpired these past few nights, Vauquelin questions whether he is in the proper frame of mind to be an anchor: but Clove had taken Éric and he had taken Teal, and as masters they must do what they can to save them.

He tilts his head and lifts Teal's chin. He had been unable to extract the truth from his own beloved... how can he expect this fragile one, with his broken wings, to speak to him of it now?

'I am not angry with you, Teal. Please do not ever think I could be. Like Clove, I have been walking the earth for many, many years, more than I care to imagine, and I know love is not something a heart can control. Do you understand my meaning?'

Vauquelin's finger under Teal's chin is the only thing holding him together. He folds his fingers around Vauquelin's arm and closes his eyes for a moment. Behind his eyelids he can hear his fireflies screaming. They know his pain and they know his strength, but they can feel it slipping away.

'I don't deserve your compassion.' His eyes flick open and Vauquelin's image blurs behind his tears. 'But love,' he pauses, '*this* kind of love I feel now, I don't know what to do with it. It's eating me from the inside, looking for a way out... and I don't know how to make it stop.'

'I must confess: you cannot stop it. This is a fact , and it has ruined many a heart throughout the annals of time.'

Vauquelin slides to the floor and sits at Teal's feet. It is not a time for posturing, or even for dispensing ancient wisdom.

'I, too, know this all-encompassing love, my sweet one.' He looks up to Teal and takes his smaller hand, folding it within his long fingers. 'Éric. May I tell you something about him, why he is so special to me?'

Teal can only nod. There's a deep hollow inside him that needs to be filled with anything he can learn about Éric. Because this is what will nourish him when they return to Gehenna.

'I have only had myself to rely on for most of my existence. I have always left myself open for love, for the fleeting intervals I could find it. Yet I would never have been prepared for Éric had I not met you, Clove, and your brothers in Gehenna. I am not as strong as Clove... I never will be. Your protector and I are quite different. What I am about to say no one else has ever heard besides Éric, and now you. When I met him, I knew I could no longer exist without him. I knew it at once. I am quite certain you understand this, no?'

Vauquelin draws a fingertip across Teal's jaw, and he knows some of Teal's pain is reflected on his own face.

The room starts to spin and Teal has to grip the edges of the sofa to stop himself from whirling into oblivion. He wants to look away because the openness in Vauquelin's face is almost more than he can bear. Teal has come into this house and stolen part of its beating heart. But he will answer the question, because Vauquelin deserves honesty.

'It was only one moment,' he whispers, 'but he took my heart in his hands and,' now he glances away and his voice catches in his throat, 'I gave it willingly knowing he could never be mine, because he belongs to you.'

Vauquelin parts his lips.

He had worried himself sick speculating over what physical act — or *acts* — might have led up to this catastrophe.

'Only one moment...' He repeats Teal's words in a whispered refrain. His heart settles, just a little. '*Mon ange*,[†] the very night I met him I told him everything about myself, that I am vampire. You know the cost for an immortal to reveal this. I flayed my heart open for him, I begged him — *begged* him — to stay with me. And then I sent him away. The decision had to be his. This is the choice I gave him which Moth raged against in the salon. Yet Éric is among us now... you know his answer. I have never loved another as I love him. Éric...' His voice breaks and he rises again to sit next to Teal. 'Éric is a one-of-a-kind soul, Teal, as you are. I will not fault you for seeing inside his heart, as I have. How could I?'

Teal lets Vauquelin's words wash over him.

'It wasn't a decision to fall in love with him. It just happened.'

Clove and his brothers know Teal's truth, even though he has desperately tried to hide it. But he's not sure if Vauquelin knows it, too. He takes a long, shaky breath.

'Éric opened something inside me that no one else ever has. I *wanted* him, do you understand?' A note of anguish breaks his voice. 'But then the moment passed because I'm not wired like that. I don't feel need like that.' His shoulders sink. 'I will never know that kind of connection.'

Vauquelin closes his eyes.

Éric opened something inside me... he had uttered this exact phrase to his beloved. He had not wanted to believe that Éric and Teal... he could not even bear the thought. And Éric could not tell him, because this is so precious, so phenomenal that he could not explain it — he had refused to define it in front of the entire gathering.

'Teal... revenants do not love like mortals, and we cannot abide by their rules. I will tell you this: you must not be ashamed of the way love

---

[†]- MY ANGEL

comes to you. Nor must Éric. He has been very reticent about what has transpired. Now I understand his reasons. When we spoke, I told him you were made of magic. I have believed this since the moment I first met you. Teal, I would die without Éric. Do you feel this way about him?'

Teal meets Vauquelin's dark, intense gaze. He doesn't need to think. But he can't say the words. They burn along the linings of his throat, cauterising his vocal chords, so he does the only thing he can: he drops his mind shield and unleashes his despair.

Vauquelin lifts his fingers to his lips, drawing in as much air as his lungs will allow.

As he studies Teal's face, the young vampire's anguish reflects into his soul: it is identical to his own. Teal's light — a radiance which could illuminate the darkest revenant night, a light which Vauquelin has held in his heart since they met long ago in Gehenna — has been snuffed out.

The magnitude of Teal's longing plunges Vauquelin into the recesses of his own memories, to the fateful morning he watched the still-mortal Éric sleep, curls tumbled across the pillow, the fist of one hand curled over his head.

At that time, Vauquelin could not articulate the reasons behind his own yearning for Éric: he could only nurse the wounds that had settled in his heart — which he knew would never heal were Éric to vanish from his life.

This is precisely what Teal is suffering, what he has given Vauquelin free rein to witness, and its intensity scorches into the elder vampire's psyche.

Vauquelin has faced losing Éric once before. Then it was beyond his control — and it was a time-slip that separated them, placing them centuries apart. He can easily ascribe his and Éric's first meeting to fate: how can he possibly see what has transpired between Éric and Teal as being any different?

He lifts a quaking hand to brush a lock of hair from Teal's forehead. His beloved is god-knows-where in the bowels of the house with Clove, and here Vauquelin sits with another who loves Éric.

It is a devastating concept.

The night of the hunt he had been so concerned with Éric's physical safety, so confident in the love that he and Éric share, that Moth and Gabriel share, that Clove has barricaded himself against.

Teal was the vulnerable one — the one left unsheltered with his heart in his hands.

Vauquelin had not recognised it.

None of them had: with the exception of Éric, who had been powerless to turn away.

Éric's open heart... the heart that had been denied love so often... he finally encountered one so equally starved, and he saw it through the lens of his unpractised revenant soul.

A fire spreads through Vauquelin's veinery, and it delivers the understanding that he had *not* taken Éric too young: he had taken him at the moment he most needed love, and he will not deny him this beauty he has discovered.

'Teal. What do you want? How will you be happy?'

Panic spirals in Teal's gut.

How can I ask for what I want?

He's not used to asking for anything: he's always simply content to walk with his brothers on their midnight road. But Éric has changed everything. He has to ask, even though it will crush him if he is denied.

'I just want to be able to be close to him,' he whispers. He reaches for Vauquelin's hand, brings it to his lips in a silent plea. 'I just want him to be able to hold me. That's all I ask.'

Vauquelin moves his hand to Teal's cheek.

Teal's blatant implorations, his vulnerability... it is something he also recognises in Éric and loves about him — yet he can also acknowledge how pain-riddled Teal is by asking for something so raw.

'*Mon ange*,[†] when I invited you all here, I did not know that the heart of Éric would be on the line, nor yours. I do not bring anyone into this house I cannot trust, and I trust so few. Earth-shattering events have occurred between these walls in a few short nights. This is my sacred space — but now it is also yours, and Clove's, Moth's and Gabriel's. But I will have you know that your love for Éric is a gift. And should it have been anyone else's heart he had captured but yours, I would not have these words for them. You, Teal, I want you to have this with Éric. I am not cruel enough to keep him from you, because you must know I love you as well. And I will not allow either of you to suffer, not a minute longer. No other will ever have him. He is ours.'

Teal's eyes widen.

He clutches at Vauquelin's sleeve. His heart is pounding in his throat because he can't believe these words fell from Vauquelin's lips. Does this mean he can let Éric hold him without judgement? He thinks it does, but so much emotion has been drained from him that this beautiful beam of light spears through his core: and he is completely undone.

Sobs begin to wrack his body and try as he might he can't keep them in.

Vauquelin takes Teal into his arms, rocks him gently.

'Teal, Teal... you are the only other who is worthy of loving my beautiful boy.' He kisses the top of Teal's head, his lips caressing golden gossamer hair as he holds the source of his beloved's torment. He wants to take the anguish away from them, to erase the pain that has suffocated them both these past nights. But it cannot go unheeded — it is a crucial component of the passion that took flight in their souls.

'Do not fear this love, Teal, because now we all have one another to lean on. None of us will fall... I pledge this to you. I will always lift you.'

Teal never thought he would feel another master vampire's arms around him. Vauquelin's touch is so very different from Clove's. It has its own

---

[†]- MY ANGEL

uniqueness; he would know this touch amongst a thousand others.

Vauquelin's hair drifts across Teal's face and with it comes the scent of sandalwood.

For the first time in two nights Teal feels safe.

Safe with his own feelings.

Safe in the knowledge that he can return to the salon, return to Éric.

The thought curves his lips into a smile.

'Thank you,' he says, wanting to throw his arms around Vauquelin, wanting to drop to his knees in front of him in adoration, wanting to somehow force his legs to run from this room, this place of books and his heart, run down the staircase and into the salon.

To find Éric's embrace.

Vauquelin rises, towering over the ethereal young vampire.

'This love will make all of us strong, Teal. I have scarcely believed anything so fervently in my life. Will you take my hand? Let us go find him.'

As Vauquelin's fingers enclose his own, a lightheadedness engulfs Teal: as though, if he wasn't holding onto Vauquelin, he would float towards the ceiling and become one with the fresco for eternity.

He's not sure what the others will say — what Moth and Gabe will say — but that doesn't matter.

He's on his way to Éric.

A Conclave of Crimson

A QUEER VAMPIRE ROMANCE

BOOK TWO ANNOUNCEMENT COMING SOON

Follow us on Instagram for news:
@nicoverleybooks

ACKNOWLEDGMENTS

✝✝✝

Our most gracious thanks to our alpha readers:

Nataly Rosen
and
Sarina Langer

Your insights and passion for our vampires are sealed in our hearts for eternity.

As they say, it takes a village to get a book out into the world and we are so grateful to our early readers, who gave us valuable feedback on our little vampire multiverse: Julia, Matthew Coxall, Alex Pearson, Lisa Niblock, Josh Radwell, Samantha Di Prizito, Danielle Klassen, E.G. Smith, Brian Bowyer, G.R. Thomas, Ruth Miranda, and Jen Young.

Grazie mille to Miranda Caudell and Samantha Di Prizito
for their assistance with Italian translation.

To Anndee Laskoe, Ian Hughes, and the boys from the crypt at Box of Kittens for making our cover dreams a reality and bringing them to life so beautifully.

A Conclave of Crimson is our heart project. *Conclave* began as a love letter to our characters. It has been years in the making, and almost wasn't published. The warmth and enthusiasm from our early readers often gave us courage when we doubted ourselves on this story that demanded to be told and refused to be pigeonholed. And to those who are new to our work, or have come to us from the other books that precede *Conclave*, we welcome you into our deliciously dark vampire world ♥

ABOUT THE AUTHORS

Beverley Lee (she/her) is a bestselling dark fiction author who lives close to the dreaming spires of Oxford, England. Her work specialises in atmospheric horror, creeping dread, and broken boys — sometimes altogether — but is always filled with heart and the tenuous threads of relationships pushed to the brink. All the Feels all the time. Vampires are her first love and occasionally they stop whispering long enough for her to write other books. When she's not writing you'll find her rambling through the countryside, dreaming about male vampires kissing, and exploring time-worn graveyards.

Visit beverleylee.com for more information about her books.

✝✝✝

Nicole Eigener (she/they) is a lifelong student of French history and the macabre. After gaining degrees in literature and history, their love for haemovores became a beautiful marriage to their obsession with French culture, specifically of the seventeenth-century, which (along with themes of historical queerness) features prominently in their work. When they aren't writing, they are most likely editing, reading, dreaming about male vampires kissing, trying to avoid the sun, and/or desperately missing Parisian cafés and rainy walks through Père Lachaise cemetery.

Visit thevampire.org for more information about their books.

CHARACTER MENTIONS FROM THE PREVIOUS BOOKS

From the Gabriel Davenport Series:

Elijah — former leader of the Vampire Hunter's Guild, now ally to Clove and the Bloody Little Prophets

Olivia — paranormal investigator from The Manor; ghost whisperer

Sasha — one of Clove's fledgling vampire charges (deceased)

Noah — A reverend; Gabriel's mentor and friend (in his human life)

Carver — Gabriel's mentor and guardian (in his human life), owner of The Manor (deceased)

Beth — Gabriel's mother (deceased)

Ella — housekeeper of The Manor

From the Beguiled by Night Series:

Olivier — Vauquelin's former valet and friend, later turned vampire and chosen brother (deceased)

Yvain — Vauquelin's maker (deceased)

Maeve — Vauquelin's former human lover, turned vampire in his second timeline (whereabouts unknown)

Céline — vampire wife of Olivier

Clément — Yvain's lover (and briefly Vauquelin's)

BEFORE YOU GO

✝✝✝

Thank you for reading! If you enjoyed *A Conclave of Crimson: Book One*, please consider leaving a review on Goodreads, Storygraph, BookBub, or the platform of your choice. Even if it's just one line to say you liked it, it helps others discover independent authors and helps us to continue to create books for you to fall in love with!

THE PREVIOUS BOOKS IN THE CONCLAVE UNIVERSE IN ORDER:

The Making of Gabriel Davenport ♥

A Shining in the Shadows ♥

The Purity of Crimson ♥

Beguiled by Night ⚜

Crimson is the Night ♥⚜

Citizens of Shadow ⚜

{ ♥ by Beverley Lee | ⚜ by Nicole Eigener | ♥⚜ by both authors }

You can find links to all of our work here:
thevampire.org | beverleylee.com

Keep up with news from us on Instagram @nicoverleybooks.

To the love of vampires!

Most sincerely,
Beverley & Nicole

SOUNDTRACK

✟✟✟

To enjoy the official Spotify soundtrack for *A Conclave of Crimson*, scan below or go to https://nicoverley.bcns.ai/OST-book-one

Milton Keynes UK
Ingram Content Group UK Ltd.
UKHW021119030324
438613UK00007B/79